Praise for Specters in the Glass House

"The novel's exploration of the delicate and [obscured] the human experience is hauntingly beautiful."

Booklist

"From the opening line, *Specters in the Glass House* captures your senses, coaxing you deeper into a troubled yet compelling world bridged over a century. This story will permeate your imagination long after you've finished the last page."

D. J. Williams, author of *King of the Night*

"Readers will be eager to take this twisty, suspense-filled ride."

Publishers Weekly

"Jaime Jo Wright is a master craftswoman of the dual-timeline suspense novel. She switches between characters at just the right moment to keep building tension."

Historical Novel Society

Praise for *The Lost Boys of Barlowe Theater*

"Once again, Wright outdoes herself as the preeminent expert in impactful eeriness. This tale takes on fresh frights with dizzying skill."

Booklist

"*The Lost Boys of Barlowe Theater* is a story that stays with you long after you close the book, leaving you with a strong sense that we all have a need to belong, to feel like we have value, a reason for being born—and that it's not impossible to find this when we trust that God has a plan for our lives. I love that Jaime brings this truth home with such care. Read this story. You won't be sorry."

Lynette Eason, bestselling and award-winning author

The BELL TOLLS at TRAEGER HALL

Books by Jaime Jo Wright

The House on Foster Hill
The Reckoning at Gossamer Pond
The Curse of Misty Wayfair
Echoes among the Stones
The Haunting at Bonaventure Circus
On the Cliffs of Foxglove Manor
The Souls of Lost Lake
The Premonition at Withers Farm
The Vanishing at Castle Moreau
The Lost Boys of Barlowe Theater
Night Falls on Predicament Avenue
Specters in the Glass House
Tempest at Annabel's Lighthouse
The Bell Tolls at Traeger Hall

The BELL TOLLS at TRAEGER HALL

JAIME JO WRIGHT

BethanyHouse
a division of Baker Publishing Group
Minneapolis, Minnesota

© 2025 by Jaime Sundsmo

Published by Bethany House Publishers
Minneapolis, Minnesota
BethanyHouse.com

Bethany House Publishers is a division of
Baker Publishing Group, Grand Rapids, Michigan

Printed in the United States of America

All rights reserved. No part of this publication may be reproduced, stored in a retrieval system, or transmitted in any form or by any means—for example, electronic, photocopy, recording—without the prior written permission of the publisher. The only exception is brief quotations in printed reviews.

Library of Congress Cataloging-in-Publication Data
Names: Wright, Jaime Jo, author.
Title: The bell tolls at Traeger Hall / Jaime Jo Wright.
Description: Minneapolis, Minnesota : Bethany House, a division of Baker Publishing Group, 2025.
Identifiers: LCCN 2025004878 | ISBN 9780764243806 (paperback) | ISBN 9780764245787 (casebound) | ISBN 9781493451364 (ebook)
Subjects: LCGFT: Christian fiction | Detective and mystery fiction | Novels
Classification: LCC PS3623.R5388 B45 2025 | DDC 813/.6—dc23/eng/20250403
LC record available at https://lccn.loc.gov/2025004878

Scripture quotations are from the King James Version of the Bible.

This is a work of fiction. Names, characters, incidents, and dialogues are products of the author's imagination and are not to be construed as real. Any resemblance to actual events or persons, living or dead, is entirely coincidental.

Cover design by Jennifer Parker

Published in association with Books & Such Literary Management, BooksAndSuch.com.

Baker Publishing Group publications use paper produced from sustainable forestry practices and postconsumer waste whenever possible.

25 26 27 28 29 30 31   7 6 5 4 3 2 1

To my sister, Brooke

I love you more each day,
and I will never love you less.

WAVERLY

In an interview shortly before her death in 1950; memories from two weeks prior to the murders:

Darkness encased Traeger Hall like a shroud. The darkness never lifted either. It hadn't lifted since I arrived a year ago at the impressionable age of eighteen. It wasn't an altogether awful place, of course. In fact, it was a mansion in comparison to the surrounding farmhouses and cottages in its vicinity. But, even if the sun was shining, somehow Traeger Hall remained in the shadows, perched on the top of a hill overlooking the small town of Newton Creek. And it was that shadowy, secretive lordship that gave my spirit pause.

Leopold Traeger, my uncle by marriage, settled in Newton Creek decades earlier as a young man. He built his sawmill, soon realized great success, and as a result the town rose up around the creek that powered the mill. Besides owning and operating the sawmill, he eventually became owner of the Newton Creek Bank plus several other properties, a veritable lord of his own fiefdom, all nestled among the rolling farmland of the state of Wisconsin.

Uncle Leopold made sure everyone knew who owned the bulk of Newton Creek when he moved into what became known as Traeger Hall, erected on the area's highest hill and flanked by oak trees on its eastern and western ends. The great house was rectangular and crafted entirely of brick, including a veranda that featured right angles only and a bell tower on its east side.

This bell tower—or so my aunt, who married Leopold five years prior to my arrival, told me—was added on to the house shortly before their wedding. Its massive bell had never been rung and was so heavy the wind couldn't budge it even in the fiercest of storms. It was quite certain, then, that human hands were ringing it when a person heard the Traeger Hall bell. However, I was told it would never be rung except in the event of an attack of a deadly foe, which was something Leopold Traeger predicted *would* happen sooner or later.

Because he'd lost his mind. At least that was my theory. The demons Greed and Ego had eaten his faculties—if I gave them names—leaving his mind riddled with decay. Why else would he run back and forth in the halls at all hours of the night, sneaking around in the shadows one moment and all but howling at the moon the next? I was convinced he was so consumed by himself that the ultimate stroke to his arrogance was to believe someone, somewhere, was devising his murder.

Oh, that we could all be so famous as to be first on the list for someone to kill!

On second thought, I preferred my anonymity, although even that was hard to come by now that I lived in Traeger Hall and put up with the pompous, heavy-handed dominance Uncle Leopold lorded over my aunt and myself as her ward.

"Remember your composure, Waverly." Uncle Leopold's stern voice raised goose pimples along my arms. I was not a mild-mannered niece by any stretch, and yet when it came to my uncle, he could silence me with a look from those steel-gray eyes of his—and a strike from the back of his hand, which had been executed a few times. I therefore learned my lesson: I listened—or seethed rather—in silence.

"I have given you respite here at Traeger Hall, and you are representative of our entire enterprise."

Uncle's gray sideburns twitched along with his jaw. His mustache covered his upper lip and hung down on either side of his mouth like inverted antlers. Under my quiet perusal, his face hardened.

"Have I made myself clear?" he added.

"Yes, Uncle." My meekness was not feigned. I quailed under his sour expression. There was a reason Uncle Leopold had been awarded such influence over Newton Creek. There was nothing so intimidating as a man with a heightened sense of omnipotence, especially when time and again he'd been proven to be in the right.

That was both the gift and the problem of Uncle Leopold. He only argued when he knew for a fact he was correct, and it seemed he was *always* correct. He was beyond mathematical equations of rational thought, common sense being his primary demand of others, and he reserved little space for unreasonable emotion. And yet I still believed he was verging on a state of insanity.

I, however, was not.

Still, Uncle Leopold was confronting my display of tears or, as he put it, my "irrational emotional outburst." For which there was little grace.

I had dared to mourn my dead sparrow. A little feathered creature I had nursed along all summer after it had careened into the window of the front parlor. It had been a tiny ray of sunshine in this otherwise questionable world of Traeger Hall, and now it was dead. No gratitude was given to Mrs. Carp's cat who roamed Newton Creek as if equal in authority to Uncle Leopold, master of the house.

"God is aware of all His creatures, Uncle." It was my attempt to put him in his place.

Uncle Leopold was unimpressed.

"And He understands that when they die, such is the wages of sin."

Uncle's eyes bored into my own. I lifted my chin, then tilted it back down as his eyebrow raised. Where was my aunt when I needed her? She and I weren't particularly close, but she at least would take my side on occasion. Rarely, though, and probably not in defense of a dead bird.

"Am I not allowed to grieve?" I realized immediately that I should not have asked such a question.

Uncle Leopold cleared the space between us, his face pressing downward and terribly close to mine. He reached to grip my upper arm with a bruising effect that made every nurturing moment with my beloved sparrow a luxury not worth the price.

"It was a bird," he gritted out, far more furious than he should be over my show of emotion.

That my existence made him so angry confused me and, to be honest, frightened me as well.

"Birds come and go," he continued in a patronizing tone. "Crying about it is a ridiculous waste of time when we have more important things to attend to." Another raised eyebrow was the exclamation point at the end of my uncle's sentence.

In that moment—and not for the first time—I wished him dead.

1

WAVERLY PEMBROOKE

**NEWTON CREEK, WISCONSIN
SEPTEMBER 1890**

One would think coming upon the scene of one's uncle and aunt's brutal slaying would be enough to send one into a dead faint. Instead, it was the cut of the trocar into her uncle's corpse that caused Waverly Pembrooke to slide off her seat and onto the floor in a pile of black mourning silk. She was brought to by smelling salts and the perturbed tapping of male fingertips against her cheek. First a blurry face with skin darker than most of the area's European descendants came into view, and then vivid blue eyes narrowed into irritated slits.

"As I said before you became one with the floor, Miss Pembrooke, the embalming process is not for the faint of heart, let alone a female, and certainly not in one's own home."

Waverly blinked and tried to gather her senses. She wasn't fond of weakness and simpering and the poppycock that went along with it, perhaps because her aunt—her very murdered aunt who lay awaiting her own embalming—had always encouraged it.

"No man will ever feel needed if you laud yourself to be as intelligent and strong as they are."

Waverly struggled into a sitting position, batting off the undertaker's hands of assistance. That was precisely the point she *wanted* to make to men. She was as intelligent as they were, yet her body had betrayed her strength.

"I'm . . . I'm quite all right." Waverly reached for the chair she'd been sitting in and pulled herself up.

"You aren't." The undertaker's gravelly vocal cords grated on her nerves.

"You're not a doctor, Mr. Fitzgerald. You're merely an undertaker." Waverly hoped it would put the man, a mere ten years her senior, in his place. She had known him since her arrival at Traeger Hall a year ago. They were acquaintances, perhaps bordering on hesitant friendship. But now? This was quite embarrassing indeed.

His mustache quirked, and Waverly had no idea how to interpret the expression on his face. That her words seemed to have no effect irked her. "And yet here I am, applying the smelling salts." He shoved the cork back into its vial. "As I stated before, Miss Pembrooke, you should take your leave during this process. It is unseemly at best. Your uncle is barely clothed at the moment, and the inappropriateness of your presence will be gossiped about for the next decade."

Her uncle. Waverly allowed her vision to rest again on his body. Wiry gray hair sprung from her uncle's chest that had been recently bathed from the crusted blood that had covered it. All fourteen stab wounds now seemed like small cuts in spongy flesh rather than the violent marks of death. His face was gray in pallor. His arms lay by his sides, and a white sheet covered his nether regions.

"My uncle has no opinion at the moment," Waverly muttered, swallowing the nausea she felt. "His requests prior to his death were very clear. His body was not to be removed from Traeger Hall, and a member of the Traeger family must be present with his body until lowered into the grave."

And that responsibility fell onto her shoulders, the only remaining heir—all gratitude given to her aunt—to the Traeger Estate, bank, sawmill, and subsequent authority earned by status over the town of Newton Creek, Wisconsin.

"That is hardly unusual, hence the term *wake*. But do you truly, Miss Pembrooke, intend to sleep beside the corpses until a dead man's wishes are appeased? I hardly imagine your uncle meant his words to be taken so literally as to deny you the privilege of leaving the room. It's ungodly. A ridiculous request, if I may say so." Mr. Fitzgerald retorted and returned to the side of the deceased Leopold Traeger.

"You may not." Waverly folded her gloved hands in her lap and straightened her posture.

"And how long did your uncle say he was to remain unburied?" Mr. Fitzgerald's voice was muffled as he bent over the body.

Waverly swallowed back another wave of nausea. "Seven days," she answered, "to be certain of his state of death."

"Seven days. Four, I understand, is traditional, but seven?" Mr. Fitzgerald jabbed the trocar into the abdominal cavity once again, intent on releasing the embalming fluid that contained a mixture of arsenic and herbs. "If this hasn't killed him and he awakens in four, I will resign from my position as undertaker. We'd best double the request for floral arrangements. I would also advise you to consider obtaining incense and the like and burning it slowly." He lifted his head and gave the spacious front parlor of Traeger Hall a once-over. "This room is going to be quite ripe by the end of seven days."

"At which point *then* we shall rest," Waverly added.

His oceanic blue eyes locked on to hers. "Miss Pembrooke, only God rests on the seventh day. We, on the other hand, shall be busy burying the dead."

2

Jennie Phillips

Newton Creek, Wisconsin
September—Present Day

She had buried her dead—and that was okay. It was this mud, the flooding, and the earth beneath her feet making sucking sounds with each step that was overwhelming her. But wasn't that a lot like life? Just when you thought you were getting back on a path that was solid, more predictable, finally pursuing your passion, another catastrophic event derailed it all.

Jennie Phillips had spent her early twenties in France, the Louvre her playground, sending pics to her mom of the works of Delacroix and Jean Auguste Ingres and Rembrandt and, well, pick an artist who embodied their very soul on the canvas they painted and that was the unbreakable tie Jennie had experienced with her mother. But today? Today she was thirty, her mom's passing from cancer only months in her rearview mirror, she'd lost her ties to the art world in the last two years of caring for

Mom, and now she was still cleaning up after her dead father—a task she'd unwillingly inherited after Mom's death.

Dad had left an unending dossier of historical property investments throughout the United States. He'd left a lot of money too, so Jennie didn't have to work ever again if she didn't want to. Still, even five years after the heart attack ended his narcissistic reign of oppression, his lawyers were still trying to sift through all he'd left behind.

Jennie lifted her foot as her rain boot sank into the soggy earth. Water flooded the boot's imprint in the mud. The farmland of central Wisconsin was about as far away from Paris as she could get. The phone call she'd received from Dad's attorney had changed her plans—and her flight. Paris and reentry into her cocoon of classical studies had been shelved once again.

All because of this place.

Newton Creek.

Or more specifically, Traeger Hall.

Movement snagged Jennie from her internal musings. She scanned her surroundings as if just awakening to them. The land to the north rose in a steady slope leading to the hilltop, the highest point of the township of Newton Creek, all the way up to the imposing, boxlike edifice called Traeger Hall with its unusual bell tower. She had yet to visit the mansion because the unexpected and rare fall flooding hadn't affected the house and grounds like it had everything else.

A shadow slipped behind an oak tree in the path ahead of Jennie. The tree's bark had turned black from the rain, and its branches were already losing their leaves. Jennie tilted her head, narrowing her eyes as she peered at the small form behind the oak.

"Hello there!" Jennie called out, infusing a lighthearted warmth into her tone that she didn't feel inside. Beyond the tree, she saw more trees dotting the flatland and, in the distance, the dilapidated remains of Traeger Sawmill.

Jennie could make out the form of a boy, maybe eight years old, hiding behind the tree, craning his neck to eye her with curiosity. She sloshed her way forward on the trail that ran around the base of the Traeger hill, toward what had once been the primary economic support for the community back in the 1800s: the sawmill.

All that was left of the sawmill were the skeletal remains of one of the buildings along with the mill wheel, still poised over Newton Creek. It was as if the wheel wanted to return to work, but its elderly and fragile condition prevented it from doing so.

"Hello?" she called again, and the boy stepped into full view but didn't return her greeting. He stared at her with large brown eyes, framed by circular glasses that might have given him a Harry Potter vibe if he wasn't so lanky and his hair so unruly with black curls. He wore a white Pokémon T-shirt with a Poké Ball at its center. His blue jeans were cuffed high, and his green rain boots sported Pikachu faces.

"Are you okay?" Jennie tried to engage the boy, wondering where the boy's parents were and why he was roaming the countryside alone.

The boy motioned with his hand, waving toward himself. He looked over his shoulder at the sawmill and then back to her.

"Is something wrong?"

The boy didn't seem to have any intention of responding. But as she came alongside him, he beckoned for her to follow. Curious and concerned about the boy's welfare, Jennie pursued him, their feet slopping through the muck. It grew muddier and slicker as they neared the old sawmill.

Newton Creek had been blown out entirely by the flooding. What had once been a delightful small stream that fly fisherman could wade in and catch brown trout from its undercuts, was now a wide swath of clay muck. The rains had caused the creek to swell, overfilling its banks until the small, man-made dam above the mill gave way, leaving Newton Pond to finish the job of destroying the landscape.

The flood had forever changed the creek. Now only a trickle of water remained, a few feet in width and shin-deep.

The boy hopped across the creek by stepping strategically on exposed flat stones, revealed by the draining of the creek. As Jennie struggled to keep up with the child, her foot slipped and landed with a splash. Her boot was barely tall enough to protect her jeans, and mud splattered over the front of the purple galoshes. The clay earth tried to swallow her foot like quicksand, but she tugged it free with a watery *squelch*.

"Wait up!" Jennie called after the boy.

Ignoring her, he continued on, scampering toward the mill wheel.

The ruins of Traeger Sawmill marred the otherwise natural surroundings of meadow and rocky earth. What had once been an area rife with workers, roads, wagons, and domestic animals was now nothing more than a demolished creek, bordered by a meadow on one side and a soybean field on the other.

Newton Creek had died right along with Leopold, Traeger Hall's original owner, back at the turn of the century. What had supposedly been a burgeoning village and a growing economy was handed down to the few folks left behind, leaving them pieces of ghost-town memorabilia and not much else to speak of.

The boy balanced on a rock that was dotted with lichen the color of mint. Spring water gurgled past it as though trying to keep Newton Creek alive. He pointed toward the mill wheel.

Jennie stood on the bank and leaned out. "I don't see anything." She squinted. That wasn't entirely true, as she saw rusted tin cans half buried in the mud of the former creek bed. And she saw scraps of wood and old iron spikes littering the area, with water trickling over and around everything. The worst part was the fish. A few small trout flopped and flipped in puddles, trying to make their way to the deeper part of the water's flow to survive the demise of their creek.

It already stank of rotted dead things and algae mixed in a cocktail of amoebas and frogs.

The boy shook his finger as if to mime what his mouth could not voice. *There!* He pointed once more toward the base of the sawmill wheel that tilted precariously from its moorings and appeared ready to collapse alongside what remained of the mill's building.

Jennie craned her neck to better see what the boy was pointing at. Her breath caught in her throat. She focused on the five brownish-white *things* sticking up in the mud. A claw. A wild grasp, frozen in time as if reaching for the sky.

In a split second, Jennie grappled for the boy, twisting him toward her and away from what she hoped was not the grisly reality she imagined. She squatted in front of him, locking eyes with the boy and gripping his upper arms.

"Do you live nearby?" She searched his face, hoping he'd finally speak to her.

The boy nodded instead.

"Okay." Jennie tried to steady her nerves by sucking in a deep breath. Bones. Was she overreacting? Was that really a hand, unearthed and clawing the air? She glanced over the boy's shoulder. It would be hard to tell for certain until she got closer, but there was no way she wanted the kid to see it any more than he already had. "Can you run home and get help? Your mom or dad? I'd like them to come and help me." She applauded herself for the calm in her voice.

Again, the boy nodded.

Jennie released him and gave him a reassuring fist bump. "All right then. Why don't you—?"

Before she could finish, the boy skirted around her and sprinted off as though the earth was made of granite and the slippery mud not an obstacle.

Jennie straightened, rubbing her sweaty palms on her jeans. She scanned the old sawmill, the creek, the land on each side, and Traeger Hall on the hilltop in the distance—all of this was hers now. Dad had purchased the Traeger Estate, which included hundreds of acres. The township of Newton Creek, now just a patchwork quilt of farmland and private homes that met in the middle of the tiny village, sat in the shadows of everything Traeger.

As the new custodian in charge here, it was Jennie's responsibility to investigate the potential appendage sticking up from the sawmill's ground. She might not be a Traeger by ancestry, but she was the rightful owner of this place. And she didn't want to call the cops just yet. If it turned out the appendage was only sticks, then she'd feel like an idiot.

Jennie was nowhere near as adept at maneuvering around the obstacles as the boy. She attempted to balance on a log that was slimy from years of being underwater. Her foot slipped, and she yelped as she sank ankle-deep in the mud. She tugged at her leg, the clay from the creek bed pulling determinedly at her boot. Crying out, Jennie lost her balance, her captive foot sinking deeper into the muck. Her hands splashed into the cold stream of water. Mud painted her chest and face as she finished her downward trajectory with a *splat*.

She lay prostrate in the creek bed for a moment, considering her options. Traeger Hall and its legacy was as murky as this creek bed—ruined and marring anything and everything that encountered it. She hadn't even had time yet to reconcile why she was here at Newton Creek, let alone deal with Traeger Hall's burdensome history.

She lifted her face . . . and froze.

Not far away, the five protruding *things* still scraped the air. Jennie recognized the unmistakable shape of knuckles and joints, stretching, palm upward, from the mire of the creek bed, as if the unfortunate soul had, with a last breath, frantically raked at the air above.

Jennie winced but forced herself not to look away this time. It seemed the thick mud was the only thing holding the skeletal hand in place, and whatever else remained of the unfortunate one beneath the mud was completely out of sight. She changed her mind then, deciding it was time to call the authorities. Meanwhile, she'd be careful not to disturb the scene.

Thank God she'd sent the boy to get help—not because anyone he returned with could help her so much as this vision would have etched itself into the child's mind for life. The innocence in his eyes having communicated he'd discovered something out of place was enough. He didn't need to know he'd identified a dead body.

Jennie's hands sank deeper into the mud as she pushed herself up from the creek bed, away from the offensive appendage. Her ankle twisted in the clay, her knees sinking down and scraping against buried rocks. Scrambling to extricate herself caused clay to squish between her hands and release the stench of rotting earth.

"I gotta get out of here," she muttered to herself. She twisted, grappling for a wooden beam that had broken off the mill and was stuck halfway out of the creek. Wrapping her hand around it, Jennie hoisted herself to her feet. As she did, more mud and silt slid from beneath the mill wheel nearby. The skeletal hand moved as if it still had life within it. The index finger and thumb curled inward.

She gasped as more horror was revealed.

Turned toward her, half buried in the clay, a hollow eye socket stared back at her, and she recognized the unmistakable breadth of a skull's temple.

A scream echoed across the meadow, resonating in her ears as a shrill siren of terror. It was her own scream. And now she screamed again for the corpse—for the human remains whose own screams had long been silenced by the creek.

3

WAVERLY

Traeger Hall
September 1890

"The terms of the will are quite simple, really." The attorney overseeing the estate of Leopold Traeger lifted the sheaf of papers on end and tapped them on the tabletop to straighten them. Like any respectable attorney, his gray eyes communicated shrewdness. The strands of white hair combed over his balding head were obedient to his ministrations, as was his mustache that hugged the sides of his mouth and almost met the muttonchops that framed his round face.

Mr. Grossman was, after all, trustworthy. There was no way that Leopold Traeger would have ever gifted any man the time of day, let alone his confidence, were he shifty or unscrupulous.

"But, Mr. Grossman . . ." Waverly lifted her chin and peered down her nose at the man, hoping to convey a modicum of self-confidence by summoning the authority her uncle had always drawn upon. Traeger authority. She cleared her throat and began again. "I am quite concerned regarding the terms of my uncle's will. They're highly . . . irregular."

Mr. Grossman eyed her, then shifted his gaze to the empty chair beside her. More than likely he was wishing for a man to be sitting there, someone to speak on her behalf. Someone with more than half a brain instead of a blond, curly-haired young woman with the innocent blue eyes and rosebud lips of a china doll. That was how Waverly Pembrooke had always been described by the matrons in her boarding school for young ladies and in the social section in the newspaper. And never did the critics mean it as a compliment. They either seethed with female jealousy and contempt, or they alluded to a flighty nature and feminine disposition that would be better off serving tea and cakes than receiving legal advice regarding carrying on the business of a profitable estate.

Mr. Grossman cleared his throat, seeming to contemplate his response considering the lack of another male in the study. Leopold Traeger's study. Uncle Leopold's desk. A desk that *she* should be sitting behind as the new mistress of Traeger Hall. Instead, she had ceded her seat to the attorney.

"Irregular as it may be, it is binding by law."

"I cannot contest it?" Waverly asked.

A flicker in Mr. Grossman's eyes told her she was remarkably close to either impressing him or offending him. She guessed it would be the latter.

"No, you can't contest a last will and testament." Mr. Grossman smoothed the papers with his hands—papers drafted according to the expressed wishes of Uncle Leopold. "Your aunt's and uncle's remains are to stay at Traeger Hall for a full week. Upon the surety of their deceased state, they will then be interred in the Traeger mausoleum at Newton Creek Cemetery."

There was only one mausoleum in the otherwise modest cemetery. Waverly had no need for Mr. Grossman to identify it as belonging to the Traeger family. Uncle Leopold had built the marble mausoleum in preparation of his death, much as he had the bell tower. There, he would assume his position as founder of the village, in death just as he had in life.

"Once the funeral has concluded, you will have forty-eight hours to gather your personal things, leaving behind all that belonged to your aunt and uncle and taking nothing with you but that which you brought here."

"My trunk of clothes and hats?" Waverly pressed her lips together, disdainful of her dead uncle's lack of concern for her welfare. "And what of Traeger Hall? I'm not allowed to stay, to make it my home just as it has been for the last year? What provisions have been left for me? I was, after all, under his guardianship."

"My dear . . ." Mr. Grossman leaned forward, folding his hands and resting them atop the will. "After said forty-eight hours, Traeger Hall is to be closed forthwith upon your departure." The attorney then rephrased his statement as though Waverly were incapable of understanding the legal verbiage. "The Hall is to be sealed, and it is not to be reopened."

"Until?" Waverly pressed.

"Until what?" Mr. Grossman appeared peeved at her question.

"When may I reopen Traeger Hall?"

"You may not."

"What do you mean I 'may not'?" Waverly straightened her already quite prim figure. The padded velvet seat of the wooden chair on which she sat creaked as a spring protested the shifting of her weight.

Mr. Grossman released a heavy sigh that communicated how sorely Waverly's feminine mind was trying his last shred of patience. "Miss Pembrooke, must I read the will again? It cannot be that difficult to understand. Traeger Hall is to be sealed. It is to remain so. The windows and entryways shall be bricked shut. The roof will be maintained by someone appointed by my firm to help it avoid the rigors of time. Aside from that, no other means of upkeep will be spared for the estate. Under no circumstances is anyone to enter Traeger Hall again."

Waverly adjusted the lace cuff of her crocheted gloves. It was absurd. It was utterly ridiculous. Uncle Leopold had been a force while alive, but now that he was dead, he'd become a monster. "You're saying that this house shall remain abandoned?" She repeated what she had heard but didn't genuinely believe.

"Until there are no longer any Traeger descendants to claim rights to it or a century has passed, yes," Mr. Grossman concluded, a look of relief apparent on his face.

Waverly seemed to finally grasp the authority of the will. "But my aunt and uncle had no children. I am from my aunt's side, and I bear no Traeger blood. My uncle had no siblings nor cousins!" Waverly's frown removed the relief from the attorney's expression.

"Then Traeger Hall will stand closed for a century, Miss Pembrooke."

"A century? That is complete absurdity! Traeger Hall will be in complete ruins in a century." It wasn't that Waverly wished to become queen of sorts over her uncle's amassed businesses and wealth. It was just that she was desperate to have a place to live and her base needs met. Uncle Leopold wasn't the only one who had no more relatives. Waverly would be destitute if what Mr. Grossman stated was upheld.

Mr. Grossman cleared his throat, followed by an uncomfortable twitch of his mustache. "What is absurd or rational matters not in light of this being the instruction of Mr. Traeger's last will and testament."

Waverly had already considered the seven-day wake over her aunt's and uncle's corpses uncomfortable at best and gruesome at worst. But this latest revelation was personal, Uncle Leopold's last slap of abuse. She tried again in the blind hope that she had somehow misunderstood Mr. Grossman. "So Traeger Hall will be closed with all of its furnishings and my aunt and uncle's belongings? With their mementos? The family portraits, my uncle's art collection, the *books* . . . ?" Waverly could feel her disbelief turning into emotion, and she fought against it while still presenting her argument. "The books will be left here to decay and be eaten by mice and moths. What about the fireplace poker?" She waved her gloved hand toward the cold fireplace and the iron poker that rested in its holder. "I must leave that too?"

An eyebrow rose. "You have sentiment toward the fireplace poker?" Mr. Grossman inquired.

"Well, if it's the only thing I can take, then *yes*. Yes, I do!" Waverly cursed herself for becoming unreasonable, but it was anger, not a supposedly witless feminine nature, which spurred her on. "My uncle is leaving me destitute. With no home, no place to go, nothing but the trunks I brought with me from my boarding school. I can no more return there than I can turn back time and become sixteen again. On my eighteenth birthday I aged out of the school, and my aunt took me in."

"Much to the chagrin of your uncle, might I add," Mr. Grossman inserted.

He needn't have. Up until his murder, Uncle Leopold had made it clear from the moment she had arrived that she was not wanted here. Her aunt Cornelia had also made it clear she had not taken Waverly in out of the goodness of her heart, but out of familial obligation as was customary.

Waverly attempted to calm herself. She cleared her throat. "Mr. Grossman, I am an orphan. My aunt was my last remaining relative on my mother's side. Where am I to go?"

Mr. Grossman blinked and then had the decency to lower his eyes as he straightened the papers again. "The will does not give instruction as to what you should do, Miss Pembrooke, only what shall happen to Traeger Hall and the Traeger Estate."

"And my uncle's business interests? The sawmill? His logging company up north? The bank?" Waverly scrambled to remember everything her uncle owned. He held the monopoly on Newton Creek. The Newton Creek Bank held most of the mortgages and loans for the area. The sawmill was just one spoke in a finely crafted wheel, attached to the northern logging company he also owned. Not to mention his copious amounts of other investments.

Uncle Leopold had made no secret that his investments were none of Waverly's business to even know about. He had his own partners, his own board of managers, and even his own hobbies. Waverly glanced at the painting on the wall behind his desk. Uncle Leopold had dabbled in the fine arts. She had no idea who had painted the landscape, but he had given strict instructions regarding its care. Yet there was more than just Traeger Hall to be considered; there was the financial foundation of Leopold Traeger himself.

She snapped her eyes back to Mr. Grossman. "All of my uncle's assets—what is to become of them?"

Mr. Grossman made the pretense of stuffing the papers into his satchel as though to imply the conversation was all but over. "They will be managed by my firm."

"Your firm?" Waverly digested that information. "On behalf of . . . ?" She let her sentence hang.

Mr. Grossman paused and met her eyes. "On behalf of your uncle's last will and testament, of course."

It was an extremely unsatisfactory answer. Waverly pursed her lips, refusing to release Mr. Grossman's gaze.

He coughed, visibly uncomfortable. "Each asset has its own set of instructions. It would take me hours to educate you, Miss Pembrooke, and it would all be for naught. None of it concerns you, nor is it allocated for your benefit."

"For whose benefit then?" The pit in Waverly's stomach grew larger with every sidestep and denial from Mr. Grossman.

"The village of Newton Creek will absorb the continued profits into the community. Mr. Traeger wished for the town to thrive in his absence. Now if you'll excuse me—"

"Who will *manage* my uncle's assets?" Waverly ignored the man's attempt to shut down the conversation.

Mr. Grossman snapped the latch on his satchel and leveled a severe look on Waverly. "Miss Pembrooke, to give you the briefest of explanations in a way that I pray you will understand, my *firm* will manage your uncle's assets until the time of my own personal passing, at which point all assets will be sold and the profits dispersed into various outlets within Newton Creek. In this way, Leopold Traeger will ensure that Newton Creek will have a promising future, just as he had envisioned it and spent his life bolstering its economy."

"But I will not," Waverly shot back.

So her uncle had left his business assets to Mr. Grossman. That was essentially the truth of what the lawyer was skirting. The lawyer would profit. His firm would become the reigning authority over it all. And to put the final nail in his legacy's coffin, Uncle Leopold had made sure no one person would gain from his vast wealth and philanthropy. He would make certain, even from the grave, that he was never forgotten and that Newton Creek's very survival as a town rested on a dead man's shoulders.

Mr. Grossman lifted his satchel and rounded the desk. He paused by her chair, looking down his nose at her and giving her an affected expression of pity. "You have several days yet. I'm sure you will figure something out."

The door closed behind him as he left the room.

Waverly lifted her eyes to the painting and was reminded once more that Uncle Leopold had only ever cared for that which benefited him. It was very apparent—not that she was surprised—that Waverly was worth less to him than a painting. For the one above his desk would still be ensconced in

Traeger Hall for at least a century, collecting dust like a miser hoarded his riches.

&pspace;

Even her reflection unnerved her. Waverly sat in her nightgown before the mirror on her dressing table, the orange glow from the fireplace behind her keeping the bedroom warm, causing shadows to distort her features. It was beyond difficult to be at peace in a home where your relatives had been brutally stabbed to death. Every creak, every moan of the house, every tree branch against a windowpane was the possible announcement that the killer had returned. Waverly attempted to calm her spirit with prayer, for God had promised to watch over the sparrow, and wasn't she more important than a bird?

Waverly stilled, her horsehair brush halfway down her lengthy corn silk tresses. Deep shadows beneath her azure-colored eyes created hollows in her face, ghoulish shadows making her cheekbones razor-sharp and her skin colorless. The fire flickered and snapped. The four-poster bed behind her boasted broad spindles and a thick mattress that should have been welcoming. Waverly's attention shifted to the bed, then to the dark corners where spirits could be hiding, waiting to haunt her when she retired for the night.

Traeger Hall was a crypt of silence.

The fire gave off a loud snap, and Waverly jumped, her brush tangling in her hair and pulling it. She blinked rapidly to clear her vision and her mind from the unsettling imagination of someone who now shared a house with corpses. The bodies of her aunt and uncle were posed in their death sleep in the front parlor, surrounded by fresh flowers with their heavily perfumed scent.

Waverly would have gagged had she not known that in another day or so, that perfume would be a saving grace to Traeger Hall. She should be there right now, standing vigil over them in the event her aunt and uncle miraculously returned to life.

It was a superstition—a wake—but it held some merit. In the event a person was not truly dead, they would prefer not to be buried alive. Waverly had heard of one man who'd been buried only to awaken later, six feet underground, the weight of earth holding down the lid of his coffin. His salvation was the string tied to his toe that traveled to the open air above him, which if pulled would ring a bell.

A bell.

Waverly stilled, her brush held against her chest, staring at the mirror, her reflection her only companion.

"Bells pronounce what is and what is to come, don't they?" she asked herself. Her mind traveled to the bell tower Uncle Leopold had built.

"When someone comes with the intent to murder and take my life, ring the bell."

She'd questioned her uncle's paranoia. Her aunt had never addressed it. His reminder came almost daily. Waverly knew he'd reiterated it frequently in town among men of importance. Among the authorities who would send their policemen to the aid and service of Uncle Leopold.

"Who would even want to come to Uncle's rescue?" Waverly resumed brushing her hair. "No one liked him. They merely *needed* him."

And that was the wily wickedness of Uncle Leopold's death. His brutal slaying had been not only the affirmation of Uncle's prophetic conviction that the bell would need to be rung one day to save his life but the revelation that even in his death, Uncle Leopold had arranged his assets in such a way that Newton Creek would still need him, would still be reminded of him every day.

"You were crafty, Uncle. Suspicious and crafty and in complete admiration of yourself."

Waverly set the hairbrush on the dressing table. No. She would not perch overnight by her aunt and uncle's bodies. She would not give Uncle Leopold the satisfaction of commanding her from the grave. If she had a plan, if she had anywhere to go, Waverly would leave Traeger Hall tonight. She wouldn't stay here in this tomb of terrible memories, in this place of violence and death. She would embrace the comfort of another human life and the warmth of a pleasurable host's fireplace.

But no. Tonight she had nowhere to go. No one to turn to. The people of Newton Creek had associated Waverly with her uncle's domineering authority. To them, Waverly *was* a Traeger—even though she wasn't.

So tonight, she was alone.

Traeger Hall's servants had retired to the servants' quarters, a smaller, separate building on the property, because, in Uncle Leopold's words, *"Only idiots share habitats with people they cannot trust with their lives."* But as the chimes of the grandfather clock reverberated from the first floor through the cavernous rooms and hallways, Waverly would have gladly shared the empty manor with a complete stranger.

Well, unless that stranger was the unknown fiend who had broken into Traeger Hall and stabbed her aunt and uncle with the vehemence of someone who reveled in the sight of blood. Perhaps a stranger wouldn't be preferred right now, but Waverly would have been thankful to have even the stableboy sleeping outside her bedroom door. It would mean there was someone living and breathing in Traeger Hall besides herself. It would mean the moments she sensed someone breathing behind her and just out of sight could be accounted for.

But alone in Traeger Hall, Waverly had no one she could blame for the feeling that eyes moved to follow her as she shifted in her chair. She had no one to blame for the sound of a door closing somewhere down the hallway. She had no way to explain the garbled chime of the grandfather clock, halting at the chime of nine when it should have gone on to the stroke of midnight. The echo of the aborted chime rang in the distance, causing

Waverly to freeze. Her eyes met her reflection, and she stared at her companion self. The grandfather clock in the front hall had chimed relentlessly since the day Waverly had arrived at Traeger Hall.

"The only reason it would malfunction tonight was if someone—some hand—had stilled it mid-stroke." Waverly's whispering only unsettled her more. Her voice was hoarse, but it was also loud in the stillness.

The termination of the clock's chimes had stopped time. Or at least that was the conclusion Waverly came to.

Her bare foot brushed against something soft but solid, and she startled, recoiling at what must certainly be her dead aunt's roaming ghost. Instead, Waverly met the blue-eyed stare of the long-haired, orange-and-white cat that had come to rub against her leg.

"Foo!" She bent down and swept the feline into her arms, ignoring his muted meow of protest at being held like an infant. Waverly pressed her face into the cat's silken fur belly, its fur tickling her nostrils.

The cat was real.

It was alive.

It was biting her!

"Ow!" Waverly tossed the rebellious thing to the floor, where Foo landed on his four feet. He didn't bother to scamper away but sat there on his haunches, cleaning his fur with broad strokes of his tongue. Waverly's unwelcome attention had apparently left Foo quite filthy according to his standards. Even now, Waverly noted his narrow-eyed glint of censure. It wouldn't be until later, when she curled up in her bed, that Foo would forgive her and position himself on top of her, his purring resuming and their friendship restored.

"Come with me, Foo," Waverly said. The heat from the fireplace had become almost oppressive. She paused, her hand poised on the knob of the bedroom door. She eyed the cat, who obviously had no intention of following her. "So I must go alone? There will be milk, and I shall share with you."

The cat blinked at her before flopping onto his side on the rug in refusal.

Waverly craved a glass of milk from the kitchen to settle her nerves. But with no one to ring for, she would have to get it herself. And the idea of walking from her second-floor room to the kitchen frightened her. She would need to traverse the broad staircase, pray that phantoms weren't waiting to claw at her, and then—the horrors—she would need to make her way through the back hallways that were typically left to the help to maneuver. Kitchens weren't normally thought of as fearsome places, but any room in Traeger Hall tonight was potentially frightening.

She would need to be careful to slip past the parlor and her aunt and uncle's remains and hope their eyes were still closed, not open and staring lifelessly at the ceiling.

The undertaker, Mr. Fitzgerald, would have made sure they stayed shut, wouldn't he? With glue perhaps? How did one shut a dead person's eyes and make sure they didn't pop open by accident? *Could* a dead person's eyes spring open by reflex?

Already halfway down the staircase, Waverly shivered. The grand entryway rose from the ground floor to the roof in a curved, elegant fashion that should have boasted a chandelier with hundreds of candles, if Traeger Hall were a castle. But it wasn't a castle. It was a manor. Therefore, the house was graced with a more modest light with carved wooden arms that held lamps that were rarely lit. Usually, gaslights illuminated the hallways. But it was midnight, so the house was dark.

She should have brought a lantern or a torch with a gigantic flame that she could jab at any wraiths who dared lunge at her from the parlor just off to her left. The parlor doors stood open, a cavern of shadows inside. Through the doorway she spotted her uncle's feet pointing toward heaven and his trouser-clad leg. The rest of his corpse was out of view.

The doors should have been closed. Who had left them open?

A hand closed on Waverly's upper arm, and she released every pent-up bit of terror that had collected inside her stomach, her chest, and even some stored in her toes—she was sure of it. Her scream pierced the night and rattled the glass somewhere in the parlor.

"Great Scott, woman!"

The hand let go of her, but the very male, very *alive* voice held enough force in it to pin Waverly to the wall. She palmed its green-striped wallpaper as though there would be something to hold on to. There wasn't. Waverly crumpled to the floor, bending her knees into her chest, exposing her bare shins and feet to the invader who had returned to Traeger Hall to thrust his knife in her as surely as he had in her guardians.

"Miss Pembrooke!" A wool coat flew through the air and draped over her body. "Cover yourself!"

Waverly grabbed the coat, catching a whiff of sandalwood and vinegar. Vinegar? No. Ether?

She squinted through the darkness at the looming figure standing over her. "Titus Fitzgerald!" Waverly's cry was one of relief, of stunned surprise, and of anger.

She preferred to address Newton Creek's undertaker as Mr. Fitzgerald, but tonight? His full name slipped from her mouth with indignation. Waverly clutched the wool coat, drawing it over her legs and up to her neck to hide her décolletage, exposed due to the scooped neckline of her nightgown.

"W-what are you doing here?" she stammered, bewilderment muddying her thoughts.

The man shook his head in disapproval. But this was her home—for now—and he was an intruder.

He had broken into her home in the middle of the night!

"You fiend!" Waverly stared up at him accusingly. "You . . . did *you* murder my uncle?"

He stared down at her, expressionless. "You're speaking nonsense, Miss Pembrooke. I am here to do what you obviously are not doing. I'm keeping watch over your uncle's remains," he explained in his baritone voice. "And keeping watch over you," he added under his breath.

The undertaker extended his hand to Waverly to assist her to her feet. "You will be pleased to know your dead uncle has not moved. Not a millimeter. He is still definitively dead."

4

His footsteps collided with the floor like ominous threats—left, right, left, right. And yet, in the darkness, Waverly found herself almost hugging the back of Titus Fitzgerald—which was most improper—only because he seemed safer than the marauding spirits she was certain existed in the house. Her earlier accusation that he was her uncle's killer was ludicrous, she realized now. If he had returned to finish her off, he would have already done so. What motive would an undertaker have to murder someone? Perhaps that was an unfair question. After all, undertakers were in the business of dealing with the dead.

As it was, Waverly's initial fright and anger had dissipated into not a small bit of relief at having human connection. She stayed as close to him as possible. He was tall and his shoulders were broad, his legs long, and his dark hair made darker by the lack of light. Truth be told, Mr. Fitzgerald was dark all the way around, and once light met him, only his blue eyes would illuminate brightly.

There were rumors that his grandfather was of African descent. Some locals curled their lips at the idea while maintaining their holier-than-thou charade that declared all men to be equal. Others, particularly those raised with Southern influence, were less forgiving, and less likely to care if anyone, including Mr. Fitzgerald, knew their true thoughts. Waverly, if given the opportunity, would argue that it was no one's business, and didn't everyone have a little bit of someone else in their blood? And if Waverly was being honest, she found Titus Fitzgerald to be enticing in a dangerous sort of way. Perhaps because his occupation made dead people a large percentage of his social interaction. Was it not strange to find a man who wielded ether attractive? His appearance reduced her insides into a quivering puddle of nonsense. His deeply toned skin was offset by the ice-blue of his eyes, and he—

"Miss Pembrooke." Mr. Fitzgerald's voice brought Waverly back to the present, and it was those very ice-blue eyes that bore into hers. He had lit a lantern. "You wished to retrieve a glass of milk?"

He extended his arm, offering her passage before him into the kitchen. Where he'd retrieved a lantern and when he had lit it only proved how lost in her thoughts she had been. A terrible habit. Waverly found herself wandering far into them at times, reliving events in the past as though they were happening just seconds ago. Her aunt Cornelia had claimed there was something "flighty" about Waverly. At times such as these, Waverly was hard-pressed to disagree. It was as if she were entering another world entirely.

"Miss Pembrooke!"

Waverly gave her head a little shake. "Yes. Yes, thank you, Mr. Fitzgerald."

"You may as well call me Titus," he grumbled as she slipped past him, clutching his coat around her body.

Waverly's stomach did a little flip. Such familiarity with the undertaker was rare. Mr. Fitzgerald—*Titus*—was not known for being friendly, warm, or inviting. He was an undertaker. He was eyed with suspicion. He was—

"Miss Pembrooke?"

There. She'd done it again. Traveled down a rabbit trail in her thoughts.

"Yes, Mr. . . . Titus. Milk. It's supposed to be good for one's constitution before one lies down to sleep."

"You'll sleep tonight?" He crossed his arms and leaned against the doorframe.

Waverly was acutely aware that Titus was watching her as she retrieved the bottle of milk from the icebox, allowing the heavy door to click shut so as not to waste the cool air given off by the blocks of ice inside.

"I will *try*," she reassured him. A little bit of irritation rose in her. Did he think she was squeamish? Well, she was, but Waverly had no intention of letting the undertaker in on her secret. She was no simpering female. No, she had willpower and—

"*Miss Pembrooke*." This time the annoyance was undisguised. "Do you often drift away into your thoughts and stop all movement?"

Waverly realized then she had the milk bottle poised over a glass and had frozen in that position. She could sense the warm blush rising up her neck. She stiffened as she poured the milk. "I could ask that a little mercy be extended to me." The milk sloshed in the glass. "My guardians were just murdered in this very house." Waverly set the bottle on the wooden table centered in the kitchen. She met Titus's stare and lifted her chin. "Any other woman would have disregarded her uncle's last wishes and left his remains here alone while taking comfort in the home of a friend or acquaintance. Please give me some credit for not doing so."

"You *should* do that." Titus pushed off the doorframe with his shoulder and strode across the kitchen, the lamp in his hand the only light in the room. Its flame danced in the glass chimney, turning his features warmer than his tone. "You should leave this house at once."

Waverly's brow furrowed. "Leave? And defy my uncle's will?" She decided not to add *And who would take me in?* She would prefer that Titus view her as stubborn, not on the verge of destitution.

"Anyone in their right mind would see how ridiculous Leopold Traeger's last wishes are. No one should leave a woman to stay in the place of his murder without protection."

"I don't need protection," Waverly retorted.

"Yes, you do."

She narrowed her eyes as the shadow-shrouded kitchen closed in on her and reaffirmed Titus's observation of the potential dangers of remaining in Traeger Hall alone. "I will get a dog."

Titus's laugh was more of a snort. "A dog? You have a bell tower. Why not camp out there and, at the first sign of danger, ring the bell as your aunt did and then pray that the men of Newton Creek run faster to your aid than they did for your guardians?"

He was being facetious.

"You're quite rude," Waverly countered.

Titus set the lamp on the table and leaned toward her, bracing his palms on the tabletop. "This place is unsafe, Miss Pembrooke. You know it. I know it. Even your uncle's attorney, Mr. Grossman, knows it. You're an intelligent woman, as you've claimed on numerous occasions in our acquaintance this past year as we've rubbed shoulders at social gatherings and at church on Sunday mornings."

"You've noticed?" Waverly quipped.

"Your intelligence or you?" Titus asked.

Waverly felt warmth creep up her neck again.

Titus spared her the need to respond. "Prove to me your

intelligence has not gone to waste. Find somewhere else to stay."

She wasn't sure why the undertaker cared so much. He had no right to invade her private home in the middle of the night, but beyond that, his excuse that he wished to watch over her relatives' dead bodies was above and beyond the role of an undertaker. And had *he* been the one to stop the grandfather clock's chimes? That was another liberty not his to take. Although there was a chance he was merely trying to do what no one else was doing—offering her protection. The police had done nothing of the sort.

Perhaps Titus was here, invading Traeger Hall in the dead of night, for self-serving reasons. Perhaps he had imagined her lying on his undertaker's table, dead as a doornail. Her skin cold, staring at the ceiling with blank unseeing eyes, and her wounds would be—

"Waverly!" Titus's voice was sharp, and he was not disguising his mounting frustration. He snapped his fingers in front of her face, and Waverly startled.

Blast her wayward thoughts!

She lifted her glass and took a long drink of milk. The coat Titus had given her for modesty's sake slipped from her shoulders, exposing her neck and upper chest. Embarrassed, Waverly tried to put the glass back on the table while adjusting the coat to cover herself. The glass wobbled, then tilted, finally finishing its dance by tipping over and spilling the milk. It flooded the tabletop and dripped onto the floor and her bare feet.

Waverly glanced at Titus, whose mouth was set in a firm, disapproving line. His eyes flickered downward to her exposed neckline.

The air grew thick, even as it remained cool between them.

Titus reached for the lamp. "Cover yourself, Miss Pembrooke. Your clavicle is showing."

Ignoring the spilled milk, Waverly struggled to cover herself with the wool coat, not missing the fact that Titus Fitzgerald was remarkably boorish and bossy. No wonder he worked with the dead. No one alive would want anything to do with him, even if he *was* the most handsome creature on earth.

Waverly

In an interview shortly before her death in 1950; memories from two weeks prior to the murders:

The tension between Aunt Cornelia and Uncle Leopold was thicker than local gossip Widow Gorski's midsection, which was no small accomplishment.

I took a sip of my morning tea as I eyed my guardians over the rim of the cup, sitting quietly on the springy settee in the parlor. Their conversation was cordial but laced with so many undertones that I was hard-pressed to ascertain who was more aggravated by the other.

"You really mean to have Preston Scofield stay with us again?" Aunt Cornelia was not fond of Uncle Leopold's assistant, who came to Traeger Hall from time to time and invaded the place as another pompous male figure.

Uncle Leopold's mustache twitched, and if I were Aunt Cornelia, I would have bitten my tongue then and there because that twitch was a warning sign that Leopold would soon transition from coolly polite to wickedly stern. The wickedly stern was the part that was intimidating, and only twice had I seen him move beyond that to the violently awful part. The result was a broken vase that Aunt Cornelia claimed was from her great-great-grandmother's estate, and it almost ended with a slap to my aunt's face. She'd dodged it, of course, and afterward Uncle Leopold had marched from the room. The second time . . . well, I'd rather not recall that time.

"When or why Preston comes to stay at Traeger Hall is none of your concern." Uncle Leopold's eyebrow winged upward. "He is pivotal to my business, which is something you would never understand."

The insult was well aimed and very clear. No one was to question Uncle Leopold about his businesses and investments, ever, especially not a mere woman like his wife.

I took another sip of tea and watched.

Aunt Cornelia stood ramrod-straight and unyielding in front of her husband, her deep violet taffeta dress as frozen as she was. The high collar looked as if it might choke her, and maybe it did because she was turning a little purple in her cheeks.

I saw my aunt swallow, and then her mouth twitched with what I guessed were repressed retorts.

"Very well," she managed. "I will make sure Aveline prepares the indigo room for him. As usual."

Aveline was the housemaid.

Aunt Cornelia didn't like her either, but I hadn't figured out why yet.

Without a word of gratitude, Uncle Leopold took a few strides toward the door, apparently assured the matter was settled. But he paused in front of me and stared down at me as though he'd forgotten I was there.

"You're not to try to impress Preston with your wits or wiles, is that understood?" he said.

Of course it was. I nodded. I had no intention of trying to attract Preston Scofield's attention. He was a lanky man, maybe ten years my senior, with a handlebar mustache that hung just below his chin and thinning hair that would likely be gone completely by the time he reached forty. Besides, Preston reminded me of a rat, and I quite hated rats. Shifty, beady-eyed creatures that scampered in the shadows, and no one actually knew what they were about. A rat could be—

"Is that understood?" Uncle Leopold barked, and I startled.

Tea sloshed over the rim of my cup and dotted my rose-blush silk dress.

"Yes, Uncle," I replied obediently. He needed a yes, not an explanation.

Eyeing me as he stood over me, I felt small, as I often did around my uncle. And he'd been my uncle such a short time really. Aunt Cornelia had been married once before, and that uncle had been kinder. Mostly because he was absent or did not give notice to anyone around him. But he had died of a burst appendix—an awful way to go, or so I've been told—and after that, Aunt Cornelia met and married Leopold Traeger. My life would have been so much different had my parents not passed away when I was eight.

"Do you really think I don't see through you?" Uncle Leopold's question curdled my insides.

"I'm sorry?" I feigned innocence, though I was quite aware that *he* was quite aware that I was *very* aware that he was not a good man.

"Stay busy with what you must but stay away from my business. Is that understood?" Uncle Leopold's eyes threw invisible daggers at me, but I still felt them. And I knew enough to surrender.

"Yes, of course, Uncle."

He stared at me a moment longer, then exited the room.

I turned toward Aunt Cornelia, who stood across the room from me. She was displeased, that much was obvious, and she was also defeated. Though she wasn't a particularly warm person and in some ways seemed suited to Uncle Leopold, I felt bad for her.

"I cannot stand that man." Aunt Cornelia finally allowed her distaste to be heard.

"Uncle Leopold?"

Aunt Cornelia cast a startled glance toward the doorway, where Uncle Leopold had exited. "No! Preston Scofield."

"Ah." I nodded.

Aunt Cornelia stepped toward me, her skirts sweeping the rug. "You must stay far away from him, or I fear he'll drag you right along with him into the muddle that is your uncle's world."

"Muddle?" I feigned innocence, all the while understanding that Uncle Leopold had his fingers in so many aspects of Newton Creek that one could hardly unravel the tangled knot. That he owned the majority of Newton Creek hadn't won him any friends, but it had earned him the right to hold his secrets, wield his authority, and essentially bind people to him not unlike a lord and his fiefdom.

"You know what I mean, Waverly, so don't play coy." She pursed her lips as she sank onto a chair opposite me. "If we knew exactly what was going on in your uncle's world, we might both fear for our lives."

I blinked.

Aunt Cornelia waited as if she expected me to respond, yet I wasn't sure what to say. Fear for our lives? This was the first time I'd seen a flicker of alarm in my aunt's expression. Fear of whom? The coarse men who worked at Uncle's sawmill? Preston and his rodent-like personality? Or maybe it was Uncle Leopold himself. He owned the bank, the sawmill, and he held the lives of many of Newton Creek's residents in his grip merely because they owed him money or were bound to him for their livelihoods. But was there more I didn't know about but Aunt Cornelia had an inkling of?

I attempted a smile to try to comfort my aunt, but it fell short.

That was when I realized the strict and uptight personality of Aunt Cornelia was only a charade. She was frightened, anxious.

Sometimes you knew what you were afraid of, and you fretted over the consequence of knowing. But not knowing who or what exactly to fear was far worse. The foreboding that something horrid was about to come down upon you and you were incapable of doing anything about it, well, that would cause anyone anxiety. Especially when the bad had an inevitable arrival date.

Looking back, maybe I should have seen it. Maybe I should have understood it all. But it was far too complicated at the time. And now? Now I marvel at how it all transpired. And, for better or for worse, Aunt Cornelia had no way to escape what was coming any more than I did.

5

JENNIE

NEWTON CREEK, WISCONSIN
PRESENT DAY

There were times that Jennie wished her mind didn't attach paintings to current circumstances. Maybe it was a form of escapism, though, and it made some moments a little less real and more palatable. Like the moment her mom was placed in hospice care and Jennie began traversing the perils of death, only a year ago. She had thought of the painting *The Cradle – Camille with the Artist's Son Jean*, where Claude Monet had brush-stroked the image of his mistress and later wife, Camille, as she bent over their infant son, Jean.

The image had carried Jennie through those final weeks, that of a mother lingering over her babe as Jennie nurtured her own mother through the journey toward death. She hated how the cancer had stolen her mother from her, the one person on earth who understood Jennie's passions and dreams. Not only understood them but shared them.

Now Jennie was again at death's door, only this time she envisioned René Magritte's *L'Assassin menacé*. A contemporary painter, Magritte had painted a murdered woman—depicted nude and not something Jennie would hang on her wall—and yet there was so much story in the painting. The murderer, the bowler-hatted men waiting to pounce, the voyeurs at the window of the scene of the crime—all were interdependent with each other. In this moment, Jennie was one of the voyeurs. She had been the one to discover the grisly skeletal remains at Traeger Sawmill; she the one to have to slop her way through the muck, extricate her phone from her pocket, and call the police; and she the one now forced to sit there waiting in a folding camp chair with a blanket wrapped around her shoulders.

Police vehicles had made their way to the scene of the old crime on the dirt road, now mud, that wound through the former Traeger property Jennie now owned. The coroner had arrived as well. The place was crawling with strangers, as Jennie was new to Newton Creek. This wasn't her home; rather, it was her mess to clean up, and her mother's dream to conclude.

"Did you move the remains at all?" Detective Darrow jerked her out of her thoughts. He'd introduced himself moments before and offered Jennie the camp chair.

"Um . . ." Jennie blinked rapidly, clearing her mind of Magritte's muted colors of a crime scene to the equally dull colors that surrounded her now. Browns, grays, blacks—even the trampled grass and waterlogged creek bank was a grim green. Dying. It was all dying. Because of the floodwaters or the autumn temperatures or just—

"Miss Phillips?" Detective Darrow squatted by her chair to bring himself to her eye level. He had kind eyes, brilliant blue, which were in stark contrast to the dullness of this real-life impressionist vision Jennie was trying to awaken from.

Jennie sucked in a breath of cool fresh air, marred by the distinct scent of rotting algae. "I'm sorry. What did you ask?"

Detective Darrow offered a comforting smile. "I wanted to know if you moved or disturbed the remains at all."

"No." Jennie had come face-to-face with the empty eye sockets of the skull and then all but face-planted in the muck trying to get away from it. "I might have . . . I mean, the mud and silt are slippery, so my getting back to the creek bank may have disturbed it some . . ." She let her sentence hang, not knowing what they were looking for exactly. It was obvious this wasn't a recent accident. Or was it a crime? "Was the victim . . . ?" Jennie was about to say *murdered*, but she couldn't form the word.

Detective Darrow glanced toward the group of people photographing and analyzing the remains. There was a stretcher with an empty bag on top of it, waiting for when they removed the deceased from its current burial ground.

"We don't know yet." Detective Darrow opened his mouth to say more but then snapped it shut, swinging his attention to the road as a beat-up, rusted truck fishtailed through the mud to a stop behind the other vehicles.

A man flung open the driver's side door.

"Oh, great," the detective muttered. "Zane Harris. Where'd he come from?" As if just realizing Jennie was there watching, he shuttered his frustrated expression and patted her knee. "Hang tight here, okay? I have more questions for you." He straightened and strode to intercept the newcomer.

Jennie studied the man who'd just arrived. He was an older version of the boy she'd sent off earlier—the boy who'd led her to the remains. The same black curly hair and black brows that made his deep-set eyes appear a bit severe, at least from where Jennie was sitting. He was attractive, athletic looking, unshaven by a few days, and wearing a blue flannel shirt that hung open over a gray T-shirt.

Even though they were several yards away, Jennie could hear the man as Detective Darrow approached him.

"Is it her?"

Darrow held his palms up as if to calm the man. "Zane, we don't know."

Zane pushed forward toward the mill, but Detective Darrow's hand landed square in the middle of the man's chest.

"Hang back, Zane." Darrow's tone was stern, and yet, Jennie noted, it didn't carry the dogmatic insensitivity she would have expected from a police detective. Instead, there was a hint of empathy in his voice, threaded through the two simple words *hang back*—as in *don't look*.

Jennie knew then that the body she'd found was somehow related to this man Zane.

Zane eyed her over Detective Darrow's shoulder. He shoved the detective's hand off his chest and marched toward Jennie.

She shrank into the camp chair as the man approached.

"Zane!" Detective Darrow shouted.

"Were *you* the one who sent my son to come get me?" Zane's green eyes bored into hers, but he didn't sound accusatory so much as desperate.

Jennie nodded, grasping the blanket the police had provided her and holding it tight around her shoulders. She wasn't cold; the blanket just made her feel safer.

"I can't believe . . ." Zane paced a few steps toward the mill and then spun back toward her. He looked at Detective Darrow as he came up alongside them. "Ben, you gotta tell me if it's her."

Detective Darrow's mouth was set in a grim line. He shook his head. "I don't want to speculate until we know—"

"Milo *found* her!" Zane interrupted. He pointed behind him at the mill wheel and creek bed. "My son found her, Ben."

"I thought—" Detective Darrow bit off his sentence and turned to Jennie.

"It's true," Jennie acknowledged. "I was on the property, and

I noticed a boy. It was . . . Milo?" She looked at Zane, who responded with a curt nod. "He led me here. When I saw what I thought was a . . . a hand, I sent Milo for help." She swallowed back a sick feeling rising in her chest. "I wanted to protect the boy from seeing anything."

"Good thinking," Detective Darrow affirmed.

"So?" Zane spun toward the detective. "Don't mince words—what do you know, Ben?"

Darrow hesitated, and then with a sigh he reached into his coat pocket and pulled out a plastic bag. Jennie saw the glint of metal.

Zane's features fell. He reached for the bag, but Detective Darrow held it away from him. "Do you recognize this?"

"It's Allison's necklace. The one I gave her," Zane said. The hollowness of the man's voice filled the air around them. Jennie could sense the raw pain that was building. She didn't know who Allison was. She didn't know how Zane Harris might be related to her, yet she had a gut feeling that Allison was the person whose remains she had come face-to-face with.

Detective Darrow continued, "We won't know for sure until we run DNA, but yes—we think we found her. Finally." As soon as the words left the detective's mouth, he reached out to steady Zane. Zane stumbled as though strength had been stolen from his legs. He bent low, gripping his knees for support. The detective patted him on the back.

Jennie blinked away tears. It was quite obvious that this Allison had been important in one way or another to Zane.

"Again, we can't know for certain until DNA is confirmed," Detective Darrow stated, "but the necklace was found near the remains. If you're sure it was Allison's—"

"I'm sure." Zane slid closer to the earth, crouching with his forehead against his knees. A guttural moan escaped from him, which carried across the creek bed to the mill and to the body, now in a black bag and being lifted. The bag sagged as the skeletal remains proved just how small a person became after decomposing, the earth having claimed the deceased one and leaving behind only the frame that had once housed a soul.

Another groan, and Jennie's eyes immediately filled with hot tears. She didn't know Allison who'd died, or Milo the boy, or Zane who'd collapsed to the ground. But she knew death and grief, and worst of all, she knew the lack of resolution. People thought answers brought closure. They didn't. They just compounded the infection in the already seeping wound of loss. Whether from cancer or something more inexplicable like a body being found at a dilapidated sawmill, loss was loss. Memories were seared into a person. The good, the bad, and the horrifying.

Yes. Jennie knew what this man was experiencing.

He was experiencing the black hole of loss, and once a person was sucked into that black hole, they could never get out.

6

Sleep had never been a good friend of Jennie's. When she was eight and her dad had awakened her one night, that was the first time but not the last that the night became filled with monsters. Afterward, there was always the belief that just out of view, hidden in the darkness, lurked a monster. Monsters were real. She kept coming face-to-face with them too.

That was when Mom had given Jennie a coffee-table book with beautiful photographs of paintings from the Renaissance to Postimpressionism. As a child, Jennie had lost herself in the paintings. She'd searched for their hidden meanings, consuming the artists' pains and joys, and if Jennie was honest with herself, she was bitter that Mom had chosen to give her an art book to abate her fear of her narcissistic, abusive father. Yet as she grew older—and as Jennie had told her therapist many times—she understood why Carol Phillips hadn't stood up to her husband, even on behalf of her daughter, Jennie.

The reason the monsters were so frightening was because she couldn't scare them away, no matter what she did. Besides, more often than not, a person simply traded one monster for another, and at least with her father, Jennie and her mom had their needs more than met. Wealth became a bandage, art became their vacation, and Dad the beast they tried to keep in the closet as much as they could.

Jennie's first experience with death had been five years ago when her dad died. She'd not cried, not once. Her therapist told her that was just fine—at first—but now her therapist kept trying to coerce tears from Jennie because they'd be "healing." Jennie wanted to scream at her to make up her mind. A person couldn't cry on demand, and a person didn't weep over dead monsters.

She'd cried, however, when her mom died. She'd wept at Mom's burial, wept when she read Mom's journals, and wept when she explored Mom's notes of her studies of Traeger Hall. Somehow, Mom had linked the place to the classical art world, and it was the only piece of Dad's estate that her mom ever cared about preserving.

Jennie had ignored it all. Instead, she'd focused on Paris and the Louvre Museum. She'd gone to school for art. She'd visited New York and toured the Museum of Modern Art for hours. This was art she could see and feel, the art that had saved her night after night. Unlike her mother, Jennie was no treasure hunter. She didn't want to explore ancient tombs with stories of lost art and treasure. She wanted what was already established, predictable. Jennie understood its beauty and pain. She saw nothing but chaos in a treasure hunt.

But today? Today Traeger Hall was one last weight Jennie needed to be free of. She needed to cut all ties to her father, to his greed and his need to own anything and everything he came across. She was ready to be free of Traeger Hall once and for all, as well as the surrounding properties her father had invested in, because Jennie needed to let her mom go. Let go of Mom's dreams of opening up Traeger Hall, which had been sealed for over a century.

Mom was not alone in believing the stories that the original owner, Leopold Traeger, who'd been murdered in the Hall and whose bell tower had pronounced his murder to the town of Newton Creek, was also a secret hoarder of valuable art pieces. Maybe under different circumstances, Jennie would have loved to treasure hunt here with her mom. But Mom was dead, Dad was gone, and Traeger Hall was an unwitting reminder of abuse and of boarded-up dreams.

In a way, Jennie felt bad for the old mansion and its bricked-up windows and doors. It was a victim of sorts, being barred from having occupants all these decades. Traeger Hall had been abused and misused. The place hid so many secrets that Jennie thought it too much like her. Traeger Hall was Jennie Phillips; and Jennie, Traeger Hall.

Now, Jennie braced herself. Yesterday had been awful. A few hours of being questioned by Detective Darrow, feeling the stare of the man who had been introduced to her as Zane Harris, the little boy Milo's dad, and then returning to her rented Airbnb for a night's sleep? Nope. She couldn't afford to take on more trauma. It was morning now and here she was, where she originally intended to be but without the emotional hangover of yesterday.

She was sitting outside an attorney's office, wrestling with that same premonition of doom she often had and that always seemed to be correct. Jennie glanced at her phone and reread the email. Her attorney—no, Dad's attorney—wasn't able to meet her in Newton Creek as promised. She wanted to clear up a few questions surrounding the Traeger property, such as why her father had bought it to begin with, and whether she could sell the place or was it tied to some ridiculous, ancient will the attorney's office determined was still binding.

Now she was attorney-less, heading into a meeting with no legal expertise. She'd take detailed notes, not make any snap decisions, and per her attorney's instructions call him later that evening to discuss the matter. That was the problem with having high-powered lawyers from her home in the Twin Cities. They had other clients too, ones with more pressing issues and who brought in more money to the law firm than a case like hers—cleaning up an old estate in Wisconsin.

Jennie took a last look in the mirror at her SUV's visor. Her brown eyes were rimmed in black, and her dark blond hair was up in a messy bun, a thick fringe swept to her temple. She'd skipped her contacts this morning and opted for her studious-looking glasses with their brown tortoiseshell frames. They made her look more put together. She hoped.

Jennie exited the vehicle and straightened her clothes. Cuffed blue jeans, ankle boots, a button-up silk blouse in navy blue, and silver jewelry to accessorize. She was ready. She hoped.

The air was permeated with the sweet scent of lavender, blowing from an oil diffuser in the corner of the small law office. White walls, black stuffed chairs, a couple of abstract paintings hanging here and there. The decor was all rather clinical, more modern than Jennie had expected. That included the woman behind the desk, who looked only a little older than Jennie. Her hair was styled in a short bob that emphasized her fine-boned features. She had the appearance of a model. Jennie had been wrong in assuming the law office would give off the same aura as the rest of Newton Creek: Midwestern rural. Instead, the woman now lifting dark eyes that matched her hair color gave off New York chic. She even had tapered red fingernails, and her blouse definitely sent an Yves Saint Laurent vibe.

"Welcome!" Her smile was warm, her voice accented with an Eastern European finish. "How may I be of assistance today?"

Jennie braced herself and answered, "I'm Jennie Phillips. I have an appointment regarding my property, Traeger Hall and Estates."

"Oh, yes!" The accent grew thicker. Russian? Latvian? It didn't matter, as it was exotic and beautiful and intimidating regardless. As the woman's smile reached her eyes, she appeared completely nonjudgmental. "I am Lisbet. I work for Mr. Wellington, and I am so glad you came. Give me one moment to see if he is free?" She held up an index finger to indicate the number one and smiled again.

Jennie nodded politely and then waited, shifting from foot to foot.

Lisbet returned in a whiff of subtle perfume that reminded Jennie of lilacs. "He will see you now." She tilted her head. "Do you want water or coffee?"

"No, no. I'm good." Jennie just wanted to get this over with. She followed Lisbet down a short hallway and into a small office. In the center was a conference table of dark walnut. A painting of red tulips greeted Jennie, and she took the offered seat in a sleek black chair on wheels.

"He'll be right with you," Lisbet said, then strode from the room with her shapely legs, black heels, and bright red soles.

This was definitely not what Jennie had expected from a small-town law office.

And then her expectation came through the door.

The attorney was short and round with a balding head, a plaid shirt, khaki pants, and brown leather shoes that were badly scuffed. He hugged a portfolio and a few manila folders that looked as though with one puff of air, papers would go flying everywhere.

"Ah!" His gray mustache tweaked upward with his smile. "You must be the proud inheritor of the legendary Traeger properties. Miss Phillips, is it?" The man dropped the portfolio and folders onto the conference table, and they slid into a disorderly pile. Unaffected, he sank onto a chair, releasing a sigh that indicated he enjoyed his job and was completely unaware how out of place he looked. "I'm Percival Wellington. Most people call me Percy around here. Born and raised in these parts. Lisbet is my daughter-in-law, and this room is one hundred percent Lisbet's doing, her way of bringing my law office into the twenty-first century." His chuckle was throaty, jovial. "I told her that I draw the line on remodeling me, however." Percy stuffed papers that had slipped from one of the folders back inside it. "Like they say, you can't take the country out of the man."

Jennie didn't think that was quite how the saying went. No matter, for she found herself relaxing. With Lisbet's appearance and the overall look of the office, Jennie had braced herself to meet with a smooth-talking attorney in a black suit and silk tie, with a square jaw that was set firm by the clenching of his teeth.

She could work with Mr. Wellington—Percy. He had to be in his mid-sixties, and the friendliness he exuded was contagious. Still, Jennie was cautious. She had to be. Life had taught her that.

Percy folded his hands in front of him on the table, and his shoulders lifted and fell in a deep breath. "I heard about yesterday." He clucked his tongue. "Such a shame they discovered Allison that way."

So it was confirmed to be Allison? Jennie didn't dare voice the many questions she had concerning the dead woman.

"And to think you found her?" Percy's rubbed his forehead in disbelief. "It's been years since . . . well, no one here thought Allison would ever be seen again."

Jennie smiled politely. It felt rude and intrusive to ask anything. Besides, for a lawyer, Percy was remarkably forthcoming.

He shook his head as he reached for the portfolio and folders, putting them into some semblance of order. "She and Zane Harris were going to be married, but then she just vanished. Shortly after Milo was born."

Jennie squirmed. Something didn't feel right here.

"Her parents were old-fashioned that way, wanting the two of them to get married. I don't think Zane or Allison actually wanted it themselves. Of course, having a kid together adds a new dynamic and, well . . ." Percy settled his hands on the pile of documents, meeting Jennie's eyes. "A lot of us hoped

Allison had simply left town to get away from it all. It was a nicer thought than what actually happened."

Jennie nodded. What else could she do? She didn't care to revisit yesterday's grisly discovery, and she didn't want to intrude on a stranger's loss. But if what Percy said was true, that meant the boy Milo had actually discovered his mother's remains! The thought sickened her to the point of nausea. Jennie swallowed hard and pressed her palm against her midsection.

"Mr. Wellington, I'd like to—"

"Yes. Yes, of course." Percy smiled, thankfully taking her cue. "The Traeger Estate. Your attorney isn't joining us?"

"He couldn't make it." Jennie managed a smile.

"Well then, let's get down to business, shall we?" Percy's eyes widened in question. There was a brief moment of silence, and then Jennie realized the question was not rhetorical.

"Um, yes, please."

Percy flipped open the portfolio. On the right side, Jennie noticed a legal pad with scribbling taking up most of the page. To the left were photocopied papers, written in old-fashioned handwriting. "We have here copies of the original last will and testament of Leopold Traeger." Percy slid a document across the table for Jennie.

Retrieving it, she right away noted the date at the top of the page: October 9, 1890. "This is one hundred and thirty-five years old." She couldn't hide the awe in her voice. Mom would have enjoyed seeing this.

"Yes, it is." Percy cleared his throat. "Now, keep in mind there's the rule against perpetuities, and in Wisconsin perpetuities and the suspension of the power of alienation. Therefore, what was written in Mr. Traeger's will in 1890 would not technically still apply today because it is, well, over a century old."

Percy was making assumptions that Jennie understood the law or anything he'd just said. But if he was saying that the will had expired, she was fine with that. It still didn't account for why she was here.

"Is there something else I'm unaware of or missing? If the original will and testament no longer applies, then what exactly are we meeting about?"

There was a short pause, and then Percy responded in a clipped manner, "Right." He riffled through the papers of the portfolio until he found whatever it was he was looking for. "According to Mr. Leopold Traeger's will of 1890, the manor house, Traeger Hall, is not to be reopened until there are no Traegers left to argue any rights to the property or until after a century has passed."

Jennie waited, but Percy said nothing more. She felt as if she were pulling teeth. "So, from what I understand, both situations have been met regardless of the fact I'm not required by law to meet them?" The rural lawyer's inability to communicate his point was trying her patience. "Mr. Wellington, I'd like to sell the Traeger Estate. My father purchased it as an investment, along with many other historic properties. I've no desire to keep any of them." She wanted to be free of everything her father had been involved in.

I'm sorry, Mom.

The apology passed through her mind uninvited. She knew her mom would have wanted her to hang on to the Traeger properties. To explore them, to see if the rumors associated with the Hall's history were true or not. Was there really valuable art hidden away in the sealed-up mansion on the hill?

Percy cleared his throat nervously. "Actually, it's the *codicil* that is creating the issue."

"The what?"

"Think of it like a P.S. to your father's last will and testament." Percy's eyes landed squarely on Jennie.

"A P.S.? You're not my father's lawyer. How would you know anything about . . . ?" Her words trailed off as she stumbled to a halt.

Percy drew a long breath and released it, as if gathering the strength to dumb down his explanation for her. "And that is the difficulty of a codicil. They make wills confusing, especially if they're not kept with the original will. Not to mention there are legal guidelines that must be considered." The man must have noted Jennie's blank look. He tried again. "I'll put it in simple terms. When your father purchased the Traeger Estate, he created—through my office here—a codicil specifically regarding the Traeger properties."

Jennie frowned. "That doesn't make any sense. Dad's other attorneys surely would've known about this. All of my father's assets were willed to my mother, including his properties. And with her death, they're inherited by me."

"You're correct," said Percy. "His attorneys *should* have known. But if your father never communicated it, and they never received the codicil to file with the will, then . . . well, I'm not sure what may have happened. There are other legal questions to consider as well. We weren't aware of your father's death until you arrived in Newton Creek a few days ago. While it appears that the codicil is valid and binding, the legalities of everything must be sifted through. I'll need to confer with your father's attorneys before asserting the codicil be followed explicitly."

"What does this *addendum* say precisely?" Jennie almost choked on the words. That her father might be able to affect her even now was outlandish.

Percy lifted a manila folder and handed it to her. "A copy is included here. Your father drew up an addendum that says the Traeger Estate and holdings cannot be sold or ownership transferred until after a period of fifty years following the date of his death."

"Say that again?" Jennie fought back tears. Her father was always close by, lingering, even though he'd died—her disgusting and manipulative and narcissistic father.

"You can't dispose of Traeger Hall or your ownership of the place."

"I *can't*?" she said in a high-pitched voice.

"No. At least not the way I understood the codicil to mean when we drew it up years ago. Again, I must confer with your attorney."

"But it's *my* property," Jennie argued.

Percy nodded, a wisp of hair falling over his forehead. "Yes, the Traeger properties are yours through inheritance via your father's will. But if it turns out the codicil is legally binding, then you can either leave Traeger Hall and the other properties of the estate alone or by all means fulfill the deepest desire of many from the last century and open the place up to see what's inside."

"That's ridiculous!" Jennie sagged in her chair, unable to hide the tears welling in her eyes. Tears of exasperation. "Why would my father even care?"

Percy shrugged. "We don't question the why; we merely draw up the papers."

"And you drafted the addendum for my father?" Jennie asked.

Percy shook his head. "No. My father did that. And now that you're here, it's my duty to bring this to your attention. Your lawyer and I must now look at the legalities involved regarding the will and codicil to determine whether it is indeed valid."

Jennie skimmed the photocopied will, searching for the words that would pop off the page to verify Percy's claim. "I-I don't know what to say."

He continued, "I understand it's confusing. But as I said, you can still make use of the place." Percy tapped the copy of Leopold Traeger's ancient will. "This has no bearing on the matter, despite what the locals may tell you."

"What do you mean by that?"

Percy chuckled. "Well, just because the Traeger will is no longer in effect, that doesn't mean the impact of its contents expire. The influence Leopold Traeger had on this area was monumental during his time, and the lore and speculation surrounding his death and Traeger Hall have always been of interest to the citizens of Newton Creek. The manor has been an important landmark for over a century. It's the primary reason people travel through here."

"You're saying Traeger Hall is a tourist attraction because of the cold-case murder associated with it and the fact it's been sealed shut for a century?" Jennie stared at Percy, incredulous.

"In short, yes. I mean, the estate itself doesn't generate income, but the people who pass through our area because of the story surrounding it boost the economy of our businesses."

"What's your point, Mr. Wellington?" Jennie pressed.

"Only that you're sure to come up against some resistance if you decide not to reopen Traeger Hall. It's been a point of division for years. There are those who believe the manor still holds Traeger's treasures and wealth. The man was rumored to have had his hand in much more than just the sawmill and bank."

"You're referring to the art." Jennie's statement made Percy's eyebrows rise.

"You've heard the rumors, I take it."

"That Leopold Traeger supposedly dealt in the fine arts? Yes." Jennie couldn't help but recall her mom's journal, which was filled with notes on various works Traeger might have bought and sold, evidence both for and against the theory that he'd been deeply involved in the art world during his time. That was what had intrigued Mom the most, and maybe if Jennie was in a different frame of mind, it would have captivated her also.

"You understand, then," Percy concluded. "There are those who want Traeger Hall opened to the public, who are looking to have their own Indiana Jones experience of viewing old, never-before-seen treasures. And there are others who want the manor to be left alone. They don't care for the sort of tourism the Hall attracts, with it being the setting of a vicious, unsolved murder.

Even a century later, the murder that occurred there still has a distinct distaste for many around here, what with the superstitions and bad omens the crime has evoked over the years."

Jennie blew out a pent-up breath. "What I hear you saying is, while we wait to sort out this *codicil* my father has on file with your firm, I can either offend half of Newton Creek by opening Traeger Hall or offend the other half by leaving it sealed shut."

"Yes." Percy was unapologetic in his answer. "You've inherited a hornets' nest, so to speak. It's been made worse by what you discovered yesterday."

"How is that?" Jennie's stomach was in knots.

"Allison, Zane Harris's deceased fiancée. One of the contentions surrounding her disappearance was that Allison had been a local connoisseur of the Traeger legend. She was convinced Traeger Hall held old artifacts, with other monetary wealth stored in a safe somewhere within its walls. Allison was hellbent on figuring out how to get inside the manor. Zane, on the other hand, took the opposing view. As did his family. They felt Traeger Hall should be left alone."

"Because of its impact on Newton Creek's economy?" Jennie leaned forward, curious as to where all this was going.

"That," said Percy, "and because they'd helped to maintain the property just as it was. They believe strongly that Traeger Hall has been sensationalized and has stirred up the kind of division that breaks down a community like Newton Creek. It's also been suggested that the Harrises are distantly related to a young woman who was once under Leopold Traeger's guardianship—a Waverly Pembrooke."

"I see." Jennie mulled over this new information.

"Some say Zane and Allison got into an argument, and Zane . . . well, there's the question of whether he had something to do with Allison's disappearance."

"But what would his motive be?" Jennie asked.

"If there was a way the Harris family could legally prove they had some claim to the Traeger Estate through Waverly Pembrooke, then whatever was inside the manor would be theirs to share. They didn't want treasure hunters gaining access to the place, and they didn't want Allison digging up anything that might disprove they had any such claim to the Hall's alleged treasure."

"Did they have any claim to Traeger Hall?"

Percy shook his head slowly. "Highly doubtful. But the rumors persist nonetheless. And by finding Allison yesterday, you just brought them to mind again with everyone in Newton Creek."

"No matter what I do, I'll be kicking that hornets' nest." Jennie leaned back in her chair.

"Actually, you've already kicked it. The only way now to avoid the worst of the fallout is to get Zane Harris and his family to support whatever you decide to do with the place—and that's only if Zane is free of any further suspicion, or, God forbid, there's no evidence he had a hand in Allison's death."

"I don't see why I need their backing. They've no legal rights to the estate," Jennie protested.

"No. They don't. But they have many of the townspeople on their side, regardless of the suspicion cast on Zane. They're longtime pillars of the township, and loyalties run deep in a rural community like Newton Creek. We like our simple life, our happy little secrets and old stories, but once you make them real and wake them up? It's not simple anymore. People get angry. Heck, they'll fight over a two-foot difference in a century-old property line. Imagine what they'll do when Traeger Hall is finally reopened—or left alone? Either way, people are bound to be upset."

Jennie wanted to leave, go back home to the Twin Cities. But she couldn't. Not now. Not with this codicil business hanging over her head, needing to be figured out. If she couldn't sell Traeger Hall or any other properties because of her father's addendum, then she had to decide what to do with it. It seemed as though her mom had been right about one thing in particular: Traeger Hall came with an entombed mystery that was still haunting Newton Creek today.

Life was never simple. In fact, it was downright complicated.

7

WAVERLY

Traeger Hall
September 1890

She had not found somewhere else to stay, as Titus Fitzgerald had so insistently urged her to. There was more at play than he knew, and leaving was not as simple when one had no place to go. Waverly was still at Traeger Hall the afternoon following her midnight interlude with the undertaker. Who had no business being in Traeger Hall to begin with—especially in the middle of the night.

Soft footsteps echoed in the vacant front hall of the mansion, and Waverly turned from her position beside her aunt and uncle's bodies. "Aveline." She offered the mousy housemaid a smile that was meant to be comforting. One needed comfort, didn't they, when the corpses of their former employers were laid out in their Sunday best, hands crossed over their chests, eyes shut, and cheeks turning hollow? "Did you need something?"

Waverly prompted the maid to speak, noticing Aveline's stare was fixed on Uncle Leopold's still form. She was probably as worried as Uncle Leopold had been hopeful that he would rise from the dead or somehow be alive two days after his murder.

It was not to be.

"Aveline?" Waverly pressed.

"Hmm?" Aveline startled, her blue eyes widening. "Oh, Miss Pembrooke, apologies." She gave a small curtsy that impressed neither deceased Aunt Cornelia nor Uncle Leopold. Waverly waved the action away.

"We can dispense with that nonsense now. We're not in England, this isn't a castle in the countryside, and I'm as unsettled as you are by all of this." Waverly felt far more composed around Aveline. There was no intimidating presence nearby, no bossy undertaker, and no sense of anxiety in speaking to the housemaid. In fact, speaking to the help was something Waverly thought came quite naturally. There were no airs to be put on. Well, Aunt Cornelia would argue with her there.

To her aunt, airs were important to maintain even with the help, as it showed you were in authority and they were your inferiors. Waverly didn't hold to the same lofty aspirations. What good could be gained by lording over another woman simply because Aveline dusted the furniture Waverly made use of?

"I wanted to ask what more you might need from me, Miss Pembrooke." Aveline's question brought Waverly back to the situation at hand. She understood that the housekeeper, the valets, and the other maids had not returned to Traeger Hall. So it was quite admirable that Aveline had come back, even though she'd refused to sleep in her quarters.

"It's not uncommon for the deceased to remain in their home until their burial," Waverly stated aloud, not responding to Aveline's question but trying to answer the one that had been bouncing around in her mind this morning.

"No, miss," Aveline said.

"Why then have the servants employed by my uncle taken their leave of Traeger Hall?"

"I suppose, miss, it's because we are afraid."

Of course they were frightened. Waverly swallowed the sudden anxiety that surged within her. She had found her uncle lying in a pool of blood that night, and her aunt . . . "Yes. No doubt that's it." Waverly interrupted her own thoughts. "Aveline?"

"Miss?"

"Have you heard any rumors or suspicions among the staff as to who the killer might be?" Waverly understood that if anyone knew the goings-on in a place like Traeger Hall, it was the help.

Aveline's expression was impassive. "No, miss."

"What, nothing?"

"Not a peep, miss." Then Aveline added, "The detective in charge asked all the pertinent questions of us, so he knows as much as we do."

Assuming the staff had been forthcoming with their answers.

"And you never saw anyone suspicious yourself?" Waverly pressed.

Aveline shook her head. "Only Cook was confronted by the man, and she said she did not recognize him or see much of his face because of his hat."

"Is the staff afraid of my uncle and aunt's killer returning?" Waverly asked.

"Yes, Miss . . . and the length of it."

"The length of their murders?" Waverly choked out. She'd assumed death had come quickly. But in retrospect she knew that wasn't the case at all. Screaming would have echoed through the halls. The jab-jab of knife into flesh. Uncle Leopold's cry to ring the bell. Waverly could imagine it all. Glassware being shattered as her uncle fought his assailant. Her aunt's desperate attempt to reach the bell tower. The stabbing . . . Aveline was right—the murders would not have been swift.

"No. The length of the wake, miss. They're lying here with

no one but you to watch over them if they were to come back to life." Aveline's assessment jerked Waverly from her imaginings.

Oh. Yet resurrection was mainly associated with Christ, or with Lazarus, and weren't there a few other resurrections mentioned in Scripture? Waverly hadn't heard of any modern-day resurrections, only the dead not really having been so in the first place.

"And no one is preparing funeral arrangements," Aveline continued. "You've not had the mirrors covered or stopped the clocks—except for the grandfather clock."

Yes, the grandfather clock had stopped mid-chime. Waverly never asked Titus if he had been the one to cease the clanging.

"Am I supposed to stop all the clocks?" Waverly glanced at the clock sitting on the mantel in the front parlor. She had not even thought of it. Aunt Cornelia would have, but she was dead. Waverly had never been a part of someone's death and funeral or the rituals involved, let alone carried out the vigil of a wake all by herself. "I suppose we should do what is required then." Waverly hoped the maid would volunteer to assist her more as an equal for the sake of her uncle and aunt.

Aveline was barely five feet tall, and her petite form was nearly swallowed by the black uniform Aunt Cornelia had insisted the maid always wear. At Waverly's question, Aveline's shoulders straightened, the woman's self-confidence seemingly buoyed.

"That would be wise, Miss Pembrooke. It's been two days, after all. We can begin by hanging a wreath of boxwood on the front door. I believe Mrs. Braun has a supply of black veils I could use to wrap around it. Out of respect for the Traegers and the community."

Waverly's eyes met Aveline's, and Waverly found some relief in the suggestion of a wreath. "Yes. That would be good."

"I will cover the mirrors with the veils as well. To avoid Mr. Traeger or the missus from being caught in them."

"Of course." Waverly was careful to temper her expression. The idea of her uncle's spirit being sucked into a mirror and stuck there for eternity was both laughable and utterly terrifying. "Cover their portraits as well, please." There was that awful one of Uncle Leopold glaring from the canvas. She could accept that being covered quite happily.

Aveline nodded.

Waverly was grateful the maid didn't ask questions, but Waverly was sure she didn't want to see her uncle or her aunt staring at her as she passed by them. It was enough to stand over their remains and gawk at them. Dead as they were.

"And shall I send to town for more ice, Miss Pembrooke?"

"Ice?" It seemed the young woman was attempting to nudge Waverly's sense of responsibility by bringing up another item on the list of things to do.

"Yes, miss. For Mr. and Mrs. Traeger . . ."

Waverly turned to the bodies laid out on cooling boards, balanced over two tubs of ice. The cooling boards were draped with black coverings, with pots of fresh flowers placed on iron stands—two at their heads, and two at their feet. The gruesome fact was that the ice and flowers were necessary to put off decomposition and its accompanying stench.

"Please do. As much ice as you think is appropriate," Waverly answered. "And perhaps more flowers."

"Yes, miss." Aveline nodded. "Will there be anything else?"

Waverly considered for a moment. "Do tell the staff it is safe to return."

But she could see on Aveline's face that the maid didn't believe her. How could she? The killer hadn't been caught, let alone identified. There was no motive known to anyone—well, that wasn't entirely true. Waverly shoved aside the nagging questions and waved a hand to dismiss the maid.

As Aveline took her leave, Waverly returned to watching over her uncle and aunt.

"You left me seven days plus two to get your affairs in order," Waverly muttered, recalling the terms of Uncle Leopold's will.

Forty-eight hours after the burial and Traeger Hall would be sealed shut. A crypt. With two days having passed since their murders, that left five days remaining until their burial. But how was Waverly to find the opportunity to go through their belongings if she was bound by the will to stand vigil at her guardians' coffins? Or was she bound? Who would know if she left her post? For though she believed in God's ability to work miracles, she felt guilty in that she hoped the good Lord would forgo the resurrection of her guardians.

"How awful," Waverly chided herself. They had been viciously mutilated by a killer's knife, and here she sat, disrespecting her uncle's last wishes and wishing that he'd stay dead. "I'm a horrible person," she concluded, while not believing it at the same time.

Waverly pushed to her feet.

There was a murderer to catch. There was her own life to protect and her future to plan for. If Uncle Leopold wished to haunt her for leaving her post, then so be it. His ghost could throttle her while she slept. But if she didn't do something—anything—she was likely to be the next on the list to die in Traeger Hall, if from nothing else but boredom.

"Your vigil has already ceased?" Titus Fitzgerald's baritone came out of nowhere and caused Waverly to straighten with a yelp and a wave of the trimming shears in her hand. Titus reached forward and pushed down the shears with his hand. "Do lower your weapon, Miss Pembrooke. I've no intention of violence."

"You have as much if not the most motivation for violence, Mr. Fitzgerald." Waverly raised the shears again.

"And how do you come to that conclusion?" he challenged, his blue eyes flashing.

"You make a good living by the deaths of others, yes? Perhaps there's been a shortage of late, and you need more bodies to invest in your services? Are you eating well, Mr. Fitzgerald, or perhaps needing money with which to pay your mortgage?"

His lips thinned at her sassy retort. "Unlike most in Newton Creek, I am not beholden to your uncle's bank for my property. And yes, I dined quite well on pheasant last night, thank you for asking. As for committing murder in order to gain corpses to tend as my career requires, perhaps if I were terribly bored, I might consider it. But as it stands, no, I did not, nor have I ever, committed a heinous crime to fill my time or coffers."

Waverly set the shears on an iron bench nearby. "Well, someone did. Murder my uncle and aunt, that is, and I'd like to find out who is responsible."

The undertaker glanced between her, the bench, then back to her. "As I recommended last night, getting yourself to a safer place would be more prudent—"

Waverly held up a hand to stop him. "Is visiting the home of your deceased clients on a daily and nightly basis typical?"

"When they have a flibbertigibbet for a niece, then I do consider it an added service, yes."

Her question hadn't fazed him in the slightest. Waverly pursed her lips.

A tiny smile played at the corner of Titus's mouth.

Waverly looked away.

"Now, Miss Pembrooke, or may I call you Waverly and be done with the pretense? It's not as if we've not known each other for months now and not run in similar circles."

Waverly gave him a curt nod. He had invited her to call him by his first name last night, while she had cavorted through the halls in her nightgown in search of a glass of milk. Truth be told, it was all terribly indecent of her.

"And what of your uncle and aunt? Who is watching them

now?" Titus's inquiry made Waverly recoil. He needn't act as if he were a schoolteacher and she a delinquent student.

"I am quite aware I should be keeping vigil, but I am also aware that certain things must be seen to. I have Aveline covering the mirrors and such, and I offered to cut boxwood for a wreath." She didn't mention that she was also engaged in seeing if there were any footprints beneath the windows. How had the murderer entered Traeger Hall? If he had broken in, then it might be a nefarious business deal gone wrong with someone sent to kill her uncle. If, however, the killer had been *invited* inside through the front entrance, that brought with it a far more intimate motive, did it not?

Titus responded, "I shall not tell Mr. Grossman of your lack of attentiveness. Between last night and now today, it must be kept secret between us." He dared a wink that was more patronizing than flirtatious. "If your uncle and aunt should see fit to break from the coma they fear and they return to the land of the living, I daresay we'd hear them if we were a mile away from Traeger Hall."

Waverly couldn't argue with that. If for whatever reason the copious stab wounds were not enough to end their lives, neither Uncle Leopold nor Aunt Cornelia would be subtle in their coming to. She could hear them now. The boorish and mean bellow from Uncle Leopold, couched in words that were unrepeatable and delivered with such condemnation that whoever had dared to stab him to death would probably suffer a stroke for fear of him. Aunt Cornelia would instantly begin to complain that her dress had been ruined, and who would be so emboldened as to shove a knife through silk, let alone her abdomen?

"Miss Pembrooke."

Waverly blinked, returning to the present. She stared at Titus Fitzgerald and then made her decision. "Please, I gave you permission. Call me Waverly. The Miss Pembrooke formalities are more tiresome than sitting for hours on the chair in the parlor."

"You know you could ask for a more comfortable chair."

"I could, but it would be asking the air because only Aveline has returned to work, and she's as light as a feather. I doubt she could move a chair any more than a mouse could. I will retrieve one myself, if I see fit." Waverly brushed aside Titus's interference. "And you really didn't answer my question. Why are you here again?" She should bite her tongue, but the silence she'd endured today—aside from her interlude with Aveline—had become painful.

Titus held his hat in his hand, and the breeze ruffled his dark hair, giving him a boyish appearance. Tight curls at the nape of his neck indicated he needed a trim, and the shadow of whiskers along his chin and cheeks was evidence he was not fond of bothering with the etiquette of shaving daily. But then who was he to impress? Dead people?

"Have you taken my advice into consideration?" Titus ignored Waverly's question regarding his appearance at Traeger Hall and posed his own.

She snatched up the shears from the bench and turned her back to him. He was unsettling. If she was being honest, he made her lose her nerve. She wanted to be in control of the situation at Traeger Hall to prove she could manage things herself and maybe prove to Mr. Grossman that they needed to contest her uncle's will and allow her to remain at the Hall instead of sealing it up like a vault. Not to mention she wanted to find her uncle's killer and be assured she was no longer in any danger. It was easier not to look at Titus while she talked. She positioned the shears around a branch of boxwood and snipped it.

"I will not leave Traeger Hall."

Snip.

"And you believe you're safe here alone at night?" Titus inquired.

"Of course," she lied, "so long as you don't intrude under the guise of doing your duty, since you refuse to give me an honest answer for your repeated visits."

Snip. Another branch fell.

"And if the killer returns?"

"I shall be waiting with an ax." Waverly responded more haughtily than she felt.

Snip.

"Might I suggest the trimming shears instead?"

Waverly paused and looked over her shoulder at the exhausting man. "I think an ax would be more effective."

"And yet you wield those shears so well." Titus pointed at the pile of branches on the ground. "You've enough boxwood there to make five wreaths, and I'm assuming only one is needed?"

Waverly looked at the pile and did everything in her power to squelch the heat that rose in her cheeks. She nudged the branches with her toe. "Since I have extra, I thought I might offer them to you. You could sell them as an added accessory with your services. Other dead people need wreaths for their front doors, don't they?"

"You're quite exasperating." Titus stated his truth, and in no way did Waverly feel as though she won the back-and-forth conversation. In fact, the way he said it made her feel as though she were naive, foolish, and quite missing the point that she was, in fact, not safe at Traeger Hall.

"My uncle always said as much about me," Waverly quipped, turning to face the undertaker, her nemesis. His black suit was badly wrinkled. The man had no shame.

"Waverly."

Her name on his tongue stilled her completely. Little bumps rose on her skin, and unwelcome tickles in her stomach betrayed her. Oh, she'd had them before where the undertaker was concerned. Last month she remembered the precise moment they had been in church and their eyes had met. So disconcerting and in church no less! She had felt embarrassed at her reaction then, just as she did now. Her cheeks warmed.

"Yes?" Waverly gripped the shears as though Titus himself were the murderer, returned to finish the job.

Titus drew his brows inward, annoyance marking his expression. "The police have not yet uncovered who broke into Traeger Hall and inflicted such violence upon your aunt and uncle. Your uncle feared such a thing would take place, though most people don't assume their death will be at the hands of a murderer."

Waverly swallowed, apprehension overtaking the attraction she'd sensed earlier. What kind of woman was attracted to an undertaker?

Titus took a step toward her as if to emphasize his point. "You know that your uncle predicted he was going to be murdered. It's no secret that there was a dangerous *incident* before the night your aunt rang the bell in the tower."

He referenced a night not long before the murders. Everyone in Newton Creek had heard of it. Waverly had pushed it from her mind. The gunshot, the broken window, the lack of attempt to ring the bell.

Waverly lifted her eyes to the bell tower that her uncle had built a few years prior to his marriage to her aunt. He'd insisted the bell tower was needed, its purpose to ring for help in the event of an emergency. All of Newton Creek knew that if the bell tolled, they were to rush to Leopold Traeger's aid. And it *had* finally tolled, two nights ago, and they *had* come . . . only they came too late.

She shut her eyes against the memory of racing back to Traeger Hall. Where she had been and why she had been there was nobody's business. Least of all Titus the undertaker's. Waverly would never forget the shame and guilt she felt upon stumbling into the bell tower to see her aunt lying there with her eyes open in a death stare, a pool of crimson beneath her.

If she had been at Traeger Hall when the murders occurred, she very well might have stopped them—or been a victim herself.

"Will this be the last of it?" Titus voiced the question the authorities had raised to Waverly the morning after the murders.

"I don't know." Waverly bounced the shears against her leg. It didn't matter if they soiled her dress. It was a black mourning bombazine, and she hated it. "I don't know if I am safe. I don't know who did it. I don't know what is to become of any of this. I am merely trying to cut boxwood branches, Mr. Fitzgerald, and have a moment of peace amidst the sorrow. I'd rather not be hounded by questions I cannot possibly answer!" Tears stung her eyes. Waverly swiped at them and continued, "I have five days left here at Traeger Hall, if you must know, and then I've nowhere to go. I have that to consider as much as my own personal welfare."

"If you could stay at Traeger Hall, would you?" Titus's eyebrow winged upward.

Waverly sucked in a breath in an effort to regain her emotional balance. "Once more, I don't know."

Much to Waverly's surprise, Titus's eyes softened, and his voice gentled. "Don't you think that *knowing* something for certain would be far better? And if you want to take control of your future, you have your uncle's entire estate at your fingertips."

"For the next five days only."

"And what happens after five days?" Titus asked.

"Traeger Hall is to be closed up. Nothing sold, nothing brought to storage or moved with me. I can take with me only what I came to Traeger Hall with. I'm afraid three hats, six dresses, and a few other personal items will not go far in providing for me."

Titus crossed his arms over his chest and eyed her. "Then take it upon yourself to make sure you're still *alive* in five days. Assume this was no random slaying, that there was a purpose behind it, and maybe, if you refuse to take refuge elsewhere, at least take ownership of the time you've been given to find out why your guardians were murdered. Don't you wonder why your uncle would make such irrational demands in his will? Whose purpose does it serve if he is dead? Perhaps if you can learn the why and the who behind the killing, you might be able to figure out the answer as to your future."

Waverly opted to ask Titus outright. "Why do you, of all people, care so much anyway?"

"Because these circumstances are not normal, Waverly. Your uncle and aunt were brutally slain. Your uncle predicted as much would happen and made no secret of this. It indicates this was no accident, no impulsive act. It's no secret your uncle's holdings are vast and extend beyond Newton Creek and his sawmill enterprise. Who knows what all is at stake here? So you are evicted from Traeger Hall, but what of your uncle's holdings? Are there large sums you're to inherit that Mr. Grossman is not informing you about? You're acquiescing, taking the lawyer at his word? Maybe instead you should fight back, take control of your future, and investigate for yourself what happened. The authorities aren't as motivated as you are. They have little to lose, whereas you have everything to lose."

Waverly's legs became as wobbly as a molded Christmas jelly. She fumbled for the iron bench and sank onto it, staring up at the undertaker. What he said made sense. His words mirrored where her befuddled thoughts had been circling but had been unable to put into order.

She lifted her eyes to the man who stood over her. "You believe I should try to solve my uncle's murder?"

Titus's brilliant blue eyes locked on hers with confidence. It was as though he had looked into death's future, seen it, and not even the prospect of it seemed to rattle him. "I believe you should try to find out why someone wanted him dead. Knowing the answer to that could very well change your future."

"It could also kill me," Waverly countered.

"Either way," said Titus, "I will be available should you need me."

She gave a sigh. It was not a comforting promise coming from an undertaker.

8

She wasn't sure where to start, but logic told her to begin by looking into her uncle's business dealings by scouring his office. It was on the first floor of the mansion, not far from the front parlor where he lay.

Waverly knew she'd won no points in her friendship with Aveline when she'd assigned the maid to watch over the bodies. But someone needed to satisfy the lawyer, Mr. Grossman, should he visit unannounced to verify the terms of Leopold's will were being honored. Now, her quest to find answers—as Titus Fitzgerald had so compellingly argued—would be even more difficult.

Because Preston Scofield had arrived.

Her uncle's former assistant, a rat, had returned to Traeger Hall shortly after Titus had left. She stood a safe distance away from the man in the sitting room. No one could fault her for harboring suspicions about everyone she met these days. Waverly eyed the man. Had *Preston* murdered her uncle? And if so, why? The fact he'd come back to Traeger Hall after a rather convenient absence only made Waverly question his motives.

"I cannot believe this happened!" Preston's face was ashen.

"Have a seat, please." Waverly extended her arm toward a stuffed chair, and Preston slumped onto its cushion like a man with no strength left in his legs.

"Is he truly dead?" Preston asked.

Waverly took a seat opposite the man and assessed him for a moment. Could a person fake such stunned surprise and mortification? she wondered. "You saw him in the parlor, yes?"

"I-I did," Preston stammered.

"And were you away on business on my uncle's behalf?" Perhaps Preston would be forthcoming, and Uncle Leopold's business holdings could be explained by his right-hand man.

Preston stilled, and a bit of color came back into his angular face. He hesitated, his mustache twitched, and then his focus shifted to the ceiling.

Was he hiding something?

"I was," he finally answered, "but that is beside the point. To return to this . . . *nightmare* is appalling." He pushed to his feet, and Waverly was quick to follow suit. "I must speak with the authorities! Press them to tell me what they know!" He stalked toward the door with purpose.

"If they knew anything, they would have told me," Waverly said to his back.

Preston stopped, turned around, and shot her a doubtful look. "Why would they tell you?" It was an honest and insulting question posed with no intention of receiving her answer. He bent and swept his hat from the floor where, in his distress, it had fallen. He brushed imaginary dust from its brim. "Leave everything to me," he advised. "I will visit with the authorities on the matter. I will also arrange a meeting with Mr. Grossman. No doubt there are legal matters to be tended to."

Waverly held up a hand to stop Preston's arrogant assumption that he was now in charge. "I've already met with Mr. Grossman. As my uncle's *heir*, his business holdings are my responsibility."

It was a lie, but she felt it necessary—at least until she could further gauge Preston's motives and state of mind.

"Preposterous!" Preston's eyes widened, and Waverly wasn't sure if this was due to outrage or fear. Perhaps both.

"And for the record," she added, "*you* are thusly employed by me now." Well, that was a stretch, seeing as Mr. Grossman retained control of her uncle's assets. But Preston didn't know this.

His voice hardened. "You have no attachment to the Traegers except through your aunt. I was close enough to your uncle to know he would not have left *you* in charge of his business interests."

Waverly hesitated. Perhaps she should be more careful talking about herself as an heir. If someone was willing to kill her uncle and aunt, why wouldn't they do the same to her if she stood in the way of whatever it was they were after?

"Well," she said, "I have spoken to Mr. Grossman nonetheless."

Preston settled the hat on his head, and it did nothing to improve his appearance except to cover his balding scalp. Which really was not the part of Preston that made him unattractive. It was that horrendous mustache.

"Be that as it may, I will still be meeting with Mr. Grossman." He lifted his chin, staring down his nose at Waverly with a lofty air. "In the meantime, your role is to continue with the funeral arrangements. Coordination with Reverend Billings is of utmost importance. I would be comfortable leaving the religious elements of the service under your care."

"How kind of you." Waverly offered him an exaggerated smile of compliance. "However, Uncle Leopold isn't to be buried for five days yet, according to his wishes outlined in the will. The will Mr. Grossman has already gone over with me."

Preston stiffened, his eyes narrowing. "Five days? Why, Leopold will be quite . . . I mean, that's a bit eccentric, don't you think?"

"Perhaps," said Waverly, "but it was written in my uncle's

will that he and my aunt must remain here at Traeger Hall for a certain duration before being taken to their mausoleum." She didn't indicate the events that would take place afterward.

Preston's chest heaved as he sucked in an irritated breath. "I've things to do, Miss Pembrooke, starting with setting up a meeting with Mr. Grossman." His conclusion was firm, communicating that he intended no further debate. "I will see you this evening."

"This evening?"

Preston's eyes glimmered. "Yes, Miss Pembrooke. Leopold assured me on numerous occasions that I would always have a place at Traeger Hall. I will be staying here in the interim as a guest, at least until Leopold is properly buried."

Waverly shrank back. "That's hardly proper!"

"Neither is murder proper," Preston said with a smirk. "It only stands to reason that I would be the one to stay at Traeger Hall and see to your well-being. After all, you are the presumptive heir, or so you say. Who is to argue over propriety when your life might be in danger? As your uncle's right hand, I insist." He paused and flashed her a grin. "So then, I will take rooms in the east wing of the mansion. You have a maid, I assume. See that she stays with you, and all will be well chaperoned. See? Already I have proven that you have need of me."

After Preston took his leave, Waverly sank back onto the sofa and tried to catch her breath. So she and Preston Scofield would be eating dinner together this evening, one at each end of the table. Well then. She would keep her steak knife within reach at all times, just in case Preston was even more devious than he appeared to be.

WAVERLY

In an interview shortly before her death in 1950:

When I was eight, my mother died from tuberculosis. Shortly thereafter, my father followed her, dying of a broken heart. That might be one of the few true acts of love I ever witnessed because from that time forward, Aunt Cornelia and her then husband became my guardians. Not ones to be saddled with a child not their own—they had no children of their own—they enrolled me in a school for girls on the East Coast.

I graduated with moderate academic scores and with even more average skills in art, music, and other such roles assigned to young women. By then, Aunt Cornelia's first husband had passed away. She later married Leopold Traeger and joined him at Traeger Hall in rural Wisconsin and the small town of Newton Creek.

It all sounded pleasant enough, so upon my graduation I accepted their kind offer to join them there. When I arrived in Newton Creek, I saw that Uncle Leopold had made the town and surrounding area into his own little kingdom. I wasn't surprised by my uncle's success and wealth, but I was surprised by the amount of influence he wielded because of this. Should his business ventures suffer bankruptcy due to a streak of bad luck or should he ever decide to shut down Traeger Sawmill, the town of Newton Creek would soon become economically unstable. My uncle's enterprises were a Midwestern gold mine of sorts, the loss of which would turn Newton Creek into a veritable ghost town.

This was why I also wasn't surprised to see that Uncle Leopold had built a brick bell tower just before his marriage to my aunt. It was attached to the side of Traeger Hall and rose one story higher than the manor house. The bell that hung in the tower had been forged of copper. By the time I moved into Traeger Hall, the weather had already begun the bell's transition to a coppery-green color.

Uncle Leopold's bell never rang. Its purpose was not to mark the time of day. Instead, it was there to function as a warning in the event of an attempt on his life. I found this disconcerting to say the least. To live under the supposition that attempted murder was not only possible but *probable* was more than unsettling.

One day I asked Aunt Cornelia, "If there's an emergency, how will Uncle get to the tower to ring the bell and alert the people of Newton Creek when he's in the middle of being attacked?"

The look of censure from my aunt did nothing to endear her to me. Her eyes narrowed, and there was a lift of her chin, and yet I saw a flicker of something in her expression akin to embarrassment. "Don't be daft, Waverly. The bell is there for *our* safety. And the staff is well trained in the event of an emergency."

Even so, it was indeed eccentric to believe such a thing. Attempted murder? Somehow, though, I got used to living under such a vague threat and even came to dismiss it altogether. It is apparent now that I shouldn't have. It is also apparent that my actions of that night should forever remain a secret, as something I take to my grave.

Upon hearing Aunt Cornelia's odd explanation, I did what most might do. Curious, I went into the bell tower to take a look for myself—not for the first time—and confirming that no one ever frequented it, I took refuge there.

Even the servants avoided the bell tower. They were superstitious that it represented a bad omen. Like Uncle Leopold, the servants didn't care to be murdered either, and the bell tower was a constant reminder that death lurked just around the corner. I learned too that some believed the bell tower to be haunted. I found this belief strange. How could the tower have become haunted when it was less than a decade old and no one had died in it? Well, maybe a field mouse had, or an insect or spider, but aside from being plagued by the spirits of roving rodents or angry arachnids, one could hardly be afraid of what wasn't in existence.

Regardless, the bell tower became my retreat. I would often sit on its brick steps leading to the loft, my back against the cool wall, a book propped on my knees. It was completely silent in the bell tower. There were no growls from Uncle Leopold, no moaning from Aunt Cornelia, and with the servants terrified of the place, I was left alone. Marvelously and splendidly alone.

Until I wasn't. I had my conscience with me, plaguing me.

Therein begins my secret. The secret I never wanted Uncle Leopold to know that I knew. The secret no one in Newton Creek should ever be privy to. The secret that now I must bite my tongue until it bleeds to keep quiet.

Even now I wonder: had I not fallen into subterfuge and cooperation with this secret, would my uncle even be dead? I find it hard to believe my secret contained that much influence, but one should never underestimate the unlikely. I have found that the unlikely often becomes the likely, while the likely often never sees the light of day.

9

JENNIE

Newton Creek, Wisconsin
Present Day

She didn't want to be bound to Traeger Hall, but even without the various elements complicating matters, the place pulled at her soul with a voracity that both frightened and irritated her. It would be so simple to just walk away. To leave everything as it had been for over a century. To ignore Percy Wellington's announcement about her father's codicil, to allow the deceased woman she'd discovered in the creek bed to rest in peace, and to put a cap on her life as it had been up until Mom's death. She could go back to Paris as she had planned. Or she could travel to New York. There were a thousand ways she could lose herself in the many museums, the paintings and artistry that resonated with her soul. Traeger Hall didn't have to be master over her life.

She could do that, couldn't she? Brick up her past the same

way Traeger Hall had been bricked up? All the memories, the secrets, the stories would be trapped inside, and she could move forward. Start a new life. Take with her only the good pieces she wanted to hold on to. The good memories of her mother's adoration and loyalty. She could leave behind her father's abuse. His gaslighting, narcissistic way of promoting himself. His vile, secret addictions that had left her scarred.

Abuse from a father came in multiple forms. Hers were emotional, psychological, and the physical kind no daughter should ever have to speak of, let alone remember. She would have chosen broken bones over the wounds she'd suffered, although Jennie knew there was no way to weigh one abuse as worse than another. Her therapist for the last several years had been helping Jennie traverse the maze back to healing. Faith had become a part of her life. God had been wrestled with. She was still wrestling with Him and the problem of evil. How could a good God allow such things? The typical answer of "we live in a broken world" just didn't cut it for her on a bad day. On a good day? It didn't really help then either.

A young man in one of her classes at college had mentioned that Vincent van Gogh was a complicated painter, that *Starry Night* might be beautiful but *Wheatfield with Crows* was messy. Jennie had glared at him, his lack of insight bothering her to her core. Her life wasn't unlike a Van Gogh, and that was why art spoke to a person. What was messy to one person could be beautiful to another. Each brushstroke was purposeful and meaningful and made sense to the painter. That was where Jennie had settled with her faith. God was still painting her life's portrait. She just prayed that when He was finished, it would make sense to her too.

And now she was here. Standing at the bottom of the stone steps of Traeger Hall, one foot perched on the first step. She could turn and walk away, or she could march up the steps and run her hand along the brick, investigate the windows sealed shut by more brick, and question who had kept the roof from rotting and collapsing these past hundred years or so.

"It makes a person wonder, doesn't it?"

Jennie spun at the sound of a man's voice. Her hand clutched the front of her shirt as though doing so would somehow save her from whatever threat he posed. "Oh! You scared me!"

It was Zane Harris. The one person she wasn't ready to meet because she really didn't know what to say to him.

His eyes were so green, they reminded her of *Green Wheat Field with Cypress* by Van Gogh. The meadow and the trees, the varying hues with yellow highlights almost dancing, the shadows deeper than a Christmas tree.

"Sorry to scare you!" His voice was a bit gravelly. "We met two days ago."

Jennie nodded. "Yes, it was . . . nice meeting you." She grasped for the right words. What was she supposed to say to him?

Sorry I found your dead girlfriend.

Sorry your son discovered his mom's skeleton.

"I wanted to say thanks." Zane crossed his arms over his chest and fixed his attention on something over her shoulder. His Adam's apple bobbed, and it was apparent he was fighting emotion.

Jennie waited, more than a little awkward herself.

"For protecting Milo and sending him away from . . . from the mill." Zane's eyes met hers.

She recalled Milo's large brown eyes, his silent gestures to get her to follow him. "Is he okay?" Jennie had been wondering. Milo had to be reeling from what he'd seen—if they explained it to him.

Zane's chest lifted in a heavy sigh. "Yeah, Milo's good." He released his cross-armed grip on himself and rubbed the back of his neck. It was obvious he was upset but trying to maintain his composure. "Milo has autism. He's high functioning, but he doesn't talk much, and emotional situations don't affect him like they might other kids."

Jennie nodded. She hadn't much experience with kids like Milo, but she knew emotions could sometimes be either extremely volatile or almost nonexistent.

Zane gave a small laugh. "I guess that's a blessing, considering..."

Jennie knew the sentence left hanging was a reference to the fact Milo had been the one to discover his mother's remains.

Zane turned his attention to the Hall, bending his head back to peer up its height. "This place holds nothing but curses." His condemnation was matter-of-fact. "It should be demolished." There was an edge to his voice, and Jennie remembered Percy Wellington's advice that she'd do well to have Zane Harris and his family support whatever she decided to do with Traeger Hall, whether she opened the mansion or kept it sealed shut.

"I hope I'm not intruding." Jennie felt like she should apologize.

He gave her a shrug. "It's your property."

"I know, but me being here, the flooding... it's all such a—"

"Mess," he finished for her.

"Yes, a huge mess."

Nervous laughter passed between them. Zane Harris had a nice smile, Jennie noted. He had a long dimple in his right cheek. She couldn't imagine him being nefarious and playing a part in Allison's disappearance and death, but then no one ever thought her father capable of the abuses he inflicted on her and Mom. There was much more to a person than a pretty face.

"Our family has been caring for this place since I can remember."

She recalled Percy Wellington mentioning that in their meeting yesterday.

Zane craned his neck to look up at the Hall. He motioned toward the tower, the bell inside weather-beaten. "That's the only glimpse we have of what's inside Traeger Hall. A few people tried to scale the tower, but the belfry windows are partially bricked up too. There's not enough space between the bell, the openings, and the wall for a person to squeeze through.

"You've never been inside?" It was a stupid question, and Jennie recognized that the moment it escaped her lips.

Zane's eyes narrowed as if he were stuffing back not-so-good memories. "No."

A moment of silence stretched between them.

The autumn breeze was tipped in the last remnants of summer's warmth. A few leaves that had fallen from the surrounding maple and oak trees blew across the lawn. An acorn fell from one of the top branches of an oak, landing on the grass a few feet away from where they stood.

"Like I said, I think the place should just be destroyed along with whatever's in it." Zane's words sliced the air between them.

"That seems rather extreme, don't you think?" Jennie retorted before she could measure her words.

"Is it?" Zane shot back. "It's just an old building with bad memories that breeds more bad memories. And now?" He glanced in the direction of the ruined creek bed, the tilting mill wheel, and the muddy earth his fiancée from years prior had just been removed from. "Right after Milo was born, I told Allison to leave it alone. Traeger Hall doesn't have a kind history, and for all the lure of a treasure inside, well . . ." He laughed, but it was humorless. "Watch any movie that includes a treasure hunt, and we all know how the story ends."

"How does it end?" Jennie couldn't help but ask. The movies she'd seen ended with the treasure revealed, the guy getting the girl, and typically a favorable ending.

Zane seemed to read her thoughts. "Forget the Hollywood *happily ever after*. It's the stuff leading up to an unrealistic end. There's always a curse, or a villain, or a war over the treasure. There's danger and imminent death." His sentence had a hard stop after the last word.

"So you think there's some truth to the claim that there's treasure inside Traeger Hall? Valuable paintings?" Maybe her mom's research of the place before she'd died hadn't been misguided after all. Maybe Leopold Traeger *had* been involved in much more than just logging and milling.

Zane's stare was a brilliant emerald that speared her. "That's not the point, is it?" he challenged. "What really matters is what a person *does* if they believe in the treasure." Zane pointed toward the creek. "And what happens to them when they try to find it." His conclusion wasn't one of threat or warning so much as it was of resignation, resentment. "Treasure is an elusive fairy tale that ruins what's beautiful. It's greed plain and simple. It's . . . messy."

Messy.

His statement jolted Jennie back to her thoughts before Zane had surprised her with his company. Messy. Like the guy in class had said of Van Gogh. Like she often said of God.

"But can't messy be beautiful too?" she asked, not because she thought Zane would give her a satisfactory answer but because Jennie ached to voice it. To a stranger. To someone who'd experienced the gross abuse that life had to offer. She longed to believe that somewhere in the muck of it all, there was hope.

When Zane didn't respond, Jennie could almost sense another brick settling into place, solidifying the truth that, yes, the bad should remain closed off and bricked over. Opening it would release the demons and the ghosts. And no one wanted to go to war with those creatures.

※

Zane hadn't left her like she'd thought he would. Instead, after she'd delivered her unanswerable question, he'd motioned for her to follow him as he bordered the foundation of the Hall.

"Newton Creek used to be a growing town. It had a promising future." He paused at the base of the bell tower and looked out over the valley, a haphazard patchwork quilt of trees, cornfields, red barns, and weatherworn farmhouses. In the distance was Newton Creek, or what was left of the town, with its small grocery store, two gas stations, five bars, and a residential area that included Jennie's Airbnb. "That all ended," Zane continued, "when Leopold Traeger was murdered."

Jennie glanced at him, stuffing her hands into the center pocket of her red hoodie. She then looked down to see water springing up around her rain boots. The earth was still so saturated from all the rain. She hadn't expected Zane Harris to give her a lecture about Newton Creek history, but then the information might aid her in determining her next steps.

"My mom was studying the Traeger murders before she died," said Jennie.

"I'm sorry she passed," Zane responded.

Jennie offered a little nod in acknowledgment. "It was cancer."

"Merciless," he said, then pointed toward the old sawmill. "Traeger owned the mill and the bank," he continued, as if sensing Jennie didn't want to elaborate on her mother's death. "When he was killed, the manor was bricked up and sealed according to his last wishes, and the town went on as though all was normal—at least for a while. Eventually, though, the sawmill declined due to mismanagement, and with the Great Depression the bank was rendered worthless. Newton Creek suffered as a result." The sarcasm in Zane's voice trailed behind him as he took a step back to peer up at the bell tower. "No one really knows what happened with Leopold Traeger."

"Wasn't there a young woman he was guardian over?" This might be her chance to garner Zane's support.

Zane nodded as he squinted up at the brick belfry. "Yep. Waverly Pembrooke was her name. She was a distant cousin to my family. My mom could tell you more—she knows our family tree."

"So she's not a direct relation to yours?" Jennie confirmed.

Zane shot her sideways glance and sniffed. "Don't worry. We've no interest in claiming Traeger Hall as ours."

"I didn't mean—" Jennie started.

Zane shifted to face her. "No, but it seems everyone in Newton Creek has a theory about how we're related and deserve the place, as though I'm willing to do anything to keep people out because I think the treasure belongs to my family."

"None of that's true?" Jennie felt bad asking so outrightly, but she felt she hadn't much of a choice.

Zane drew a deep breath, leaning his shoulder against the base of the tower. "Listen, I'm sure it's already been made clear to you that this place is an important landmark to Newton Creek, and what side you're on with opening it up or keeping it closed depends on your outlook."

Jennie nodded, her silence urging him to continue.

Zane obliged. "For me, it's personal. Because of Allison."

She hoped the expression she offered Zane was appropriately empathetic, but she couldn't tell if the man was heartbroken over Allison's disappearance and now confirmed death, or if he was something else entirely that Jennie couldn't put a finger on.

"Allison disappeared from Newton Creek eight years ago," Zane stated. There was a catch in his voice that made Jennie believe he was compartmentalizing emotions while communicating facts. "She was . . . a great friend, a young romance gone too far, and . . ." Zane seemed to measure his words and then he met Jennie's gaze. "Her folks were old-fashioned and insisted that we marry because of Milo. I was willing to, Allison not so much."

"Oh." Jennie wasn't sure what else to say. She was surprised to learn that Zane had been agreeable to do the stand-up thing by a woman he apparently hadn't been in love with, while Allison was the resistant one.

"Allison was a free spirit, full of life, and she had big dreams. She thought this place was the gateway to adventure." Zane slapped the side of the bell tower. "Some adventure. It got her killed."

His sentence hung between them for a long moment until Jennie felt she should say something. "I'm so sorry," she whispered hoarsely.

Zane shook his head. "You're not to blame. I thought Allison had tired of trying to figure out a legal way to get into Traeger Hall to do her treasure hunting. Instead, she abandoned Milo and me to go do it somewhere else. But after yesterday, I can no longer blame the wanderlust of a young woman of twenty-two who was full of dreams. Now I don't know who or what to blame . . . and that's maybe the worst part of it all."

Jennie frowned as Zane's words sunk in and confirmed one of her worries. "Allison's remains . . . they don't think she died naturally?" She'd hoped that whatever had trapped Allison Quincy beneath the sawmill wheel had been accidental. A horrible, freak accident Jennie had yet to hear an explanation for.

But this was different. This meant—

"A concrete block was tied to her ankles." His voice was flat. "The block was wedged beneath the mill wheel. They said Allison probably drowned. But—" Zane swallowed hard—"they don't know for sure. Either way, it was no accident."

Jennie wanted to reach out to Zane but hesitated. He was hurting and bitter toward Traeger Hall. She slowly lifted her fingers and grazed his arm. "I'm so, so sorry," she murmured. And she was. Horribly sorry.

"I don't know what you hope to achieve here," Zane said, stepping away from Jennie's empathetic touch, "but it would be best if you left Traeger Hall alone. Newton Creek has let sleeping dogs lie here for years. It's better that way. Allison tried to awaken them and look what happened." His face contorted as he attempted to collect himself. "For *eight years* we didn't know what happened to her. But I always suspected it had to do with this house with its stupid bell tower and its—" He bit off his words.

"Its what?" Jennie asked.

"You see the top of the tower?" Zane pointed up, and Jennie nodded, following his index finger. "Everything's bricked up to keep trespassers out. You might be able to see the bell, but like I said, you still can't squeeze your way inside. No one since has been inside the tower or the Hall itself. Yet the roof has been maintained over the years. My dad helped to install metal roofing over the old roof. There's been no evidence that anyone has stepped foot inside the place since the day it was sealed shut."

Jennie waited, a heaviness settling over her chest with the expectation of something coming she was not going to like.

"And yet somehow," Zane went on, "the townspeople heard distant echoes of a bell the night Allison disappeared. It's enough to make folks wonder if Leopold Traeger still has some hold over the manor—and over Newton Creek. It's almost as if Traeger's ghost is locked away inside the house, and he dares anyone to disturb its peace."

"But how would the bell ring if no one can get to it?"

"There's the mystery," Zane concluded. "Did anyone *really* hear the bell ring, or was it just our imagination because of the stories?" He paused and leveled his gaze on Jennie. "And why do some people swear that they heard the bell the night Allison disappeared?"

10

"Do you know why your father purchased the Traeger properties?"

Jennie brushed by the one who fit the stereotype of small-town newspaperman to a tee: round glasses perched on his nose, balding head with a wisp standing straight up in the middle like Alfalfa from *The Little Rascals*, and a skinny little neck she really wanted to wring.

"I'm trying to get some coffee." Jennie elbowed her way to the coffee bar at the little shop that boasted fresh-brewed coffee in carafes and an admirable but sad attempt at making a good latte. She'd tried one yesterday, tasted the watery milk and vague hint of espresso, and tossed it. Today, Jennie was opting for a black coffee. Columbian. Nothing fancy. Definitely not with a side of newspaper reporter.

"Do you think your father had anything to do with Allison Quincy's murder?"

Jennie froze.

The entire six hundred square feet of the shop stilled.

All five coffee drinkers at tables stared at them.

The barista behind the counter made a pretense of studying her receipt book.

Jennie prayed for grace. No. Why should she have grace? Hadn't she learned over the past thousands of dollars of therapy that setting boundaries was an important measure for self-protection?

"How dare you?" She allowed herself to grind out the words the reporter deserved.

He took a nervous little jump backward, but his eyes narrowed all the same. "You have to admit that your father purchasing the estate properties around the same time Allison went missing is a bit peculiar."

It was new information to Jennie. All she knew was that her dad had bought the properties in another one of his sweeps to obtain historic sites that could potentially be monetized in the future. If anyone studied her father's business dealings, it was no secret the man had made a mint investing in property across the United States. His attorney had told Jennie that Dad simply hadn't gotten to dealing with Traeger Hall yet. With quite a few properties with the Phillips name still awaiting a finalized business plan, Dad had died and left them all just sitting there. Most of the properties had since been sold, though Mom hadn't wanted to get rid of Traeger Hall. Not after she read about its possible link to the art world.

But eight years ago?

Allison's disappearance?

While Jennie wouldn't put much past her father, murderous activity had not been on his list of sins.

The reporter's eyes had turned shrewd. "Do you recall your father visiting Newton Creek around that time?"

Jennie turned her back to him and pumped coffee into a paper cup. "No comment."

That made it worse.

"So you *do* agree the timing of the purchase of the properties from the township of Newton Creek and the disappearance of Allison Quincy appears to be more than mere coincidence?"

Jennie didn't want creamer, but she poured some into her coffee anyway. That way she wouldn't have to look at the newsy little worm next to her.

"I said *no comment*," Jennie repeated.

"Do you think Allison might have uncovered something your father wanted kept secret? Everyone knows she believed there was treasure of some sort inside the Hall."

"Mr. . . ." Jennie whirled, coffee spilling from her cup.

"McSwigen," the reported provided.

"Mr. McSwigen, yes. My father didn't have secrets to uncover." Well. That wasn't true. But it was when it came to Traeger Hall. "As for Allison Quincy, I don't know a thing about her. I'm sorry for her family, for the grief they must be experiencing now that her body has been found, but I—"

"You found Allison's body, correct?" Mr. McSwigen interrupted.

She should have remained true to her no-comment declaration. Now Mr. McSwigen stood directly in front of her, pinning her between himself and the coffee bar at her back.

"We know you did find her," the reporter continued. "What can you tell me about the remains?"

"Nothing!" Jennie's voice cracked. The man had no sense of decency.

"There was a necklace taken off the body, and—"

"Stop." Jennie felt her rarely unearthed temper rising to the fore. She'd learned from childhood to be compliant, not to upset the apple cart, to be a peacemaker. That was what Mom had always done. Smooth things over so that Dad didn't get too upset. Don't rock the boat. But this? Jennie could see the potential victimization of Allison's family, of Zane Harris, and of his son, Milo. There was no way she was going to play a part in that or allow someone to hurt an innocent child.

Mr. McSwigen's eyes rounded at Jennie's bold command.

She took a step toward the reporter, thankful she was taller than him. "Your insensitivity toward the families involved is abhorrent." Jennie didn't bother to lower her voice. The entire, intimate coffee shop had already heard every word and were still unabashedly listening. "Allison Quincy has a *son*. A little boy. Show some respect."

Jennie shoved her coffee cup into the newspaperman's chest. The hot liquid slopped over the side, staining his shirt. He instinctively took the cup she'd jabbed at him and held it away from himself like a hot iron. He stared at Jennie as though she'd lost her senses. She glared down at him and then swept the room with her eyes, meeting the stunned gazes that stared back at her.

"I don't know what it is about Traeger Hall and why you all have put up with such nonsense for so long. It's a *house* for Pete's sake. An old house with an old crime, and you all want to sensationalize it for, what, *news*?" She shifted her anger back to McSwigen. "Maybe I'll just have the place bulldozed. Then you and your nosy little paper can go back to your puny little desk and write about the cow tipping that took place at Farmer John's on Friday night. Leave Allison Quincy to rest in peace. Leave my father and my family alone. And for all that is decent and right, don't drag Allison's child through a muddy investigation into some rumored treasure."

Jennie's shoulder pushed against Mr. McSwigen's as she marched from the coffee shop. She waved her hand in the air as she walked. "My father might have been rich, and he might not have splashed his business across your paper's front page, but if you want to find your monster, look to Newton Creek. Look at yourselves. I'm willing to bet you have so many of your own monsters, there's no need to adopt mine."

The worst part about her verbal onslaught, Jennie realized with a sickening feeling as the coffee-shop door slammed behind her, was that she'd just handed McSwigen a juicy piece for his paper: *Woman Goes Berserk in Coffee Shop, Assaults Reporter with Hot Coffee.*

This was why her mom had always justified to Jennie why she'd never raised the roof to get out from under Dad's thumb. When you tried to fight a monster, they always came back stronger. It was better to hide under the blankets.

She just didn't want to hide anymore.

Mr. McSwigen had shown her that.

11

WAVERLY

TRAEGER HALL
NOVEMBER 1890

Preston was indeed a most oppressive man. Aunt Cornelia had been right about that when she was alive, and though she now lay lifeless in the front parlor, Waverly was certain her aunt's opinion had been the truth.

It was half past nine, and dinner had gone well enough, she supposed. Preston had done exactly as he'd said, moving into Traeger Hall as though Uncle Leopold himself had issued the invitation.

"Mr. Grossman picked a fine time to go out of town on business." Preston dabbed at the corners of his mouth with a napkin. "I'm not sure how I'm supposed to manage affairs without meeting with him to get the specifics of Leopold's last will and testament."

Waverly bit her tongue.

Preston prattled on. "But you mustn't worry. I will handle everything."

Oh, she wasn't worried. Not about that at least.

Waverly refused to respond. Instead, she eyed their used dinner plate settings still on the table. There was no one to clear the table except for Aveline, who had been resistant to Waverly's instruction that she must stay at Traeger Hall and not leave at night as she'd been doing. Waverly knew Aveline didn't wish to sleep in a mansion with dead people. She could hardly blame her. But there was the issue of Preston's insertion now, and the thin grasp Waverly had on maintaining decency rested on the poor maid's shoulders.

Waverly pushed herself up from the table and eyed the dirty dinnerware. Aveline would clean it up after they left. Dinner had been made quickly after Waverly sent an impassioned plea to the cook, who agreed to come back to Traeger Hall once before breakfast and once before lunch, leaving enough rations for Aveline to serve dinner. But now Aveline had disappeared, and Waverly couldn't blame the young woman. She knew the maid wouldn't reappear until she could do so alone and without eyes on her.

Waverly marched from the room, her head held high as though a throng of onlookers were watching to see what Waverly would do next. As it was, she entered the front hall, crossed it, and peered into the parlor.

Had Uncle Leopold's eyes begun to sink into his head? She tiptoed to his body to observe more closely. Sure enough, it looked as if the regions of his eye sockets were hollower. It had been only a few days since death, so at least Uncle's skin wasn't falling off yet. Waverly sniffed the air. The flowers seemed to be doing the trick, although there was an odd, pungent undercurrent to the perfumed orange, purple, and yellow potted chrysanthemums.

She rounded Uncle Leopold and bent over Aunt Cornelia.

For some reason, Waverly was certain she saw her aunt's hand twitch. She leaped back and stared at it.

"Aunt Cornelia?" Waverly's whisper sounded loud and intrusive in the otherwise empty room.

The dead woman didn't move or respond. Which was good. Maybe it was normal for the eyes to play tricks. Waverly sensed a coolness come over the room, and she shivered, wrapping her arms around herself.

"Well, that is unkind," she chided Aunt Cornelia. If the woman's spirit was hovering over her body now, Waverly would not have been at all surprised. She could feel the censure in the marrow of her bones. "I merely left the room to cut boxwood and eat my dinner," she explained to Aunt Cornelia's ghost. "And you of all people should know that shirking my duties would be the one thing to bring you back from the dead." Waverly tilted her head and looked down at her aunt's face. Pale. Unearthly. Spongy. "And I certainly do not want that," she added with a curl of her lip.

A swift and sudden rush of cold air blew across her face, and Waverly yelped. Without staying to investigate, she hurried from the parlor and slid the pocket doors shut. This time, if her aunt and uncle really did wake from some unresolved comatose state that made them appear dead, they could do it alone. She was not going to fulfill a part of her uncle's last wishes merely because he'd stated them in his will.

Waverly hurried down a short hall to the left of the main staircase. The entire front hall was rich with cherrywood—the floors, the banister, the molding. In fact, as she stopped in front of Uncle Leopold's closed study door, Waverly realized the entire wall leading to it was paneled with cherrywood as well. There were no wall coverings and no decor but sconces for lighting. It struck her how little she noticed details until she was alone.

And yet there was Preston.

He was seated at Uncle Leopold's desk as if the man were not just yards away, lying on his iced bed of deathly rest.

"What are you doing in my uncle's study?" Waverly heard the edge in her voice. She also heard the quiver, which undermined her attempt to sound confident.

Preston gave her a look that indicated her question was out of line. "I'm doing what needs to be done. Your uncle's businesses do not just stop with his death. Many are reliant on the sawmill, on the logging company up north, and so on. There's the board of trustees at the bank to be met with. Certain things must be put in place to avoid complete economic havoc for Newton Creek. Have you considered that?"

Of course she had considered it, and Mr. Grossman had crushed any hope that she might benefit from any of it. Grossman and his firm now retained a controlling interest regarding management of the estate's assets, which was something Waverly had no desire to reveal to Preston. No doubt he would find out soon enough. Still, she'd let Mr. Grossman be the one to drop the heavy news on Uncle Leopold's assistant. She could almost see the greed in Preston's expression. The expectation that somehow he would benefit from her uncle's death. Was Preston assuming he'd been included in the will? Did he think he'd be taking Uncle Leopold's place at Traeger Hall?

Waverly saw a gleam in the man's eyes, and a sudden realization washed over her.

"No," she stated firmly.

"No?" He raised his eyebrows and folded his hands in front of him, elbows resting on Uncle Leopold's desk.

"There will be no marital alliance between you and me." Waverly was determined to nip that notion in the bud.

"But it could be beneficial—"

"I said *no*." Waverly bit her tongue. Beneficial? How? Once Preston found out she would be evicted from Traeger Hall and the estate sealed up like a tomb in no more than a week's time, she would be as worthless to him as a discarded penny. She had no idea how the man would respond once faced with the truth of Uncle Leopold's will.

"You're being shortsighted, Miss Pembrooke," Preston said and tapped his index fingers together.

"And you're being presumptuous."

Preston shook his head slowly. "I think not. I am only doing as your uncle would wish me to do in his absence."

Waverly debated telling the arrogant assistant everything, but then he continued before she could speak.

"I intend to do as Leopold wished and ensure that his interests are seen after." He stood and rounded the desk, dragging his index finger along the edge of it. "You can tend to the burials. If there are terms to the will that require further discussion, I'm certain Mr. Grossman will call upon me." He drew to a stop in front of Waverly, leaving mere inches between them.

"I'm sure he will." Waverly lifted her chin. My, how stunned Preston would be when Mr. Grossman returned to Newton Creek and told him everything. She kept her arms crossed over her chest now for a different reason—one of self-preservation—and she wondered how she had never noticed the vitriol in Preston Scofield's eyes before today. He had always given the impression of being the one to do her uncle's bidding, not one who held any real authority. But now, in the wake of her uncle's death, Preston was transforming into someone else entirely.

"I'm not going to argue with you," he added, giving her a wave of dismissal. "Right now, there are business matters to be seen to. You must realize the importance of that as well as your inability to tend to them."

Preston must have read submission in her silence, as a conceited look of satisfaction came over him.

He gave a short nod. "Now, I am going to retire for the night. I strongly advise you return to your place beside Leopold and his wife, for there is no one else here to carry on with the vigil."

He pushed past her and made no apologies when his shoulder brushed hers. Pausing at the door, Preston dared to offer her a patronizing smile. "Go through your uncle's papers if you wish. If you come across anything confusing to you, simply set it aside. I believe you will find yourself quite overwhelmed within a few minutes, and perhaps later we can explore how I might be a *partner* with you in the future."

The interloper exited the room, his long legs marching into the innards of Traeger Hall without hesitation. The very insinuation in his closing statement rankled Waverly. Preston was probably correct in that she wouldn't understand the ins and outs of Uncle Leopold's business ventures. Even so, she had no intention of entering into a partnership with the man. She knew very well that he was referring to marriage, which was a wild grab for the inheritance he believed Waverly to be in possession of.

The memory of the night she burst into Traeger Hall, the bell's echo still ringing over the valley, was enough to seal her lips. The blood that had soaked her uncle's chest from the stab wounds, the gruesome scene of her aunt splayed on the bell tower's steps . . . No, Waverly couldn't trust Preston any more than she could trust, well, she could trust very few people. And the more she considered this, the more her trepidation grew.

Yet Preston had suggested one thing that, after careful consideration, made some sense to Waverly.

"Very well." Waverly spoke to the empty study, lifting her chin and feeling more confident now that Preston had departed. She looked toward the door and addressed the man who was no longer there. "I *shall* look through my uncle's papers."

With that, Waverly stepped behind the desk and looked down at the many papers lying there. Leopold Traeger didn't appear to be a well-organized businessman when it came to his notes. She thumbed through a few pages and was loath to admit that indeed they made no sense to her. Reaching for a ledger, she opened it and saw columns of numbers and scribbling in the margins and even bits and pieces of dried tobacco leaves jammed into the spine. Waverly brushed them away. The only thing she understood in this ledger was the tobacco remnants, as well as the smell of the tobacco that permeated the pages of the ledger. Waverly was disappointed that the only thing she could glean from what she'd seen so far was that Uncle Leopold was also quite messy when he rolled his own cigarettes.

Preston was right. She knew very little about how to interpret her uncle's records. The ledger appeared to be a list of loans given, debts owed, and the like.

Waverly sat in her uncle's chair and slumped forward over the desktop, thankful Aunt Cornelia was not there to reprimand her about her posture. Of course, her corset did enough reprimanding as it was, and Waverly shifted in her seat so she could breathe. As she did so, a page fluttered from the desktop as if an invisible hand had lifted it into the air and made a show of its floating to the floor.

She reached down and picked up the page, then turned it over. It was written in Uncle Leopold's hand. Waverly frowned as she read her uncle's words.

> *To the members of the Newton Creek Council:*
> *It is no secret I have undergone the construction of a bell tower addition to my home at Traeger Hall. Be aware and be forewarned of its purpose, which is as follows:*
> *When you hear the bell toll, hasten to Traeger Hall. Summon the best and the strongest and urgently come. For if you dare to hesitate, all within will be dead, and the people of Newton Creek will be dismayed. My blood will seep into the soil, rotting the earth, and when the last turn of the mill wheel comes to a halt, you will perish with me.*

Waverly's hand trembled as she lowered the page. These were the words her uncle had been known for in the last days of his life. These were the words—in writing—that had sealed his reputation of eccentricity, but now were the exclamation mark on his true prediction.

Newton Creek had heard the tolling of the bell. *She* had heard the tolling. It was an unfamiliar sound, the bell having never rung before. It sounded deep and mournful, as though already grieving the violence taking part in its shadows below. Waverly remembered vividly where she was at the time, what she was doing, and with whom she'd shared that moment. She had startled, met the eyes of her companion, and whispered, "Surely not!" in utter disbelief.

Maybe it was her hesitation to act, something the townspeople had in common with her that night, which had resulted in their aid coming too late.

And yet Uncle's letter didn't make sense. Hadn't Mr. Grossman said that Uncle Leopold had assigned the lawyer to be in charge of his assets, so that the town might continue to thrive in Uncle Leopold's absence? Even after death, it seemed her uncle still wanted to have his mark on the town's economy. Had provisions been made, she wondered, with the town given access to the profits of her uncle's businesses?

And wouldn't that mean—contrary to Uncle Leopold's prophesy that without him, the sawmill would cease to exist and Newton Creek would perish—that the entire town had motive to kill him? He held most of the loans, he employed the majority of the townspeople. They were all under his rule, so to speak. With Uncle Leopold gone and Mr. Grossman's firm managing the assets, wouldn't that lend hope that the dominant force of Leopold Traeger would be dissolved and the town continue to grow? That way they would be free of Leopold, but not of the benefit of his assets.

Waverly pushed up from the chair and turned to eye the painting on the wall behind her uncle's desk. It was one of many that hung in Traeger Hall. It appeared Uncle Leopold had a hobby of collecting fine art. Aunt Cornelia, too, had a strong interest in it. Preston's efforts were centered on the sawmill and logging company, while Mr. Grossman was focused on the business assets, namely the financial foundation of Newton Creek, including her uncle's bank. But the paintings? Surely no one had forgotten to consider those. If the Hall was sealed with the paintings inside, that meant thousands of dollars' worth of art had been left behind.

Waverly considered her uncle for a long moment. He was devious. Savvy. He was thrilled by the fact he was in control of Newton Creek, and he was so sure of his eminent position that he believed someone would try to murder him. So if he left his business assets to Mr. Grossman's management, and he left nothing to Preston or her, then what was the one thing that her uncle upon his death would still retain control of, the one thing that might be to the detriment of the town?

She lifted her hand and, though instructed many times never to do so, ran her fingertips across the oil paint, feeling the tiny bumps and ridges made by the painter's brush. Her uncle had entombed his art collection so that no one would come to possess it, but what was it about the paintings in Traeger Hall that could ruin the town of Newton Creek?

Sleep was fitful. Waverly had barred her bedroom door by wedging a chair beneath its handle. Foo the cat had lain down beside her so close to her face that she was breathing in fur fluff. But Foo's familiar scent was comforting, and tonight, God knew she needed comfort.

The small fire Aveline had started in the fireplace before reluctantly retiring to her quarters had gone out. Every minute, it seemed, Waverly awakened to squint into the darkness to make sure Preston wasn't looming in the shadows, hoisting a knife high above his head to bring down on her.

What would it feel like to be stabbed? For a blade to slip into her body and then withdraw only to be thrust in again? She hoped it would happen so quickly she might not have time to feel the pain. And it mattered where the knife entered. If her abdomen, she would slowly bleed out. But if her chest, it might pierce a lung and then breathing would be near to impossible.

If Preston was the wicked culprit, motivated by a quest for wealth and influence, then why had he bothered to leave her alive? He could have been rid of her in private over dinner or in her uncle's study. He could hide her body in the cellar. Or, because no one was at Traeger Hall besides herself, Preston could drag her through the hallway and out the back door into the woods. Few people would notice her missing, not while she was supposed to be holding vigil over the bodies of her guardians. Preston would have plenty of time to leave her to be taken care of by coyotes or bobcats or even black bears.

As Waverly considered all of this while under her bedcovers and comforted by a cat who probably would take part in the disposal of her remains, she drifted in and out of sleep. It was little wonder why it was so disturbed. No one in their right mind could sleep when they feared their impending murder.

Had this been what Uncle Leopold had endured?

A rush of empathy filled Waverly as she drifted off to sleep once again.

It was the sound of the floorboards creaking that awakened Waverly for what must have been the eighty-seventh time that night. Her eyes fluttered open. Her hand reached for Foo, but the pile of feline fluff had disappeared. The traitorous cat had left her alone. Waverly lay frozen in her bed, her head resting on the pillow. If she lay perfectly still under the quilts, whoever had caused the floor to creak wouldn't see her.

Her childish reasoning was foggy with sleep, and Waverly fought disorientation as she peered into the darkness. The two arched windows on the far wall were shuttered, their gauzy white curtains undisturbed, as if they were ghosts hanging there to oversee the night. The wardrobe at the far end of the room was outlined by what little moonlight filtered through the shutters.

The floor creaked again. It was the obvious creak of a carefully placed foot on a floorboard unwilling to bear the weight.

Someone was in the hallway outside her room.

Waverly's fear from her earlier imagination overtook her. This time, however, it was real, not just the result of an overactive mind.

Someone was there...

As she stared into the shadows, it was the form of a man that stole her breath. She couldn't have moved or screamed or pleaded for help if she'd had the inclination. All reason had taken flight.

Another creak.

The man stilled.

Or was it a man?

For a terrifying instant, Waverly thought she could see right through her bedroom door to the figure beyond.

"Wavvverly..." The voice, indistinguishable as male or female, dragged out her name, the whisper drifting through the keyhole and floating toward her like an invisible fog. "Open your door."

Waverly squeezed her eyes tight, but knew it would serve her no good. She had left her uncle and aunt's sides in the parlor and gone to her own bed, sought her own comfort, hidden from a man she feared. But now?

She opened her eyes. Maybe if she peeked out her door, just enough to confirm the ghost of Uncle Leopold was not taunting her from the beyond, from outside her bedroom door. But her body was exhausted, her mind heavy with worry, fear, the puzzle of her uncle's estate, and the motive for his murder.

The whispering had ceased. The floor's creaking had subsided. All was as it should be...

Fully awake now, Waverly sat up in bed. Sunlight pushed its way through the shutters, lighting her room with morning's kiss of promise.

"Uncle Leopold?" The sound of her voice spoke reason into the room. It was real. *She* was real.

Uncle Leopold was not.

Or he hadn't been.

Or . . . maybe he had.

12

Preston's voice filled the front hall and drifted up the staircase to where Waverly was perched below a painting. He was entertaining a visitor, but Waverly was less concerned about his goings-on than about investigating her uncle's art collection. This painting before her depicted a woman standing in a pasture with a dairy cow. Softly muted pastels. Spring colors. It was beautiful. The artist had signed the work in the bottom right corner in red paint: *Vallée*.

The name sounded significant. A French artist? Of course, Waverly didn't know one painter from another, and Uncle Leopold had never included her in his dabbling in the art world.

But perhaps there was something about this painting that would give her a clue as to why her uncle thought Newton Creek would perish after he died . . .

"Miss Pembrooke!"

Waverly jumped, and Aveline mimicked her reaction. They both stared at each other in a moment of terror. Aveline's hand flew to her throat while Waverly's covered her mouth.

Recognizing the maid, she quickly dropped her hand to her side. "You frightened me!"

"You frightened *me*, miss!" Aveline said. She bit her lip, and when Waverly released a nervous giggle, Aveline joined her.

"I fear we're both convinced we're also to be murdered," Waverly stated.

"Or haunted," Aveline added.

Waverly nodded, then dared to ask, "Did you hear anything strange in the night?"

Aveline's eyes widened. "Should I have?" She swallowed visibly.

"No, no," Waverly replied and swept a hand through her hair nonchalantly. No reason to alarm Aveline at the moment, yet Waverly couldn't shake the idea that she'd heard Uncle Leopold's voice last night, hissing through the keyhole of her door, beckoning her to open it . . . tempting her to believe in ghosts.

Waverly then remembered that Aveline had probably approached her for a specific reason. "Did you need something?"

"Yes, miss. Mr. Scofield has requested your presence in the sitting room."

"Requested or demanded?" Waverly retorted. She noted Aveline's cheeks go pale again. "Never mind. I'll come."

On her way to the sitting room, she stopped at a mirror to check her appearance, pushing aside the black veil that hung over it. Shadows under her eyes made her pale skin look even whiter, and her white-blond hair gave her a ghostly aura. At the bottom of the stairs, she glanced at another painting momentarily before turning her attention to the sitting room.

On entry, Preston Scofield offered a disingenuous grin. "Ah, there you are!" He stood near the door with two gentlemen. "Waverly, Constable Morgan is here to see you."

Constable Morgan? Perhaps he had captured her uncle and aunt's killer, and tonight she could sleep in peace!

Waverly half smiled, straightening the black cuffs of her mourning dress. Preston spoke with too much familiarity as he drew her farther into the room. As he did so, Waverly took notice of the second man, Titus Fitzgerald. His frigid eyes met hers. Why was the undertaker here? Was this regarding funeral plans?

"Welcome to Traeger Hall, Constable." Waverly pulled from every memory of Aunt Cornelia's example of hospitality. She looked toward the room's pocket doors that remained open, searching across the entryway to the parlor. She noted, with a small bit of consternation, that someone had opened the parlor doors that she'd closed the evening before, and she could see Uncle Leopold's feet pointing toward the ceiling.

It was evident Constable Morgan had noticed them as well. He cleared his throat, his gaze dodging between Preston and herself.

"Mr. Fitzgerald." Waverly nodded to the undertaker. It was all so formal and stiff, much like Uncle Leopold and Aunt Cornelia . . . She sniffed as she righted her thoughts, and Waverly caught a whiff of sandalwood drifting from Titus's person. Sandalwood was much preferred to the undercurrents that were beginning to become more prominent in the parlor of death.

All three men stood until Waverly lowered herself onto the padded velvet chair closest to the door. After last night's bad dream or all-too-real haunting, she was as relaxed as a mouse under the stare of a cat. Regarding cats, Waverly noted Foo's fluffy white tail sticking out from his hiding spot behind the violet draperies that flanked the windows. Foo lifted the tip of his tail as if in salute to her well-being. It did little to calm her nerves.

Both Constable Morgan and Titus Fitzgerald took seats across from her on a stuffed sofa in a pinkish mauve that made both men appear very out of place. Preston stood at the fireplace, propping his elbow on the mantel with an air of authority as though quite pleased by the events unfolding before him.

Constable Morgan announced the reason for his visit with a

loud, phlegm-filled clearing of his throat that turned Waverly's nervous stomach. "Miss Pembrooke, please accept my condolences once again regarding your uncle and aunt."

Waverly stuffed down the wave of annoyance that sliced through her. "Thank you," she managed.

"I also appreciate your taking the time to see us. I've asked Mr. Fitzgerald to be here, as I believe he may help me in making sense of a few lingering questions I have."

A *few* lingering questions? Why, she had a *hundred* lingering questions! It didn't bode well if the constable had only a few.

"Have you found the one who murdered my uncle and aunt?" Waverly asked pointedly. She dared not look at Preston right now.

Constable Morgan cleared his throat again, only this time with less drama. "Ah, no. No, I have not. However, I do have *questions*."

"So you said." Waverly tried to be cooperative, though her mind was racing with all the possibilities, not the least of which was the likelihood the murderer stood right here in this room, his elbow on the mantel, a smug look on his face.

She caught herself. Was she being unfair to Preston? As much as she disliked the man, perhaps the constable himself had murdered Uncle Leopold and Aunt Cornelia. Or Titus! In fact, anyone in Newton Creek could have motive to kill her uncle. It didn't appear he was appreciated by them when alive, and his death might bring some financial relief to the town. But that would mean they would've had prior knowledge of her uncle's will and that Newton Creek stood to benefit from his death. Waverly sank into her seat. If true, that only muddied the waters further. Who would know about the will? Mr. Grossman? She couldn't imagine the older man being agile enough to commit two murders just to gain access to Uncle Leopold's estate. But then Grossman could have hired someone . . .

She glanced up at the oil painting near her in the sitting room. It was of two English Setters in full point, tails extended, noses in the air. Another Vallée painting?

Constable Morgan leaned forward in the sofa. "Miss Pembrooke, might I ask: where were you the night of the murders?"

Waverly was jolted back to the present conversation. Three sets of eyes were focused on her. She tempered her reaction, but her heart stopped. It stopped for so long, she surmised, that she should probably drop dead in about five more seconds. Or so it felt.

She looked at Titus. He stared back at her, unblinking. She glanced at Preston, who waited for her response, his expression also blank.

At last, she returned her gaze to Constable Morgan. "Why, I was . . . I was in town when I heard the bell toll."

"Where in town, Miss Pembrooke?"

Well, that was an entirely different matter altogether. "I-I . . ." She managed to get out the one word, but all others instantly erased themselves from her mind.

Constable Morgan exchanged a look with Preston. "I have it on good authority that you were seen in the company of an unidentified man outside the stables of the Fairfield Inn."

Waverly knew exactly whom Constable Morgan referred to. She only wished he hadn't, as she wasn't sure how to cover for herself, nor how to cover for the man she had no intention of identifying to Constable Morgan.

"Miss Pembrooke?" The constable was watching her. So were Titus and Preston.

Waverly remained still so she couldn't be accused of squirming. She folded her hands in her lap and lifted her chin. "In passing, yes, but it was of no consequence."

"I've a waitress who will attest to your sharing coffee with the man inside the inn. That's hardly a passing hello," Constable Morgan stated firmly.

Well, that was unfortunate. She never should have agreed to meet with the man in public. Waverly managed not to react in a suspicious manner. "I didn't know sharing coffee with someone was a crime, Constable."

"It's not." Constable Morgan sniffed and leaned back on the sofa. A spring in the velvet seat made a popping noise. For an irrational moment, Waverly hoped the spring would poke through and prod the man in the backside.

"I may have had coffee with him, but it was for a short period of time. Again, nothing of consequence." Waverly silently prayed that she'd be spared from further questions on the subject.

"You're aware that Mr. and Mrs. Leopold were both stabbed numerous times?" the constable asked, moving away from the topic of the unidentified man.

Apparently, God had heard Waverly's prayer.

"Yes," she answered.

The constable twisted in his seat. "Mr. Fitzgerald, would you please enlighten us as to the weapon you believe was used?"

"I'm not a doctor, mind you," Titus replied, his eyes still fixed on Waverly. "However, as I prepared the bodies for burial, I noticed the wounds were not consistent with what I would consider to be stab wounds inflicted by a typical knife."

"No?" The constable's question was leading. He had a point to make, and he wanted Titus to be the one to make it for him.

"Not as such. More specifically, the wounds were inflicted by a *dagger*." His eyes shuttered then, which gave Waverly no consolation as to whether he was still of the mindset to assist her or if he had shifted loyalties and was now acting like a witness in court against her. Against her for what reason, she didn't yet know, but Waverly could sense an accusation coming as strongly as one could sense an approaching thunderstorm.

"But isn't a dagger also a knife?" Constable Morgan smacked his lips as if tasting his inevitable conclusion.

"Technically, yes. But most knives are not daggers."

"For pity's sake, you're speaking in riddles." Waverly didn't bother to suppress her exasperation but released an unladylike sigh.

"It's hardly a riddle," said Preston with a pompous tone of assumed expertise. "A knife is a tool created for cutting or slicing things, hence one might loosely call it a dagger. But an actual dagger is created for one purpose only—stabbing. It is double-edged, symmetrical, and made with the intent to drive its sharp point into something by using a thrusting or a stabbing motion."

"Yes, thank you." Titus's mouth thinned. He appeared a little annoyed by Preston's interruption. "It is also the tool of a gentleman in many cases," he added.

"A gentleman," Constable Morgan reiterated. "Much like the unidentified man, Miss Pembrooke, with whom you met the day of the murders, the same man who was seen leaving in a fine carriage and wearing a well-tailored suit—this according to the waitress at the Fairfield Inn."

Waverly straightened in her seat. "What are you implying, Constable Morgan?"

The constable folded his hands in his lap, breathing in and releasing a great sigh. "One wonders why, on the night your guardians were so brutally attacked by someone wielding a dagger, you would be in town having coffee with a stranger who, since that day, has not been seen again."

"I still do not understand what it is you're implying." Waverly preferred to make the constable state his case clearly.

"Do you or do you not share an acquaintance with a gentleman who may have wished your uncle dead and who may have carried a dagger?"

"Shall we create more stories!" Waverly erupted. She glared at all three men, lingering for a few seconds on Titus before swinging her attention back to the constable. "Do you think I conspired to have someone assassinate my *family*?"

"Is that your answer, Miss Pembrooke?" Constable Morgan's eyebrow lifted.

"I did *not* conspire with anyone! If you have a witness who places me with said unidentified gentleman, then you will note it was during the very time the murders were being committed. How could he have been your culprit? How could *I*?" Waverly prayed this would resolve the matter. Logic would serve its purpose, and no more questions need be asked. Because those questions were ones she could not answer.

"Miss Pembrooke?" The constable demanded her attention.

"Yes?" Waverly weighed her words, her expression. She couldn't tell them everything. The consequences of honesty would be catastrophic. She bit her tongue, squeezing her folded hands together until her knuckles turned white.

"Going forward, I would recommend that you be very cautious regarding those with whom you associate." Constable Morgan took on the tone of a father. A father who didn't believe the claim of innocence he'd just heard. "As to your relationship with this gentleman—"

"I don't have a *relationship* with *any* gentleman," Waverly interrupted.

"For now, Miss Pembrooke, I leave you in the care and oversight of Mr. Scofield."

Waverly drew back and eyed the constable. "I don't need Preston's *oversight*."

Constable Morgan shrugged. "Be that as it may, with your being a grown woman, there are moral parameters. You, Miss Pembrooke, have stepped a toe outside those lines, which is raising questions on multiple levels. If you are, as you claim, innocent of any deviousness of late, then you will only benefit from the reputation of a man of business such as Mr. Scofield and his endorsement on behalf of your uncle."

It was revolting to Waverly. The very idea that they would consider her as having anything to do with the brutal slayings of her uncle and aunt. But what she would never admit aloud was that she wasn't innocent when it came to the unidentified gentleman. She wasn't. That was the worst part of it all. Yet to free herself from speculation, which was misplaced and yet founded in some truth, meant that she would have to endanger someone else. And that was completely out of the question.

WAVERLY

In an interview shortly before her death in 1950; memories from twelve days prior to the murders:

Now that I am old and have lived through two world wars, one might question my recollections. But I'll never forget an evening almost two weeks prior to the murders. This particular evening, Uncle Leopold was in fine form for dinner. While he wasn't engaging in any sort of conversation with Aunt Cornelia or me, he was congenial nonetheless. Pleasant would be too far of a stretch. But to eat in silence without thick tension or the impending threat of a verbal explosion? Well, that was practically a gift! Aunt Cornelia and I gladly received it.

A fire crackled in the fireplace at the end of the dining room. The sconces with gas lamps created a warm glow that bounced off the wood-paneled walls. Four narrow arched windows were opposite me and looked over the back gardens of Traeger Hall. Night had already settled, and we were all wandering in our thoughts over a dinner of roast chicken, sweet potatoes, and the last remaining green beans from the garden.

"I saw Margaret Fultch this afternoon," Aunt Cornelia offered by way of introducing a new conversation, one that was interesting enough to be shared at the table but not controversial enough to cause an argument. "She said that her daughter is getting married next spring to a man from Cambridge."

"Cambridge?" That snagged Uncle Leopold's attention, and he looked up from his plate.

"Wisconsin," Aunt Cornelia clarified. "Cambridge, Wisconsin."

"Oh." Uncle Leopold returned his focus to his plate of food.

I stifled a smile. On evenings such as this, a sort of peace came over Traeger Hall. It was tentative and teased of what could be if only its inhabitants could get along. If it took Margaret Fultch's daughter getting married to accomplish that, then I would personally see fit that every eligible young woman in Newton Creek followed suit and gave us all something to muse upon.

"Margaret stated that the young man has quite the mind for business." Aunt Cornelia gave Uncle Leopold a side-eye. "Perhaps you could . . ."

Uncle Leopold set his fork down with a clank against the plate. His brow furrowed. Peace winged its way from the room. "Ah! I see what this is about. Are you attempting to insert yourself in my business? I never asked you to suggest a replacement for Preston."

"I never suggested such a thing!" Aunt Cornelia clutched at her throat in an overblown show of mortification. That was exactly what her intent had been.

"Bah!" Uncle Leopold swiped the linen napkin from his lap and threw it on his plate. "Now my appetite is ruined." He glowered at her. "I don't know why you have a predilection to dislike Preston."

"I don't trust him." Aunt Cornelia dabbed the corners of her mouth with her napkin.

"Poppycock! I—"

At that moment, everything at Traeger Hall shifted and not for the better.

I'm not certain which I heard first, or if both sounds came simultaneously but were also distinct enough to be different. One was a gunshot. Not a large gun like a rifle. I had heard plenty of those in the past during the seasons when the locals hunted. No, this gunshot was sharp and not far from the mansion. The second sound was the shattering of window glass. It scared all three of us who were sitting around the dinner table. Glass exploded into the room, the bullet having pierced the window and hitting the wall behind me. Its trajectory, we would soon discover, had been a mere one inch away from traveling through Uncle Leopold's head.

Aunt Cornelia screamed and then landed face-first on her plate, the sweet potatoes pillowing her head as she fainted. I flung myself to the floor because that seemed the wisest thing to do—although far too late had the bullet been meant for me.

Uncle Leopold pushed back from the table, surging to his feet. "It's happening!" he bellowed. "Get my gun! It's in my study." He delivered the order to a white-faced servant, who rushed from the room to retrieve Uncle Leopold's pistol.

"Aha!" Uncle Leopold's cry encouraged me to raise my head. I saw what he had spotted: the silhouette of a man in the darkness, darting off into the night.

Uncle Leopold charged forward, rounding the table and knocking into it with his leg. The chinaware clanked, and shards of glass crunched under his shoes as he raced for the front door.

An hour later, once Uncle Leopold returned, and with Aunt Cornelia having disappeared into her bedroom to recover and to wipe sweet potatoes from her décolletage, it had become apparent that my uncle had been right. Someone wanted him dead. They had attempted to kill him tonight during dinner. What caused them to miss their target, we would never know.

But in the chaos of the moment, no one had thought to ring the bell in the tower and alert the townspeople for help. This fact had incensed Uncle Leopold, so much so that for the next three days he'd ranted about it to his staff, had lectured Aunt Cornelia to the point of exhaustion, and had made it clear to me that he'd had the bell tower built for just this purpose. But no. No one had bothered to race to the tower to ring the bell, to summon assistance from the town.

While Uncle Leopold ruminated and obsessed over this life-threatening dereliction of duty, the rest of us were consumed by a much different question. *Who?* Who wanted Uncle Leopold dead, so badly that they would risk exposure by standing outside the dining room window to administer their failed kill shot? And who had Uncle Leopold chased through the gardens that night, but to no avail?

One might argue it could have been any number of persons. Preston, at this point in time, had not made my personal list of suspicious characters. I also knew that there were others who harbored grievances against Uncle Leopold. But to murder him? Either way, it fit precisely into Uncle Leopold's prediction of his demise and was as potentially broad as to include anyone from a farmer whose loan Uncle's bank had foreclosed on, to a disgruntled sawmill worker, to a businessman Uncle had bested in some way.

The list could be lengthy if one truly wanted to examine it.

I was worried, yet I didn't say anything. Sometimes knowing and *knowing* were two entirely different things with horribly different consequences. And silence was often the best recipe because speaking out could cause so much more trouble.

13

JENNIE

NEWTON CREEK, WISCONSIN
PRESENT DAY

Tires squealed to a stop on the street outside the rental house. Jennie stared at the black truck with its tinted windows as she froze on the tiny porch, her keys in one hand and the morning newspaper blaring up at her in the other. Someone exited the driver's door, slamming it loudly behind them.

"Now what?" Jennie muttered under her breath, adjusting her grip on the paper. Mr. McSwigen had penned a fact-less exposé reviving all the legends and lore, ignoring Jennie's plea to respect the grief of Allison's family and friends. He'd included a pile of insinuations as to why Jennie Phillips had arrived in town. Perhaps to protect her father's interests? As if! Was it coincidental that Allison should go missing after Jennie's father purchased the property and then be discovered upon Jennie's first time visiting the property eight years later?

Well, she could sue for libel. She'd spoken with her attorney just that morning. He was now working on it, along with investigating the codicil. But for now? Now, there was an angry person stalking around an unfamiliar truck, and . . .

Zane Harris?

But this Zane Harris had an entirely different demeanor from the one at Traeger Hall yesterday. This Zane Harris had flashing eyes that had brewed into a stormy *Emerald City* rage. His scowl was so fierce that Jennie found herself taking a step back as he stopped just below her on the sidewalk. The newspaper was held tightly in his fist, and he lifted it with a jerk and waved it at Jennie.

"Real classy of you," he gritted out through clenched teeth. Zane tossed the rolled-up newspaper at Jennie.

She stepped away from the paper's intended path even though it wouldn't have hurt if it had hit her.

"If it helps any, I didn't give that reporter an interview." But going by the look on his face, her words didn't seem to make much difference.

"You didn't give—" Zane bit off his sentence and stepped onto the bottom step of the porch. "Just engaging with McSwigen was a big mistake. Heck, the entire town is talking about it since your outburst in the coffee shop. And now this." He dug into the pocket of his jeans and pulled out a piece of paper. "Leaving messages in a high schooler's locker? On school property? I should call the cops is what I should do."

"Hold on!" Jennie shot back. "I was *never* at the high school. And what high schooler are you talking about?"

"My sister, Hannah!" Zane shook the paper in the air. That he didn't believe her was obvious.

"Let me see that." Jennie hurried down the steps and snatched the paper from Zane's hand and made quick work of unfolding it. It was printed off an inkjet printer, the words on the page making a short paragraph. But it was the final sentence printed in red that jumped off the paper at her:

What happened to Allison can happen to you. Stay out of Traeger Hall.

Jennie frowned. "You think I'm responsible for leaving this in your sister's locker?"

He cocked his head, and his expression implied his accusation.

"Don't be ridiculous. Why would I do that? Besides, what does it even mean?"

"You tell me," Zane demanded. "The newspaper comes out this morning with that crap, and then my sister leaves school in a panic because she gets this?"

"Why would I have anything to do with that? I'm the one trying to figure out what to do with Traeger Hall! Why would I threaten someone to stay out of it, and why would I threaten your sister of all people?"

Maybe it was a look on her face or something in her eyes, but Zane's anger abated a bit. "Because you know Hannah wants to be just like Allison and open up the Hall to find the Traeger treasure?"

"I didn't even know you *had* a sister, let alone where she goes to school!" Jennie threw her hands up in the air. "You're being completely irrational!"

A moment of thick silence passed between them, eyes locked in defiant stares. Finally, Jennie shoved the ominous threat back at Zane. "I'm sorry someone is messing with your sister, but I didn't do anything. I was cornered by Mr. McSwigen at the coffee shop, and I made quite a fit about him leaving everyone alone. Ask anyone who was there at the time."

"What about the connection he made between your father and Allison?" Zane's dark eyebrow rose, his jaw set.

"Do you really think my father would have wasted his time on Allison? She would have been *nothing* to him. If she had been in his way, nosing around the Hall as McSwigen implied, my father had plenty of other legal options he could have turned to." Jennie snorted derisively. "Look, my father wasn't a good man, and I've *no* desire to defend him, but he wouldn't have dirtied his hands by killing anyone. He loved himself too much to risk getting caught."

Maybe something in her abhorrence of her father convinced Zane her statement was believable. He took a step back, eyeing the paper with the note that he'd snatched back from Jennie's extended hand.

"Then what's this?" His lost expression doused her temper.

"I don't know. Still, I would never threaten your sister." Jennie reached out her hand again. "May I see it again?"

Zane handed the note back to her.

She took a moment to scan the rest of the page.

To the members of the Newton Creek Council:
It is no secret I have undergone the construction of a bell tower addition to my home at Traeger Hall. Be aware and be forewarned of its purpose, which is as follows:
When you hear the bell toll, hasten to Traeger Hall. Summon the best and the strongest and urgently come. For if you dare to hesitate, all within will be dead, and the people of Newton Creek will be dismayed. My blood will seep into the soil, rotting the earth, and when the last turn of the mill wheel comes to a halt, you will perish with me.

"What *is* this?" Confusion rippled through her.

"It's the original and *legendary* letter sent to the Newton Creek town council shortly after Traeger built his bell tower and a few years before he was murdered along with his wife."

Zane's explanation made no sense. "Why would someone

leave a copy of that old note in your sister's school locker?" Jennie asked.

"I don't know, but something in the news article set them off. Hannah was my son Milo's age when Allison disappeared. She worshiped Allison and always wanted not just to pick up where Allison left off in the hunt to get inside the Hall but to find Allison. Being a teenager, she reads those books and watches the shows where teens go around solving crimes, cold cases mostly. She was stoked when you came to town. Hannah was going to get ahold of you to see if you would let her into the Hall if you decided to open it."

"She wanted to get justice for Allison and finish what Allison set out to do. Get inside Traeger Hall and uncover the mysteries within it," Jennie said. She blew out a breath of pent-up tension. "I get it. So someone read the newspaper this morning and knew I was in town, and suddenly Hannah's interest in Allison's disappearance and Traeger Hall is no longer just a teenage girl's whimsy. It's a legit threat."

"Right. Whoever was threatened by Allison eight years ago is threatened again—this time by Hannah."

Jennie didn't blame Zane one bit. She'd have been furious too if she were in his shoes. She also didn't blame him for accusing her. The timing of her dad's purchase of Traeger Hall and Allison's disappearance, and now Jennie's arrival in Newton Creek and finding Allison's remains, was awfully coincidental. But that was all it was—coincidence.

"Who then wants to keep Traeger Hall closed bad enough to kill someone over it and now threaten a teenager?" Jennie combed through possible theories she could offer Zane. "Would the lawyer, Mr. Wellington, have a motive to want me to keep the Hall closed? His firm helped my dad add a codicil to his will, essentially stating I'm not allowed to sell Traeger Hall or the properties associated with it for another fifty years. My own attorney is investigating the validity of the codicil and the reasoning behind it."

Zane contemplated for a moment. "Why would your dad not want you to sell his properties?"

Jennie rolled her eyes. "That's one of the things I'm trying to find out. My dad didn't exactly share his world with me and my mom."

Zane eyed her. "You and he didn't get along?"

It was a fair question, considering. "Not at all. But Dad was also self-serving and self-*preserving*. Not only did he have the codicil drawn up to safeguard his own financial interests but he also wouldn't have done anything illegal. Everything he did with his businesses was approved by lawyers."

Zane's brow furrowed as he studied her.

"He was far from a good dad," she added, dropping her voice. There. Maybe that would stop him from questioning why she'd emphasized his ethics on the business side of things and nothing else.

Zane simply nodded. "I shouldn't have gone off the handle on you."

"It's okay," Jennie assured him. "I'd feel the same way if I were you. You've been through a lot in the last forty-eight hours." She hoped he could see the empathy in her eyes. "Is Hannah all right?"

Zane released a heavy breath in agitation. "I told her to go home. My mom will call the school."

"You need to file a report." Jennie's suggestion seemed to dissolve more of Zane's anger. She handed the paper back to him, and he took it. "The school and the police should know about all this. With what happened to . . . your fiancée, it's not safe to assume this is an empty threat."

"I fully intend to," he said.

"You can name me in the report if you need to," Jennie stated. "I'll answer any questions. I don't want to see Hannah hurt."

The more she spoke, the more obvious it became. If the note was any indication, finding Allison's remains had stirred up something. Maybe there was some credibility to the Traeger Hall curse the locals believed in, or maybe it was something more recent . . .

"I'll make sure to keep Traeger Hall in the same condition it's been in. If opening the place up will cause more harm, I'll gladly leave it alone."

"But that's just it," Zane said. "If you keep it closed up, then we'll never know why whoever sent this note wants the Hall kept sealed. We won't know what Allison—and maybe Hannah—were close to uncovering. And that's going to hang over our heads like a bad omen. Who's to know when it'll become an issue again?"

Jennie held up a hand. "Let's just leave things be for now," she suggested. That was probably the best thing to do. The police might have their own recommendations. Opening the Hall would bring a ton of local interest just when the authorities were trying to figure out what had happened to Allison Quincy. Jennie thought again of the woman she'd found in the creek bed. That had been traumatic enough. And now this?

If Jennie was convinced of anything, it was that her mother—and probably Allison—had been correct. The allure surrounding Leopold Traeger, as well as the cold case of his and his wife's murders, had never died. Its suppressed heartbeat had thudded quietly for decades, and now it seemed it was coming back to life.

Jennie knew from personal experience that one way to avoid more trauma was to smother it. Shut it down. Ignore it. It might not go completely away, but at least the possibility was there that the hidden monster might be lulled back to sleep.

14

The Traeger Sawmill looked as forlorn, if not more so, as Traeger Hall.

Jennie stood on the creek bank, away from the yellow tape that still cordoned off the area where Allison's body had been found. Part of the tape had come loose and blew in the evening breeze like a yellow ribbon with black lettering. But this was no celebration. Allison was dead, and she'd not just drowned in the creek. She'd been murdered. The very idea sent chills through Jennie and grabbed at her emotions, clogging her throat with tears. She couldn't fathom the feelings that must be coursing through Zane at the discovery of his son's mother's remains. One thing Jennie had learned long ago was that, in spite of family dynamics and the dysfunction of relationships, death still brought with it mountains and valleys to traverse. Grief had many faces.

And then there was the mansion. Jennie shifted her attention to Traeger Hall, which stood on the hilltop, a crypt of memories and stories. Opening it would be like entering a time capsule, one that had waited more than a lifetime. What had happened during the days leading up to its windows being bricked and mortared? Who had been the last person to walk out of Traeger Hall, perhaps watching as the bricks were placed at the entrance as a permanent guard?

The notion that Allison's death could be tied to Traeger Hall beyond just her body being found near the sawmill unsettled Jennie in ways she couldn't quite define. Maybe Zane had been right. Maybe it *was* better to open Traeger Hall and then summon the courage to face the monsters. The unknown monsters that lurked around corners and in closets, as well as the monsters that were known all too well, those that taunted and prevented one from sleeping. But keeping the Hall closed forever meant the monsters couldn't escape, right? Or if she demolished the Hall, would that destroy the monsters altogether without the need to face them?

"What happened to you, Allison?" Jennie heard herself whisper aloud. There was no one there to hear her. Just the trickle of the creek as its significantly smaller presence tried to remind onlookers that it had once, until just a week ago, flowed wide and deep. Deep enough to successfully hide Allison's body for seven years. Deep enough to support an entire sawmill at the end of the nineteenth century.

Jennie turned at the sound of tires crunching on the gravel near the dilapidated sawmill's main building. It was where she'd parked her own car when she came here to get away. To be alone. To think. But it seemed that everywhere she went, someone came along to disturb her peace. She stifled a sigh and debated climbing the hill toward Traeger Hall to get away, but then decided against it. She'd be smart to post some *No Trespassing* signs.

An elderly woman exited the car. Her shoulders were curved from age, her spine bent, osteoporosis maybe. Her gray hair was tightly permed and close to her head, and she wore a blue blouse that hung over darker blue polyester pants. Jennie found her anxiety diminishing some at the sight of the elderly woman. The woman had to be in her eighties. A retired individual was unintimidating, and Jennie could hardly be upset with her for trespassing.

Jennie wove her way around the cordoned-off area and up an embankment to the gravel drive. The newcomer, looking very fragile, stood near the steeper part of the bank where part of the mill wheel still remained. The area that had been disturbed by the authorities was still visible, though Allison's body had since been taken away.

"Hello?" Jennie approached the elderly woman with caution so as not to frighten her.

The lady turned and gave a tiny smile, which was outlined with bright pink lipstick. "Oh, hello," she said in a wobbly voice. "I'm sorry. I didn't know anyone was here." The woman's golden-brown eyes were pleading as though she didn't want to leave.

"You're welcome to stay," Jennie said, offering her hand. The elderly were vulnerable. She knew what that felt like, and every part of her wanted to make this woman feel safe. "I'm Jennie Phillips."

The woman took Jennie's hand, and her skin was papery soft and cool. "Jennie." She said the name as if trying it out. It sounded soothing coming from an elderly woman. "I'm Gladys Quincy."

Quincy . . . Allison Quincy.

Jennie must not have hidden her surprise well enough. The sadness in Gladys's smile verified the relation before Gladys spoke. "I'm Allison's grandmother. I came here to see where she . . . where she spent her last moments." Tears glistened in Gladys's eyes, and Jennie stood beside her as they both turned to look down at the creek bed, at the clay and silt and the rotting mill wheel.

"I'm so sorry," Jennie breathed. It took everything in her not to put her arm around the delicate woman next to her.

Gladys was barely five feet tall. A stiff wind would probably blow her away.

"You're the one who found Allison, aren't you?" Gladys asked, her voice ending on a higher pitch with a quivering vibrato that was customary with old age.

"I am." Jennie shuddered again at the memory, not bothering to mention that actually it was a boy who'd found Allison. Her son. Zane had said Milo had autism, but that didn't mean it wouldn't impact the boy, who struggled with emotional disassociation. If somehow Jennie could bear Milo's distress, she would do so. Regardless, she knew she would never forget the moment she saw Allison's skeletal remains. It was a real-life horror movie. She didn't want to admit to Gladys that she'd already had nightmares because of it.

"Thank you for finding her." Gladys patted Jennie's arm. "For eight years I have prayed for Allison. In my heart, I knew she had probably gone home to be with the Lord, yet I still hoped to see her at least one more time." A tear trickled down her wrinkled cheek. "A mother should never have to bury her child, but a *grandmother*? It feels as though death played a wicked trick. I'm ready to go be with my Lloyd—my husband who passed twenty-one years ago—and to see my sister and my parents. So many relatives and old friends."

Gladys turned and looked up at Jennie. "When you're my age, you're ready to go. But Allison had a baby boy, our Milo, and she had Zane. He's such a good man. He treated Allison well, and with her need for adventure, well, my granddaughter didn't deserve him. Zane was willing to do right by her and Milo, and I get where my son and daughter-in-law were coming from as Allison's parents. They wanted Allison to marry, to give that baby a solid family. I don't think it would've lasted, though, to be honest. Allison and Zane were so young; they didn't share the kind of deep love like Lloyd and I shared. You can just tell when you see a couple, you know?"

She met Jennie's eyes with frank honesty. "You can tell if that lifelong love is there or not. Zane was a good man, while Allison was impetuous and full of spirit, but oh how I loved her." Gladys clicked her tongue and drew a shuddering breath even as the tears flowed more easily. "Nothing was ever the same after Allison disappeared."

Jennie bit her bottom lip and followed Gladys's line of vision over the creek and toward Traeger Hall. The bell tower affixed to the mansion's side was an architectural anomaly that looked out of place.

Gladys continued, "Some folks have said they heard a distant bell ringing the night Allison went missing."

Jennie nodded.

Gladys lifted a shaky hand and pointed toward it. "Now you tell me how that bell would ring if the place is all fortified like a castle and no one can get inside to ring it!"

Jennie waited, but Gladys didn't continue. Dare she ask? Jennie didn't want to upset Gladys any further, and yet . . . "Do you think Traeger Hall had something to do with Allison's disappearance and . . . her death?"

Gladys swallowed, her thin lips making a fine line. "The mansion itself? No. Its ghosts? I would bet my retirement on it." She looked at Jennie, her eyes narrowing behind her glasses. "Now, I'm not saying some spirit wafted down and killed Allison, but this place—" she clicked her tongue again—"since I was a little girl, this place has had an unhealthy aura around it. Like it was asleep, and someone needed to wake it up."

"And you think Allison woke it up?" Jennie ventured.

Gladys drew back, shaking her head. "I don't think she woke it up. I think she disturbed whoever wanted to keep it asleep, that's what I think. 'Leave it alone'—that's been the warning given about Traeger Hall for generations. Leave it alone. How else do you explain a mansion being intact after a century and no one ever breaking in? It's because of fear. And superstition.

Except for a few over the decades who got a bee in their bonnet, who tried to break through the bricks. They either gave up or got caught. With every generation, there seems to be that one person who can't let the mystery go—in spite of the warnings. And that was my Allison. She thought she was some adventurer or . . . what do they call those folks who dig up history?"

"Archaeologists?" Jennie offered.

"Yes. That's it. Allison wanted to know not only what happened to the man and his wife who were murdered there back in the 1800s but why the place had been sealed like a tomb."

"Do you know why it was sealed after the Traeger murders?" Jennie knew the stories her mom had researched. The lost art, the possible safe with money in it. But hearing from an aged local might bring a new perspective.

Gladys waved her right hand limply in dismissal. "Oh, there's all the rumors. My father swore he'd heard that Leopold Traeger had a pile of Monets stored in the attic. Some say the only treasure in there are copies of all the land deeds Traeger held because he owned the bank. They'd be worthless now, of course. Others say the only things inside are old furniture, antique relics from back in the day. No one would be foolish enough to seal up a house filled with treasure for no one to find. What would be the point of that? Especially when Leopold's will intended for Newton Creek to benefit from his profits long term. He wanted to be remembered as the cornerstone of this town. Too bad that failed. Newton Creek is but a whisper of what it once was. The Great Depression made sure of that."

Gladys had summarized the theories behind Traeger Hall, which coincided with what Jennie had read in her mother's research. Only her mom had included a few other artists besides Monet. Which, if true, begged the question of how a lumber baron like Leopold Traeger of Wisconsin would have had enough connections to the art world to bring a haul of valuable art to Newton Creek.

"Do you . . . ?"

Jennie hesitated. She didn't want to push her luck by asking the poor, grieving grandmother too many questions. Yet there were so many repercussions to consider. Not just for Zane and Milo, but now with the threat to his sister, Hannah. But Allison Quincy had her own family. She had relatives. Now that she'd been discovered at the sawmill, they might have an opinion about opening the Hall.

"Do you think it would be a bad idea if the Hall was opened?"

Gladys shook her head, leveling her sight on Traeger Hall. "I think it would be better if the place didn't exist anymore. Or is the house just the shell of something much deeper?" Her question speared Jennie, who swallowed hard. "Maybe," Gladys added, "Traeger Hall is not the reason for all the darkness around Newton Creek."

"What is the reason then?" Jennie asked, genuinely curious.

Gladys looped her thin arm around Jennie's, hugging it tight as if pretending for a moment that Jennie was Allison back from the grave.

"*People*, Jennie Phillips. People are the ones who create the darkness. Traeger Hall is just the place where they lock it up so it can't get out."

※

Everything bad happened at night. That was when monsters woke up, when poltergeists came out to exact revenge, when memories posed as nightmares and replayed without asking "Are you finished watching?" like a polite streaming service would. At least during the day, a person could distract one's mind and manipulate life to follow a path that steered clear of the frightening.

Jennie hadn't left the Traeger property after Gladys pulled away in her car, going at least twenty miles under the speed limit and barely able to see over the steering wheel. Instead, she'd been lured up the hill to Traeger Hall, as if an invisible force were pulling her there. With dusk fast approaching, it went against her comfort and security to face Traeger Hall in the dark. Whispers drifted in and out of the trees that dotted the overgrown front lawn. Whispers of the past, the voices of those who had died here. Jennie could almost hear them audibly. The words muttered were unintelligible but still heard.

She craned her neck to look up the two stories of the mansion made of brick. Every window was merely an outline, multicolored bricks filling in the space where panes of glass used to be. The front door that had once stood majestically was blocked in, and the stone stairs that led up to it were filthy from years of disuse and neglect.

Jennie meandered to the right of the building and paused in front of the bell tower. It reminded her of a squat version of Rapunzel's Tower from the popular fairy tale. It rose one story above the mansion, built of matching brick, with the large copper bell, its patina green from oxidation, hanging quiet and still.

Who in their right mind built a bell tower attached to their home?

Leopold Traeger, that's who.

Jennie lowered herself to the dying autumn grass, crossing her legs like she did years ago in school. Darkness was thoroughly setting in now, and part of her was anxious to return to her car and drive back to Newton Creek and her rental house for a cup of decaf coffee. But something held her here. Something that linked her to this place—to its history—though she couldn't identify what it was.

Was it the lure of art and treasure?

Did it have to do with fulfilling her mom's dream of exhuming the Hall's secrets?

Was it because this place was connected to her father and her still unresolved issues concerning him?

She wanted to move on. She *ached* to move on. Jennie wanted

God to make her messy beautiful. To infuse life with hope and peace. There were scriptural promises that said He would. Then there was the reality of life as well as the confirmation from the culture around her that she was perhaps misguided and naive for believing that God was somehow good.

Jennie plucked a blade of grass and rubbed it between her thumb and forefinger. She stared up at Traeger Hall. "You were a house of horrors, weren't you?" She thought of the mansion's history, the murders, and the ensuing mystery, the *whodunit* speculation . . . Jennie could feel the horror in the earth beneath her.

Bad things had happened here. Things no one spoke of, and now no one remembered.

Traeger Hall was more than just a house that had witnessed murder. It was a house of monsters. So how could anything good come from opening it?

15

WAVERLY

TRAEGER HALL
SEPTEMBER 1890

One thing Waverly had noticed about Titus Fitzgerald was that he was not one to be coerced or bullied into something. He was far too opinionated for that. On one hand, it was no surprise he remained behind when Constable Morgan took his leave; on the other hand, Waverly was aggravated that Titus presumed she'd wish to speak to him. He had, after all, just given the constable added weight to the ludicrous theory that she had something to do with her uncle's and aunt's deaths.

"Might I have a word with you, Miss Pembrooke?" Titus addressed her but also included Preston, who sauntered back into the sitting room after showing the constable to the front door.

"Ah!" Preston exclaimed. "I see. You are not here to speak with me." He looked between them, seeming to enjoy exerting an air of self-importance. "I shall leave you to it then." With a slight bow of his head, Preston took his leave, which surprised Waverly. She'd expected him to want to be included or at the very least to stay, to pretend he had some tie to Waverly as a potential suitor.

"A stroll outdoors, perhaps?" She extended her arm toward the door, recalling a few months ago when she'd engaged in polite conversation with Titus at a social event in Newton Creek. At that time, she'd been enamored with his icy eyes, his deeply toned skin, his remarkable features that were so unlike what one might imagine an undertaker to be. Enamored? She might have been. They had sparred verbally from time to time, but that had been the extent of it. Until now when her guardians were dead, and when Titus seemed far more invested in the situation than one might find necessary.

"The fresh air will do us good." Titus held his hat under his arm. "It's stifling in here."

Within moments, they had moved to the outside and were strolling along a path that led to the gardens in the back.

"I don't believe you personally wielded the dagger that slaughtered your uncle and aunt," Titus proclaimed with all the finesse of someone terrible at navigating polite conversation.

"How kind of you to place such faith in me," she retorted.

Titus halted on the path, his dark brown suit emphasizing the bright blue of his eyes. "I do wonder, however, if today's conversation underscores for you the danger you are in? As I've stated before and will not cease stating."

"Danger?" Waverly feigned surprise. "What with the magnanimous Preston Scofield in residence now, who believes he can determine my future and take over my nonexistent inheritance? On the contrary, I'm quite protected now." She didn't care if Titus heard the anger in her voice.

"Are you insinuating that Mr. Scofield isn't aware of the terms of your uncle's will and your soon-to-be destitute future?"

Waverly frowned. "No. He is not aware. He has yet to meet with Mr. Grossman."

"And you haven't informed him?" Titus's deep baritone held a hint of surprise.

Waverly looked up at him. "And have him murder me too? For all I know, *he* is the one who fired the shot through the window not three weeks ago, and *he* is the one who finally succeeded in killing Uncle Leopold and Aunt Cornelia. What if this was part of his grand plan? To swoop in and merge his life with mine and take over my uncle's assets. I'd be a fool to reveal to him that I—and, in turn, *he*—will inherit nothing from my uncle. Preston just might turn his wrath on me, and then I would be the next body you prepare for burial."

"Waverly—" Titus began.

She held up a hand, cutting him off. Waverly knew he was about to reprimand her for staying at Traeger Hall and putting her life in danger. "I'm trying to make plans for myself. I have *questions* of my own, you know? And your keeping me from investigating the motives for my uncle's death is hindering me. Also, I have my maid, Aveline, to add an element of safety, and I'm not unaware of what is going on around me." It was a weak defense, and Waverly knew it. Reason told her to flee Traeger Hall now. But where would she go, and with what money? Besides, she had more than just herself to think about; she had someone else to consider as well . . .

"I am not witless, you know. I can be cunningly cautious," Waverly finished with an emphatic lift of her brows.

"And yet you meet with unidentified gentlemen." Titus looked into her eyes with a bit of accusation.

Waverly felt her cheeks become warm and sensed apprehension squeezing her heart. "It was nothing untoward." She could at least assure Titus of that, if nothing more.

Titus regarded her for a long moment and then gave a shake of his head. "This morning, I took into my possession the remains of an elderly man. I doubt you would know him personally. He was more than likely *beneath* you in station and in company."

"Oh, for pity's sake," Waverly spat under her breath.

"I did so because I was responding to a writ of replevin," Titus concluded with an expression that insinuated Waverly should understand.

She didn't.

Titus, appearing to gather that, continued, "In short order, Mrs. Hammish, who owns the boardinghouse in Newton Creek—"

"I know who she is," Waverly interrupted, not wanting to appear completely removed from the community over which Traeger Hall seemed to lord.

"Good. Well, Mrs. Hammish offered room and board to an elderly couple only a week ago, and shortly thereafter the gentleman's heart gave out and he passed on. I was arranging for a coffin for the deceased when I witnessed Mrs. Hammish's attempt to receive payment for the time the couple had stayed at her boardinghouse and for the food eaten there."

Waverly had no idea where Titus was going with all of this.

"In the end, the dead man's wife offered to pay half of the total cost, not believing the full price was fair, seeing as her husband had died and their visit cut short."

"I'm not understanding the relevance," Waverly said.

"Mrs. Hammish had taken the man's body hostage," he added.

Waverly had no words at this point.

Titus continued, "Mrs. Hammish stated she would keep the body in her front parlor for as long as it took the man's wife to pay their bill in full. It was then that the wife took it upon herself to seek assistance, and Constable Morgan was called upon. She requested that the constable administer a writ of replevin—a case made in writing to retrieve property that has been wrongfully obtained."

"The old man's corpse?" Waverly was dumbfounded and at the same time still bewildered. What on earth did this situation have to do with her?

"Precisely. Due to the writ of replevin, and at the rather forceful insistence of Constable Morgan, Mrs. Hammish agreed to relinquish the body to me."

"Sir, what is your point?" While the story was morbidly fascinating, she had become thoroughly exasperated.

"My point, *Waverly*," said Titus, making a show of using her first name, "is that those who believe something rightfully belongs to them will stop at nothing to retrieve it."

"Well, I should think so, especially with respect to a loved one's remains!"

Titus nodded. "And if one is willing to do that for a corpse, imagine what someone might do to retrieve what they believe to be their own wealth being unjustly kept from them."

"Are you implying that I would have my guardians killed under the assumption I would then be able to lay claim to my uncle's estate?" While Waverly saw only a thin correlation between Titus's story and her own situation, she did not like it nonetheless.

"I'm not implying anything," Titus snapped. "I'm merely stating what I've observed about human nature. And what will inevitably be part of Constable Morgan's reasoning. Like it or not, you are more of a suspect to him and with more motive than anyone else. Your clandestine meeting with the unidentified gentleman, your arrival at Traeger Hall barely a year ago, the fact your aunt had married Leopold just five years prior to your arrival—all of it is suspiciously convenient, appearing like a wily plan concocted by two women who stood to gain quite a lot by one man's death."

Speechless, Waverly could only stare at Titus.

"That you've yet to take your leave of Traeger Hall when a murderer is still on the loose shows a serious lack of caution,"

Titus added. "Unless, of course, you already *know* who the murderer is, and you have no fear of the person."

"I don't!" Waverly protested. "Besides, you know as well as I do—I stand to gain nothing!"

"An unfortunate and unpredictable turn of events," Titus said. "Your master plan has gone awry."

"You think I orchestrated this with my aunt?"

"No, I do not think that. Nor do I think you double-crossed your aunt by having the unidentified man kill her also. But I guarantee you the constable believes this, and he's looking for evidence to back it up."

Panic swelled within her because everything Titus said made sense. Horrible, awful sense! She could see how it all appeared now. And in good conscience, for the sake of another, she couldn't defend herself!

"Oh, bother!" Waverly whirled away from Titus and marched to a bench several yards away, flanked by rosebushes that had already finished blooming for the summer.

Titus followed her to the bench. "I hope you see now the urgency for you to protect yourself and for you to be honest, telling the authorities everything you know, so that we might clear your name before this becomes entirely blown out of proportion."

"I have nothing of which to clear my name!" Waverly glared at Titus, who stared back at her in return. His expression held little empathy.

"Tell me who the unidentified gentleman is, Waverly, and allow me to assist you."

"I-I cannot." She tugged a handkerchief from the pocket of her black silk bombazine. It was an awful feeling to realize the only friend she might have was the undertaker of all people, and even more awful that she simply *could not* say another word.

"You cannot, or you will not?" Titus pressed.

"Both." Her voice was small and strained.

"Did this stranger hurt or threaten you in some way?" Titus's features darkened.

"No!" Waverly hefted an unladylike sigh.

"I think it would be best if you came into town with me."

The sudden shift in conversation took Waverly by surprise. "Why?"

"Because we must determine what you wish to acquire for your guardians' coffins. Funeral arrangements must be made. And perhaps"—Titus extended a gloved hand to her—"I may in time earn your trust."

"My trust?"

"Yes. I would like for you to see that I am more than just an undertaker."

"What are you then?" she whispered around the emotion that made her throat sore.

Titus took her hand and squeezed it. "At the very least, Miss Waverly Pembrooke, I am a friend. Let's start there, shall we?"

The funeral parlor was a newer addition to Newton Creek. Funerals were typically held in the parlor of the deceased's home. That she could host the funeral was obvious, that she *would* host it was not. Waverly didn't even know how to pretend to grieve for Uncle Leopold, and with the impending hardship of losing her home once the Hall was closed forever, well, there was no reason to exhaust herself with hostessing duties.

To serve as the funeral home, Titus Fitzgerald had purchased a two-story, white pillared house in Newton Creek's valley. The house featured black shutters, a black porch, and a black front door. A circular drive looped to the right of it, with a portico at the side door that was large enough to allow for a horse-drawn hearse. But then who would order a hearse for their funeral in a small town like Newton Creek? Few people cared for such pomp and circumstance. Or perhaps Uncle Leopold would have, as he could easily have afforded it. But, for all the eccentricities of his will, Leopold had left no instructions regarding the funeral itself.

That, unfortunately, had been left up to Waverly. Her undying curiosity rose to the fore as they neared the funeral home. "Do you live here as well?" The idea of sharing a residence with the dead was quite macabre.

"I do. The upper level is my living quarters." Titus helped Waverly from his modest carriage. With her feet planted on the walk, they approached the home. The front door opened with a subtle flourish as Titus pushed on its handle.

A middle-aged housekeeper, dressed respectably in mourning, met them at the door and took his hat.

"Tea, Mr. Fitzgerald?"

"Yes, please, Agatha. And show Miss Pembrooke into the office. I will be there directly."

So formal. So businesslike. Waverly eyed Titus as he turned to address her. Did he know that many of the townsfolk questioned his heritage, wondering why he'd decided to settle in Newton Creek since he had no immediate family in the area? Yet it didn't seem to bother Titus what other people thought of him. It only bothered him what other people thought of *her*, and that bothered Waverly. She was, after all, nothing more than a paying customer on behalf of the Traeger Estate. And yet he claimed to be her friend, this after all but accusing her of murdering her own kin.

"I'll be right with you." He dipped in a solemn bow and then disappeared into a side room, leaving Waverly at the hospitable mercy of Agatha.

"This way, Miss Pembrooke."

Waverly followed Agatha down a hallway that was whitewashed and had an assortment of gilded-framed paintings of countryside, farmland, and even one of a cow. The art was nothing at all like Uncle Leopold's.

Agatha swung open a heavy wood door, and a burst of sunlight met them in the hall, along with the scents of sandalwood and tobacco.

"Please, have a seat, Miss Pembrooke." Agatha motioned to a stuffed chair near a bay window with a table between it and another matching chair. "I'll be back shortly with tea."

"Thank you." As Agatha took her leave, Waverly settled into the chair, adjusting her skirts and pulling off her black gloves.

Titus strode into the room, leaving the door open behind him. "Do forgive me for keeping you waiting."

"I've been here all of a minute, not long enough to succumb to death from boredom." Her response was meant to lighten the mood, but instead Titus frowned as he took the chair opposite her.

"Do be serious, Waverly." He gritted the words through his teeth, and he cast a glance over her shoulder at the door, presumably left open for propriety's sake.

She felt a pang of remorse. Her previous interactions with the undertaker had her expecting bluntness from him, even a cutting sense of humor. Perhaps his aloof manner was meant to mask an awkwardness between the undertaker and a young unmarried woman. Both were all too aware of the other's eligibility. Or maybe, Waverly thought, irritating the other brought some satisfaction to the one doing the irritating.

But now Waverly could see the facade of etiquette had fled from Titus's features. He leaned forward with a sternness that demanded her attention.

"I am begging you to trust me."

"We've already spoken of this." Waverly released a breath of exasperation, wishing Titus would leave it be. "I'm here to plan my uncle and aunt's funerals."

"You don't understand—"

"Here we are." Agatha entered the room carrying a tray with a teapot, cups, and a small plate of cookies. She slid it onto the table between them. "Would you like me to pour?"

"No, Agatha, thank you." Titus attempted to shoo her away discreetly.

Agatha looked between them, and her lips thinned. "Would you like me to stay and assist with notes?"

Titus cleared his throat uncomfortably. "No. I am quite capable of recording the wishes of Miss Pembrooke for the Traeger funerals."

"Very well then." Agatha, who seemed a tad presumptuous and uptight to Waverly, straightened her back and exited the room.

"She means well," Titus said as he reached for the teapot.

"Allow me," Waverly offered.

Titus sat back as Waverly took it upon herself to pour the tea. It gave her something to do and something else to look at besides Titus's face, which was once again turning concerned and adamant.

"Do you not see what is happening?"

His persistence might have been endearing had he any expression other than one that scowled at her as if she were an imbecile.

"You already made it quite clear back at Traeger Hall. You haven't *stopped* at making it clear." Waverly gave a short nod and set the teapot down with a plop that made the teacups and saucers clank together. "I came here to discuss caskets." She tried to ignore the anxiety welling within her. "I would like satin lining for my uncle and aunt's caskets, I hear it is all the rage," she prattled. "And a stuffed turtledove as well, posed along with a bouquet of daisies and sunflowers in honor of Aunt Cornelia's fondness for orange and pigeons."

"Turtledoves and pigeons are hardly the same bird."

"Then I want both. Stuffed. With glass eyes."

"Glass eyes?"

"Glass eyes." Waverly handed a teacup and saucer to Titus. "And I would like the caskets to be made of cherrywood. Uncle Leopold would have nothing less, I'm sure of it."

"And would you like windows placed in their coffin lids so you can see their expressions when you suddenly fall into the grave along with them after someone returns to Traeger Hall to finish the job you seem so bent on ignoring?"

Waverly stilled, her teacup halfway to her lips. She wondered if it were possible to hurl daggers from her eyes at the man. Likely not. But it would be a nice addition had the Creator seen fit to give her such a talent.

"I'm not ignoring it," Waverly capitulated. There were certain consequences for taking Titus into her confidence, not the least of which was that he might discover more than she wished him to. He was an intelligent man who was far more invested in her situation than seemed necessary for an undertaker. She ran her finger along the rim of her teacup, allowing the silence between them to build. He had offered friendship, yet there was something more in his eyes, in his tone . . . as if he truly cared about her. She wasn't sure why, but that frightened her as much as it caused her heartbeat to race. She didn't hold many precious memories of being cared for. Aside from . . . No. Waverly cut that thought short.

Would trusting Titus be the wisest course of action? Doing so could possibly assist her in solving the mystery of why Uncle Leopold believed he would be murdered, not to mention address her suspicions that it had less to do with her uncle's businesses and more to do with his dabbling in the art world.

And then there was the incident last night. The whispering through the keyhole of her bedroom door.

The beckoning . . .

Waverly, open the door.

She leveled a frank gaze on Titus Fitzgerald. Sometimes trusting cost more than one was willing to pay.

Waverly decided to change the subject. "In regard to the satin-lined caskets . . ."

WAVERLY

In an interview shortly before her death in 1950; memories from twelve days prior to the murders:

I was going to die.

At least that was what Uncle Leopold had told me.

That night, after the bullet had shattered the window, after Aunt Cornelia and Uncle Leopold had retired to bed, I tiptoed through the Hall. I stood at the door that led into the bell tower, staring down at the brass knob, and finally twisted it.

Once in the tower, a draft of fresh air wafted down the narrow, winding steps that led up to the belfry. It was also cold and damp. I wanted to take comfort there. I hoped I would find it in the bell tower at night just as I did during the day. A place of solace and quiet. But at night, the tower took on an ominous feel, an oppressive weight on my chest. I had barely made it up the first few steps before I decided to return to my bed.

That was when I heard them, the footsteps. They were heavy and echoed in the tower. Someone above me was descending the stone steps. Fear rippled through me, and I froze in place. My palm was spread against the cold wall as I stared up into the darkness, certain the one who had fired the gunshot earlier had returned to finish the job.

But it was Uncle Leopold who wound his way down the stairs. He stopped, visibly surprised that I was standing there at the bottom in my white nightgown, looking very much, I suppose, like a ghost. He held a lamp in his hand, and its light cast shadows around him, deepening his eyes and emphasizing the grim set to his mouth.

"What are you doing here?" he demanded.

"I-I come here . . . sometimes," I managed in reply.

Uncle Leopold descended the final steps to stand beside me. He held the lamp up and stared into my face. "Sneaking about the Hall at night will sign your death warrant."

His voice was stern, commanding. So I did what I always did—I nodded my acquiescence.

"Go to bed before the killer decides you will join me in the afterlife."

My response surprised even me. "Why do you believe you're going to die?" I asked.

Uncle Leopold's eyes narrowed. He seemed to consider whether I deserved an answer and then decided I did. "Because I must die. That's the way of it when one has wealth."

"I don't understand," I said.

"You're not supposed to understand." He pushed by me and stalked into the passageway beyond.

I followed him, closing the bell tower door behind me. When the latch clicked shut, confirming the door was sealed, I looked up to see Uncle Leopold still standing there.

His eyes were hard and drilled into me so insistently that I could almost feel their glare.

"You must stay out of the business of Traeger Hall. Death doesn't play favorites and will have no mercy."

"What business?" I breathed.

It was then I thought Uncle Leopold might actually know my secret, the one I hid especially from him.

"You know of whom I speak."

He knew!

"Go to bed. Lock your door. Stop roaming the Hall at night. That is foolishness."

"Yes, Uncle." My response trailed behind me as I hurried back to my bedroom. I shut and locked the door, then went and sat on the edge of the bed, staring at the door.

It wasn't the first time I'd seen Uncle Leopold roaming the halls in the middle of the night. I always assumed he couldn't sleep or that he was still about his work. But tonight was the first time I saw him in the bell tower. Perhaps he was assessing why his instructions had not been followed—why, after the gunshot, no one had tried to ring the bell and alert the town about the need for help.

But there was something else about Uncle Leopold that night, something I could not put my finger on. It became the first of several nights that I lay awake, considering, before it all ended in a bloody massacre heralded by Uncle Leopold's bell.

As I sat on the edge of my bed, I knew that if I dove beneath the bedsheet, I would still be seen. I would still be vulnerable. I was not safe in Traeger Hall, and that feeling had been with me since the day I first arrived. So I did the only thing I could do—I faced my fear. I faced the monster who roamed the halls as Uncle Leopold. And that night I whispered my final response to my uncle.

"What are you all about?" I asked. And I was worried that I would never find out.

What I didn't know then was that, in a matter of two weeks, Uncle Leopold's predictions would come true and I would be flirting with death myself, not realizing how imminent it really was.

16

JENNIE

NEWTON CREEK, WISCONSIN
PRESENT DAY

Rain pelted the ground and with it came uninvited flooding. The saturated earth, the already muddy creek, and the fallen leaves that had collected into moldy, wet piles were all drowning. Though it was nine o'clock in the morning, the sky remained dark as if it were already dusk.

As the autumn storm raged on, thunder rumbling in the distance, Jennie sat watching it all from the top step at the entrance of Traeger Hall. Thankfully, her body was shielded from the rain by the veranda's overhang.

He wasn't going to show. She didn't blame him. It didn't surprise her that Zane might have second thoughts. Heck, *she* had second thoughts. The fact she had even called Zane to meet her here was giving her a fit of nerves, but somehow it didn't seem right to open Traeger Hall alone. Then again, none of the options felt right, whether to keep it sealed, open it, or even bulldoze it.

And she was alone in making her decision. She'd called her attorney, who stated that it was up to her. Even if her dad's codicil checked out as legal, that had to do with selling the property only. What she did with the Hall while she owned it was up to her.

There was the added pressure of Hannah, Zane's sister, and the threatening note she'd received. That worried Jennie more than anything. If she opened up the century-old tomb of Traeger Hall, what other Pandora's box elements would be released? Would whoever wrote the note to Hannah exact some form of retribution?

Jennie shifted on the step, drawing her shoes further under the shelter of the roof as the rain increased in intensity. The weather seemed to oppose her decision. Jennie scanned the sky. Gray, unyielding, judgmental. Opening Traeger Hall was not a small thing, and Zane had suggested they meet privately. His concern was if anyone got wind that they were going to remove the bricks and enter the Hall, the entire township of Newton Creek would show up to watch. So it was to be just them present: the owner of the Traeger property and the man who seemed to have lost the most because of Traeger Hall.

At that very moment, Zane charged toward her through the sheets of rain, a green raincoat hoisted over his head.

Jennie stood to greet him, being careful to stay well under the veranda's roof that spanned the length of the mansion.

Zane pounded up the stone steps, leaving behind muddy footprints. "It's a torrent!" he exclaimed. A wet behemoth of a sheepdog chased after him. The dog shook itself, spattering rainwater across Jennie's jeans.

"Midas!" Zane scolded.

Jennie laughed, wiping off her pantlegs. She was glad for the distraction and pleased to see the shaggy dog.

Midas lumbered toward her, sniffing and licking her outstretched hand. Then he padded away to explore the veranda further.

Zane shook the water from his jacket and hung it over the paw of a marble lion that ornamented the front entrance. Midas shook with a fury once again, sending more water and mud spraying in all directions.

"Sorry about my dog," he apologized.

"It's okay. I love dogs," Jennie said, not knowing what else to say.

Zane didn't look happy to be here. Traeger Hall came with a lot of baggage for him.

Jennie hesitated, then decided it was only right to ask, "How is Hannah?"

"Hannah?" Zane gave a crooked smile. "Oh, she's sixteen and fine. She didn't take the note too seriously, I mean once the panic wore off. I wish she did. But my mom is acting like a raging mama bear, and she aims to ransack Newton Creek until she finds who left the note. My dad? He's, well, he's a dad."

Jennie didn't know what that meant. It was as if Zane assumed all dads were the same. She was pretty sure that Zane's dad wasn't like hers had been.

"And you?" he asked.

His question took Jennie by surprise. She was already uneasy being alone with Zane, mostly because she didn't communicate well with people in general. But men—especially good-looking ones—were downright intimidating.

Fly under the radar. It's safer there. That was her unspoken motto for years. She'd never dated and never wanted to.

She finally replied, "I'm . . . making it."

He offered no assurances that all would be fine, and Jennie appreciated that. After everything that had happened in the last couple of days, they'd been given ample proof to the contrary. There were no guarantees that things would work out.

"I'm making it too," Zane said.

Jennie took a step away from him. She was taken off guard by the sudden urge to give the guy a reassuring embrace. He wasn't just trying to be kind to her during his own turmoil, he was also being honest. There was too much vulnerability in his admission to be anything but. That thought floored her. It felt foreign to have a man stand before her and admit to any sort of weakness.

"So how do you want to do this?" Zane's question stunned Jennie, and she stared at him. He raised his brows, waiting. When she didn't reply, he cocked his head to the side with a questioning expression.

Jennie had to get herself together. But courage was hard to find, and the very thought of taking charge? This was no small thing! They were literally breaking into a house that had been shut up since 1890! And this was her *mom's* dream. Carol Phillips had read old newspapers, scoured the internet for anything she could find about Traeger Hall. She had been her own type of Indiana Jones, and Jennie was just the sidekick who'd gotten sucked into the adventure. But now Mom was gone, and Jennie was left holding the proverbial Ark of the Covenant. Was it smart to open it?

"I don't want my face to melt off." Were those the only words she could think of to say to Zane Harris?

Zane stared at her, then let out a short laugh. "Is that an Indiana Jones reference?"

Jennie nodded, avoiding Zane's eyes and making a pretense of studying the closed-up entrance. Bricks of various colors had been used to shut out the world. Now they were old with crumbling mortar, and dirt piled in the corners between what should have been the door and the floorboards of the veranda.

"My mom liked the Indiana Jones movies."

"Best ever," Zane said.

"Yeah, I just . . ." Jennie hesitated, but something in Zane's eyes coaxed her to go on. "I just wonder if we're not opening up a curse. Maybe this isn't a good idea."

"I highly doubt our faces will melt, although I can't say for sure we're not inviting a curse." Zane shifted his attention to the doorway. It was about seven feet high and eight feet wide, the frame blocked entirely by the brick. The large double doors that once hung there had long since been removed. "But curses don't hold any power unless we give it to them. I guess I need to remember that." He seemed to be talking as much to himself as to Jennie. Zane ran his hand along the bricks in the doorway. "Allison swore there was a way inside the mansion, and she was going to find it." He crouched and picked at some mortar that was crumbling in the bottom corner.

"Did she find a way?" Jennie asked.

He gave her a sideways look. "Not that I know of. But folks say they heard the bell the night she went missing. The bell can't ring unless someone is inside the tower to ring it."

Jennie wrapped her arms around herself, feeling not the first ghostly premonition hovering around the place. "Do you believe in ghosts?" she ventured.

Zane grimaced. "No. Do you?"

"I . . . no." And she didn't. But sometimes ghosts seemed like a good explanation for the unexplainable.

He planted his hands at his waist and stared at the bricks. "I don't know what we're going to find inside, Jennie. The place could be falling apart. But I want you to know I'm not out to gain anything from this. You own the place, so I'll be fine just walking away if you don't want me here."

Didn't she want him here? She hadn't considered that. It also hadn't entered her mind that Zane would break down the wall and then leave her to explore the abandoned mansion by herself.

Her hand flew to grip Zane's wrist. His skin was hot beneath her palm, and she blushed as she made contact, shocking herself that she'd grabbed him. But somehow she couldn't let go. He seemed to understand. For a long moment, the air between them grew heavy. Shared grief, pain, and questions hung between her and Zane, a binding force she hadn't expected. Jennie tried to release Zane's wrist but found herself tightening her grip instead.

"Please. Don't leave me," she whispered.

Zane twisted his wrist so that his hand could clasp hers. As their palms met, he offered her a small nod of reassurance. "I won't leave," he promised.

Jennie badly needed to hear those words. From someone. From anyone.

I won't leave.

Now the trick was believing them.

The first impact of the sledgehammer brought the crumbling of clay and mortar to the veranda's stone floor. While the rain continued to pour upon the earth, Zane and Jennie were shielded by the roof that had been maintained by Zane's family.

She had been the one to bring the sledgehammer. Jennie had bought it at the hardware store in Newton Creek and was glad the guy at the checkout hadn't asked why she needed it. Apparently, it wasn't uncommon to buy a sledgehammer, though it had never been on Jennie's list of items to shop for.

Zane swung the hammer again, and its force cracked more bricks. He set the tool down and glanced at Jennie. "Let's hope this doorway isn't holding up the entire building."

She smiled at the thought. "That's not a concern. Still . . . maybe we should make a gap big enough for us to squeeze through and stop there for now."

"You mean not the whole doorway?" Zane said.

"Well, if we tear out all the brick in the doorway, people will for sure notice, and then how will we keep them out? And if the threat against Hannah was real . . ."

"You're right." Zane raked a hand through his hair and made the black mass stick up every which way. He assessed the doorway again. "If I take out just this portion here"—he pointed to it—"then we should be able to slip inside. We can fill it with a makeshift enclosure for now, and I'll come back later tonight with some supplies to make it look sealed again. Until we can get a security system in place, that is. I should have thought of that."

Jennie eyed him.

"What?" Zane said.

"You're coming back tonight?"

"I said I wasn't going anywhere, remember?" His smile was quizzical, as though he didn't understand why she'd doubt him.

If only he knew.

Her dad had made a zillion promises. She couldn't remember one that he'd kept. Not that keeping a promise would have bought him any forgiveness for his other sins against her.

Jennie shoved away the bad thoughts. "Let's keep going."

"Yes, ma'am." Zane wielded the sledgehammer with precision, and this time a layer of brick fell inward.

They both stilled as a puff of musty, century-old air escaped the house. The looks exchanged between them sent a shiver through Jennie and for an entirely different reason than before. This time it had nothing to do with Zane and everything to do with Traeger Hall.

"This is actually pretty crazy," Zane admitted.

Jennie nodded, and together they both stood on tiptoes to peer through a hole that was no bigger than half a foot square.

"It's dark," Jennie whispered, sensing a reverence in the moment. She pulled a flashlight from her back pocket and held it up to the hole. The beam pierced the blackness inside Traeger Hall and revealed what appeared to be wood paneling on a wall opposite them.

"I wish Mom were here," she breathed.

"And Allison," Zane added.

They shared a look of understanding, and Jennie found comfort in the camaraderie.

"Stand back," Zane instructed. He took a couple more swings of the sledgehammer, and within seconds the hole in the bricked doorway grew larger.

They stood shoulder to shoulder, staring into the mansion. Jennie aimed her flashlight at the walls, the floor, a staircase, and then a gust of chilling air whipped through the newly exposed opening. The smell of time, of must, and of mold assaulted their senses. Jennie pressed her nose into her elbow, her hand still holding up the flashlight.

A flutter of gray swept past the opening. Jennie saw it and knew it for what it was, and she released a scream that tore at her throat.

They had opened a tomb, and its ghosts were set free.

17

"Jennie. Hey. Jennie." The gentle tapping of fingertips on her cheek were matched with the wetness of a dog's tongue licking the other cheek. "Midas. Go!" The dog was pushed away as Jennie managed to open her eyes. Zane came into focus, concern creasing his face. "Hey," he said again.

Jennie tried to collect her muddled thoughts. She'd never fainted before. Well, not that she could recall. But the stone-cold veranda floor she lay on told her that she had passed out.

Traeger Hall.

The opening.

The specter that had flown before their faces.

Jennie struggled to sit up, scooting herself farther away from Traeger Hall's opening.

"Here, take my hand." Zane helped her sit up enough so that she could lean back against the wall.

Midas sniffed her neck, her ear, his tongue lapping at her face.

"Midas, leave her alone," Zane commanded.

But Jennie wrapped her arm around the dog's shaggy neck, drawing him close despite his damp fur. There was comfort there, security. She'd always wanted a dog.

"What *was* that?" Jennie asked.

"What was what?" Zane looked confused.

"Didn't you see it?" Jennie frowned. "The ghost?"

"Um . . . no," Zane replied. "There was a tapestry or something that fell down when we opened the place. It wasn't a ghost."

Mortified, Jennie closed her eyes and drew a deep breath. She had passed out because of a falling tapestry? She leaned into Midas, who licked her across the nose.

"It's okay. This is all very creepy." Zane patted her shoulder. "The adrenaline rush is greater than when I rode the wildest roller coaster at a theme park down in Florida."

"A roller coaster sounds tame compared to this," Jennie muttered. She didn't have a future career in tomb raiding, that was for certain. Everything in her screamed to close up the entrance again and pretend they'd never opened it.

"Yeah," said Zane. "I'd go with you. But for now, how about we check it out?" He extended his hand once more.

Jennie eyed it. Part of her wanted to take his hand and continue. Another part didn't want to touch him, to feel the warmth of his hand and then try to decipher why it made her feel a certain way. Yet another part of her wanted to run.

"For Hannah." He kept his hand extended to her. "Let's figure out why whoever left that note for my sister doesn't want us to disturb this place."

For Hannah.

Motivated by the teenage girl she'd yet to meet, who didn't deserve to be caught up in some old ghost story and cold case, Jennie took Zane's hand. And with the stabilizing presence of Midas, she pushed to her feet.

Sure enough, once she aimed her flashlight through the opening again, Jennie could see the pile of material lying on the floor. Gray and riddled with holes, probably from moths and mice.

"Can you slip through?" Zane asked.

"I think so." Jennie turned her body so she could lift her foot and step over the remaining bricks that hadn't been cleared. She eased her way through the narrow opening, very aware that she was the first person to set foot in the mansion since 1890, mere days after Leopold Traeger had been murdered.

Not releasing Zane's hand, Jennie managed to get her other leg inside, and then she was inside completely, her feet planted on the hardwood floor. The entryway was pitch-black. With all the windows sealed, there was no light in the house but her flashlight. The beam spread ahead of her like a tunnel, revealing dust motes in the air, shadows, and dark shapes and forms. Jennie half expected something or someone to jump out at her. It was the perfect setting for a horror movie. A ghoul crawling from behind an inanimate object. Skin peeling away from its face. Rags hanging from its body as it slunk toward her, arms outstretched, a leering expression with a toothless mouth that gaped wide enough to be a pathway to the pit of—

"We're in." Zane's announcement in Jennie's ear caused her to yelp. She jumped sideways, and he steadied her. "Are you going to be okay?"

Jennie nodded. She would be if things stopped going bump in the dark! They stood, side by side, until Jennie shifted the beam of light to look up at Zane. "Where do we go from here?"

He held up an arm to shield his eyes from the beam of light, and Jennie quickly lowered it with an apology. "Want me to take that?" he offered. She accepted, and Zane removed the flashlight from her grip. He swept the beam slowly across the room. "So this is Traeger Hall." He gave a low whistle as their eyes adjusted, the light revealing a space no one had seen since before the Wright brothers had flown their airplane.

Jennie took in the dark wood floor and wall paneling. The floor was covered with layers of dust, cobwebs hung from the ceiling, and mice nests and droppings were piled in the corners.

Aside from what one might expect to find in a closed-up house, there was also furniture.

Zane stepped forward, bouncing a little to check the stability of the floor. It must have felt safe enough because he took a few more steps, and Jennie determined she wasn't going to be left too far behind. She followed him close, reaching forward and grasping his shirttail. A light *woof* sounded behind them.

"Stay, Midas." Zane's voice echoed in the large room. He leveled the flashlight on the main staircase and the long table beside it. The table, also covered in dust, had curved legs with hand-carved sides, indicating an elegance from a different time.

They walked toward the table, Jennie holding on to Zane's shirt. He shone the light on the top of the table.

"There's a pot of old dirt," he observed.

"Maybe it held a plant at one time," Jennie said.

He pointed the beam at a few other trinkets, one of which was a china bowl. Thick dust clinging to the bowl made it difficult to see any sort of pattern. Inside the bowl was a pair of cuff links.

"Cuff links," Zane muttered, then lifted one into the light to see it more clearly. It was made of gold, the letter T engraved in it. "T for Traeger," Zane guessed.

Jennie nodded, then reached out and touched it cautiously.

Zane put the cuff link back in the bowl and moved to a small pile of material. It was black, torn and chewed, and when he went to pick it up, the material crumbled beneath his touch.

"Gloves," Jennie murmured. "Those were someone's leather gloves."

The fact they were touching articles of clothing and accessories from a hundred and thirty-five years ago, tossed onto a side table by someone, was surreal. If these items belonged to Leopold Traeger, then they were remnants of the last time the man had returned to his home, removed his gloves and cuff links, and then walked further into his house only to be stabbed to death.

Jennie froze where she stood. She could almost feel, almost *see* Leopold Traeger just out of reach of the flashlight's beam. An outline of a face, a shoulder, a torso . . . But no. It was only a coatrack she'd been staring at.

Zane moved the light as if he, too, had sensed a presence. But instead of Leopold Traeger's ghost finally being set free, it was the same wooden hall tree. A wool coat hung from one of its arms and was in no better condition than the gloves. And yet it was a coat! When a family vacated a house and had it sealed shut, one would think they'd take not only their keepsakes and furniture but their clothes. Instead, this one tiny section of Traeger Hall exposed something about its last moments in the daylight.

Whoever had been behind the sealing of Traeger Hall hadn't bothered to take with them these personal items. They had deserted the place quickly as though they were fleeing from danger.

Zane swung the light toward the staircase, and it shone on a portrait hanging on the far wall. A set of eyes peered through layers of dust. Eyes that watched them. Eyes that had witnessed Traeger Hall's final days, and now greeted them with a dull expression. A hopeless expression.

Jennie took a step toward the portrait, then hesitated. It appeared to be of a woman. She could make out a slender neck, bare arms and upper body, hair piled on the top of her head. She was young, beautiful, and . . . Mesmerized, Jennie moved toward it, barely hearing Zane cautioning her to watch where she was walking. When she reached it, Jennie lifted her hand to brush away the years that collected on its face.

"Jennie, maybe don't—"

But Zane's warning came too late. She swiped her hand lightly over the canvas. She knew better than to do that. If this was to be the first of the rumored works of fine art, one mustn't remove the dust from it with a bare hand. And yet Jennie had done just that without thinking it through. The swath cleared by her hand revealed more detail. It opened the woman's eyes even more, a deep azure, and her hair was a chestnut color.

"Who was this woman?" Jennie breathed.

Zane came up beside her and directed the flashlight squarely on the portrait. "No idea."

"Well, she was beautiful."

"She was," Zane agreed.

They both stood there as if under the woman's spell. Then Jennie was sure she heard a soft whisper just behind her ear. A voice that lifted the small hairs at the nape of her neck.

Come, know my secrets, the whisper taunted.

The moment dissipated.

Jennie realized Zane was eyeing her, and she swallowed back a sudden rush of nausea.

Come, know my secrets.

Jennie heard the words again, this time in her mind. But instead of heeding the woman's plea, she turned and stumbled her way back toward the entryway and the daylight that promised they could still reenter the real world. That this time machine of sealed memories and curses could be left behind.

She wasn't feeling well. Not at all. Something from inside the house had left her feeling dizzy, disoriented. Zane helped her to his car, and by the time she was inside the vehicle, they were both soaked through from the rain. He called for Midas to hop onto the back seat, and within a few minutes he was driving her away from Traeger Hall.

"I'll return later and board up the hole we made," Zane said.

Jennie turned toward the side window and leaned her forehead against the glass. She could sense him casting concerned looks in her direction.

"I wonder if there was something noxious in the air. I should have brought along face masks for us."

Jennie waved away his worry. "I'll be fine. I think I just got overstimulated or something. Fear, adrenaline . . . I'm not sure."

Midas pushed his nose against the back of her neck.

"I should at least take you to urgent care to get checked out. The air has been sealed inside that house for decades. It could be infested with mold and who knows what else? That wasn't smart of me, Jennie. I'm sorry."

Jennie smiled weakly. It was sort of cute the way he was chiding himself as though she were his responsibility. She wasn't used to that kind of attention. "It's okay. We weren't in there long enough to have any permanent damage done. I just need to rest, inhale fresh air, and drink some water."

"Well, my parents' place is closer than Newton Creek. They're just down the road a couple of miles away. If you're okay with it, I'd like to take you there."

She wasn't. She didn't know Zane's parents, hadn't met his sister Hannah, and they might hold her responsible for the chaos that was erupting since her arrival in Newton Creek. "I-I don't think—"

"Please." Zane shot her a look before turning his attention back to the road ahead. "I'd feel a lot better about it."

She nodded. She didn't have the gumption to argue with him. All Jennie could think about right now was the whispered words, *Come, know my secrets.*

"Did you . . . *hear* anything when we were inside?" Jennie ventured, hesitant to ask but knowing she'd feel better if he admitted he had in fact heard the whisper too. Then she'd at least know she wasn't losing her mind or under the influence of some century-old poisonous gas or something.

"Hear anything? No." Zane shook his head. "Just Midas, outside barking."

So much for feeling better. Jennie rested her head against the window again.

Just minutes later, Zane pulled into the gravel driveway of a ranch-style house with blue siding, untrimmed bushes, and a small flower garden by the front door. While it wasn't anything fancy, she could tell by just looking at it that whoever lived here valued family. A few lawn chairs faced a metal fire pit made out of a barrel. Children's bikes leaned against the side of the house. Jennie could see lace curtains in the front windows and the glimmer of a lamp breaking through the gray day with its dismal rain.

Zane let Midas out of the car. The dog leaped out and raced around behind the house somewhere. He hurried to Jennie's door and opened it. "You can hold on to my arm if you need to," he offered.

She shook her head. "I'm fine." But when she stumbled, Zane ignored her and slid a supporting arm around her waist.

"Yeah, you're not fine," he said without reproof.

He helped her to the front door, which opened before they arrived. A woman in her mid-sixties peered out through the screen door and then pushed it open.

"What on earth happened?" Genuine concern touched her expression. Shoulder-length, graying black hair waved around her cheeks. She had Zane's eyes. It had to be his mom.

Jennie glanced up and offered an apologetic smile. She didn't want to be a bother. She would have preferred to sink through the floor. Something was wrong with her. She'd heard that whisper, and now she could hardly stand up. If it was toxic air or mold, Zane would suffer the same effects. Wouldn't he?

"Sit down in the recliner there." Zane's mom, who introduced herself as Trixie, waved toward the chair before continuing forward on a mission. As she left the room, she was still talking. "I'll get a cool cloth and some water. A little peppermint oil too. For under your nose, and that will . . ."

Jennie couldn't hear the rest as Trixie disappeared around the corner.

Zane's eyes were smiling when he explained, "My mom, she's a fix-it person. She'll make sure you're feeling better and soon."

A shuffling from the hallway alerted them both. Jennie saw Milo before his father did. The little boy from the creek. The boy who'd led her to Allison. Would he remember her? What if her appearance in the living room triggered an emotional reaction from the memory of what he'd discovered?

Zane extended his arm toward his son. "Hey, buddy."

Milo hurried forward and leaned into Zane, but didn't remove his dark-eyed stare that was leveled on Jennie's face.

"Hi, Milo." Just seeing Milo encouraged her to take a deep breath—deeper than she had since they'd left Traeger Hall. The oxygen filled her lungs and then she released it. Only then did she realize Milo had done the same in unison with her. He breathed in again, and Jennie followed suit.

Zane noticed, and a flicker of something crossed his face. He squinted in thought and looked between the two, then addressed Milo, "Can you watch over our friend Jennie here while I go help Nana?"

Milo didn't shift his focus. He didn't give any sort of physical or verbal response, but Zane must have taken that as an affirmative. He ruffled Milo's hair and finished with, "Thanks, I'll be right back."

For the next couple of minutes, Jennie and Milo locked eyes with each other and breathed together—in and out, in and out. She could feel herself returning to earth, so to speak. Being inside the Hall had felt like an out-of-body experience.

"Thanks, Milo," she said. "I feel better now."

Milo's only response was to rest his hand on the arm of the recliner in which she sat. Jennie watched him for a second. His features were fine, but one day they'd be darkly handsome like his dad. The few things quite different from Zane were the smattering of freckles across the boy's small nose, which tilted up at the end, and his dark brown eyes. Jennie wondered if those traits came from his mother.

"Do you do breathing exercises a lot?" Now that her mind was clearing, she knew that's exactly what Milo had been guiding her through.

He tilted his head to the side, watching her.

Should she communicate differently with him? She wasn't sure. She didn't have much experience with kids and autism, but she knew, in a hugely different way, what it was like to be inside of oneself. She knew she wouldn't want to be patronized or talked down to; she just wanted to know she was valued and could trust the person speaking to her.

Why not just be honest with the boy?

"Your dad and I went into an old building today, and I think something in it bothered me."

Milo blinked.

"I thought I heard someone whispering to me, but no one was there." Jennie winced the instant the words left her mouth. She was probably going to terrify the child.

Instead, she stilled as Milo lifted his hand from the recliner and pointed to his ear.

"Do you hear whispers?" Jennie asked. Another question she maybe shouldn't ask a small child.

Milo grunted, then clapped his hand over his ear.

When she didn't say anything, he reached out and picked up her hand. She allowed him to guide her as he brought her hand to his ear. He grunted again. This time his lips pursed as though he might try to say something.

"Do you—" Jennie stopped. She didn't dare ask again.

The little boy pushed her hand from his ear and then put it back. "Ma . . . Ma . . ."

Jennie stared at Milo as his attempt at communication began to sink in. "Do you hear your mama?"

His eyes brightened, then came a slight nod.

"Here's some water and a cool cloth." Trixie breezed into the living room. She looked between Jennie and Milo.

Milo's expression settled back into being placid and unreadable.

Jennie shifted her attention to Trixie and took the glass of water. While Trixie placed the cool cloth on her forehead, Jennie found herself searching to meet Milo's gaze again. When she did, the corner of his mouth turned up in a little smile.

She might not have learned Traeger Hall's secrets that day, but Milo had just trusted her with one of his.

Milo Harris heard his mother's whispers.

What that meant, Jennie didn't know. Did he hear her audibly, or was it more in his soul, like a memory? Did it really matter? They had both lost their mothers, though for different reasons. Once again, Jennie was reminded that even after someone had passed from the earth, their voice still echoed in the hearts of the ones who loved them the most.

Come, know my secrets.

She realized then that she wasn't finished with Traeger Hall. Not yet. Not while someone's echoes could still be heard.

18

WAVERLY

TRAEGER HALL
SEPTEMBER 1890

"Reverend Billings!" She shouldn't have allowed herself to sound so surprised when Aveline showed the man into the parlor, where she sat vacantly staring at Uncle Leopold's dead face.

The reverend, all five feet of him, gave her a quizzical look as he turned his black hat in his hands. His white clerical collar looked as if it might choke him. He was rotund and ruddy and known for enjoying his pastries. "Miss Pembrooke, thank you for receiving me."

"Of course." She tempered her voice.

"I know I called shortly after your uncle's and aunt's passing away, but I felt it prudent to return and see to your spiritual welfare." He cast a glance at Uncle Leopold and Aunt Cornelia and then took a few seconds to approach them with a grave expression. After a moment of silence and reverent studying of their features, which were sinking into themselves, he sniffed.

Yes. It was getting . . . what word had Titus predicted it would become? Ripe? That was it. Waverly reached out and gave one of the bouquets of flowers a shake, hoping their perfume might release more prolifically into the room.

"And are you well?" Reverend Billings still eyed Aunt Cornelia specifically as he asked the question.

Waverly followed his gaze. What was she supposed to say? *Oh, Reverend Billings, my uncle has left me destitute. We've no idea who murdered him and my aunt. I may also be in danger for my very life. And it's of little comfort that the only one who seems to care is the undertaker. I believe he's waiting for his next customer because if I am murdered, that is what I will be!*

"I'm faring well," she lied because she was convinced the reverend didn't want an honest reply.

"Good." He tipped his head, still perusing Aunt Cornelia's features. Waverly frowned, thinking it a bit odd that her aunt was the center of the man's attention. He cleared his throat as if realizing he was acting peculiar. "Your aunt was a valued member of our congregation."

"Mmm." Waverly offered a soothing response just in case the reverend was getting emotional. She hoped he wasn't.

"Why, just last week she promised the funds needed to have installed in the church custom stained-glass windows." Reverend Billings dipped his head, shaking it in dismay. "And to think, with such an expense . . . we would never be able to make up for it had I already proceeded with the order."

"I'm so sorry." What was she to do? She couldn't offer the funds herself, which she knew the reverend was fishing for. But she also owed him nothing, for it sounded as though the windows were merely a wish now than a future reality.

Reverend Billings sniffed when she didn't offer what he was hoping for. "Well, I suppose it was all for naught anyway."

"For naught?" Waverly absently picked at a dying daisy in one of the funeral bouquets.

"Yes." Reverend Billings shifted his attention toward Uncle Leopold, who lay with his hands crossed over his chest. He looked remarkably more porous this morning than he had yesterday. The minister's expression soured. "Your aunt had just sent me word that I was not to worry. Yet her husband had indicated he was not willing to donate the necessary funding for, and I quote, 'the blistering wastefulness the church squanders on architectural beauty as human souls rot from sin.'"

For the first time, Waverly could almost agree with her uncle. Churches did seem to put an awful lot of importance on their buildings, while destitute people stood in their shadows unnoticed.

"I found it more than insulting." Those last words were spoken directly to Uncle Leopold's corpse.

Uncle Leopold had no response, which was probably just as well. For that would have frightened them both and then where would they be?

"Be that as it may . . ." Reverend Billings moved away from both Uncle Leopold and Aunt Cornelia. "What may I do to offer the church's support during this time of sorrow? Will you be needing me to facilitate the funeral services?"

The funerals. Yes. She had three more days of vigil, and then not only would her uncle and aunt take up residence in their mausoleum at the cemetery but she would have only two days remaining before she might find herself without a place to—

"Miss Pembrooke?" Reverend Billings said, interrupting her thoughts.

"Yes. I . . . of course. Your ministrations will be needed at the funeral."

"And when will that be? Has that been determined?"

Waverly floundered. She'd not come up with a firm plan as yet. She had been busy trying to stay alive, trying to uncover what had gotten her uncle and aunt killed to begin with, and to protect her own desperate secret. "No, it has not. I am meeting with Mr. Fitzgerald in the morning to finalize the details." And she was. That wasn't a lie. She could only imagine what Titus would say when he heard of the reverend's visit and his taking offense regarding the funds for the stained-glass windows his congregation had hoped to get.

Were stained-glass windows enough of a motive to kill for? Waverly wasn't sure, and she felt a pang of guilt for questioning if the reverend might have anything to do with the murders.

"Well then, if you've the time, we could discuss the eulogy?"

Oh, that.

Waverly cringed inwardly and then hoped it didn't show on her face. How was she to compose a respectable last remembrance of her uncle and aunt when their memories were not pleasant ones? "I may need more time to consider the eulogy," she said at last.

Reverend Billings's small, blue eyes narrowed. "Miss Pembrooke, have you prepared *anything*?"

If the reverend meant to sound disdainful, he'd succeeded.

He continued, "Because, in any other circumstance, the funeral would be taking place either today or tomorrow. I am aware there are *exceptions*, however, what with your uncle's last wishes, and so here we are. But, my dear, while our grief is a consuming thing, one must move forward."

Grief was not the primary emotion she felt. If Waverly was as independent, strong, and courageous as she wished to be, she might have glowered at him. As it was, she attempted a sad smile and hoped she appeared appropriately sorrowful.

"Perhaps give me another day or two. I must collect myself."

That seemed to appease Reverend Billings, and he gave a short nod. "Yes, yes. That is reasonable. Meet with Mr. Fitzgerald and make the final arrangements. Once you're prepared, send me a message, and I shall return to discuss the funeral services."

"Thank you." Waverly extended an arm toward the front door in a polite gesture to indicate she believed their conversation to be over. As Reverend Billings was a busy man, she gave her permission for him to take his leave.

He accepted the hint, and they left the dead behind as they returned to the front entrance. Waverly's gaze skimmed the painting hanging on the wall at the bottom of the staircase. She wanted to jump into it and run away. Maybe there would be a little cottage or a farmhouse, and she could make it her home. Just her and her terribly adored cat Foo, who now brushed up against her leg and trilled. Apparently, the cat thought it was his turn for attention, and he leveled disdainful cat eyes on the reverend for the man's interruption.

"Miss Pembrooke . . ." Reverend Billings paused at the door and looked down at the hat in his hands as if gathering some supernatural power of persuasion. As he returned his attention to Waverly, she was almost certain she read something unfriendly in his countenance. "Would there be opportunity after the funerals to discuss the matter of the stained-glass windows? I know your uncle was opposed, but your aunt—who is your direct relation—was quite committed to the idea."

Waverly didn't want to tell the man no and then be compelled to offer a reason as to why not. So she gave him the only answer she felt she could give. "Certainly." She dipped her head, and a light flickered in the man's eyes.

"Thank you, Miss Pembrooke." He puffed out his already large chest. He was attempting to show his dominance, and while she wasn't typically afraid of ministers, Reverend Billings suddenly seemed . . . hostile. "I shall look forward to that conversation and setting things to right."

Setting things right?

As though Uncle Leopold's refusal to fund the church's stained-glass windows had been a wrong.

Waverly closed the door behind the reverend and leaned

against it. She lifted her eyes at the sound of movement, and she met the frank and open stare of Preston.

He raised an eyebrow and tapped the mouthpiece of his pipe in the air. "Reverends are greedy men, Waverly," he said. "Be careful of whom you trust."

She watched Preston turn and disappear into the bowels of Traeger Hall.

Yes. Be cautious of whom she trusted.

His warning was a bit disheartening at the moment. Knowing that even she kept her own deceptions hidden, she could conclude there was no one on earth who didn't have secrets.

※

With Preston slinking around Traeger Hall, together with the visits from Titus, the constable, and Reverend Billings, as well as her attempts to play the role of a grieving family member, Waverly hadn't had a free moment to return to the scene of the crime.

The bell tower.

What had once been a refuge for her, a place in which to dwell on her innermost thoughts, was now violated by Aunt Cornelia's bloodstains. She had been the last to be *daggered* to death, if Titus and the constable's assumptions about the murder weapon were correct.

Waverly left Reverend Billings behind and ignored the fact that Preston was roaming about Traeger Hall. He had informed her at breakfast that he was to meet with Mr. Grossman today. He needed access to certain accounts, and there were some loose ends with the sawmill that required his attention. Waverly could not shake the trepidation she felt in knowing that in just a few hours, Preston would receive the news that she was to inherit nothing, and he had no part in Uncle Leopold's will or future business plans.

"Aveline?" She caught the attention of the maid, who was descending the staircase, a duster in hand.

Aveline's eyes widened and then returned to normal size. "Yes, miss?"

"Would you sit with my uncle and aunt for a bit? We should try to honor their final wishes to the best of our ability, and I have some things that need tending to."

She also wanted to be sure that Aveline didn't see where Waverly was going. Waverly wanted to be alone and unnoticed. Not only did she want to retrace the night of the slayings but she needed to make certain an important piece of her life was in order. She had stored it in its place in the bell tower because no one had ever visited it. Or so she'd thought. Until the night almost three weeks ago when she'd come face-to-face with Uncle Leopold there. Waverly found her anxiety heightening.

She was about to make her leave when a solid knock on the door interrupted her. "Bother," she mumbled under her breath. If things continued in this manner, the only privacy she would be able to muster would be sitting in the parlor with her dead relatives. That wouldn't help at all.

Aveline hurried past Waverly and opened the door. "Mr. Fitzgerald."

"Is Miss Pembrooke at home by any chance?"

He hadn't seen enough of her yesterday?

"I'm right here." Hiding would solve nothing, not to mention the increase of her heartbeat betrayed her. The sound of Titus's voice gave her heart a leap of pleasure, which was out of place in such times.

"Ah." Titus stepped inside, and Aveline closed the door, bobbed a curtsy, then hurried toward the front parlor to sit with Waverly's uncle and aunt.

Titus swept his hat off his head. "May I?" He motioned to the coat tree by the staircase and, without waiting for Waverly's approval, made himself at home by placing the hat on one of the hooks. He busied himself with a cuff link at his wrist, removing it and tossing it into a bone china bowl with a scowl. "Blasted thing broke." He removed the matching one and disposed of it likewise.

Waverly waited impatiently.

When Titus turned his attention back to her, she noticed his eyes sweep the length of her, and she regretted that she could only wear mourning black. She had a lovely pale pink silk that complimented her ivory skin and white-blond tresses. But no, she must wear black, buttoned to her chin, with black lace and black cording, and the black made her appear as if she, too, were on the way to the grave.

"I had a revelation." Titus approached her, his eyes earnest.

Waverly glanced up the staircase to make certain Preston wasn't lurking. "Not here," she hissed, and Titus gave a quick nod, following her into the sitting room. Though it wasn't appropriate, Waverly slid the pocket doors shut. "Preston is here, and Aveline is as well."

"I see." Titus seemed to choose his words carefully. "I don't wish to invite more angst, but I thought if we revisited the events of the night of the murders, it might be helpful in our figuring out what happened—that is, if we were to investigate your uncle's dealings."

Waverly didn't bother to tell him she had been about ready to embark on her own mission to reassure herself that her concerns were still in order. While she hadn't exactly accepted Titus's friendship and offer of assistance, she hadn't outright shunned him either. It appeared he was taking that quite seriously.

"All right then," she complied, then instantly wondered if it was such a good idea when he brushed by her and his hand accidentally touched her skirts. What would it be like to have those strong hands at her waist? To feel those arms slip around her and draw her toward him? To feel his breath on her neck and his lips at her throat—

"Good heavens!" Waverly exclaimed to herself.

Titus's abrupt halt was accompanied by a look of concern. "What is it?"

Waverly stared at him, swallowing hard and wishing she had better control of her wandering thoughts. Her mind seemed to explore and contemplate so many things, and now he was staring at her as if she'd come upon a great revelation. She had, but she certainly wouldn't tell him that she suspected being kissed by an undertaker would be terrifying and most interesting at the same time, yet she would be willing to try. Hence her exclamation, and now the blush that crept up her neck.

"Nothing. I-I saw a spider." She made pretense of investigating the floor.

"A spider." His tone indicated he didn't believe her, but if she'd told him the truth, he'd not believe that either, she supposed. He would most assuredly think less of her. "Very well," he went on, dismissing the threat of arachnids. "Who else besides yourself has a witness account of what happened?"

Waverly set aside her memories. The unidentified man. Their conversation. She had slipped from Traeger Hall without Uncle Leopold or Aunt Cornelia knowing. Had she instead stayed at Traeger Hall . . . she didn't want to consider the outcome of that.

"I do, sir." Aveline's voice in the doorway startled Waverly. Hadn't she asked Aveline to sit with her aunt and uncle? She had disobeyed and had eavesdropped by sliding open the pocket doors a few inches.

Waverly glared at the maid.

Aveline's face remained innocent and sincere. She latched her gaze on Titus. "I talked to Cook, sir, the night of the killings."

"And?" Titus was unaffected by the maid's sudden and uninvited appearance in the doorway. Instead, he gave Aveline his undivided attention. "What did Cook say?"

"She told me 'twas a man who had pushed his way into the kitchen after he knocked on the kitchen door—the door where we take deliveries and the like. Cook answered it."

"Show me." Titus motioned to Aveline, and to Waverly's surprise and annoyance, Aveline smiled and nodded. She spun on her heel and headed off toward the kitchen as if she'd acquired a new sense of importance. Waverly trailed behind. Where had this rather confident Aveline come from all of a sudden? A rather sneaky little thing and a side of her that Waverly hadn't seen before.

Once in the kitchen, Titus looked around the room, addressing Aveline, "Is anything amiss or out of order?"

"I don't think so, sir," Aveline answered demurely.

Waverly frowned.

Titus strode to the door and opened it, looking out over the path that led from the main driveway. "So the man came through this door?"

"That's what Cook said," Aveline affirmed.

"A man knocks on the door, and Cook opens it." Titus put his hands up as though battling an imaginary assailant. "The brute forces his way into the kitchen but does no harm to Cook?"

"Well, he shoved her," Aveline said. "Shoved her hard and she fell into that side cupboard there."

Waverly and Titus both turned to look at the cupboard Aveline pointed out.

"But Cook wasn't harmed?" Titus asked.

Aveline shook her head. "Not really, no."

Titus nodded, his face the epitome of concentration. "So then, gaining entrance, the killer leaves the kitchen and goes where?"

"To the library. It is where Uncle Leopold and Aunt Cornelia were spending the evening." Waverly answered as quickly as she could to shift the conversation away from Aveline.

"The library." Titus marched out of the kitchen with Waverly on his heels. "He comes through here on his way to the library. What does Cook do?"

Aveline skipped after them. She spoke up without being

prompted directly. "Cook told me she chased after him, screaming out a warning to the master of the house."

Titus rounded a corner. "Did she give a description of the man? I've heard only that he was athletic and tall and *unidentified*." He shot a meaningful glance at Waverly.

She colored.

Aveline nodded. "Cook said as much and that he was dark. She couldn't see much more. He had a hat pulled low on his head. He wore a nice coat, though, and expensive shoes."

Waverly looked away just as she felt Titus turning toward her again.

The unidentified man. Aveline had basically described him just as Constable Morgan had. And yet Waverly knew it wasn't him. It *couldn't* be him.

Titus stepped into the library. Floor-to-ceiling bookshelves lined the room's walls. A dark green carpet covered much of the wood floor. A chess table stood in the corner with two chairs. Three stuffed leather chairs encompassed a small area by the fireplace. But it was the far corner, now void of furniture, that Waverly averted her eyes from.

"The murderer barges into the library, Cook on his heels." Titus whipped into the room, flailing his arm in dramatic fashion. "He produces his dagger, threatening the lives of Leopold Traeger and his wife. What does Cook do?" Titus looked over his shoulder at Waverly, his arm still held up as though holding a dagger.

"She—" Waverly started.

"Fainted," Aveline interrupted, obtaining Titus's attention once again.

He eyed the maid. "And where were you?"

"Me?" Aveline paled.

"Yes. Were you in the kitchen too? Or upstairs? Where were you at the time of the stabbings?"

"I-I was not h-here, sir," Aveline stuttered. "I'd been to visit my mother in town. When I heard the bell, I came running back. That was when I heard Cook's account."

Titus swung to face Waverly. "Can you confirm this?"

Waverly's voice caught in her throat. She couldn't say yes or no. She had no idea where Aveline had been that night. Waverly herself had not been at Traeger Hall to keep watch over the staff.

It was apparent by the look on his face that Titus knew she could not provide confirmation of Aveline's claim. He continued, "Cook faints to the floor and is no longer aware of the horrors about to occur." He steps around an invisible form of Cook lying unconscious on the floor. "Ah. The killer clears the sofa here with one step and a leap." Titus stopped in front of a green sofa that sat in the middle of the room with a small table of books in front of it.

"How do you know that?" Waverly asked.

Titus pointed. "A footprint, there on the sofa. I would daresay you're not making it a habit to walk on the cushions?"

"Of course not," Waverly responded.

Aveline stifled a giggle.

Waverly pressed her lips together and moved around the maid, nearing the sofa. Sure enough, there was a footprint, albeit rather faint, in the middle of the pillowed seat.

Titus moved to the back corner that Waverly was uncomfortable looking at. "Apparently, the killer is so intent on getting to your uncle that he leaps over the sofa rather than going around it. And it is there your uncle and aunt were sitting at the time?"

"Yes." Waverly swallowed back nausea as she finally focused on the empty space. The two chairs that had been arranged in the small reading corner had been disposed of. But she recalled that night all too clearly. "When I came into the room, there were all sorts of people here by then." She recounted the memory, closing her eyes as her mind took her back to the previous week's events.

"I remember Cook was just coming to where she'd fallen."

Waverly kept her eyes closed. "Near the fireplace, there were two men from town. I'm not sure who, but one was retching into the coal bucket, and the other looked as if he might follow suit. I had just arrived at the Hall. I was out of breath from running after I heard the bell. I saw my uncle on the floor. My aunt was not in the room—as you know—since she was found in the bell tower, having been the one to ring it."

"We can conclude the killer had chased after your aunt in order to stop her," Titus acknowledged. "Which indicates not only was he well aware of the threat of the bell tower's purpose but there was a strong possibility he was familiar with Traeger Hall itself. If your aunt outran him, which stands to reason since she did in fact ring the bell, he would have needed to know where to go to chase her down and kill her too."

"Gracious!" Aveline breathed, grasping her throat, her face white.

Waverly cast her an impatient glance. Titus had finished asking the maid questions. There was no need for her to remain.

"What else did you see?" Titus asked. When Waverly didn't answer—distracted by Aveline, who was clearly unaware of Waverly's growing annoyance—Titus tried again. "Waverly?"

"Hmm?" Waverly snapped around to face him.

His eyes had a flicker of mirth in them, and he tipped his head with a reassuring look. "What else did you see?"

"Oh." Waverly glanced at Aveline again and then determined not to allow the maid's simpering to affect her. "Well, Uncle Leopold was . . ." Waverly cleared her throat from the bile that had risen in it. She pointed. "His chair was in the corner, but it had been tipped over. I could tell there had been a struggle, as a floor vase of fern had fallen and broken into pieces. The dirt from the vase was soaking up . . . Uncle Leopold's blood." Tears sprang to her eyes. Not because of any fondness for Uncle Leopold, but because the violence of the scene demanded as much—unless one was heartless.

"I need to sit down." Aveline plopped onto a nearby chair.

Titus nodded, then turned back to Waverly. "Where exactly did your uncle fall?"

"There." Waverly pointed. "He was lying with his head turned toward the door, as though in his last breath he was calling for Aunt Cornelia to run." Yes, now she was crying, and it was only fair. No one, no matter how unlikable, should experience such horror.

"Bear with me, Waverly." She startled as she felt Titus's warm hand cover hers and give it a reassuring squeeze. But he released it just as quickly, and the moment of tenderness passed. "Did it appear your uncle had been stabbed where he lay?"

Waverly nodded. "Several times," she said hoarsely.

"Yes, well, I'm quite familiar with his wounds." Titus hefted a deep breath and motioned toward the wood floor that was exceptionally clean. "Was there a rug there the night of the killings?"

"Yes." Waverly nodded. "It was disposed of. Someone rolled it up and took it away. The chairs too. There were bloodstains on the chairs. Quite a lot of them."

"It was one of the valets, sir, who got rid of the carpet," Aveline inserted. "He left right after the constable said he could. Most of the staff did. What happened frightened all of us!"

Titus ignored the girl. "There were stains on both chairs?"

"Yes," Waverly said.

"We can assume your uncle tried to ward off the attack, during which time your aunt may have come to his aid at first. If there were bloodstains on both chairs, it was likely the attacker also went after your aunt and wounded her, spattering blood on her chair as well."

It stood to reason, yet all Waverly could hear now were her aunt's screams echoing in her ears. Though she hadn't been here, it was too easy to engage her imagination and replay the events.

Aunt Cornelia received a blow, the anger of the dagger driving into her body. She screamed, a gargling scream of panic and horror.

Uncle Leopold, half incapacitated, pointed from his position on the floor. "Go! Ring the bell!" he commanded in one last attempt to thwart his own murder.

At the sound of Uncle Leopold's voice, the killer swung his attention from Aunt Cornelia and stood over her uncle, straddling his body with both feet before bringing the dagger down.

Aunt Cornelia, injured and bleeding, scrambled for the door, succeeding in escaping. But her injuries curtailed her speed and agility. As she fled through the hallways and rang the bell, the killer finished the job. The thrusts of the dagger into her uncle's body could be heard throughout the house, over and over again, until Aunt Cornelia thought she was alone.

"Let us go look at the stairway where your aunt would have fled." Titus held out his elbow, and Waverly took it, thankful for his support.

Aveline popped to her feet to join them.

Titus said, "Thank you, Aveline, for your assistance. You may return to your duties now."

"Oh," she responded, her voice small. Aveline glanced at Waverly, who said nothing before slipping away.

Waverly didn't miss the young woman, although she felt a tad guilty for being jealous of her. The poor thing. Titus cut a handsome figure, and it was a natural reaction. Still, the way she had inserted herself into the conversation was unsettling.

They climbed the stairs, and upon reaching the top, Waverly pointed to the bloodstain on the upstairs hallway wallpaper.

"There. That is where she must have fallen against the wall."

"Wounded and bleeding already," Titus observed.

Waverly nodded, then continued down the narrow hall, passing her uncle's suite of rooms to the left and her aunt's on the right. "The door at the end, that is the entrance to the bell tower." She pointed, pausing in her step. Titus moved past her and twisted the knob.

The door gave its familiar creak upon opening. In the past, Waverly had welcomed the sound. Like a greeting, friendly and warm. Now it was ominous.

"What do they believe happened next?" Titus turned back to Waverly, who closed her eyes to remember.

"Aunt Cornelia managed to get into the bell tower and climb the flight of steps until she reached the rope kept wrapped around an iron anchor. She unraveled the rope and began ringing the bell."

Waverly could almost imagine what that had been like for her aunt. Too soon there were footsteps behind her, the killer scaling the tower's steps. Aunt Cornelia had dropped the bell's rope and whirled toward him, raising her arms to protect her face . . .

"Right there is where she was found." Waverly gestured to a bare spot on the floor. The bell was quite large, and it hung above them a few yards away. Its rope had once again been wound and anchored to the wall, but she could make out the patches of dark rust that stained it. "Aunt Cornelia was slain here," Waverly finished.

Titus was silent for a long while. They both stood there peering out from the bell-tower windows. They were relatively large, open and without glass or shutters. Cool air wafted in through them, chilling Waverly through her dress, reminding her of the hours she had once spent here. She dared to glance in the direction of one of her primary worries. All seemed untouched. She dropped her gaze as Titus addressed her.

"The killer had to have been strong."

Waverly blinked, thinking that should have been a foregone conclusion.

"But also speedy," Titus added. "To do as he did and then escape down these same stairs, carrying his weapon with him and fleeing Traeger Hall. He moved with athletic skill and, I must say again, with some familiarity of the place."

Waverly swiped at her eyes, which had suddenly become clouded with tears again. That was quite baffling. She wasn't grieving; she didn't *miss* her uncle and aunt, and yet she never would have wished this upon them. Yes, there was a time when she'd wanted her eccentric and cruel uncle dead. She was certainly not innocent of wanting retribution . . .

Waverly cut off her thoughts as Titus stepped toward her. In the confined space of the bell tower, she could feel him—*feel* his presence more than him—and it was close, overwhelming.

The air between them grew thick, the scent of his sandalwood intoxicating.

His glass-blue eyes latched on to hers. "Waverly," he said, his voice taking on a hint of hoarseness.

She leaned toward him instinctively. "Yes?"

Titus's eyes narrowed with emotion. He leaned toward her. He reached out and touched her hair, then pulled back his hand, holding it up so she could see it. "You've a spiderweb in your hair."

WAVERLY

In an interview shortly before her death in 1950:

There were some things I didn't know to be important about my uncle's behavior leading up to his murder. Yes, we had met the night of the gunshot in the bell tower. But as I've mentioned before, I'd seen him other nights too. I hadn't put the puzzle pieces together because, aside from the secret I was already aware of and was harboring in my own silent vault of loyalties, I didn't know there were more puzzles to be solved.

But I will admit there was something about Uncle Leopold that bothered me from the moment I arrived at Traeger Hall. I always thought it was the unpredictability of his moods that I abhorred. But there were times like the night I saw him in the hallway outside the library, only a few months after I'd arrived at Traeger Hall. I had slipped through the house to retrieve a glass of milk to help me sleep. On this particular night, he stood in front of a painting, his face drawn into a scowl.

I must have made a sound because he turned, and his expression softened briefly and then hardened. He grabbed another small painting that rested on the floor against the wall. He carried it into the library and out of view from my eyes.

"Go get your milk," he advised. He didn't sound angry or even intimidating. This was the contemplative side of Uncle Leopold that confused me the most, when it seemed as if he were trying to understand something, calculating, and yet it was subtle. Instead of demanding anything, he became impulsive, forceful.

When I didn't move, Uncle Leopold turned to face me and crossed his arms. He studied me for a long moment before he stated, "You were not part of the equation."

At first, I assumed he meant he didn't like my presence in Traeger Hall. But then he added, "What to do about you?" As if I needed to be disposed of.

"Please," I heard myself plead shamelessly, "leave me alone." It was one of the first and only times I dared to give Uncle Leopold instruction.

"I shall," he grumbled. His deep voice made my insides quake. "I have already said my time here will be cut short. Will you ring the bell, I wonder?"

The hall clock ticked and filled the air with its rhythmic keeping of time. I couldn't answer my uncle.

"Will you?" He pursued an answer. Uncle Leopold came no closer. He merely stood by the painting on the wall and stared at me.

"Will I what?" My voice quivered, already forgetting what he'd asked because of the sheer intimidation of his person.

"Ring the bell?" Uncle Leopold asked again.

"Yes, of course." I told him what he wanted to hear. "I will ring the bell."

Then he surprised me. In fact, he terrified me. He crossed the space between us and ran his finger down the side of my face. I could feel the coldness of his skin, the scratch of his fingernail. He bent, his breath wafting over my face, the smell of stale coffee gagging me.

He pressed his mouth to my ear and whispered four words, and I've never forgotten them. I didn't forget them the night of his death; I haven't forgotten them now. I never told anyone this the night of his death either, even after we were all trying to ascertain what had happened. Because it was a puzzle piece. A piece that made no sense.

"Don't ring the bell," he'd told me.

His words befuddled me, but before I could regain my senses and my composure to clarify, he'd pulled away and strode from the hallway into the library. He shut the door behind him.

Don't ring the bell? I questioned his command even as my body trembled from the fright of his presence. But hadn't he built the bell to call for help not if, but when, someone came to slay him? To give me instructions to ignore the bell was to give me instructions to let him die. And until now, everything Uncle Leopold did was to ensure that he lived on. In fact, the Uncle Leopold I knew would prefer to live forever and never be forgotten.

This was the first time I questioned if Uncle Leopold was not suffering from some malady we had not yet been made aware of. There were places for minds like his. The ones who did not know up from down. The ones who screamed to live and then begged to die. It was a "place for the insane," and they called it an "institution."

19

JENNIE

NEWTON CREEK, WISCONSIN
PRESENT DAY

The rain was still coming down in sheets, but Jennie was more content than she had been in weeks. She looked to her side at Milo. He had initiated her move from the recliner to the couch by summoning her with hand motions. Now he sat close to her, his knees pulled up and his feet perched on the edge of the seat. A book filled with glossy pictures of dinosaurs was propped against his legs, and he was engaged in its content.

"He likes you." Zane entered the living room and took Jennie's vacated spot in the recliner. He'd changed into dry clothes and now clutched a YETI tumbler of coffee. Trixie had given Jennie some dry clothes as well, which left her feeling cozy and content. Strange considering what had already happened that day.

"I like him too," Jennie replied, watching Milo enjoy his book.

"We should probably talk," Zane said and took a sip of coffee. His words weren't intended to sound ominous, but they did to Jennie nonetheless. Her peace evaporated.

"May I join you?" Trixie asked, entering the room with her own cup of coffee. Without waiting for an affirmative answer, Trixie sank onto another recliner in the corner of the living room. The furniture in the plain ranch-style house was well broken in, comfortable, in various shades of brown, with the sofa being a navy blue. The lace curtains added a feminine touch. The wall opposite Jennie was a collage of family photos hung in assorted frames.

The Harris house was a *home*.

Jennie could feel it. And she longed for it. And with Milo tucked into her side? Strength emanated from the boy in a way Jennie couldn't understand, let alone decipher.

"What happened?" Trixie wasted no time. Though her directness was obvious, the way she held her cup with both hands, her expression relaxed, somehow made her approachable.

With a glance at Jennie as if seeking her approval, Zane filled Trixie in on the events of the morning. His mom's eyes widened with concern and not a little amazement.

She stared at Zane. "You went *inside*?"

Jennie wasn't sure if Trixie was upset or just stunned.

Zane didn't appear rattled by her reaction. He took another sip of his coffee, then nodded. "Yeah. It was . . . surreal."

Jennie now wished she had a cup of coffee, something warm to hold on to, and something to keep her hands occupied. But she'd refused it earlier for fear the caffeine would make her nerves even worse. Instead, she stuffed her hands into the center pocket of the hoodie sweatshirt that belonged to Zane. A freshly laundered scent clung to it that enveloped and reassured her.

Trixie looked between them, then settled on Jennie. "And you didn't think to wear a face mask?"

Zane shook his head. "That's on me."

Trixie shifted her attention to him. "Well, if I were you, I wouldn't go back inside that house without the right gear. And what if the flooring isn't safe? We've no idea what condition the structure is in. Just because we've kept it up on the outside doesn't mean the inside isn't crumbling."

"I'm sure it is. Crumbling, I mean." Jennie looked up and met Trixie's questioning gaze and then Zane's. "Anything locked up for so many years . . . well, its brokenness has been hidden from everyone."

A softness entered Trixie's eyes. She sipped from her mug of coffee, studying Jennie over its rim. Jennie could tell she was being assessed, and when Trixie lowered the mug, she offered a smile. It was kind. It was knowing. "Yes. Yes, that's true," she said.

Zane seemed to miss the subtle interaction between the women. "The floor seemed stable enough—at least in the entryway."

"What happens next?" Trixie leaned forward.

Milo turned a page in his book.

Zane looked at Jennie expectantly.

She tried not to squirm beneath their focused attention. What happened next? She was woefully unprepared for all of this. Mom would have had a plan. An adventurous course of action. But at least Jennie knew Mom's main goal would have been to solve the age-old mystery of Leopold and his wife's murders. To hunt for any elusive pieces of art. But it seemed heartless to mention now that Allison's remains had been found at the sawmill. This was a recent discovery, and the confirmation of her death affected this family very deeply. Jennie couldn't just blurt out that she hoped to solve a historical cold case on behalf of her dead mother while this family was trying to hold it together for the sake of the little boy snuggling at her side.

"I don't know," she finally answered.

"I know!" A voice piped up from the hallway. A young

woman with pretty green eyes appeared who looked to be around sixteen. She gripped a tablet computer in one hand, her dark hair hanging around her shoulders, with the front section braided away from her forehead. No doubt this was Zane's sister, Hannah.

She curled into a recliner opposite Jennie and Milo, offering a little smile. "I'm Hannah. The girl with the school stalker."

"Hannah." Trixie's low reprimand didn't faze the teenager.

Jennie exchanged a glance with Zane and then looked back to Hannah. "Hi, I'm Jennie. Nice to meet you."

"Oh, I know who you are! You own Traeger Hall."

"Hannah, please," Trixie admonished.

Hannah shot her mom a look. "What? It's no secret, Mom."

"I know, but still—maybe be a little less blunt." Trixie's tone was accompanied by a tender expression.

Jennie was reminded of her own mom and the times they'd shared together. She missed their companionship and ached to have her mom back in her life.

"So." Hannah pulled Jennie back into the present. She set the tablet in her lap and swiped at the screen with her finger. "Here's what I'd like to suggest."

"Hannah, maybe—" Zane began.

"What?" She grinned at her brother, a quizzical frown at her brows. "I'm the one threatened if Traeger Hall is opened, and now it's been opened. I think I should have a say in where things go next."

"You're not Nancy Drew," Trixie inserted, as if to remind Hannah that amateur sleuthing wasn't actually what popular fiction portrayed it to be. "But you're right—the police haven't yet figured out who left that note in your locker, and until then—"

"I know." Hannah held up a hand and offered Trixie the resigned look of an imprisoned daughter. "I'll stay here with you, Dad, or Zane at all times until it's proven I'm no longer in danger." That she was repeating instructions was apparent.

"Which will be for a while now that you opened Traeger Hall," she added with a pointed look at Zane.

Jennie sensed Milo squirming next to her. He slid off the couch and hurried into the kitchen, where she saw him retrieve his own tablet before exiting the kitchen and disappearing down the hallway. He must have taken inspiration from Hannah, who was busy swiping at something on hers. She propped up the tablet, then turned the screen for them all to see.

"Exhibit A." Hannah's tablet displayed an image of a painting. "This is a—"

"Mary Cassatt," Jennie supplied.

Hannah grinned. "Yes. She was an American painter who studied painting in Pennsylvania in the 1860s before she moved to France. She began exhibiting her Impressionist art in the 1870s, along with artists like Monet, Renoir, and Degas."

"What's your point?" Zane didn't seem impressed by Hannah's choice of topic, nor by the painting of a little girl in a blue armchair.

But Jennie had an inkling of where Hannah was going with this. She scooted forward on the couch. "Cassatt would have still been creating paintings during the time Leopold Traeger was alive."

"Yes." Hannah jabbed the air with her index finger. "And since Cassatt was originally from the States, it's not too far a stretch to think that Traeger might've had connections to the art world."

"Right," said Jennie. "Such as through his investors and other business ventures."

"You're saying that was how Traeger acquired the rumored collection of fine art?" Zane asked. He turned to Jennie. "Is the painting of the woman, the one we saw by the staircase . . . is that a Cassatt?"

"There was a painting?" Hannah shrieked.

Jennie quickly shook her head before things got out of hand. "It wasn't a painting I recognized."

"But it still could have been by a famous artist, and you didn't recognize it because the world has never seen it!" Hannah beamed conspiratorially.

"Hold on, Hannah," Zane said. "It was just a portrait, not unlike any other portrait in an old Victorian house."

"I didn't recognize the style either," Jennie added. At Zane's questioning glance, she bit her tongue. He didn't know about her background in art. But there was no way the portrait of the chestnut-haired woman was a Cassatt or a Degas.

"Fine. But there was a painting, you said. So? That could be just the beginning. I've been researching . . ." Hannah uncurled her legs from beneath her in the chair and planted them on the floor. "Let's assume that Traeger *did* have a connection with those who knew Cassatt, and he acquired not only her work but the works of others Cassatt had rubbed shoulders with. If so, then it's little wonder that Traeger would want that art collection protected after his death."

"That's always been the story," Trixie inserted. "Fine art—treasure—hidden inside the mansion by a miser long dead. But there's no firm connection to Cassatt, is there?"

"No." Hannah wilted a little. "I've been trying to come up with a plausible way that a man in Wisconsin like Leopold Traeger could become part of the European art world."

"It's not really a stretch," Jennie said. "Fine art has always been a pursuit of the wealthy. Those who appreciate it are not only drawn to classic artists like Leonardo da Vinci but to contemporary artists too, painters who have proven to be a new inspiration."

"Like Cassatt would have been in Traeger's time," Hannah finished. Her eyes sparked with an unspoken pleasure, and Jennie was following her line of thinking. "An artist who was making her mark on the art world, who would likely become famous within those circles and beyond."

"Which Cassatt did," Jennie concluded. She looked at Zane and explained, "I went to school to study art history. I spent two years in France and one in New York."

"Bruh." Hannah's surprise was mixed with a suppressed grin.

Jennie laughed even as she pulled small bits from her past that she felt she could safely share. "My mom instilled a love for the arts in me when I was young. It's one of the primary reasons she didn't sell Traeger Hall after my father passed away. Because of the legend that art is stored inside the mansion somewhere—art of great value."

"Monet." Hannah released a longing breath. "Or I'd take a Degas. A Cassatt?"

Zane shook his head. "The odds of Traeger leaving behind an art collection of that caliber is—"

"Small," Jennie affirmed, interrupting him. "Still, it *is* possible."

"Then why," Trixie interjected, "would someone leave a note in Hannah's locker, threatening her if Traeger Hall was opened? Wouldn't people *want* to find out if there's priceless art inside the place?"

"Or they just want it for themselves. If Hannah is right—and if Allison was right—by opening Traeger Hall, anything discovered would be rightfully claimed by the owner. And that's Jennie." Zane's words gave Jennie pause as a little thrill shot through her.

What if she did find classic art that Traeger had invested in hidden in the attic, or stored in a spare room, or hung on the walls of Traeger Hall itself? This was why her mom had been so interested in Traeger Hall. The hope it might be true, the very possibility was intoxicating when Jennie let it sink in.

"But *how*," Trixie pressed, "would this school stalker get these supposed paintings if Jennie didn't open Traeger Hall? There's no way inside the house. Yes, they'd risk Jennie claiming said art collection, but whoever threatened Hannah—and whoever maybe killed Allison—they'd have no way of obtaining the art anyway if Traeger Hall was kept sealed up. And why threaten *Hannah* of all people?"

Hannah perked up, her back straightening and her hands waving as her tablet balanced precariously on her knees. "Hold up, Mom! You're getting ahead of things." Jennie noted that Hannah was disregarding her mom's concerns. "I remember when I was a kid and Allison was still with us. She believed there was a way to get into Traeger Hall—a way people didn't know about."

"A secret entrance." Zane nodded. "That's been as rumored as the fine art collection or the safe in the house that's stuffed with Traeger's money." He paused for a moment and then eyed his sister. "Does someone think Allison told *you* about this so-called secret entry?"

"I dunno. But don't you get it?" Hannah seemed unimpressed that someone had threatened her with a note in her locker. "Now we can find out if there is an entrance somewhere," she chirped. "Think about it. You asked what happens next? Bruh, it's obvious. You go back to Traeger Hall and find out."

⁂

Outfitted with headlamps, flashlights, and respirator masks, Jennie felt a little bit more prepared this time as she approached the front entrance of Traeger Hall. Zane had pulled down the plywood he'd used to block the hole in the brick they'd made with the sledgehammer. There was no evidence of tampering overnight, but then the heavy rain had probably helped with that.

Hannah had begged to come with them. She'd even offered to skip school today as though it were a big favor to them. Jennie couldn't blame the teenager. The excitement of a treasure hunt was intoxicating. But Jennie also agreed with Hannah's parents. The idea that someone had targeted Hannah with a threatening note was beyond concerning.

Now Jennie was back inside the tomb of a mansion, and she stared again at the woman in the portrait, focusing on her blue eyes, her dress that appeared to be from the late 1800s, and the wisps of reddish hair painted into an elegant chignon. Contrary to Hannah's hopes, there was nothing to indicate it was the stylistic efforts of any known artist from that era.

"I wish I knew who she was," Jennie mumbled. This time she didn't hear whispers or feel cold air on her neck, but that didn't leave her feeling any less uneasy. She knew she could only attribute the whispers to her overactive imagination, or yes, perhaps something in the air.

Zane stood shoulder to shoulder with her, the staircase rising to her left, his flashlight's wide beam illuminating the wall. He studied the edges of the painting, taking his gloved hand and rubbing years of grime from its corner. "There's an artist's name here in the corner." His voice sounded almost robotic as it came through the respirator.

A thrill surged through Jennie as she stepped closer to the painting to read the artist's signature. "Vallée," she whispered.

"Do you know of the artist?" Zane inquired.

Jennie frowned. "No. He—or she—isn't one I've heard of."

"Then I guess this isn't one of Hannah's Cassatts hidden in the Hall," Zane declared with a bit of sarcasm in his tone.

It definitely was not a Cassatt. It resembled the style of a Degas, but the name, while most definitely French, was as unfamiliar to Jennie as if a stranger on the street had painted it. "If there are any works from famous artists in the house, I would imagine they'd be in a more secure environment than near the front entrance," Jennie said.

"Why?" Zane side-eyed her. "What better place to show off your wealth and appreciation of fine art than to display it right here? It's the first thing a guest would see after entering the house."

Jennie considered that and then nodded. "I guess you're right.

And back then, they wouldn't have necessarily taken into account such things as humidity, temperature, and sunlight to best preserve the art."

"Art was for show. It was about status," Zane mused.

Jennie met the vacant eyes of the young woman in the painting, "If that's true, and if Traeger did dabble in the art world, where are the rest of the paintings, and why is this portrait the first to greet us after a century and not one from a revered artist?"

"No clue." Zane shook his head, then swung the flashlight's beam to the room to the right of the painting. "Ladies first."

Jennie smirked and took the lead, stepping into the ray of light cast there by Zane. With Traeger Hall being shrouded in darkness, Jennie wished they'd taken the time to sledgehammer more holes where the windows once were. But then that would open up Traeger Hall in a way that could prove more difficult to control.

"This must be a parlor." Zane shone his light around the room.

Jennie grabbed his arm.

He stilled. "What is it?"

"Back in the day, people used to lay out the dead in the parlors of their homes. That's where the name *funeral parlor* came from."

"Where'd you learn that?"

"History, Zane. History."

Zane pointed to Jennie's flashlight. "Turn yours on too."

Jennie hadn't done that yet. For some reason, the one flashlight made her feel as though there were some element of control. To turn on more lights meant the house became that much larger, the shadows deeper, and the ghouls more real.

She reluctantly switched on her flashlight, and between their two lights, the parlor was fully illuminated.

They stood in silence, staring.

"If I ever wondered what it would feel like to be in a time machine," Zane observed, "this is it."

Jennie couldn't respond. She was tongue-tied. The room appeared just how it must have looked the day Traeger Hall had been sealed shut. Evidence of dust and time aside, it was completely furnished, a haunting memento of the distant past.

The far wall was draped with tattered black tulle cloth, funeral shrouds that had stood the test of time enough to still cover the mirrors. She swung her light to a clock on the mantel of the cold fireplace. Its hands had long since stopped turning, and she couldn't help but wonder what or who had stopped them. Was it time itself, or had someone marked the exact moment a death occurred?

Aside from the stuffed chairs and end tables covered in gray dust, the lamps swathed in cobwebs, and a tea set sitting on a side table as though company were expected to come calling, the most interesting items were the two pedestals in the middle of the room. They were long enough to have held the bodies of Leopold and Cornelia Traeger.

"Wow," Zane said as he approached them. His footsteps echoed in the room, leaving prints behind him. Plant stands, set in groups at the head and foot of each pedestal, held pots that still contained the remnants of what must have been flower arrangements that had decayed long ago.

Leopold Traeger's will came to mind, and Jennie said, "Traeger had insisted that his and his wife's bodies be laid out here for seven days before being taken to their mausoleum in the cemetery. Someone was to keep vigil at all times in the event they 'woke up.'"

"That's creepy." Zane rounded one of the pedestals, bending to look beneath it.

"My mom wrote in her notes that it was common to preserve the bodies in the days before the funeral."

"Well, at least they removed the bodies before bricking up

the Hall," Zane said. His expression was hidden by his mask, and the flashlight cast shadows that hollowed out his eyes. "Otherwise, we would've had to report it to the state, and that'd be a whole other set of issues."

She hadn't thought of that. Their coming upon human remains from a century before—especially associated with so much history and intrigue—would have resulted in a flurry of renewed interest.

"There's no hidden treasure in here by chance, is there?" Jennie half teased. She swept her flashlight across the parlor walls. There were more paintings, mostly landscapes. Not one was in a style she recognized. Jennie neared one and eyed the artist's signature. Another Vallée.

"If it were only that easy," Zane said.

"Where to next?" Jennie was anxious to continue on. The allure of finding lost art was as addictive as the desire to run from the ghosts of the past—from the mystery surrounding murder and tragedy that seemed bent on resurfacing in the present.

"Let's head back—" Zane's words cut off by a crashing sound coming from the entryway.

Jennie grabbed for Zane's arm. He raised the flashlight, shining it back in the direction they'd come.

"Who's there?" he shouted.

No answer.

"Show yourself!" Zane yelled, and Jennie jumped. She hadn't expected the forcefulness of his voice. They left the parlor, and both of them swept the entryway with their flashlights.

It was empty—at least of other humans. Nothing appeared to have fallen or been broken. The woman in the portrait eyed Jennie through the darkness. She could feel her. Sense her. The only thing she couldn't do at the moment, thankfully, was *hear* her.

A creak from a side room opposite them made Zane freeze. He held out his arm as if to stop Jennie and shield her simultaneously.

"Who's there?" he repeated.

A shuffle. Then, emerging from a darkened doorway, the pale skin of an arm. Its hand was extended, an index finger pointing at them. A low moan filtered through Traeger Hall.

Jennie leaped forward, burying her face into Zane's back. She couldn't do this anymore. The place was haunted! There were demons and ghouls and specters and poltergeists and zombies and—

"*Milo?*" Zane's incredulous exclamation filled Jennie's ears. "What are you doing in here?"

Jennie peered around Zane, and sure enough, the young boy had slipped from the darkness of the other room, his arm reaching for his father. His eyes were wide with fright, his glasses cockeyed on his little face. He moaned again, and Zane launched forward to comfort the boy who had come out of nowhere so unexpectedly.

But Jennie wasn't watching Zane, nor were her eyes fixed on Milo. She was looking beyond them to where the shaft of her flashlight shone into a sitting room. A sitting room in perfect order, with chairs and draperies, along with the large, looming portrait of a man she could only assume was Leopold Traeger. The man's eyes were but narrow slits in his painted face. His mouth was set in a grim line, split in half by a jagged slice across the entire canvas. It was a callous act of vandalism, ripping through the portrait with an unspoken vengeance.

Leopold Traeger had been despised. And before they sealed Traeger Hall, someone had seen fit to make sure his memory would be marred forever.

20

WAVERLY

TRAEGER HALL
NOVEMBER 1890

Titus had taken his leave. She was convinced he was the worst sort of man. Picking a spiderweb from her hair? How was this gentlemanly when he made her heart thud with his movement and the intensity of his eyes? She was surrounded by boorish men. And the only feminine influence in her life was Aveline, whom she was less fond of now that she'd witnessed Aveline's desire to gain Titus's attention.

Still, with Preston away from Traeger Hall and meeting with Mr. Grossman, the world would soon implode once again. Waverly needed to prepare for Preston's anger. If he was responsible for the original attacks and so positioned himself to have a part in a supposed inheritance, what might he do if he returned to the house after hearing there was no inheritance to speak of? And why hadn't she thought to ask Titus before he left? Her oversight could only be blamed on the way her nerves went in seventy different directions when he was near her. It was hardly fair to blame Aveline either, yet part of Waverly did just that. Aveline had distracted her. Aveline had made her feel jealous.

How petty of her. Waverly wished she hadn't been so snippy. Aveline was merely trying to help, and a woman would have to be cold-blooded not to be affected by a man like Titus Fitzgerald.

Waverly would make things right with Aveline should the maid react as though she'd noticed Waverly's irritation, and then she would prepare for Preston's return.

Oh, and she needed to finish what she'd set out to do before Titus had once again descended unannounced on Traeger Hall. She simply *must* get to the bell tower and assure herself that what she'd hidden there had not betrayed her by being found or moved.

Agitated, Waverly hurried through the halls, peeking into unused rooms. Traeger Hall was large, yes, but it wasn't a cavern that swallowed its help. For goodness' sake, Aveline had to be in the servants' quarters then!

"Bother." Waverly hitched up her skirts and climbed the narrow steps to the attic, where two rooms were designated for the help. She thought of calling out, but it seemed ridiculous when she could just peek into the rooms. The first room, complete with three cots, was empty just as she'd expected. The room at the far end was the one Aveline had occupied with Cook prior to Uncle Leopold's death.

"Aveline," Waverly said as she pushed open the door, "I need to—" She broke off her words with a high-pitched gasp.

Preston leaped from the bed, a blanket around his waist, his bare, thin chest as revolting to Waverly as a side of pork. Aveline sat with her back against the iron headboard, a sheet pulled up to her neck.

"Waverly." Preston held out his hand.

She whirled and fled from the room.

"Waverly!" Preston's shout followed her as she made quick work of escaping the attic.

The resounding thud of someone falling shook the floor, likely from having been entangled in the bedsheets while attempting to exit the bed.

Waverly didn't bother to investigate. How on earth had . . . ? She and Titus had only just left Aveline to return to her duties less than an hour ago! When Aveline had all but swooned in the presence of Titus. And Preston? He was supposed to be with Mr. Grossman, not bedding her housemaid like a lecher!

Waverly rushed to the first floor, taking refuge in the . . . oh, where could she take refuge? This was a house of murder and now *scandal*! She decided to slip into the sitting room. As she paced in front of the windows, she wondered if perhaps Preston and Aveline had run off somewhere and married secretly. That might justify what she'd just seen and—

"Waverly!" Preston marched into the sitting room.

She couldn't look him straight in the eyes. He was mostly dressed now. Trousers, shirt hanging untucked around his hips, a tie hastily knotted—as if a tie would make him appear respectable! Waverly had never found him attractive, especially not now that she'd caught sight of him half naked in Aveline's bed. The shameful image made her feel nauseated.

"There is no reason to overreact," Preston instructed, a lofty bluster in his voice. "What you happened upon was—"

"Was *what*?" Waverly lifted her chin. "Have you married her?"

"Heavens, no." Preston waved her off, as though Waverly's question was sheer foolishness. "Don't be naive, Waverly. The world is not a perfect little package."

"You're taking advantage of her then." Waverly glowered at the man who had inserted himself into Traeger Hall's business with no invitation and who now had violated her only remaining housemaid.

"I did no such thing." Preston's mustache twitched with offense. "She was quite willing."

"Are you in love with her?" Waverly demanded, although she wasn't sure in this circumstance if that even mattered.

"Certainly not," Preston scoffed.

"Did you seduce my housemaid?"

Preston moved closer, and Waverly stepped back. Her foot landed on the furry mop of Foo's tail, and the cat, unnoticed until a second ago, yowled and raked at Waverly's dress. His front claws caught in her skirt, and Foo wrestled to release them. When he succeeded, a small tear was made in the black silk of the skirt.

Waverly was beside herself. She glared at Preston. "Look at what you've done!"

"What I have done? Your *cat* did that. If you want to avoid such mishaps, then put him outside and let him be a normal cat chasing after mice. Not the pampered little prince that he is."

Waverly could accept plenty of insults. If this man was like Uncle Leopold and intimidated her, she was likely to cower for fear of abuse. But she would allow no one to threaten her cat. She hauled back and slapped Preston across his thin face.

"Why, you little minx!" He reached for her, but Waverly dodged him and took refuge behind a wing-back chair.

"You must marry Aveline now," she insisted. She was flustered. The man was pretending nothing untoward had occurred, and now she was fighting off a churning stomach, frayed nerves, a clawed dress, and the sudden realization that Preston perhaps had never met with Mr. Grossman and was still in the dark about the lack of her inheritance.

"I will not marry the girl." Preston rubbed the cheek Waverly had slapped.

"Well, I certainly will not marry *you*! Not for all the tea in China and India and England combined!" Waverly sputtered, stating aloud what had been merely implied by Preston to this point.

"*Your* future is another matter entirely." His face darkened.

"And you will say nothing of my little dalliance with your housemaid. What I do is my business. Aveline was quite willing, and I will give no further explanation."

"Was she truly?" Waverly challenged.

Preston's smirk unnerved her more than she wanted to admit.

"Aveline and I have had an arrangement for well over a year now."

Hearing this news, Waverly rounded the chair and sank onto it.

Preston glowered down at her with all the power and control he deemed was his own. "You will stay out of my business. I am a man. Men have needs. And if you don't know this by now, then you're a foolish chit."

Waverly bit her tongue. Hard. She tasted blood.

"Do I make myself clear?" Preston leaned down, his expression suddenly reminding her of Uncle Leopold. Domineering. Powerful. Mean.

Waverly nodded.

She would need to lock her bedroom door tonight and pray that Preston had never gotten ahold of a skeleton key. Or she needed to pretend to go to her rooms and then sneak away to safety somewhere. But where? There was Titus, but how unseemly would that be?

She cursed Traeger Hall as Preston spun on his heel and exited the sitting room. She cursed the day Aunt Cornelia had married Uncle Leopold. She cursed the day she'd learned Uncle Leopold's secret, and it all began to unravel. Waverly sagged back in the chair and gave a long sigh.

Foo padded over to her and nosed her leg, then hopped onto her lap as if their kerfuffle had never taken place. The cat sat on his haunches and stared at her with his blue eyes.

"Now what do I do?" she asked Foo.

The cat blinked and then began licking his paw.

She could criticize Preston all she wanted for his lasciviousness, but when she ran into Aveline as she slunk down the staircase that night, it was all Waverly could do not to scream. The guilt and embarrassment she felt for being caught snooping were overwhelming. She clutched at her throat, her shawl slipping down around her waist.

"Now you come out of hiding?" Waverly hissed, mostly not to awaken Preston than out of anger. She wanted to believe Aveline was innocent, yet the look on the housemaid's ashen face told Waverly otherwise. Aveline was far from guiltless.

"Miss Pembrooke, I . . ." Aveline couldn't look Waverly in the eye.

"Say nothing more." Waverly held up her hand. "I've no wish to pry into what has already happened. In a few days' time, much will change anyway." She didn't expound for the maid's sake. Instead, she tried to collect her thoughts as best she could. "But do tell me one thing."

"Yes, miss?" Aveline swallowed hard, the whites of her eyes showing her nervousness.

"Was it consensual?"

Aveline reddened. "Yes, miss, it was."

Then Preston had told the truth in that matter. What other secrets were within these walls that she knew nothing about? Waverly tempered her breathing to control her emotions. "Did Mr. Scofield leave Traeger Hall today to meet with Mr. Grossman?"

"No, miss," Aveline answered.

"Very well." Waverly suddenly felt a bit more empathy for her aunt. If Aunt Cornelia had witnessed such happenings in the years she was married to Uncle Leopold—well, no wonder she despised having Preston visit. His behavior was appalling, and Waverly could only assume that Aveline was not the first young maid to receive his attention. Poor Aunt Cornelia. Perhaps her irritability was merely a facade to hide the awfulness lurking in Traeger Hall. To hide her husband's frequent shifts in personality. To hide the shame of her help's behavior. To keep secret the freedom Uncle Leopold gave Preston as his assistant.

Waverly's small smile directed at Aveline was one of pity, not friendship. Aveline's expression fell even further. "When you retire tonight," Waverly said, "you will keep your door locked, and there will be no visitors."

"Yes, miss." Aveline took a few hesitant steps up the staircase and then fled the rest of the way.

Waverly steadied her nerves. It was well past eleven, and she had battled over what to do now. Preston hadn't threatened her life like she'd half expected earlier had he met with Mr. Grossman and learned of Uncle Leopold's will and its terms. On the other hand, Preston—if he was the killer—now had even more motive to do her in.

She hurried through the hallways, a lamp in her hand. Waverly lifted it before each painting her uncle had on display.

Vallée.

Vallée.

Vallée.

Who *was* this artist? At first, she had considered that maybe Uncle Leopold had purchased stolen art or perhaps spearheaded art thefts. That would explain his death and possibly explain why Newton Creek would also perish with his murder. If it was discovered that he'd been involved in art theft or illegal dealings, such a disclosure could upset his estate. The art collection would be seized in order to make restitution to the victims and their families who had their property stolen.

But Vallée?

Waverly didn't know the name. But why would her uncle display this artist's paintings throughout the Hall if he had been engaged in subterfuge, underhanded dealings, or even art theft?

She really didn't want to be stabbed to death, or shot to death, or put to death by any other means, and by some unknown person intent on, what, revenge? Obtaining Uncle Leopold's wealth? Did they hold her responsible? Could it potentially be tied to . . . ?

Waverly drew up in her thoughts.

No.

Her meeting with the unidentified man had nothing to do with it, of that she was certain.

Waverly's position was growing more precarious by the moment. She stared at one of the paintings, a field of wildflowers. White splotches and pink pokes of paint among yellow and green grasses.

She couldn't shake the feeling that somehow the paintings were key to the mystery, and it had nothing to do with Uncle Leopold's holdings at the bank and the sawmill. The paintings were his hidden passion. They were what he'd been observing those nights Waverly had witnessed him wandering about in the Hall. But she couldn't make any sort of case for it because she had nothing to explain. A person couldn't just point to a painting by an unknown artist and claim *That is why my uncle was brutally murdered*—not unless one could explain why.

And she couldn't. The only person she could think of who might be able to shed some light on the matter was Titus Fitzgerald. She wanted to go to him, to find safety in the funeral parlor where he prepared the dead for burial. But then wouldn't her sneaking out in the dead of night to see him and beg for his insight be considered as scandalous as what she'd witnessed that afternoon? And there was no way she could tell Titus about that incident! The indiscretion made her blush just thinking about it. To describe for Titus what she'd seen . . . the censure in his eyes, his brooding frown and brow, the deep honey of his skin, the purse of his sculpted lips, and the way he—

"Lord, have mercy," Waverly whispered as she hurried down the hallway toward her bedroom.

Once there, she gathered her shawl and pulled a carpetbag from her wardrobe. Hurrying to her bedside, she scooped up Foo and stuffed him yowling into the bag, then buckled it shut.

"I'm sorry, Foo," she said, but she had no intention of leaving Foo behind to be slaughtered in her absence.

Waverly slipped from Traeger Hall into the night, shawl wrapped around her shoulders and carpetbag clutched under her arm.

She rushed across the lawn, hearing the creek in the distance and Foo's occasional growl of protest. She could see the outline of her uncle's sawmill, the wheel proud and robust as it stood still for the night. Waverly stumbled to a halt. The darkness was pierced only by the thin sliver of moonlight, and the crisp chill helped to keep the fog at bay.

Along the tree line she glimpsed a silhouette, and the vision made her stumble to a halt. Uncle Leopold? Impossible! Waverly squinted, attempting to see more clearly. Surely not—but yes. It was Uncle Leopold! He glided as if his feet didn't touch the earth. His familiar form moved quietly, shoulders back with authoritative confidence.

"Uncle?" But it came out a gargled whisper of fear and shock. She darted behind a tree, hugging its trunk as she peered around it.

His ghost.

It was so clear.

She knew Uncle Leopold was dead; she had just seen his corpse in the parlor. So it had to be her uncle's spirit.

Waverly watched as his form paused by the side of the bell tower and then, in an instant, dissipated before her very eyes.

Uncle Leopold had been there—and then he wasn't.

A wisp.

A reminder.

That he was watching *her*. Just as he always had been. Yes. He was watching her.

21

"Have you lost your mind?" Titus, shirttails hanging around his trousers, sleep still present on his face, yanked Waverly into the funeral parlor with all the grace and gentility of a farmer tugging on an obstinate donkey.

Waverly stumbled into the parlor, the carpetbag banging against her leg and Foo releasing an offended wail from inside it. Titus slammed the door behind her. Glaring at her with both incredulity and reproof, he stretched his arm toward the door. "What if someone saw you? Haven't you enough trouble at Traeger Hall than to add scandal to it?"

"Scandal?" Waverly knew she had overstepped, but what could a desperate woman do when she had no family, no guardian, no one to step in and give her counsel? "I can tell you about scandal." She pushed past the undertaker, setting the bag on the floor and unbuckling it. Foo popped his head out, blue eyes sparking.

"You brought your cat with you?" Titus exclaimed.

"I couldn't very well leave him at home. Had you been at Traeger Hall today, you would know my dilemma."

Titus moved to the windows, making sure the shutters were completely closed. Foo sprinted into the unfamiliar depths of the funeral parlor. Titus escorted Waverly into a side room, yanking the draperies shut and switching on all the lights for the sake of propriety.

She knew her coming here had been impulsive and foolhardy, but didn't the sheer necessity of staying alive justify any missteps on her part? One could hardly pass judgment when circumstances called for such unusual behavior. However, she *had* put Titus's reputation in danger of ruin . . .

"I'm so sorry!" Waverly popped up from the chair she had all but collapsed in. She made for the front door, her nerves completely frayed. Titus was right! She *had* lost her mind! She reached the door and began to open it, but it slammed shut as Titus reached over her shoulder and pushed on it.

Waverly whirled only to find herself nose to nose with him.

"You've created quite a pickle, Waverly." Though his statement was correct, his blue eyes glinted with a bit of humor now that the shock of her arrival seemed to be wearing off. It startled her and made her stomach do silly twirls.

"I know." Waverly swallowed, trying to produce a reasonable explanation for why she couldn't wait until morning. "But I fear for my life."

Titus stiffened. "Did something happen?"

"No, no! Not yet anyway." Waverly placed her palm on his chest without thinking. "But today, with Preston and Aveline, it was shameful, and I—"

"Slow. Down." Titus's expression was stern. But then she must appear an absolute mess to him, showing up at his home in such a state and in the middle of the night. But what else was she to do? Huddle in her bed and watch the doorknob for the moment Preston twisted it and then came at her with a dagger? He would bring it down and stab—

"Waverly." Titus's calming voice brought her eyes up to meet his.

She snatched her hand off his chest, now very aware that her fingers had been splayed there. Tears popped unexpectedly into her eyes, unwanted little pools.

"Come." Titus motioned for her to follow, and they returned to the room where the draperies had been pulled. "Sit." He pointed to a chair and then he sat opposite her, leaning forward with his arms on his knees. "Let's start again. Please explain to me why you came to my home at this hour, risking both of our reputations."

Waverly hesitated, looking around to gain her bearings. She was in a sitting room, likely to receive customers and not personal guests. It was good she wasn't in his personal quarters. If called on to explain themselves, they could always say she'd found herself in immediate need of an undertaker.

"Preston and Aveline," Waverly breathed. "I found them."

"Found them?" Titus raised his brows. "Are they dead?"

She could see he was genuinely concerned. "No. No, but it is quite worse than that."

"What is worse than being dead?"

"Being discovered in a compromising position," Waverly retorted.

"Ah, and you just now realized this about them?"

"You *knew*?"

"I didn't know with *whom*, but it was apparent to me that Preston is a cad. There is more than one reason I've been adamant that you should find a more secure place to live now your aunt and uncle are deceased."

Waverly sagged in her seat. "Have I mishandled everything so terribly? I . . ." Oh, how she wanted to blurt it all out. To tell Titus everything—*everything*! But she couldn't. And if she did, what would he say? There were reasons she'd remained at Traeger Hall. There were reasons she'd hid the—

Her face whitened at the realization.

"What?" Titus leaned forward.

Waverly shook her head, waving him away. "I-I just feel a bit weak." And she did. She'd forgotten again to check the bell tower. To make sure it was in its place.

Titus studied her as if to reassure himself that she was not going to faint. He must have felt relieved because he pressed forward. "Do you know if your uncle was aware of the relationship between Preston and your maid?"

"How am I to know that?" Waverly was embarrassed by how her question came out as a whimper.

Titus patted her knee and then quickly pulled his hand back, snapping his fingers to indicate his next thought. "This is another motive for Preston to be rid of your uncle. If his indiscretions with Aveline had been found out, your uncle might have been threatening to remove Preston from his position in the company. If your uncle was worried that Preston's scoundrel ways might be revealed, why . . . No, that's too obvious." Titus slouched back in his chair and clicked his tongue. "Now I wonder if Preston is innocent of your uncle's murder."

"Innocent?" Waverly could hardly keep up with Titus.

He nodded. "Yes. Think about it. Leopold Traeger was a wealthy man. Many have questioned where all his wealth came from. Surely the sawmill and logging company are lucrative, but there have been rumors of other dealings for months now. If Preston was his right hand in those dealings, and your uncle was involved in such things under the table, so to speak, then I scarcely believe he would so much as blink an eye if Preston . . . well, relieved some of the anxieties of life with the housemaid."

Waverly straightened. "There are rumors of other dealings?"

"It's not uncommon, you know," Titus said, "for a businessman to carry on his business under the table on occasion."

"Yes!" Waverly leaped to her feet. "The paintings! I've been suspicious of them, yet I could not figure out why until now."

Confusion marred Titus's expression. "What paintings?"

"The paintings in Traeger Hall. The Vallée paintings especially. Have you heard of an artist by that name?"

Titus shook his head. "I haven't," he admitted.

Waverly paced the floor, wringing her hands and wishing she could pinpoint why the paintings gnawed at her. "If only I'd had the gumption to ask my uncle when I saw him in the garden tonight—"

"Did you say you *saw* Leopold in the garden?" Titus interrupted her, and Waverly was grateful he did. The more she voiced her thoughts, the more worried she became that she might say something she shouldn't.

"Yes. I saw my uncle—his *wraith*—in the garden tonight." Waverly avoided Titus's eyes for fear he'd think she had lost her senses. "And I thought I heard him whisper through my bedroom door's keyhole the other night. I disregarded that because of course it wasn't him, but then after seeing him tonight, I wonder . . ."

"Your bedroom door?" Titus's brows drew together in concern.

"Well, yes." Waverly bit at her fingernail. "Before he died, he used to pace the halls at night. I quite thought he was losing his mind—"

"Waverly!" Titus shot to his feet. "Was he moving toward insanity?"

Realizing her blunder, she said, "I don't know. He would just . . . change suddenly. He was so domineering and forceful, and yet sometimes—at night especially—if I came upon him in the house, staring at one of the paintings, he acted differently." She hesitated as she remembered. "He would contradict himself sometimes."

"What do you mean? How?" Titus reached out to halt her pacing, his hands gentle but firm on her upper arms.

"The strangest contradiction was when he told me *not* to ring the bell," Waverly said. "It made no sense. Isn't that what the bell tower was built for? To alert the town in the event of a life-threatening emergency? To save *him* should someone come to attack him? He also told me I was a problem he'd not taken into consideration. At times I thought he wanted to die, that he hoped he would be murdered. And other times it was as though death was the most abhorrent and frightening possibility. He would often remind me and my aunt of ringing the bell should the need arise." Waverly looked up at Titus, aware of his thumbs caressing her arms where he held her. Aware of the safety his presence provided. "It is all quite a pickle, Titus." Her watery voice broke, and her shoulders sagged.

"It is more than a pickle." Titus eased her down onto the sofa and then sat beside her, his leg touching hers.

She found she liked the feeling of his closeness. As she blabbered on, knowing she needed to stop, she couldn't help but feel captivated by Titus Fitzgerald in this moment, imagining herself enveloped in the man's arms. "The fact of the matter is," she prattled, trying to determine what to do with her hands, "I've only a short time left before my uncle and aunt shall be buried. That will put Uncle Leopold's spirit to rest, I'm sure, and then I can finally be rid of him just as I'd hoped."

"As you hoped?" Titus prodded.

"Well, yes. I've lived in Traeger Hall for a year, but before that, he was a nuisance to say the least, and I—"

"But you said you never met your uncle prior to coming to Traeger Hall."

Waverly bit her tongue. She should have done so much earlier. "I-I, no. I simply said—"

"You've always said," Titus went on, "that you spent your youth in the boarding school, that you knew your aunt had married Leopold Traeger five years prior to your coming to Traeger Hall. But you didn't meet him until you came to live under their guardianship a year ago. Now you claim it was before that? Did you meet Leopold before your move to Newton Creek?" He moved his leg away from hers as if he'd just realized he was touching her and wanted a bit of distance between them.

Waverly's hands became dotted with perspiration. The unidentified man flashed through her mind's eye. She couldn't lie. Not to Titus. She could withhold the truth—she *had* withheld it—but she couldn't lie directly to his face. "Yes. Uncle Leopold did visit my boarding school once or twice."

"Once or twice." Titus cocked his head. "Which is it, Miss Pembrooke?"

Oh no. The sudden use of her formal name again meant that he was distancing himself further from her. Waverly had done more than made a mistake in coming here tonight. Acting on impulse never proved wise, and here was the evidence. "Twice," she answered.

Engaging in deceit was ill-advised. But knowing her deceit also affected Titus was a weight she was struggling to bear. If Titus knew—if he learned the full truth—Waverly wanted to believe he'd have mercy. That he would understand. That grace would be offered.

"Twice then," Titus repeated. He seemed to consider that for a long and dreadful moment. The fire in the fireplace crackled, its glow turning his face a bronze color, darkening his hair, and his eyes appeared more brilliant. "Why didn't you tell me?"

Waverly began to protest, then snapped her mouth shut when Titus's glare became even more severe.

"I don't understand why you would not want me to know that your uncle had visited your boarding school."

"I-I . . ." She fumbled for the right words, a way to explain without *explaining*.

"Please." Titus surprised her when he reached for her hands. Waverly met his eyes, which glistened an icy blue but held something else as well, something that pulsed between Waverly and this man who had refused to confine himself only to the role of undertaker. "Let me help you. I can only do so if you're honest with me."

"But if you think I'm a liar..."

"I never said you were a liar. Don't insert words where they've never been spoken."

"I-I haven't been fully honest!" Waverly choked through tears that rose once more. "You don't understand—"

"I *know* you haven't been. So does the constable. We know you met with a man the night of the murders. *I* know something greater than you has bound you to Traeger Hall or you would have left to preserve yourself." Titus leaned into her. His hands wrapped around hers in her lap and held them tightly. Waverly could feel the warmth pulsating between them. "Tell me," Titus urged, "because I do not wish to find out I've been in error about your integrity—your goodness—this entire time."

"I am good—I mean, my intentions have been nothing but good," Waverly whispered, turning to look into his eyes.

Titus's knee touched hers again.

"I'm frightened. I know things about my uncle." Titus's expression darkened, and Waverly hurried to continue. "Please don't make me tell you everything. Please! There will be repercussions if I do. I have been trying to protect... I mean, I have hidden the sins of others, and perhaps I am to blame for some of this."

"Some of what, Waverly?" Titus pressed.

"My uncle's death. My aunt's heartbreak. The secrets. The bell tower..." Waverly hesitated. "I was trying to help fix it the night my uncle and aunt were murdered."

"Fix it?" Understanding washed over Titus's face. "The unidentified man, was he assisting you?"

She swallowed hard. She supposed that was one way of putting it.

"Waverly..." Titus reached over and nudged her chin until she was looking directly at him. "What have you done?"

WAVERLY

In an interview shortly before her death in 1950; memories from a few days prior to the murders:

I was, in retrospect, probably one of the worst people to have uncovered even one of Uncle Leopold's secrets. And there were many secrets. Oh, so many more. As the days passed, following the bullet through the window and then my uncle's midnight conversation with me, I grew increasingly unsettled—as did he.

Aunt Cornelia and I both noticed. Uncle Leopold's agitation was exaggerated. He snapped at us with his words and temperament like a rabid dog. We found him pacing in his office, muttering to himself, and then, when we inquired as to his welfare, he barked and cursed at us to leave him alone.

He demanded that all the draperies and shutters at Traeger Hall be closed. Daylight was not allowed inside. It was as if he were turning into a vampire and would melt should he encounter the sun. Personally, I believed a vampire would be easier to deal with. Easier than a madman who was unpredictable and made at least four visits a day to the bell tower to be sure its rope was readily accessible and could be rung at a moment's notice. And yet he didn't seem to remember that he'd told me, *"Don't ring the bell!"*

His visits thwarted my trips to the bell tower, both to get

away from the insanity and to protect my own secrets. I was quite worried that Uncle Leopold might stumble upon what I'd stashed behind a loose brick. I was going to need that, and far sooner than I'd first thought.

It was becoming clear that my uncle wanted me dead. It was a mutual feeling, I'm sure. It seemed we were in a race to see who would succeed first. If Uncle Leopold wanted me dead for the secrets I knew, then why had he not simply strangled me in my sleep or done away with me on one of my nightly jaunts for milk?

I was certain now that something must be done about Uncle Leopold—*for* Uncle Leopold, for his own sake. And the impending arrival of Preston had Aunt Cornelia in a tizzy. She could hardly continue to bring up her dislike of my uncle's assistant any more than she could reason with Uncle Leopold to find someone else to do his bidding.

As I climbed the steps of the bell tower, looking over my shoulder to make sure Uncle Leopold didn't make a sudden appearance and startle me, I pondered what to do. I had verified he was in his study before heading to the tower. I had also made certain Aunt Cornelia was resting in her suite of rooms, seeing as I tiptoed past them on my way to the bell tower. Aveline had brushed by in the hallway, her eyes wide as they always were, looking as though I'd caught her doing something far worse than dusting the paintings.

The outside air drafted through the open belfry and drifted down the stairs. I shivered but didn't dare return to my room for a shawl. Instead, I kept climbing. I needed to ease my mind that it was still where I had placed it. It was the only proof—the only evidence—that I had. Uncle Leopold would be furious had he known I was in possession of it, and that it had been given to me out of trust. A trust I was afraid I would be forced to break, and sooner than anyone hoped.

Seeing the brick I had pried loose from its mortar, I hurried to it, working the brick back and forth until it pulled free. Setting it on a stair, I ducked to look inside . . . and breathed a sigh of relief when I saw it was still there right where I'd placed it. I reached inside and grabbed ahold of it, the cool metal matching the cold of my hands.

The chain was made of silver and dangled as I gripped the locket in my palm. This was no ordinary locket. No. I had a locket of my own—as did many of the girls in the boarding school—with miniatures and portraits of our parents, one on each side. I often visited my parents that way, keeping their memories alive since they'd passed while I was still young. At times they didn't seem at all real to me but more like a dream.

But this locket was quite different, a *memento mori* of sorts, although death hadn't yet arrived. When it would, no one knew, but isn't that the way of things? This was in preparation for that day, and in some ways I was struck by the similarities between Uncle Leopold and the secret in my hand.

I opened the locket. On the left side was a tiny lock of hair the color of chestnut, tied with dark pink embroidery thread. On the right side was a miniature of *her*.

She was beautiful and had kind eyes. We were the best of friends at the boarding school—until Uncle Leopold ruined everything that day. He ruined our friendship, our camaraderie, our trust. He ruined our future. He ruined my hope that one day I would be free of Aunt Cornelia's insistence that I be locked away in school and no longer her responsibility, that I would be free of the shadow of her new husband.

That day when I left school to come to Traeger Hall, she remained. She remained there because she would never enter Traeger Hall. She didn't belong at the Hall, not like I did. And yet Uncle Leopold knew of her.

Uncle Leopold knew . . .

As did I.

I slipped the locket back into its hiding place in the bell tower. It was why Uncle Leopold hated me. Because I knew of her, and because of the locket. And if circumstances called for it, I was not afraid to use it against Uncle Leopold, while still doing my best to make sure nothing ever touched Louisa.

22

JENNIE

NEWTON CREEK, WISCONSIN
PRESENT DAY

Milo had followed them to Traeger Hall. Now he sat in the back seat of Zane's vehicle as they drove back to civilization and away from the estate. Their exploration of the mansion was over for the day. Milo needed to go home. The fact he had followed them there was not only concerning but dangerous.

"I'm glad he's okay," Jennie stated. This was the second time since she'd arrived in Newton Creek that Milo had shown up on Traeger property. Alone.

Zane gripped the steering wheel, and Jennie noted his knuckles were white. He'd been uptight since they'd discovered the boy in the house. He'd been even more frustrated when Milo attempted to communicate something, and Zane couldn't understand what it was.

Milo had been anxious, agitated, pointing multiple times at Jennie and repeating one word, *"Man, man,"* over and over again. But without the ability to explain further, they were lost as to what Milo was afraid of.

"He doesn't understand the boundaries of safety." Zane was visibly disturbed by the situation. "He doesn't understand that he can't just run around the countryside. The thing is, my parents own the Duck Blind, which is a small café just outside town."

"I've seen it," Jennie acknowledged.

"Yeah." Zane nodded. "Well, it's not too far from here, and Milo is often there with my parents, who help keep an eye on him. But the boy's a master at slipping away." Zane maneuvered the car around a corner. "I mean, when I was his age and growing up in the country, I'd run around carefree too, but . . ." He didn't finish his thought, and Jennie understood why. There were special needs with Milo, and as smart and independent as the quiet boy could be, he wasn't mindful of the dangers the world posed.

"What do you think he was trying to tell us?" Jennie couldn't get past it. The look in Milo's eyes. The word *man*. What man? Or did he not mean this literally? And why had Milo focused on her so intently?

Zane voiced her thoughts as the Duck Blind came into view. "I'm worried about this *man* Milo kept referencing." He pulled the car to a stop in front of the café and killed the engine.

The café was rustic with camouflage material in the windows for curtains and hunting decor on the outside that gave the place more the look of a shack than a restaurant.

Zane exited the car and opened the back door for Milo, who hopped out as though everything was in the past and nothing had happened. The boy ran into the Duck Blind, leaving Zane to rest his arms on the roof of the car. "Jennie, we opened Traeger Hall," he stated. It wasn't a declaration of their success;

it was an acknowledgment that they had done exactly what the threatening note in Hannah's locker had warned them not to.

Jennie nodded. "And now Milo is scared of a man."

"Yeah. I'm not cool with any of this."

"I know" was all she could think to say.

"I'm going inside to let Mom and Dad know what happened." Zane gave her a little wave, then headed into the Duck Blind.

Jennie leaned against Zane's car and pulled her phone from her pocket. There was a missed call from a number she didn't recognize. She checked, and sure enough, someone had left a voicemail. She took a minute to listen to it.

Gladys Quincy's shaky voice greeted Jennie's ears: "Hello, it's Gladys. I got your number from my son-in-law, Percy Wellington."

The lawyer was Gladys's son-in-law? That was unexpected. Unexpected and a little too coincidental. That meant Percy Wellington, who'd brought up her father's will in the first place, was Allison's uncle.

The voicemail continued. "I was wondering if you wanted to come by my place. I have some things you might want to see. Let me know." Gladys left her number for Jennie to call her back. As Jennie finished listening to the voicemail, Zane returned to the car. She tried to nullify her look of confusion. It didn't work.

"What's going on?" Zane drew up beside her.

"I got a voicemail from Gladys Quincy." Jennie watched Zane for his reaction. Just as she expected, his eyes darkened.

"Gladys?"

"She got my phone number from her son-in-law, Percy." Jennie waited again, and this time Zane outright frowned.

"Percy? Allison never liked him."

"He's the one who presented me with the codicil to my dad's will," Jennie reminded him.

Zane sniffed. "I forgot about that. So Percy knew we were going to open the place?"

"Not exactly. I didn't tell him what I was going to do with the Hall." Jennie tried to squelch the uneasy feeling churning in her gut.

"Percy has his finger on the pulse of everything in Newton Creek." Zane didn't seem convinced. "I guarantee he knows somehow. I'd never hire him as my lawyer. He's like the used car salesman stereotype but in the legal world. What did Gladys want?"

Jennie didn't want to dredge up anything for Zane, so she was careful as she responded, "She wants to show me some things. I-I think they have to do with Allison."

"Oh."

There it was. Zane wasn't good at disguising his emotions, and the pain that reflected on his face was real. There was also a surprising and unwelcome sting inside of her. For a split second, she was jealous of Allison. Jealous that she had someone who was still loyal to her years after her disappearance and death. Envious of her little boy. Wishful that Allison's world was one that could be duplicated. One that Jennie could find refuge in.

"You should go." Zane's statement brought Jennie's eyes up to meet his. "Seriously. The Quincys haven't shared anything about Allison since she disappeared. If Gladys is wanting some closure now that Allison has been found, this might be good for her. For them."

"You care about them? Even after they blamed you and suggested you might have had something to do with it?" Jennie didn't comprehend Zane's being so understanding.

He sighed and then leaned against the side of the car next to Jennie. Crossing his arms, he looked off into the distance as though conjuring up a memory. Perhaps one of Allison. "They had to blame someone. It wasn't going to be themselves. There's no point in blaming Traeger Hall, and they sure weren't going to hold Allison responsible. I'm the best first choice."

"That doesn't seem fair," Jennie replied, dropping her gaze to her feet planted on the gravel parking lot.

"Not much in life *is* fair." Zane's words pierced her in a way he couldn't know.

She wasn't about to expound either. Baring her soul wasn't Jennie's forte, nor was it a comfortable place to go.

Zane didn't hold the same opinion. He continued, and Jennie could tell he didn't notice that she was becoming more and more silent.

"We all have to find ways to cope with trauma. Not one person is exempt from it—we just experience it differently. Mine has been the unknown, and now Allison's death being confirmed after eight years just raises more questions. Did she run away? Who killed her? Was she being held prisoner somewhere? Finding her doesn't take away the pain and the hurt from the past. Everyone who cared about Allison has to say goodbye to hope. The hope that she might turn up alive. That Milo could get his mom back."

"Do you still love her?" Jennie couldn't help but ask, even though she probably shouldn't have. She should have kept her nose out of Zane's personal life.

He looked sideways at her and gave her a crooked smile. "She's my son's mother. There were lots of opinions about her being young and pregnant, but there were two of us involved. And I would have stood by her. I don't know that what I felt for Allison was love so much as we were two kids barely out of high school, flirting with the idea of love. But I'll never regret that she gave me Milo. He's the best thing that ever happened to me. So yeah, I love her for Milo. I sometimes miss what could have been . . ."

His voice caught, and Jennie could see tears glistening in Zane's eyes.

"But, you know, life goes on. It has to. And we must learn to move on with it or we become like . . . like Traeger Hall. Closed up, our memories collecting dust, and leaving everyone around us with a million unanswered questions. I believe God helps those of us who experience trauma so we can discover the path to keep going in spite of the pain. To have faith and find strength outside of ourselves and hopefully"—Zane's gaze dropped to meet Jennie's—"find beauty again."

Jennie mused on his words for a long, quiet moment. She looked away from him as she did. She couldn't keep staring into those orbs that were so filled with strength and kindness. The men she knew didn't think like this. Dad didn't think like that. Find beauty? It sounded so simple, yet her dad had made sure to destroy everything beautiful in her life, and up until recently, Jennie thought he might just destroy her future too. His needs had sucked the life from her and had slowly killed Mom. Sure, Dad would have blamed cancer, but in the end, Jennie blamed Dad. He'd taken bits and pieces of her since she was a little girl. He was the one who had created the mess, then left her behind to deal with it all.

"Jennie." Zane twisted to lean his shoulder against the vehicle. He reached out and lifted her chin, gently turning her face toward him.

She allowed it. She allowed it because she was compliant. Compliance was a form of self-defense too—some people just didn't understand that.

"None of this is your fault," Zane assured her. "Not the note in Hannah's locker, not Milo and whatever man scared him, and especially not Traeger Hall."

Tears sprang to her eyes. *He* was the one who should be suffering right now. He was the one who had lost Allison. He was the one Traeger Hall had wounded. Yet here he was, reassuring her because—why? Had he somehow seen past her own bricked-up doors and windows?

Zane ran his fingers through her hair along the side of her head, tucking it carefully behind her ear. It was a familiar gesture, and Jennie wasn't sure he'd earned the right to show such intimacy after only a brief time of getting to know her. But somehow it felt safe. Right. It was a gesture of comfort, not of want. A gesture of giving, not of taking.

"Go see Gladys, Jen. See what Allison still has to tell us. To tell *you*."

"Me?" Jennie whispered.

"Open your door, Jen," Zane said. "Just a crack. Let us in."

⁂

A man not much older than Zane opened Gladys's door. He was quite paunchy around his waist, and he moved slow, but he had a friendly face and ruddy cheeks. "You must be Jennie!" he greeted and held out a hand. "Grandma Gladys told me you were coming. I'm Todd."

"Hi." Jennie took his hand.

Todd welcomed her inside the stuffy, small ranch house. The windows were all closed to shut out the fall coolness. In fact, it seemed that the heat was on too, and Jennie was immediately overcome by the smothering air.

"Gladys is your grandmother?" she asked, trying to make conversation as Todd led her into the house.

"Yeah, she is."

Jennie wondered if Percy Wellington was Todd's father, but she didn't ask.

Gladys sat comfortably in a recliner. She was dressed up to receive a visitor, her flowered blouse buttoned, with a string of red beads at her neck. Her hair had been carefully curled and tended, and she had lipstick on again. She reached out.

"Jennie! I'm so grateful you came."

Jennie smiled. "Thank you for having me."

"You've met Todd, then. He is Allison's brother," Gladys explained.

"Oh." Jennie offered him a conciliatory look. "I'm sorry about . . . about—" She fumbled for what to say.

"You've nothing to be sorry about." Todd motioned for her to have a seat, and Jennie did so. She sank gratefully onto a green sofa with bright orange throw pillows. Todd continued, "In fact, we're grateful to you for finding her. After all these years." He shook his head, his lips pursed. Then, snapping out of his momentary remembrance of his sister, he gave his hands a light clap. "Well, I'll leave you two to it. Whatever it is." He bent and dropped a peck on Gladys's cheek and then exited the living room.

Gladys watched him as he left. "He's been a good boy to me." She turned back to Jennie. "He lives here with me so that I don't have to go into assisted living and leave my home. Todd is a nurse at the local hospital. When he's not working, he's here."

"He seems nice." Jennie didn't know what else to say.

"He and Allison were—" Gladys winced as if she felt guilty about something, then lowered her voice. "Well, my son raised Todd and Allison right. God-fearing, service-minded, and so on. But my daughter? She married Percy, and I'll tell you, those two let my grandkids run wild. I have another grandson, Rick. He used to get Allison into all sorts of trouble. They were close as cousins growing up. But then she started dating Zane Harris, and all that changed. Zane got Allison back on the straight and narrow, for the most part. That and her upbringing kept her from letting her wild streak run free."

It was an interesting thing for an elderly woman to say, considering Allison had borne a child with Zane. But maybe the "wild streak" as Gladys called it had more to do with something else.

"Do you like Zane?" Jennie asked before she could censor her words.

Gladys looked surprised. "Well, yes. I always liked Zane. My son, Allison's father, might have something else to say about him. But then, well . . ."

"You have to blame someone," Jennie finished for her.

Gladys lifted her eyes. "Yes," she agreed solemnly. "And my son wasn't fond of Zane getting Allison pregnant. He didn't like that Zane didn't up and marry her right away. Of course, there was also the argument."

Jennie frowned. "What argument?" She still didn't know why Gladys had invited her here, but this trip down memory lane was proving interesting.

Gladys raised thin, almost invisible eyebrows. "Oh, Zane and Allison had a dreadful fight the night Allison disappeared. Everyone knew about it. They were at the Duck Blind, and Allison told Zane she was going to petition the town to have Traeger Hall opened. She believed it was owed to the town's citizens after all these years. She'd been adamant about it for days leading up to their fight, and it was all escalating."

"What happened?" Jennie was thoroughly invested now.

Gladys's voice grew distant as she recounted the events. "Well, Allison had figured *something* out about Traeger Hall, or at least she thought she had. And she wanted to prove it. That was why she was so upset with Zane that night. He told her she needed to give up on the idea, to focus on their newborn son. I can't say as I blame him for that, but it was what happened after that we've had a hard time forgetting."

"What happened?" Jennie breathed.

Gladys fingered a button on the cuff of her sleeve. Her voice grew watery and went up a pitch as she explained. "Zane gave Allison an ultimatum. Him and Milo or Traeger Hall."

"And Allison picked Traeger Hall?"

"No." Gladys shook her head. "No, Allison refused to pick. She said Zane was being closed-minded or something to that effect. Anyway, she left the Duck Blind that night in tears, and that was the last anyone saw of her. Until you came."

Until she came face-to-face with Allison in the muck of the creek eight years later. Jennie would never forget that moment for as long as she lived.

"That's not why I asked you here, though." Gladys waved it all away like a bad dream. Jennie struggled to pull her attention back from the story she'd just heard. Gladys was lifting a shoebox from the floor beside her and set it on her lap. She eyed Jennie. "Percy says you are indeed the true owner of Traeger Hall, so I believe this should be yours." She held out the shoebox.

Jennie took it cautiously. "What is it?"

"Paraphernalia that Allison had collected about Traeger Hall. It's of no use to us and—well, don't ask me how she got some of it, but she did."

Jennie shifted her attention to the box in her hands. She lifted the lid and looked inside. There were scribbled notes in feminine handwriting that had to be Allison's, a piece of paper that appeared to have a diagram of a family tree written on it, and tucked into a corner was a locket.

Jennie lifted the locket out of the box, its chain dangling between her fingers.

Gladys jabbed her index finger at it. "Allison told me she found that locket the same day she had the big fight with Zane—the day she disappeared. She didn't tell me where she found it, but she said it proved everything she'd always suspected."

"What's that?" Jennie carefully pried at the locket's clasp to open it.

"That there's treasure inside Traeger Hall," Gladys declared.

"But isn't this just a cheap antique locket?" If Allison had thought it was a piece of expensive jewelry, well, it didn't make sense.

Gladys nodded. "Oh, she knew that. It's what's inside the locket."

Jennie's thumbnail finally popped the locket open. "I don't understand."

"That right there." Gladys pointed at the locket. "Take a good look."

Jennie focused on a tiny lock of chestnut-colored hair and a miniature painting that matched the portrait in Traeger Hall. The portrait with the woman Jennie thought had whispered, *Come, know my secrets.* "This is proof of treasure?"

"Yes," Gladys confirmed solemnly. "Allison believed that miniature was painted by an artist who was growing in popularity back near the turn of the century. If that was the case, Allison believed there would be more paintings in the Hall by the same artist."

Jennie had studied art in school. She'd toured Europe and visited the best museums the world had to offer. This was not a miniature portrait that stuck out as even vaguely reminiscent of a well-known artist. Not to mention the large version she'd seen with Zane in Traeger Hall had declared the name of its artist: Vallée. An unknown artist. "I know a few things about art, and this"—Jennie held up the locket—"doesn't resemble any famous artist's work. It wouldn't carry much monetary value even if the Hall was filled with them."

"Allison had a name." Gladys seemed unwilling to give up. Jennie cringed inwardly but didn't stop the elderly woman from her passionate pursuit to prove Allison correct. She leaned forward toward Jennie and pulled out an index card from the shoebox on Jennie's lap. "See there?" She tapped on a name written on the card. "Louisa Theophilus. Now, Allison did some research on that girl, and she discovered some old records online for a girl's boarding school. The man who had paid for her room and board, at least on record, was Leopold Traeger."

"That still doesn't prove anything about the Hall having valuable art inside . . ." Jennie began.

Gladys stiffened, her features straining with annoyance at Jennie's argument. "Allison was out to prove that there was *valuable* art inside the mansion. She thought the locket with the miniature was just the tip of the iceberg."

Jennie bit back another protest.

Louisa Theophilus . . .

What about the name Vallée? Perhaps it wasn't at all like Allison had suspected. Perhaps the miniature and the portrait in the Hall were of a woman named Louisa Theophilus, and she wasn't an artist—she was the artist's muse. That was possible, wasn't it?

Jennie offered Gladys a kind smile and prayed it wasn't patronizing. In the end, the artist's signature said *Vallée*, and no matter how badly someone wanted art to be worth a fortune, sometimes an artist drifted into obscurity with the passing years, leaving their works—or their singular work—no more valuable than the tarnished locket in Jennie's hand.

23

"It's true," Hannah announced.

Zane's eyebrows winged upward at the sight of them.

Hannah slipped into the booth at the downtown ice cream shop that featured an old-fashioned soda fountain counter complete with stools and scrolled woodwork.

Jennie spooned a bite of Neapolitan ice cream into her mouth and waited, opting for silence over adding to the chaos. She'd already filled Zane in on Gladys Quincy's rather passionate revelation from Allison. She'd sent Jennie away with the shoebox of Allison's notes and the locket. Now it sat in the middle of the table with the lid on so as not to bring undue attention to it.

"Allison was right," Hannah insisted. She'd opted against ice cream in exchange for excitement. Her green eyes sparkled as she unzipped her backpack. She tugged out two high-school textbooks and her tablet computer, piling them on the table. Then she pulled out a notebook filled with sticky flags of multiple colors, jutting out from the places she wanted to revisit.

Thumbing through the notebook, Hannah selected a page with a neon-green flag. "When I was at the historical museum, the lady there helped me pull up records of the Traeger family. When Leopold was murdered, the only person left behind was his niece by marriage, Waverly Pembrooke." Hannah glanced between Zane and Jennie as if to make sure they were listening. Assured of their attention, the teenager continued, "Then we searched the online records to see where Waverly Pembrooke came from before moving to Traeger Hall. She lived at a boarding school out east. The same boarding school that Allison confirmed Louisa Theophilus had attended." Hannah folded her hands and rested them on her notebook. "Put bluntly, it appears Leopold Traeger helped finance not only Waverly's education after he married her aunt Cornelia but he sponsored Louisa Theophilus's education too."

"But Louisa Theophilus wasn't an artist, right?" Zane said.

"No." Hannah shook her head, her ponytail bobbing. "At least not anywhere I could find. I don't know what made Allison think that."

Jennie poked at her ice cream with her spoon. "What about the name Vallée?"

Hannah tapped the page in her notebook. "That's where it gets weird. Not long before Waverly Pembrooke died, a reporter sat down with her to get her account of what had happened. She mentioned that her uncle had a fascination with the artist Vallée and with fine art in general."

Zane nodded. "So it's possible Allison was right about the Hall having a treasure trove of art inside it."

"Except Vallée's art never grew in demand, and then it faded into obscurity," Jennie said.

Hannah grinned. "Maybe. Still, we don't have Waverly Pembrooke's explanation because a portion of the journalist's notes was lost."

Zane grimaced. "Let me guess. There was a fire?"

"No." Hannah laughed. "The journalist moved and took his stories with him. He never published the piece about Waverly

Pembrooke. In fact, the museum director said it was an accident they found what they did, seeing as the reporter's notes somehow got mixed in with some other paperwork and left behind by mistake."

"How do you know the documents are authentic?" Jennie asked, mouthing a cold spoonful of delicious heaven.

"Because there was a black-and-white photograph clipped to the first several pages of the journalist's notes after interviewing Waverly Pembrooke. She was in her eighties when the photo was taken, and it matches another photograph from roughly the same time period that has been confirmed to be of Waverly." Hannah thumbed through more papers. "The people at the museum in Newton Creek were a bit reticent to let me see them because—" she paused and shot a wary glance in Zane's direction—"well, the last time someone asked about them . . ."

"It was Allison." Zane saved Hannah from having to dance around the painful truth.

"It was." Hannah winced. "So while no one ever said Allison's disappearance was directly related to her research of Traeger, the museum felt it better to file away the account from Waverly Pembrooke since all it did was raise more questions."

"Did they let you see them then?" Jennie asked.

"What they had on file, yeah." Hannah shrugged. "But the only thing they'd let me copy was this." She pulled out a diagram of a family tree, which she spread out so Jennie and Zane could see it. "Tell me this doesn't set your mind on fire. This is supposedly the Traeger family tree that Waverly Pembrooke provided the journalist with."

Jennie stared at the family tree. "Louisa Theophilus?"

"No mother is listed," Zane verified.

"Nope. But this shows she was Leopold Traeger's *daughter*."

"Hold on." Zane looked sideways at Jennie. "Are you saying

the portrait we saw in Traeger Hall is an unknown daughter of Leopold Traeger?"

Hannah's scrunched up her face. "That's what everything seems to be pointing to. But no one is going to hang a portrait of their illegitimate daughter in the front hall of their home. So why is it there? Not to mention it's always been thought that Traeger had no heirs."

"Except he wouldn't claim an illegitimate daughter," Zane said, "but he *would* add a clause in his will keeping his estate from passing to any Traegers who might come out of the woodwork after his death."

Jennie didn't contribute her opinion. All she could hear was the imaginary or hallucinatory whispers, *Come, know my secrets.* She looked back down at the family tree. "What's this?" Jennie pointed to a line that extended horizontally from Leopold Traeger to the edge of the page and ended there.

Hannah shrugged. "A line? Bruh, how should I know?"

"Why?" Zane studied Jennie, but she didn't meet his questioning eyes. She kept staring at the line that led to nowhere.

"I thought every line on a family tree meant something."

"What are you getting at?" Hannah pressed.

Jennie cleared her throat. "Well, the lines are what connect people and generations stemming from the same family roots. Why would there be a line extending from Leopold's name that goes nowhere but to the edge of the page?"

Hannah and Zane both redirected their attention to the family tree.

"It's like . . ." Jennie hated to say it out loud because it would only muddy the waters, but she did anyway. "It's like part of the tree is missing."

Trixie had invited Jennie for dinner. It was the first time Jennie had met Zane's dad, Greg, who was a down-to-earth rural Wisconsin man if she'd ever met one. She was cautious around him until she was reassured by his demeanor and actions that he was authentic and kind. Bratwurst on the grill was on the menu, and Trixie was busy tending the spitting and popping sausages.

Hannah and Milo were in the backyard throwing a tennis ball, with Midas woofing and loping after it, creating a form of entertainment that seemed to have captured Greg's attention. He shouted something to his daughter, and Hannah waved at him before tossing the tennis ball his direction. Midas charged the older man, and Greg laughed and threw the ball in the direction of the cornfield that abutted their yard.

"Is this what it's like?" Jennie mumbled to herself as she stood at the kitchen window and watched.

"Is this what what's like?" Zane came up behind her so stealthily that Jennie jumped, which caused her to bang her shoulder into his chest. He steadied her.

His musky juniper scent tickled her nose. She wasn't sure if she liked it or not, but it was Zane. It was warm. It trailed along his skin and his shirtfront and enveloped her . . . and suddenly Zane was very close. Too close. Jennie jumped and hit her elbow against the window frame.

"Hey . . ." Zane stepped back. "I didn't mean to scare you." Concern emanated from him.

She hadn't fooled him for a second. Jennie knew that now. She could see it in his eyes, in the way he was careful to back away from her. He knew she was wounded.

"You can trust me," he said, his voice lowered. He didn't say anything more. Didn't reach for her. Didn't try to come closer.

They stood staring at each other in the kitchen, while the rest of the crew still congregated outside.

Jennie crossed her arms over her chest—a classic defensive position, she realized. She quickly uncrossed her arms and then didn't know what to do with them. She wanted to get away from this uncomfortable situation. At the same time, she wanted Zane to stop being so careful and to just come and hold her. She noticed the muscles in his upper arms that were partly hidden under his T-shirt, also the breadth of his chest. She hadn't ever really been held. Just held. With no other ulterior motive.

This was stupid. He had no reason to hold her. That was taking a drastic leap from being new friends to . . . she didn't know what.

Jennie sniffed and looked down at her shoes, crossing her arms again. Mom was gone. She was the only one Jennie had ever trusted receiving affection from. But something inside of her felt as though that was crumbling. Something bad and good at the same time. She didn't understand it. Didn't know how to explain it.

"Jennie."

Shoot. Zane *had* stepped closer. He *had* dared to invade her personal space, just like he had earlier when he combed through her hair with his fingers and she'd—oh, gosh! She'd forgotten she'd leaned into his hand. She'd probably sent him some sort of signal when she did that. Did he think she was—

Zane tilted her chin up, and his eyes bored into hers. She felt him step even closer until their bodies were only a few inches apart.

"I know we haven't known each other for that long, but . . . would you please open the door just a little bit?" His quiet words caressed her face.

Supper had been nice, although Jennie had hardly been able to choke it down. She'd given Zane a slight nod earlier when he requested that she be more open with him. Yet he'd already busted through the front door of Traeger Hall and unveiled a tomb of potential horrors. Why would he want to enter her personal house of horrors?

Even so, she'd nodded. That nod had been earth-shattering. Her stomach had done flips, and she ended up in the bathroom, dry-heaving over the sink. A moment any woman in her right mind would have swooned over and texted her best friend about, for not only was Zane practically a heaven-made man but he was to-die-for good-looking. And he had a sensitive soul that made him . . . what? What was she thinking? Dad had been able to manipulate women with his charm too, and that didn't make him safe. He'd been selfish and deceitful, making her believe for three-quarters of her life that everything was all her fault. But it wasn't. Mom had told her that many times. She'd urged Jennie to get counseling after her dad died. Pleaded with Jennie not to close herself away as she had done. But to embrace restoration. But what was restoration supposed to look like anyway?

Heck, Zane would need a ventilator just to take one curious step into her life, or he'd be knocked over by the dilapidated Jennie he'd find inside.

There was a song she heard on the radio now and then, something like "Let me be your hero." Yeah, that was Zane's theme song, Jennie was sure of it. But she couldn't, she wouldn't . . . no, she *had* to let him in. The contradiction was terrifying.

Come, know my secrets.

The whispers became more real as the evening wore on.

Come, know my secrets.

What if it hadn't been the woman in the painting that had whispered in her ear? What if it had been her own voice? Urging her to unveil her secrets. To explore what they were and then be rid of them . . .

Jennie jumped to her feet. They were all sitting around a table, playing a rousing game of Uno. She herself had been playing robotically.

Trixie threw down her cards in surprise.

Greg lifted a lazy eyebrow and stared at her.

"Ope!" Hannah peeped.

Jennie's eyes connected with Zane's. She sensed a storm brewing within her. The turbulence that had entered her life. She had to get away. He was busting in, using a crowbar but with gentle pressure. And she was utterly, completely terrified.

"Jennie!" He shouted after her as she whirled from the table.

Yes. She was causing a scene. She was doing everything she wouldn't have wanted to do if she'd thought about it beforehand. But she needed fresh air. She needed to breathe.

Breathe, Jennie, breathe.

Come, know my secrets.

One breath, Jennie, just one deep breath.

Come, know my secrets.

Secrets.

My secrets.

Come.

She ran into the backyard and collapsed on the ground, her chest heaving. Jennie could see the high pitch of Traeger Hall's roof far off on the distant hill and its dark, brooding bell tower. The sad little trickle of what remained of Newton Creek gurgled nearby. Though the sawmill was out of sight, Jennie knew it was there too in all of its deplorable decay and boasting the ugly fact it had hidden Allison's body for eight years beneath its wheel and water.

A hand touched her hair.

Jennie screamed, scrambling away from it. "Please, just . . . go." She lifted her eyes and leveled an urgent, beseeching look on Zane.

Only it wasn't Zane.

Milo stood there.

His little glasses encircled his deep chocolate eyes. Freckles dotted his nose and cheeks. His black hair flopped every which way. He was wearing overalls, and a purple highlighter pen poked out from the chest pocket for whatever reason.

"Milo, I'm so sorry!" Jennie reached for him, but he stepped back instinctively. Zane had said that Milo initiated physical contact; he didn't receive it. Still, in her emotional meltdown, she hadn't meant to scare the boy. Hadn't intended for him to see her charge from the house, and she certainly hadn't intended for him to follow her to the backyard.

Milo looked over his shoulder, then turned back to Jennie. "Ma . . ." he said.

Man? Or was it Ma?

"Ma . . ." he repeated.

Okay. This time it was not uttered in fear and not regarding some man. No. Milo had said "Ma" when he indicated he'd heard his mother's whispers. Allison's whispers. At least that was how Jennie had interpreted it.

Milo stepped closer and pointed to her chest. Then he poked her right where a child would imagine her heart to be. "K."

"K?" Jennie tried to understand.

"Oh."

"Oh?" Jennie repeated. "Okay? Is that what you're asking? Am I okay?"

Milo gave a tiny smile.

Jennie sniffed. Gosh. How did she give an eight-year-old autistic boy the honest answer he deserved?

No. No, I'm not okay. I was abused by my dad when I was a girl. But now I see you and your dad, Milo. I see your grandparents and Hannah and . . . my life wasn't normal, was it? I missed out on family, on all the good that can be in the world. I'm scared. It hurts. It's safer to stay closed up. It's safer to . . .

Jennie hadn't said one of her ranting words out loud, but in that moment, Milo threw himself forward. His skinny arms wrapped around her neck, and he lowered himself onto her lap and curled against her.

"Ma." While the word was a struggle for him to communicate, he was insistent. "Ma," he said into her neck.

Jennie held on to him.

She knew then that Milo knew. Knew what it was like to be closed, cut off, but also having so much inside that screamed to be heard. To be set free.

Milo wasn't saying "Ma" or "Mama." He was trying to say "Me."

See me.

Find me.

Come, know my secrets.

"Okay, buddy," Jennie whispered, weeping softly into the neck of the little boy, whose insight and perception were more healing than anything anyone had ever done for her. "I'll find you." She pulled back, and they locked eyes with each other. "Will you help me find me too?"

Milo nodded. He gave her his typical half smile that, now that Jennie was really looking, was remarkably like his dad's.

She lifted her eyes and, in the distance, saw Zane striding toward them. Milo pulled away from her. He took her hand.

"Come."

It was perhaps the first clear direction Jennie had received, and she thanked God for it.

24

WAVERLY

TRAEGER HALL
NOVEMBER 1890

The disbelief on Titus's face was perhaps more frightening, considering she still had to traverse through the night and return to Traeger Hall. Return to her uncle's marauding ghost, Preston's lascivious ways, and Aveline's frantic scurrying about. Not to mention the bodies. Oh, the bodies! Waverly would be so happy when Titus came with the horse-drawn hearse to wheel them away. She would be even happier once the mausoleum was shut and sealed, their spirits locked inside.

Titus was pacing the room.

It was his turn to pace now, and it wasn't helping matters at all.

"Please sit down," Waverly advised.

"Sit down?" Titus gave her such a look of sheer incredulity

that Waverly wondered if she might have lost him—and his friendship—forever. "How could you keep such a thing a secret?" he demanded.

She had told him everything.

She'd had little choice really, yet she now regretted it. Perhaps a night in her room at Traeger Hall, with a glass of warm milk, a sense of reason, time to think instead of reacting on impulse . . . and she could have come up with another plan.

"How?" Titus stopped in front of her and looked down with such condemnation that it stupefied her.

"You cannot see why?" she challenged.

"You *conspired* with the illegitimate daughter of Leopold Traeger!" Titus threw his hands in the air.

"Not to have Uncle Leopold assassinated!" Waverly jumped to her feet. "To have *Louisa* protected from Uncle Leopold!"

Titus gave her such a look of doubt, she knew she had much ground to make up and quickly. He backed away from her and marched to the fireplace before whirling around again. "How do you *know*, Waverly?"

"What do you mean?" Confusion was often a preferred emotion to fear, she supposed, but right now Waverly almost preferred to tussle with Uncle Leopold's ghost.

"How do you *know* that this *Louisa* is your uncle's illegitimate daughter and that he wanted her dead?" Titus shook his head at her supposed ignorance. He leaned forward and gestured with his hands to emphasize his point. "You hired a *bodyguard* using money you *stole* from your uncle's safe!"

"Yes, again to protect Louisa. For heaven's sake, Titus, I'd heard Uncle Leopold in discussion one night behind a closed door. I assumed he was speaking with Aunt Cornelia. Or maybe it was Preston. How am I to know! But he said that Louisa needed to be cut off, and all ties severed. She was my *best friend* in boarding school, Titus, and I wasn't going to let her become one of Uncle's disposable pawns."

"I understand that," he growled, "but there were other, safer ways to handle such things."

"Were there?" Waverly had to get the man to see reason. Titus was a bit naive regarding Uncle Leopold and the power he wielded. It probably came from working with dead people. Titus probably had no idea what it was like to carry secrets for others or to fear for one's own life. "I knew how to get into my uncle's safe. I wrote a letter to the Pinkerton detective agency, and your *unidentified man* met with me the night Uncle was murdered to discuss making sure Louisa was protected."

Titus was quiet for a long moment. Waverly could hear him breathing and trying to sift through other options, just as she had before finally settling on hiring a bodyguard for her friend.

He tried again. "Perhaps you could have gone to the constable when you realized that your uncle was threatening Louisa."

"Constable Morgan? The man who already suspects me?"

Titus's eyes widened. "You were *seen* with an unidentified man, and you were tight-lipped about your relationship with him."

"I don't have a relationship with the Pinkerton agent—I have a business arrangement."

"To *outsmart* your uncle," Titus added.

"You have to understand," Waverly went on, "I couldn't go to anyone for help because no one knew of Louisa's illegitimacy but Louisa! And she never told me until we came face-to-face with Uncle Leopold at the boarding school on one of his rare visits. Even then, he didn't know who *I* was until I came to live at Traeger Hall. I was just a nameless person he'd met at the boarding school, not the niece of his new wife."

"You do realize how dangerous your subterfuge was—is. Could still be! Where is this agent now?"

"The unidentified man? He is watching over Louisa per our agreement. But still, I cannot divulge this to Constable Morgan or to anyone else. I shouldn't have even told you. Louisa's future is at stake! She's been employed as a teacher in the boarding school neighboring the one we attended as girls. If her true identity was to be uncovered, she would be left destitute."

"That could very well be your future as well," Titus said.

"Well, that is neither here nor there. Uncle Leopold being killed changes nothing for Louisa. The facts surrounding her birth remain the same."

"And that is why your uncle said Traeger Estate was not to be opened until all remaining heirs were gone—he has a daughter. She would be named his direct heir." Titus pondered this for a minute before adding, "And yet he could have specifically written any Traeger heirs out of his will without requiring Traeger Hall to be sealed. That part still makes no sense."

Waverly plopped onto a chair as Titus's logic sank in. "I've not been able to make sense of any of this. If Uncle Leopold wanted to end Louisa, then who wanted to end *him*?"

"And you trust that Louisa would not—"

"No!" Waverly cried on behalf of her friend. "She would never conspire to commit murder—not to mention how would she pay for it?"

"Constable Morgan could make the argument that you and she were in cahoots this entire time."

"But, Titus, we were not!"

"When did you finally put the pieces together that Leopold was Louisa's father?" he asked.

"The first time I met Uncle Leopold was at the boarding school. He greeted me and Louisa very coldly and continued on. He would have had no idea I was Aunt Cornelia's ward. A year later, after my aunt had married Leopold, as I was passing by the headmistress's office, I saw him standing inside. Louisa was also in the room. By then, I knew his name and heard it spoken and was curious to meet my new uncle. When I spotted Louisa in the office, I realized my uncle wasn't there on my behalf, but on hers. They never saw me—except for Louisa. Later, Louisa took me into her confidence and told me that Leopold Traeger was her father. Aunt Cornelia didn't even know she existed, and that was how Uncle Leopold wanted it."

"And now your uncle and aunt are dead, and Louisa is a teacher?"

"Yes, Titus. Teaching is all she can do. Uncle Leopold released her from his guardianship on her eighteenth birthday."

"Such a generous man," Titus retorted wryly. "Does Preston know of Louisa's existence?"

"I don't know."

"Well, I understand now the reason for your deceit. But I still don't get why precisely your uncle was killed."

"Perhaps that is why he haunts Traeger Hall," said Waverly. "He wishes to avenge his enemies." Her eyes widened. "Or what if he isn't dead?"

Titus let out a laugh. "I believe you're letting all this go to your head. Don't forget—you've been keeping vigil over his corpse, and he has not moved one millimeter. I myself injected an arsenic-based solution into his body. Therefore, in my professional opinion, your uncle is most certainly *dead*."

"Yes," Waverly conceded, looking down at her hands. "You are right, I suppose."

"Now, one may make an argument for your uncle's ghost, but that's a different matter altogether. There is still Louisa and your uncle and aunt's killer to work out. How do we truly *know* she isn't behind his murder?"

"I told you!" Waverly popped her head up so fast she heard her neck crack. "She wouldn't."

"No?"

"No."

"And what of her mother?"

"Her mother?"

"Yes." Titus shot her a nonplussed look. "Who is Louisa's mother? It's not your aunt, we know that. Given how important your uncle was to the community, it is quite hard to believe he had a daughter with no one the wiser. Does the mother live elsewhere? Did Leopold travel anywhere in particular that would allow him the opportunity to father a child? Where was Louisa born?"

"I don't know the answers to those questions. I don't believe even Louisa does." Waverly wished Titus would stop probing her with questions she had no answers for.

Titus strode over and crouched before her so that they were at eye level. "My dear, *dear* Waverly, you have only succeeded in adding to the list of possible killers while implicating yourself in a serious crime, one punishable by law."

"What?" she gasped.

"Without more evidence, we can hardly go to the constable with any of this. He will conclude that you and Louisa hired the agent, the unidentified man, to have your uncle killed. Not to mention the funds you *stole* from your uncle's safe!"

"What do we do then?" she breathed.

"Do you wish for me to solve this for you?" He goaded her with a smile that both irritated her and gave her shivers.

Bother. Waverly extended her hand to Titus. She needed to stand. Sitting before him like this, she felt small and vulnerable. He tugged her out of the chair with such unreasonable force that she catapulted forward and landed squarely by smacking her palms on his chest. She would have pulled away had he let her. Instead, his arms tightened around her, and his face drew close. So very close that Waverly wasn't sure if she should close her eyes and prepare for her first kiss or keep them open in the event Titus decided to chastise her yet again.

"You, Miss Pembrooke, must not return to Traeger Hall." His words took on a soothing but stern tone.

"I-I have to," she whispered. She was quite overwhelmed. She might as well admit it. She had completely fallen for an undertaker, someone who was more accustomed to the company of the dead than to that of the living. "I certainly cannot stay here, can I?"

※

They had verbally sparred for the last thirty minutes of Waverly's visit to the funeral parlor. Titus had listed every female matron he could think of in Newton Creek whom they could approach to request lodging for Waverly. She had a reason for why each of them would not agree to take her in. The boardinghouse was the last option. When Waverly reminded Titus she had no access to monetary funds, he offered to pay for her. She'd told him in no uncertain terms that his doing so would make her appear as though a kept woman, and she would rather be murdered in her bed.

The evening had turned out to be an utter waste of time. Also, Waverly had betrayed herself and Louisa's confidence by disclosing to Titus the fact of Louisa's existence. To make matters worse, she had simpered in Titus's arms, expecting her first kiss, only to have him step away from her when she posed the question of where she would stay. He had immediately seen fit to solve that conundrum, which doused any hopes she had of a romantic connection with him.

Now he walked beside her in the darkness, the outline of Traeger Hall stark against the moonlit sky.

"I don't feel good about this," he muttered.

"Neither do I, but what else is there for me to do?" Waverly hissed a reply as if someone were watching and bearing witness to their midnight tête-à-tête.

"If I wasn't against marriage, I would give you my name for convenience's sake," Titus shot back, ducking under a branch.

The very suggestion shocked her. "Against marriage?" Waverly's voice rose.

"Shh!"

"Against *marriage*?" she hissed again. "Whatever for? Not that

I would have considered matrimony had it been proposed." She would have, but he didn't need to know that.

"I'm not against marriage *per se*." Titus pushed through a thicket of bushes that bordered the Traeger property. "I'm against an institution that is too often used as a way for society to achieve its purposes, whether for status, monetary gain, or convenience."

"Then what do you believe it is for?"

"Companionship."

"Companionship?" Waverly repeated as quietly as she could. She pushed between the bushes, following Titus. "That is about as romantic as giving a lady a bouquet of grass for Valentine's Day."

"Marriage isn't about romance. Or feelings. Or the ridiculous notion some women have who believe they need a man to think for them, which sometimes they do or they might just get themselves killed."

"I have succeeded in avoiding death," Waverly quipped in her defense, then added, "Although on occasion I will admit you have been helpful."

"Keeping you alive, you mean?"

Waverly went to slap his arm, but Titus stopped her hand.

"Waverly . . ." Titus heaved a sigh as he looked up at the bell tower, which rose three stories above them. "You're a remarkable woman. If I am called to Traeger Hall to prepare your corpse . . ." He fumbled for words.

"You said you would be there either way," she reminded him.

"Yes, but—"

Waverly stepped closer and whispered in his ear to taunt him. "You could sleep in the kitchen."

"Good heavens!" He snapped his fingers. "Why didn't I think of that?"

"Think of what?"

"I can stay at the Hall in one of the guest rooms—under the

guise of having to oversee the deceased's remains due to the irregular terms of Leopold's will. It's a bit flimsy, but it will work. Then, should anything go amiss, I will be there to protect you."

His idea was unexpected, and Waverly didn't know how to respond. "I-I am quite capable of—"

Titus held up his hand. "I'm not here to bandy about who is stronger or smarter or what is most appropriate. The fact of the matter is"—he leaned forward, and this time it was his lips that moved against the sensitive skin by her ear—"if something should happen to you, Waverly, I would be quite beside myself. Or have you not figured that out by now?"

25

Preston was not happy that Titus was joining them for breakfast, Waverly observed. He stared at Titus, then at her, and then finally stated baldly, "And you were concerned about my dalliances, cousin?"

Preston took a seat at the table and proceeded to shell a hard-boiled egg.

Titus sat as well, and for a moment, Waverly felt a renewed sense of confidence. If Preston were her uncle and aunt's killer, then she and Titus outnumbered him now. Still, sharing breakfast with a murderer was not on her list of preferred things to do.

"Actually, Mr. Scofield," Titus said to Preston as he slid a linen napkin on his lap. "I am here to tend the remains regularly now that we've exceeded the typical four days for a wake. And, well, you must admit, the bodies require a special sort of tending—that is, until the terms of the will are met."

"Terms of the will!" Preston barked. "Ridiculous. I don't know what Leopold was thinking."

"I quite agree." Titus gave him a thin smile. "I'm merely here to do my duty by Mr. Traeger and his wife, yes?"

Aveline cleared her throat from the dining room doorway. Preston shot her a look, and she paled.

"Sir, Mr. Grossman is here to see you."

"At this hour?" Preston let his spoon drop from his hand onto the table. "Well, Aveline, show him in. I believe both Miss Pembrooke and Mr. Fitzgerald should hear what he has to say."

Aveline dipped in a curtsy and disappeared around the corner.

Within seconds, Mr. Grossman blustered in, his thin face ruddy from what appeared to be a brisk walk in the cool November morning. He held a portfolio under one arm and tapped the floor with a walking stick with his other hand.

"Mr. Scofield!" He acknowledged Preston with a small smile. "My apologies for taking so long to meet with you. I had business outside of town, and then my wife took sick. But here I am!" Mr. Grossman appeared to notice Waverly and Titus at that moment, giving an understandable second look when he registered their presence. "Mr. Fitzgerald?" The unspoken question was obvious.

"I'm here to tend the bodies," Titus said without hesitation.

"Ah. Well then." Mr. Grossman turned back to Preston. "Would you prefer to meet privately?"

"No." Preston gestured to an empty chair and beckoned for Mr. Grossman to have a seat. "I do believe this is all pertinent information, and Mr. Fitzgerald, being the undertaker here, understands the need for confidentiality."

"I do," Titus responded appropriately.

Mr. Grossman appeared a bit out of his element as he set his portfolio down beside him at the table and accepted Waverly's offer of coffee. Without a full staff, and with Aveline nowhere in sight, Waverly stood and moved to the sideboard to pour a hot cup of coffee for the lawyer. Her hand shook as she poured it, and she was glad that no one witnessed it. This was the moment that would reveal Preston's true intentions regarding

Uncle Leopold's estate. She was not the heir apparent, nor would any alliance with her benefit Preston. He would not be named in the will. It all fell—if they were honest—to Mr. Grossman himself. While he didn't benefit personally from the funds and properties, he did benefit from the prestige of managing the affairs of Leopold Traeger. It was an enviable position.

"Thank you." Mr. Grossman accepted the coffee and waited for Waverly to be seated again. Once she had, he began. "Mr. Scofield, as you are aware, I've already gone over the details of the last will and testament with Miss Pembrooke."

Preston cast her a wary look. She couldn't tell if he was surprised or had simply forgotten that she had told him this fact.

Mr. Grossman sipped his coffee, then continued. "In short, the will lays out rather . . . well, unique specifics surrounding the burial of Mr. Traeger and his wife—specifics that Waverly has been requested to attend to. In addition, the will states that the Traeger Estate, its business holdings, and all financial investments are to be transferred to the care and oversight of my office."

Preston paled.

Mr. Grossman didn't seem to notice. "On my own death, the estate will transfer to Newton Creek. The town may sell or do with the assets as best suits the community at that time."

Waverly exchanged glances with Titus, who turned to Preston. He was watching the man, Waverly knew, for any sign of murderous intent. Which was a bit ridiculous because, at this point, even a kind and friendly Preston Scofield would likely feel murderous after hearing this news.

"I-I don't understand," Preston spat out.

Mr. Grossman appeared far more understanding than when he'd told Waverly the will's terms. "Miss Pembrooke didn't either. But there really is nothing complicated about it. Aside from the eccentricities surrounding his burial, Leopold Traeger left the terms of his will quite cut-and-dried."

"And this house?" Preston blustered. "What about Traeger Hall? Is *she* the one to remain here?" Preston jerked his head toward Waverly, his face a purple color.

"No," Mr. Grossman replied. "This property will be sealed, along with the entirety of its belongings, forty-eight hours after the burial of Mr. Traeger and his wife. And it's not to be reopened for a century."

Preston launched from his chair, slamming his fist on the tabletop and sending the dishware clattering. "Preposterous! How do I contest this?"

Mr. Grossman didn't seem flustered in the slightest. "You don't. It is incontestable."

"The courts may have something else to say." Preston tugged at his jacket, straightening it on his torso. "*You* cannot possibly understand the inner—" he glanced at Titus and Waverly and gritted his teeth—"the inner workings of Leopold Traeger's business interests."

Waverly noticed that Titus remained placid with regard to the scene unfolding, yet his eyes remained sharp. He wasn't missing a thing.

"I understand more than you know, Mr. Scofield." Mr. Grossman pushed his chair back and stood. "There is nothing more to discuss." Despite his professional demeanor, there was steel in the lawyer's voice.

"I will see you out," Preston stated flatly.

As the two men exited the dining room, Waverly stared after them, debating on whether to follow for the purpose of spying.

Titus's low voice kept her planted in her chair. "Both men are hiding something."

"That is apparent," said Waverly, "but what is it?"

"I would wager there is more to your uncle's business ventures than meets the eye."

"Everyone assumes that already," Waverly retorted. "Still, we've no evidence of anything, Titus. There still isn't any indication as to whether Preston or Mr. Grossman—or perhaps both—had anything to do with the murders."

"Or *Louisa*." Titus eyed her with some reproof.

Waverly was unwilling to entertain that idea. She tossed out an equally absurd suggestion. "Or Reverend Billings."

Titus laughed. "Because of some stained-glass windows for his church?"

"People have murdered for less."

"Perhaps, but whoever killed your uncle and aunt was overcome with violent rage. The killer showed no mercy or hesitation."

"So then . . . what next?" Waverly asked pointedly.

Titus lifted his cup and took a long drink of coffee. He set the cup back on its saucer and said, "I believe it is time to plan the funeral."

WAVERLY

In an interview shortly before her death in 1950; memories from a few days after the murders:

But I had no idea of the course of events I had set into motion. I had no idea of the events that were already well under way without my knowledge. The morning Preston discovered what was in my uncle's will was the morning everything became a terrifying whirlwind.

Nothing could prepare me for what was to happen next. The secrets that Traeger Hall buried . . .

26

JENNIE

NEWTON CREEK, WISCONSIN
PRESENT DAY

"Where's the rest of it?" Hannah popped her head up from the microfiche screen.

Pauline, the curator of the Brookland-Newton Creek Historical Museum, offered an apologetic smile. "I'm afraid that is all we have in the archives of the 1950 interview with Waverly Pembrooke."

"That's it?" Hannah sagged in her chair.

"Yes." Pauline's smile was understanding.

While disappointed, Jennie had expected this. If Waverly Pembrooke's testimony of the events that took place then were complete, there would be no lingering mystery surrounding Traeger Hall.

"There's nothing more at all?" Hannah asked again, as if Pauline could somehow make Waverly's remaining pages of the interview suddenly appear.

"No. Not that has been found anyway." Pauline leaned a hip against one of the museum's research tables and crossed her arms. She had to be in her mid-fifties, Jennie guessed, which meant she had enough years here not to be a novice who had missed something. "I had this same conversation with Allison Quincy years ago." Pauline grew serious. "It's why I was so reticent to show these to you. But with you"—she looked at Jennie—"being the owner of Traeger Hall and the sawmill ruins, I didn't feel right withholding them either."

"You were the one who worked with Allison here at the museum?" Jennie wanted to know more about Allison, Milo's mother, and find out the secrets of Traeger Hall—not for herself so much as for Zane and Milo. They believed Allison's death had been the result of her inquiring into the mystery of the historic house. If they were right, didn't they deserve to get some answers?

"I was." Pauline nodded. She blew a small sigh from her lips. "She was a persistent young woman, and smart as a whip."

"How so?" Hannah prodded.

Pauline looked toward the ceiling as if trying to recall the memories of her conversations with Allison. "She had an innate ability to piece things together. Such as these incomplete archives from Waverly Pembrooke and the family tree with Louisa Theophilus that she found in a cabinet with other family records." Pauline paused. "That's when I became concerned."

"Concerned about what?" Jennie rolled back in the office chair that she'd pulled up to the table with the microfiche, giving herself room to cross her legs.

Pauline pushed off the table and pulled up her own chair. There was a fervency in her green eyes that showed a deep worry, even after all these years.

"Allison's cousin Rick—he got involved."

"Rick? That's Percy Wellington's son," Hannah added for Jennie's benefit.

"Mm-hmm. He was convinced—as was his cousin Allison—

that Leopold Traeger's house had been shut up all these decades because there was treasure hidden inside."

"A very popular theory," Jennie confirmed.

Pauline waved a hand in the air. "What creepy old house *doesn't* come with a rumor of treasure? But Allison and Rick were of the mind that they had the right to open the place. So they went to Rick's dad, Percy, and everyone started getting excited because the will was no longer valid. It had expired long ago. Allison believed all she needed to do was to convince the Newton Creek council members that the mansion should be reopened."

"And?" Hannah bit her fingernail.

"And she found out that the Newton Creek council had voted only a few months prior to sell the Traeger Estate to bring in more cash for the township."

Jennie straightened. "Had they already sold it before Allison put in her request?"

"Mm-hmm." Pauline pressed her lips together. "Your father had put in an offer to buy up all the properties. The township needed the money, so they transferred the trouble and maintenance of Traeger Hall to be his responsibility, and that was that. Allison and Rick were completely out of luck because they would have to work with your father to gain access to the Hall."

Jennie's gut churned. Something was off. Terribly so. Her dad—her family—had no ties to Newton Creek. So how would Dad, not having a charitable bone in his body, have known about the opportunity to buy the Traeger Estate?

Pauline seemed to read the question on Jennie's face. "Your family has no ties to this area."

"I didn't think so," Jennie responded, still confused.

"But your father was a business associate of Percy Wellington's father, Wellington Sr. That is who let your dad in on the rather easy purchase of valuable property."

"And then Dad had him write up the codicil that keeps me from being able to sell the place." Jennie could see it now.

"But why would your dad want to do that?" Hannah frowned.

The answer was simple. "Because," Jennie said, "if there *was* potential for treasure or something valuable locked away inside, Dad would want it—or he'd at least want my mom to find it. Not because he cared about *her* so much as the principle of the matter. Dad never wanted to miss out on a good thing . . . even if he was dead."

"And Traeger Hall stood closed until you arrived," Pauline finished.

"So Jennie's dad had already purchased the property before Allison disappeared?" Hannah tried to insert Allison back into the narrative.

Pauline nodded. Her contemplative look told Jennie that whatever she said next was merely conjecture. "Your father had no motive to have anything to do with Allison's death, Jennie, and he had already left Newton Creek two days before she went missing. Allison and her cousin Rick probably made plans to break into Traeger Hall anyway. Rick is . . . well, the law doesn't apply to him, or so he thinks. And Allison was such a good girl in so many ways, and yet she could be a pit bull once she latched on to an idea."

"Do you have suspicions as to why Traeger Hall was sealed?" That seemed the biggest question at this point. What would be so worth their locking up the place for a century, and what would be worth breaking into it so many years later regardless of the law and the consequences?

Pauline's shrug wasn't what Jennie was hoping for as a response. "Leopold Traeger dealt in a lot of questionable investments. Some believe he locked away vats of money in the basement and didn't want anyone else to have it. He was a miser, they said. So sealing up his house was a last hurrah."

"Money? That seems too *typical*." Jennie felt disappointed. "What about fine art?"

Pauline laughed as she rose from her chair. "Or jewels maybe.

Who knows? Maybe it was just Leopold Traeger's last attempt to stay alive."

Jennie frowned. "What do you mean?"

Pauline settled her gaze on Jennie and summarized, "Leopold Traeger didn't want to die. Think about it. He built a bell tower so it could be rung in case there was an attempt on his life. His will demanded that his body remain in Traeger Hall for seven days to be sure he was really dead. If he was that opposed to dying, I always wondered if he thought the only way he could keep his name alive was to seal up the house like a mystery and give his property to the very town that didn't like him all that much. They would never forget him. Not for decades."

"And that way," Jennie finished, "Leopold Traeger never really died."

"Right," Pauline agreed. "He's still very much alive. At least in Newton Creek. One hundred and thirty-five years later, Traeger Hall is still the center of the town, just as Leopold Traeger wanted it to be."

―――

Jennie curled up on the couch at the Harris place, with Hannah next to her, Allison's shoebox in her lap. Zane was putting Milo to bed, night was settling in, and she had already shared the events from the afternoon at the museum with the Harrises.

"You know I don't think Pauline is right, don't you?" Hannah stated. "There *is* treasure inside. You just have to keep looking."

Jennie managed a laugh while her tired spirit sort of wanted to just be done with it all.

"So this was Allison's?" Hannah stared at the box with a bit of longing.

"Yeah." Jennie offered Hannah a conciliatory smile. "I haven't gone through it all yet. It's mostly just papers."

"I think we should call Rick Wellington and get his . . ." Greg Harris, the patriarch of the family, bit off his words as he sat in his recliner. He tried again. "I think he needs to answer for a few things."

"I tried calling the Wellingtons. Percy said Rick is overseas in Japan." Trixie eased onto her own recliner, a thermos of coffee in one hand and a chocolate chip cookie in the other. "He's hardly been around since Allison disappeared."

"That's convenient," Greg grumbled. "I bet he had something to do with her ending up in the creek."

"Greg." Trixie's voice had an undertone of scolding.

He wasn't dissuaded. "I'm just sayin' it was no accident, Allison getting trapped under the mill wheel. A person doesn't just slip into a creek and get herself wedged there with a concrete block tied to her feet like the Mafia paid her a visit."

"But we don't know it was Rick. That's a dramatic accusation," Trixie reprimanded her husband.

Greg gave his wife a dark look. "We don't know it *wasn't* Rick."

"Okay, Dad, that's enough." Zane entered the living room, leaning against the doorway. "The biggest concern right now is why someone would leave a threatening note for Hannah. What does she have to do with anything?"

"It was probably a prank!" Hannah rolled her eyes. "Like, everyone in school knows by now that Jennie is here."

"And nothing else has happened since, right?" Trixie raised her eyebrows at her daughter with a look that demanded complete honesty.

Hannah shook her head. "No. Nothing."

"Who left the note then? Who threatened my daughter?" Greg wasn't going to let up, and Jennie couldn't blame him. Not to mention she thought she might be developing a sentimental affection for the man. He was what every little girl wanted in a dad. Protective, grouchy, but soft inside and genuine.

"Maybe I *should* just bulldoze the place," Jennie stated. She couldn't help herself. It would at least end the sensationalism that surrounded it.

"Don't do that!" Hannah exclaimed.

"Hannah, it's Jennie's right to do what she wants with the place." Trixie sipped her coffee.

"Do you all want me to?" Jennie figured it was as much their decision as hers. And maybe she should ask Gladys and Allison's brother, Todd. Maybe try to meet Allison's parents and—

"I don't think it's time yet," Zane said.

Everyone looked at him, and he motioned toward the shoebox. "Allison was adamant about there being something in Traeger Hall. She wouldn't give up on it, and I—well, back then I wish she would have—but now I feel like if we give up, I'm—"

"Giving up on her?" Jennie asked gently.

Zane cast her a look of gratitude. "Yeah. That."

She wasn't going to admit she felt that way too. For Allison, and for her mom.

"So?" Hannah tapped on the shoebox. "Are we gonna look?"

"You're going to bed," Trixie said.

Hannah scrunched up her face. "Mom, I'm sixteen. Since when do you send me off to bed?"

"Since now." Greg pushed off the recliner and exchanged looks with Trixie. "Your mother and I are heading to bed too."

"Yes." Trixie caught the hint and stood.

"What?" Hannah was clueless.

"Bed. Now." Greg's commanding voice caused Hannah to leap from the couch, but then he grabbed for her as she shoved past, annoyed, and Greg ruffled her hair and gave her a sideways hug. "Let Zane and Jennie have a chance to go through Allison's papers."

Hannah stopped to look over her shoulder, and awareness flooded her face. "Oh, yeah." She finally caught on that maybe Zane would need some privacy. "Good night," Hannah chirped as she headed down the hallway.

"Night," Jennie chimed back.

As Zane's parents eased past him in the doorway, Trixie paused and put a motherly hand on her son's arm. "Just remember, Allison cared about you. Whatever priority she gave Traeger Hall over you and Milo . . ."

"I know, Mom." Zane gave a small smile.

"Okay." She patted his arm and followed Greg to their bedroom.

Zane hefted a sigh and approached the couch, easing onto it next to Jennie. "Well, they cleared out fast."

"Are you ready?" Jennie asked, her hands poised over the shoebox lid.

"Let's do it," Zane replied.

27

Jennie rolled over on the couch in the Harrises' living room, taking the fluffy blanket with her. She and Zane had stayed awake until after midnight, looking through Allison's handwritten notes, newspaper clippings, a brochure someone had printed in the 1970s about Leopold Traeger, and so on. There was nothing substantial that they'd seen to give any clue as to why Allison had been so dogged in believing there was classic art hidden inside Traeger Hall. And there was nothing to indicate why someone didn't want them to open Traeger Hall now, then had fallen silent. As if . . .

Jennie sat up. The living room was dark, but Zane had flicked on a nightlight in the hallway before going to bed. She hadn't intended to spend the night, but with it being so late, it was easier. She'd fallen into a fitful sleep. But now?

She swung her legs off the couch and fumbled for her phone. Turning on its flashlight, Jennie reached for the shoebox on the floor.

Reaching into the box, she pulled out the locket and carefully pried free the clasp that held it closed. She stared at the portrait.

The young woman. If this really was Lousia Theophilus, Leopold's illegitimate daughter...

Jennie held the flashlight up to the tiny miniature in the locket, her thumb brushing the coarse lock of hair on the opposite side. What if *keeping* Traeger Hall sealed shut was all the person had wanted? The person who'd left the note in Hannah's locker. What if by opening the house, they would be negatively affected by a Pandora's box of mysteries? What if it had nothing to do with their wanting any potential treasure for themselves? What if the person who'd written the note just wanted the Hall left alone? Nothing devious or dangerous or even deadly.

Lousia Theophilus could be the secret of Traeger Hall. Maybe Jennie had been staring at it from the moment she and Zane had first entered the Hall. Louisa could be what Leopold wanted locked up for generations, so that her existence couldn't come back to shame him. But to hang her portrait for all to see upon entering the house?

What about the artist Vallée? Jennie had pulled up the name on her phone earlier, also running a search for it in various art databases. Nothing. She decided to search the internet linking *Traeger Hall* and *Vallée* together.

She frowned as she thumbed her phone screen. The only thing of value the search had brought up was old property records from Connecticut. A house owned by an L. Traeger. The deed was linked to an 1880 census and an occupant at the same address: *Fidelia Vallée*.

Jennie jumped to her feet, a burst of energy filling her. Vallée. The person who had painted the portrait of Louisa might very well be this Fidelia Vallée. And if L. Traeger—listed as owning the property in Connecticut where Fidelia Vallée resided—was *the* Leopold Traeger, she could have just stumbled on the rumored artist of Traeger Hall's collection of paintings.

She grabbed her shoes and slipped them on. She would hike there. Starting the car might wake the occupants of the Harris house, and she didn't want to disturb them. It wasn't that far, and the walk would do her good. Jennie paused, debating on whether to wake Zane. With it still being so early, she decided to leave him a note, asking him to join her when he woke up. Scribbling on an envelope she pulled from the trash, Jennie left the note on the couch and slipped from the house.

In the predawn, a thin line of pink spanned the horizon, outlining Traeger Hall and the bell tower. She was so excited, it was hard not to bust back into the house and start rummaging through everything to find more clues and more evidence of Louisa Theophilus's life. But she tempered her anticipation, taking the time to unlock the padlock Zane had put on the heavy-duty metal gate he'd installed to keep out vandals. He'd given her an extra key, and she removed the padlock and swung open the gate.

The entrance she and Zane had created beckoned her inside. Jennie pocketed the key and reached for the respirator mask she'd grabbed from Zane's car on her way out their driveway, along with a flashlight. Once prepared, Jennie flicked it on and ducked so she could squeeze into Traeger Hall.

Jennie instantly swept the beam of light onto the portrait just off the entryway by the staircase. The woman's blue eyes stared back at her, unyielding in their persistence. She walked to it, raising the flashlight and studying the paintbrush strokes, trying to differentiate what was dust, paint, or cobweb.

"What do you want me to find?" she asked Louisa Theophilus. "Who is Fidelia Vallée?" Her voice echoed through the abandoned home and deflected off furniture and tapestries—evidence that whoever had sealed Traeger Hall had left it all behind intentionally.

Jennie scanned the entryway with the flashlight and noted the hallway that ran to the left of the staircase. She badly wanted to explore the upper level, but maybe the entrance to the bell tower was this way. There had to be some explanation for how the bell had rung the night of Allison's murder too. If she could uncover that . . .

Jennie shone the light at a door on the left. It was a study draped in cobwebs, mice droppings, and piles of chewed paper where rodents had been. She entered the room carefully, swinging the light upward to make sure nothing was going to cave in from the floor above. All looked secure. It was a museum. A moment frozen in time.

She shone the light on the desktop. An old book, gnawed and mostly destroyed, lay there. A teacup and saucer, so filthy she couldn't make out its pattern. A dry inkwell, an assortment of pens, and a tobacco pipe resting on a wooden holder. Jennie reached out and ran her finger across it.

Leopold Traeger's pipe? It had to be his. He had held it, smoked it, and here she was touching it as if it were a relic worth thousands of dollars. Jennie withdrew her hand. If Leopold had accomplished anything, it had been to immortalize his life. He was not forgotten.

She swept her flashlight along the wall. There. A painting. Two English setters in the same paint strokes and style as the portrait in the foyer. Jennie leaned closer to read the artist's signature: *Vallée*.

Of course! Now she was getting somewhere. Perhaps there were records—files of painting purchases or business transactions between Leopold Traeger and Fidelia Vallée.

Jennie pushed on the wooden chair by the desk and noted that it still felt solid. Regardless of the dust, she lowered herself onto it, sitting at the desk as though she could summon the spirit of Leopold Traeger. Read his mind. Know his thoughts. He had sat right here more than a century ago and composed the last will and testament that had begun this entire debacle. He had determined that this place would be sealed shut.

Jennie tugged open a drawer. It stuck, and she wrestled with it for a moment as she sat there enveloped in the darkness. Only the flashlight provided light, and she had her phone with her if she needed a backup. The drawer finally tugged free, and she peered inside. Old, chewed papers; another book, warped from age; a small metal box toward the back of the drawer. She pulled the box out and set it on the desk. When she opened it, she smiled. Its contents were so simple, the day-to-day life of someone in the nineteenth century. Buttons that might have come off Leopold Traeger's suit coats or shirts were among the items in the box, as well as a matchbook, a few coins that could be worth something, and a penknife.

Closing the lid, she slid the box back into the drawer, leaving the rest as it was. The rest of the drawers weren't much different in their contents. Jennie moved to the wall shelves. Books lined them, so thick with dust that she could barely read their titles. There were a few gaps where, instead of books, a vase rested, a small knickknack, and in the corner of one shelf, a compass encased in glass. The glass was grimy, and Jennie couldn't tell if the compass was anything special.

She moved on. Where would Leopold have stored information on the artist and about Louisa? Louisa's boarding school records perhaps? Records of payment to support her . . .

Jennie swept the flashlight's beam around the room until it landed on a landscape painting, hung on the wall behind the desk. Again, her flashlight confirmed it. Another Vallée. She hurried to the painting and, ignoring the spiderweb that clung to her hand, lifted it off of its wall hook.

"Of course." Her voice sounded louder than she'd imagined it would be. But being alone in Traeger Hall in complete darkness made it eerie, even to her own ears. The wall safe behind the painting wasn't even latched. Jennie's fingers curled around the door and tugged it open. She raised the light to peer inside.

Aside from a sheaf of papers tied together with string, the safe was empty. No jewels or gold coins or other such riches.

Jennie smiled to herself. Mom would have loved this time capsule of stories that had become treasures. She pulled out the papers and set them on the desk.

"What did you leave in the safe that was so important, Mr. Traeger?" she muttered to herself. "Who was Fidelia Vallée—?"

Jennie whipped her head up at the sound of the floor creaking but saw only blackness. With no light source inside the abandoned mansion, she would have expected to see a beam of light if it was Zane.

"Zane?" she called. Tugging out her phone, she glanced at the time: 5:32 a.m. He could have awakened and come to join her. But the fact he didn't answer unnerved Jennie. "Zane?" she called again, this time shining the light through the open doorway of the study. She saw the hallway and then nothing. Absolutely nothing.

Her ears must have been playing tricks on her.

Jennie brought the flashlight back to the folder and finished untying the string. The folder fell open, and she saw a sheaf of old handwritten pages in brown ink. They had to mean something to have been stored in a safe. And why had the safe been unlocked, with these pages left behind?

Lifting a page, Jennie held it toward the light. "'Girl with Chestnut Hair. Poppy Field in Oil. Dogs of the Moors,'" she read aloud. Jennie carefully examined the header of each page. They were records of Vallée paintings, at least forty of them. Jennie frowned, sinking onto the chair.

Had she missed something in her research? Was there an artist named Vallée who had become someone in the art world? Or was this Leopold Traeger's attempt to hoard paintings from one he *believed* would rise to fame? If he sealed Traeger Hall to hoard the paintings, there was no good explanation for that action either. Their beauty and value would be kept for ghosts only. Traeger in no way benefited by sealing a collection of paintings from an unknown artist in his home for a century!

Jennie froze.

The floor had creaked again.

A chill made her shiver, and she had the sudden sensation that she was being watched. She grappled for the flashlight, knocking over Leopold Traeger's pipe and stand.

"Zane?" she tried again.

This time she was answered with more distinct footsteps. The person wasn't trying to hide from her. A light flickered and then shone down the hallway.

"Is that you, Zane?" Jennie was irritated by his not announcing himself. He of all people knew how creepy this old place was.

A figure rounded the corner, and Jennie stared, confusion muddling her senses. This person's presence in Traeger Hall made no sense, and yet at the same time it did. "Oh! H-hello." She managed a wobbly smile. "You scared me."

"Yeah? Sorry about that."

Jennie eyed the visitor with suspicion. "How did you know I was here?"

"I didn't." The individual took another step into the room.

"But—"

"I warned you to keep this place shut."

Jennie stilled. Hannah's locker. The note. The pieces fell into place, but there were still several missing. She didn't have a complete picture, and fear began to trace its way up her spine.

"I just needed more time." Another step toward her.

"What is it you want?" Jennie demanded, trying to sound strong and failing at it. The words came out in a breathy plea.

"The paintings, Jennie. One at a time, and with the right connections, I can move them and make a killing."

"These?" She waved the Vallée records in the air. "They're worth nothing! No one in the art world would recognize a Vallée."

"Don't worry." The smile didn't quite meet the person's eyes. "They will. Once I'm able to move the last Degas."

Jennie ignored the unwanted visitor for a moment and quickly shuffled through the records in her hands.

Vallée.

Vallée.

Vallée.

Vallée.

Degas.

Degas.

Monet.

She jerked her head up in surprise. "There *are* priceless works here?"

Jennie was met with a laugh. "Quite a few actually. I've had to be real strategic in moving them. Even in the underground art world, selling priceless paintings is a dangerous business. Eight years and counting . . . it's been a lucrative hobby."

The individual who'd threatened Hannah really *had* wanted Traeger Hall left alone. This person had been pilfering Leopold Traeger's fine art collection for years.

Allison had been right. And if she'd been killed for her meddling, then it stood to reason they would be willing to kill again.

28

WAVERLY

TRAEGER HALL
NOVEMBER 1890

Mr. Lichton had picked the worst time to die. That and the fact Titus had been fetched to do his due diligence as the only undertaker in Newton Creek had them both, well, up a creek, she supposed. Waverly had retreated to her bedroom as soon as Titus gave her instruction. He'd eased into his black jacket and adjusted his tie, all while spearing her with his blue gaze that would welcome no argument.

"Old Man Lichton was supposed to live another week," Titus explained. "Unfortunately, he didn't cooperate. I will be gone most of the day. Until I return, you will stay in your room, do you hear me? I don't trust Preston or Mr. Grossman at this point."

"Then I'll come with you!" Waverly had started forward, but Titus stopped her with a shake of his head.

"I've no good way to explain why Leopold Traeger's niece is accompanying me to care for the deceased, and frankly, you wouldn't be welcome."

"Because I'm Uncle Leopold's niece."

"Precisely. It is best that you sequester yourself in your room. And for pity's sake, push some heavy furniture against the door just to be safe."

"I need to find Foo." Waverly looked around in search of the cat.

"Your cat will be fine. You need to care for yourself," Titus urged.

"I would leave, but I've not heard from Louisa yet," Waverly countered. It was common sense. "I'm hoping to join her once she gets word to me that she is safe and still at the school. I can secure a position as a teacher, and I—"

Titus marched toward her and gripped her arm firmly. "Don't you dare leave yet! I have a plan. But I need a little bit of time."

"A plan?" Waverly pulled back. She had to admit to some annoyance that *she* was not privy to this *plan*. "And the plan is what? To spirit me off to a secret hiding place?"

Titus tipped his head back and forth as he considered it. "That's not necessarily a bad idea—"

"It's an *awful*, ridiculous idea." Waverly gave him a little shove, and a tiny smile played at Titus's lips. He seemed up to something and almost too confident he'd succeed at it. But for the moment, Mr. Lichton was dead, and his body had already begun to decay.

Not unlike Uncle Leopold and Aunt Cornelia.

Waverly stood over their bodies now, staring down at the two of them while she ignored Titus's instruction to barricade herself in her room. Preston had left the Hall; she had seen him drive away in his carriage. Aside from Aveline, she was quite alone at Traeger Hall, and Waverly determined she would not leave her cat to the mercies of anyone unknown who might do them all harm.

"What have you done, Uncle?" she asked the body before her on its slab of wood. The bouquets of flowers were wilting, and there was a pungent, unfamiliar smell in the room that was unsettling. "Why didn't you simply welcome Louisa into your home? She is a lovely young woman."

Uncle Leopold didn't respond. In fact, he lay quite still—as a corpse should—and she noted his skin was beginning to appear splotchy in places.

"Oh, why won't you let me bury you!" Waverly muttered. She had two more days. Two more days before a funeral could be administered and Titus could remove Uncle Leopold and Aunt Cornelia from the house. "Foo! Foo!" She called for the cat even as she eyed Aunt Cornelia.

Waverly rounded her uncle's remains to peer down at her aunt. Aunt Cornelia's pinched nose seemed thinner now.

"We could have been happy, you and I, if you'd only not married Uncle Leopold. Did you know of Louisa? I am quite sure you did not."

"And yet you found out by happenstance." A deep voice from the doorway frightened Waverly, and she jumped, clutching at Aunt Cornelia's hand and then thrusting it away as she felt the cold flesh beneath her fingers.

Waverly stared at the man.

She dropped her gaze to Uncle Leopold's remains.

She lifted her eyes back to the man in the doorway.

"Your eyes aren't playing tricks on you." He stepped into the room and approached Leopold Traeger. Standing opposite of Waverly, he shook his head. "It shouldn't have been this way."

Her heart in her throat, Waverly could only stare. Stare at her Uncle Leopold—*both* Uncle Leopolds—and try to make sense of it.

Dead Uncle Leopold remained very dead.

But his ghost seemed too corporeal. He stood over himself, looking down at his features and studying them.

A sort of terror had frozen Waverly in place. Ghosts came out at night, did they not? They didn't speak clearly. But this man was no visiting spirit, but flesh and blood. He had to be, though she dared not reach across the two dead bodies to poke at him. The realization did nothing to release her from the fear that rooted her feet to the floor and stole her voice when she tried to speak.

The mobile Uncle Leopold lifted his eyes, and a dry smile thinned his mouth. "Ah. I am no ghost, Waverly. In fact, we've met before. Many times actually."

Fear was a dreadful foe, and right now it had taken from Waverly all ability to do anything but gape at the replica of Uncle Leopold.

"I am your uncle's twin brother." Another thin smile. "The silent one of the partnership."

"A *twin*?" Waverly gasped.

"Yes. Although quite some years ago now, I *died*. That was when we lived in Connecticut. Fabricating my 'death' and coming here was a strategic move on both our parts. Making use of our similar appearances as necessary was also strategic. We had different sets of skills, you see, but we were not always well received as two separate men."

And to think she'd had no idea.

Waverly decided she would fall over from fright and shock, and that would be the end of her. So this was how she would die? Literally and horribly scared to death.

"I am Theophilus, by the way." He offered a smile that reminded her instantly of the days in the past year when Uncle Leopold had seemed more at ease, less of a bark, and, on rare occasions, even congenial.

"Oh, my goodness!" Waverly clapped her palm over mouth. "You . . . you two swapped places?"

"More times than I can count." His eyes sparked, and while he seemed far less uptight than Uncle Leopold on his worst day, Theophilus also seemed far more dangerous.

"Theophilus?" The pieces of the puzzle were beginning to fall into horrible, complete place. "But that's—"

"Louisa's surname. Yes. Leopold and I had to work quickly when her mother told me she was having a child, but it was handled. Handled very well, that is, until we discovered Leopold's new wife's niece resided in the same boarding school as my daughter."

"Louisa is *your* daughter? Did Aunt Cornelia know there were two of you?"

"No." Theophilus shook his head. "That was entirely Leopold. Neither of us were supposed to marry, and when Leopold stepped outside that plan for his own purposes—whatever they were—that's when things began to unravel."

"Was it Uncle Leopold I saw at the boarding school that day I met Louisa?" Waverly continued to stare at Theophilus, trying desperately to find a physical difference in him. Something that would identify him as Theophilus and not Leopold. There was none.

"It was me," he answered.

"And when my Uncle Leopold told me not to ring the bell?"

"Also me. I came to realize in the last few months that my brother was up to his own devious plans to completely cut me out of our accrued wealth. If he were to be at risk of death, I preferred that you refrained from trying to stop it."

There was not a little venom that shot from his expression, and she was aware in that moment that there was another suspect on the list of who might have killed Uncle Leopold and Aunt Cornelia.

"Was it you who was always staring at the paintings in the night?" she asked, breathless and sincerely wishing she'd listened to Titus and barricaded herself in her room.

"Ah, the paintings. Fidelia Vallée, Louisa's mother. My mistress and a beautiful artist. I brought her pieces back here with me when I visited and hung them in Traeger Hall—much to my brother's disapproval. The other pieces of art—the Monet, the Degas—those weren't to be displayed. Those are a means to financial gain. But Fidelia's paintings? They're beauty personified. As is my daughter, Louisa. Unfortunately, my brother Leopold had grown sick of my side becoming more advantageously positioned. And your remarkable loyalty to Louisa is something that has gotten in the way of things." Theophilus began to approach her, circling the remains of her uncle and aunt. "My poor daughter has no idea of the Shakespearean drama taking place behind the scenes. Louisa believes herself to be Leopold's child. That was the safest way."

Waverly backed away, hoping to make a half circle before rushing out the door.

Theophilus eyed her. "It's not complicated. Or it wasn't until Leopold changed his will, that is. Originally, in the event of his death, I was to ease into his position, and no one would be the wiser that he'd died. Cornelia perhaps, but that was something I could work with. However, it got complicated. He rewrote his will and then that infernal bell of his!"

Waverly had made it around the bodies, and in that moment, she decided that escape was preferable to understanding what had happened the night of Uncle Leopold's murder.

She sprinted for the door, her feet slipping on the wood flooring. Theophilus Traeger launched after her, and Waverly screamed as he grasped her chignon and hauled her backward. His arm came around her front just beneath her throat, and his breath was hot in her ear.

"That infernal bell and your irrepressible inability to stay quiet. Had you been home that night . . . but no, you had to meet up with that ridiculous Pinkerton agent."

"You killed them, didn't you?" Waverly choked as his arm tightened around her throat. He pulled her backward from the parlor door toward Leopold's study.

"Don't think less of me," Theophilus chided. "I was protecting Louisa."

JENNIE

NEWTON CREEK, WISCONSIN
PRESENT DAY

Jennie struggled to comprehend. "B-but Rick—"

"Rick?" Todd, Allison's brother, looked confused. "Oh! You thought Rick was the one who left the note?"

Jennie nodded, frantically trying to concoct a plan as to what to do next. There were no windows to jump out of, no way to escape Traeger Hall but through the front entrance.

Todd laughed, and even that one action changed his features to appear friendly and unassuming. "That was me." He laughed again. "It was pretty obvious really, but people forget I sometimes work at the school when the nurse is off sick. I'm the substitute nurse, so to speak."

Jennie reached for her flashlight, but Todd waved her away from it. She noticed then the glint of steel. He was armed.

Panic welled in her throat. This was not what she'd expected. She thought she had figured it out on the Harrises' couch early that morning. There was no treasure in Traeger Hall. Instead, there was the secret of Louisa Theophilus. Fidelia Vallée was an unknown painter, and it all ended there . . .

But no.

The realization left Jennie cold. She'd been led astray by her own wish that an abusive, unfeeling father would suddenly view his daughter as a treasure. It had been a dangerously sentimental conclusion to a century-old tale of mystery and murder and betrayal.

The art records burned in her hands as if on fire. This was the treasure. Not the Vallées, but the records of the Degas and Monet.

"So you had found and were selling the paintings?" Jennie

asked incredulously. "But *how?* This place has been sealed shut for over a century!"

Todd shrugged, his face ghoulish in the shadows made by his own flashlight that he'd set on the desk. "That a grand house like this one could be closed up for so long and have no one find a way in is a fairy tale. It's not rational."

"But . . ."

Todd shrugged. "Rick and Allison had been nosing around here for years. Rick was able to dig up a set of old blueprints that matched the place. I don't know where he found them, but he did. There's more than one way to get into this place. Do you really think a man as paranoid as Leopold Traeger, a man who believed someone wished him dead, would plan that his only escape routes would be through the predictable front and back doors?"

Jennie was cold. Inside and out. She seriously doubted that Allison would have been involved in stealing priceless works of art from Traeger Hall, only to turn around and sell them on the black market. She was a treasure hunter, yes, but Jennie couldn't believe that Allison had been part of an art-theft scheme.

Todd waved his handgun as if it were a toy. "My sister was going to tell Zane all about it. That night when they argued? She was planning to fill him in on what she and Rick had found—a way into Traeger Hall and about the art. Instead, they fought. Allison was so upset that she confided in *me*." Todd gritted his teeth, and the anger he felt toward Zane was palpable.

Jennie eyed the darkened doorway behind him, the area around its frame lit only by the flashlights each of them held.

"I told her I'd help out," Todd went on. "Rick wasn't around at the time, and Allison was inconsolable. She told me she was going to the police to report everything. I tried to get her to chill out. Zane had her unraveling, and we needed to think!"

Jennie reached for the desk. The respirator mask on her face felt hot and was suffocating her. She tried taking a few deep breaths. "W-where did she find a way in?" There had to be a secret tunnel or entrance somewhere in the Hall that she didn't know about.

Todd sneered at her. "The bell tower is more than meets the eye. Built into its side are a sequence of three bricks that, when moved a certain way, open a hinged door made to look as though it's part of the tower. It's actually a secret passageway into the house."

Jennie sagged onto the chair behind her. "So you've been sneaking in and out of Traeger Hall and slowly selling off the art piece by piece?"

Todd nodded. "She wasn't supposed to die, Jennie. I loved my sister. But once she was gone . . . she'd worked too hard to find the Traeger treasure for me to just give it up." He moved to the desk, leaning over it with both hands planted on the desktop, the gun pinned beneath his right palm. "You have to understand—I didn't mean for any of it to happen. After Allison's argument with Zane, and after she said she was going to the cops to tell them about this place, she took off. Even though I'd promised to help her, she left me behind."

Todd jerked back into a standing position, still holding the gun but sending his flashlight flying off the desk and rolling across the floor. He was becoming more agitated. "Allison was calling it quits. She said it wasn't worth it—wasn't worth losing Zane over." Todd turned, shuffling back toward Jennie. He waved the gun in the air again. "They were *Monets*! You don't just walk away from something like that!"

Jennie shrank into the chair. She had to get out of there. She could easily outrun the overweight man, but it was the gun she was worried about. If he shot at her, maybe he'd miss in the dark. Then again, maybe he wouldn't.

"I tried to convince Allison." Todd whimpered a little. He sniffed and ran his arm beneath his nose, the gun held lazily in his hand. "Then she got mad at *me*! At me! I was just trying to help her, and she was walking too fast to her car. We were outside Grandma Gladys's place, but Grandma was sleeping. I can't walk that fast, and it was raining at the time. She turned around to yell at me, and she . . . she slipped and hit her head on a concrete birdbath Grandma had set near the corner of the garage."

"She slipped?" Jennie repeated. "Did you—?"

"No!" Todd shook his head vehemently, stepping back into the beam of light and tapping his temple with the handgun. "I would never think of doing that. She just hit her head—it was a freak accident. I couldn't get Allison to wake up, and she was bleeding . . . I-I panicked."

"You tied your sister to a cement block and took her body to the creek by the mill wheel and dumped her in?" Jennie imagined Todd wrestling his sister's body into the water. She felt as if she might throw up.

"I didn't want to get blamed for her death!" he shouted, acting furious that Jennie didn't seem to understand. "The whole thing was blowing up in my face. I needed time to think. To *think*!!" Once again he tapped the barrel of the gun against the side of his head.

"Todd . . ." Jennie straightened in the chair ever so slowly. She understood how to placate a narcissist like her dad, but Todd? He was emotional and irrational, and she wasn't sure what might trigger him. She held up her hands to try to calm him down. "Let's just—"

"No!" Todd dropped the gun from his head and aimed it at Jennie. The gun trembled in his hand. He wasn't in complete control, which only made him more dangerous. Yet it also made him more likely to miss.

Jennie decided to do something. She dropped to the floor and into the darkness, scrambling on all fours for the doorway.

Todd's shout split the air, which was followed by deafening gunshots.

29

WAVERLY

TRAEGER HALL
NOVEMBER 1890

Theophilus dumped her onto a chair opposite her uncle's desk. He pulled a landscape painting off the wall and slammed his palm against the safe hidden behind it. Its door was partway open. He spun back around to Waverly. "Leopold didn't keep it where he said he would."

"What are you looking for?" Waverly had no idea what Theophilus was referring to.

"The *miniature* of Fidelia. Where did Leopold hide it?"

"Is . . . is Louisa's mother dead?" Waverly breathed deeply while trying to figure out a way to escape this cold, even more terrifying version of Uncle Leopold—no, Theophilus.

Theophilus's expression was pained as he rifled through the safe's contents. "I told Leopold I was done switching places. I couldn't care less about acquiring more art, more wealth, the under-the-table deals. And he had Fidelia 'taken care of'—that's what he called it!" The veins in Theophilus's neck began to bulge. His anger and his grief were fast overpowering him. "Leopold thought Fidelia was a distraction, but she was my *life*! He was only worried about our assets, our agreements. He was afraid if I backed out of everything, if I claimed Louisa as my daughter . . ." Theophilus punched the wall. "Leopold knew that if anything came down, it would come down on him and not me."

"The gunshot in the dining room?"

"I missed," Theophilus said. "And my brother Leopold had to have the last word. He made that ridiculous change to his last will and testament, demanding that the house be sealed shut after his death, and thereby keeping me out of this place forever. He cut me and Louisa out of inheriting the estate. How am I supposed to show up now as Leopold Traeger and say it was all just a terrible accident but that I've recovered? Leopold is dead, and I can't even maneuver Louisa into place to inherit what's rightfully hers—what belongs to *me*. Why? Because my brother double-crossed me!"

Theophilus had been cheated by a dead man. Waverly tried to catch her breath and think rationally. What would Titus do? Aside from engaging in a fistfight, he'd probably throw Theophilus out the window. She wasn't capable of either. Which was a shame.

"I wanted my brother dead."

"You gave him fourteen stab wounds! I would quite agree that you did!" Waverly exclaimed. "Does Preston know?" She knew she was pushing her luck, but she had to know.

"Preston Scofield is a dimwit. He's focused only on legitimate businesses. He has no idea all that we accomplished on the side."

"And Mr. Grossman?" Waverly asked.

Theophilus clicked his tongue. "Why on earth would Leopold reveal any of this to his lawyer? Does Mr. Grossman strike you as savvy?"

Waverly shook her head.

"No. Mr. Grossman did whatever Leopold told him to do. Hence that fiendish will of his."

"Then why are you still here?" Waverly pressed.

Theophilus approached and lifted her chin with his finger. "I want my paintings. I want Fidelia's miniature self-portrait. I want what belongs to me and Louisa."

"But Louisa doesn't know about you . . ." Waverly let her sentence hang as Theophilus's features darkened.

"She will. All of this got messy quite fast. Then your aunt rang that infernal bell. By the time I got to her, it was too late. There was no way to feign injury and take Leopold's place. There wasn't enough time to get rid of his body."

Then Theophilus grabbed her and jerked her head toward him. Waverly whimpered beneath his grip.

He bent down until his nose almost grazed hers. "But there is no one here to ring the bell for you, is there?"

Jennie

Newton Creek, Wisconsin
Present Day

She heard the bell, a tolling bell in the distance.

Her leg burned where a bullet had grazed it. Jennie huddled in the corner of the study, relying on the darkness to conceal her.

Todd moaned, pacing the floor.

Jennie caught glimpses of him as he shuffled in and out of the pool of light from the flashlight he'd knocked to the floor. He held his hands to his ears.

The bell continued to ring.

The bell!

Jennie held her breath. The ringing bell was a pure miracle! It was only she and Todd in Traeger Hall. No one else knew about the secret passageway into the bell tower.

She wasn't sure just how long it had been ringing. After the bullet grazed her leg, she had blacked out for a moment. The adrenaline and shock proved to be a bad combination.

"Make it stop!" Todd sank onto a chair. He rocked back and forth. "Stop."

Jennie took the opportunity to shift onto her hands and knees again. If she could crawl from the room quietly, she might be able to get past Todd this time. She'd counted three gunshots. If he had a fully loaded clip, that meant he still had at least another seven rounds.

She felt her way across the floor. The ringing of the bell was insistent. She could almost see the old copper-green bell swinging back and forth.

At last, Jennie's hand reached the doorframe. She was careful to feel her way through in the blackness. Her leg burned from the bullet wound. She was sure, though, it was only a graze. Jennie saw a glimmer of light at the doorway. The light was coming from where she and Zane had busted through the front entrance only a few days before.

She had to hurry. By taking just a few steps, Todd would see her form crawling on the floor. She needed to stand now . . .

Jennie palmed the wall, bracing herself against it as she pulled herself up. Her right leg felt strong while her left throbbed in pain, although she found she could put her weight on it. That was good.

She limped toward the front entrance. The closer she got, the more the daylight illuminated the space. Illuminated the darkness, the secrets, the ugliness that was Traeger Hall. She glanced at the portrait of the young woman. Louisa Theophilus. She was watching. These were her secrets.

Jennie heard Todd's shout over the pealing of the bell. A thud told her he'd risen to his feet. He would be going after her. She headed for the entrance with the opening, broken through brick and mortar, an unwelcome but needed opening to a world of greed and grief.

"Jennie!" A figure at the opening appeared. He squeezed through it, grabbing her as she collapsed.

"Zane! We need to get out of here! Todd Quincy, he has a gun..."

WAVERLY

Traeger Hall
November 1890

When the bell began to peal, both Waverly and Theophilus met each other's eyes. Hers filled with hope, his with outright panic.

"Not again!" he hissed. Theophilus charged to the doorway of the study, peering up and down the corridor as if he'd find the answer as to who was ringing the bell.

Was it Aveline? Had she returned in time to have overheard them and was now calling for help? Waverly had to help her, otherwise their rescuers would arrive at another dreadful scene like with Uncle Leopold and Aunt Cornelia. The two of them slain—Waverly in the study, Aveline in the bell tower.

Theophilus turned and sprang at Waverly. Screaming, she slid from the chair to the floor like a limp rag. He had not been expecting that! Waverly rolled across the floor, twisting in her skirts until she reached the doorframe. She pulled herself to her feet as Theophilus wrestled with the chair that had toppled on him when he missed his wild grab for Waverly.

Waverly sprinted down the hallway toward the front entrance but hesitated at the staircase. Should she help Aveline first? They could both find themselves trapped in the bell tower. Waverly wasted no time and raced for the door, tugging it open and rushing out onto the veranda.

Fresh air assaulted her face. The bell continued to ring in the tower, pealing over the countryside. In the distance, she could see people running toward Traeger Hall. They were moving faster this time. Having found two murdered victims at the Hall only a week prior, no one wanted to witness such a thing a second time.

Theophilus hadn't chased after her. Waverly stumbled down the stairs. She suspected he had gone to Aveline. To the bell tower.

The first man to reach her she didn't know, but she gasped out, "Bell tower! He's in the tower!"

Constable Morgan hopped down from a carriage that barreled up the road. In the minutes that followed, Waverly found herself watching the chaotic world around her as if she were merely a curiosity seeker out on a walk. As she crossed the lawn, the bell finally ceased its ringing. Then she heard Aveline, weeping, as a couple of men helped her from the bell tower. In that moment, Waverly quite liked Aveline once again. She would need a friend once she came to realize the error of her ways and the manipulation of a wicked man. Aveline had earned that after today.

Waverly leaned against a tree, hugging herself, as the wind was a bit chilly. Preston had arrived and was watching in shock and fear as they led Theophilus Traeger from the innards of Traeger Hall. Let Preston be afraid of the specter for at least a full day or more. Let him believe that Uncle Leopold had in fact risen from the spirit world to haunt Preston for his greed.

And there was the undertaker. Titus Fitzgerald.

She smiled broadly as he swept up to her and grasped her

arms. His eyes were remarkably blue, so much so that Waverly wondered if she could see her reflection in them.

"Waverly, you're in shock," Titus said.

"No, I'm quite all right." Yet everything was a bit blurry, and he was spinning . . .

"Waverly?" Titus seemed bothered.

She reached out and patted his cheek. "You poor man. I suppose you spent the day preparing Mr. Lichten for his burial."

And then Titus turned black as night. She couldn't see him at all anymore. But she could feel him. Feel his arms. He was carrying her. At least that was what she thought before slipping into utter oblivion.

JENNIE

NEWTON CREEK, WISCONSIN
PRESENT DAY

The next several minutes were chaos. Zane pulled Jennie from Traeger Hall as Todd stumbled toward them from the hallway.

The police arrived with sirens blaring. Then came an ambulance, followed by a fire truck.

Jennie was ushered off to the ambulance, where she was immediately given oxygen. An EMT began assessing her leg. She watched, half in shock, as a few police officers escorted Todd down the steps of Traeger Hall.

But it was when a cop carried Milo from the Hall, followed by a terrified-looking Hannah, that Jennie shoved away the EMT and ripped the oxygen mask from her face.

"Milo!" she cried. "Hannah!" Staggering across the lawn, the

EMT shouting at her, Jennie rushed toward the little boy, whose glasses were half broken on his face. His dark hair was mussed and covered in cobwebs. She saw Hannah hurrying toward them with old blueprints rolled up in her hand.

Zane took Milo from the officer's arms and held the boy tight. Jennie managed to join them. She grabbed ahold of Zane's arm, feeling blood trailing down her leg.

"Why is Milo here? Milo, are you all right? Hannah? What happened!"

Milo pushed against Zane, his eyes wide. "Uh . . ." he began.

Zane was trying to squelch the boy's urgent emotions and opt for calmer ones, so that Milo wouldn't spiral downward. While doing so, Zane speared his sister with a look that told her he was both proud of her and infuriated with her.

"Did you follow Jennie here?" Zane demanded.

Hannah nodded, tears staining her cheeks. She lifted the rolled-up blueprints. "I was up most the night. I found these in the bottom of Allison's box. There's a secret passageway into the bell tower. I was planning to tell you about it this morning, but then I saw Jennie leave. So I followed. I had no idea Milo was following *me*, and then—"

"Jee." Milo pointed at Jennie, interrupting Hannah.

"Yes, Jennie." Zane exchanged glances with her but kept his hold on Milo's arms. "Buddy, you can't . . ." His voice broke. He looked to Jennie, then to Milo, and finally to Hannah. "You rang the bell?"

"We both did," Hannah said, tears rolling down her cheeks again. "Milo and I both did."

The tears were impossible to hold back. Jennie reached for Milo, and the boy came into her arms of his own choosing.

"Jee," he said again. Calmly as though nothing had happened.

Zane pulled Hannah into his arms with a gruff motion.

"They rang the bell for me." Jennie wept, hardly able to reconcile all that had occurred. "They rang the bell for me."

30

Jennie tossed into the fire a pile of papers they'd taken from their third week of going through Traeger Hall. They were old, useless papers, unlike the ones that listed art pieces that had come and gone through Traeger Hall as a part of the Traeger twins' nefarious dealings. Art pieces that had been sold a century ago, and art pieces they had yet to find after Todd had slowly pilfered them. The only works of art no one seemed to care about were the Vallées. The worthless paintings were so beautiful and compelling that Jennie wished things were different for them.

"We don't get to keep any of the art, do we?" Hannah gave a sad laugh as she stood next to Jennie, watching the papers burn. "Even if the ones Todd sold on the black market are recovered?"

Jennie shook her head, exchanging glances with the others around the barrel. Hannah, Trixie, Greg, Zane, Milo, and of course Midas the dog. "Only the Vallées."

"This has to be the first time in Newton Creek history that the FBI showed up," Greg stated.

"What if the art wasn't stolen, though? What if Traeger had

acquired it legally? Then can Jennie keep it?" Hannah's protest was laced with her desperation to keep a little bit of the treasure from Traeger Hall.

Zane gave Hannah's shoulder a nudge. "The FBI will run the art pieces through the National Stolen Art database. Either way, the papers that were found weren't bills of sale. They were inventory for trafficked art. Whoever Leopold Traeger was in cahoots with, it wasn't legal."

"When he died, he didn't want anyone finding out. Or did he not want anyone to know about Louisa Theophilus?" Hannah pressed.

Zane shook his head. "I think it's all the above. He wanted to hoard the art, protect the name he'd spent years perpetuating, and, well, I think Pauline at the museum got it right. Traeger wanted to live forever in Newton Creek's memory. Maybe he thought he was too important to be forgotten. And maybe there was more, something none of us know about. I mean, trafficking in art—he couldn't have been a good man."

"What are you going to do with Traeger Hall now, Jennie?" Trixie's question was a loaded one.

All eyes turned on her, and she grimaced. "I'd like to find out more about Louisa Theophilus and Fidelia Vallée." Jennie met Zane's gaze. "I think there's more to the story. The paintings, they . . ." Jennie left her sentence unfinished. How could she explain how the Vallée paintings spoke to her soul? It was as if each brushstroke carried with it some secret pain, one still tipped with an element of hope. Hope for something better. For love. For belonging.

That was what good art did, Jennie had decided. It could reach inside a person, unravel their emotions, and connect with their spirit. It was a song of color, its imagery a dream yet to be realized.

Trixie cleared her throat. "How about some hot cocoa? I have it inside in the Crock-Pot."

"Sounds good!" Hannah took off for the house, Milo running after her, with Midas barking in pursuit.

Once everyone had gone back to the house, Jennie and Zane stood opposite the burn barrel, watching the flames and listening to the crackling. She still owed him an apology. Her recklessness had almost ended up getting both Hannah and Milo hurt. Milo! That little boy had been her hero in so many ways already.

"Don't say it," Zane said in her ear.

Jennie startled, not realizing he'd rounded the barrel to stand by her.

"Say what?" she breathed.

"Don't say you're sorry. You didn't do anything wrong."

"But—"

"No," Zane said firmly. "Don't take blame for something that wasn't your fault."

"But I went to Traeger Hall alone. I didn't think Hannah and Milo would follow—I didn't even know they were awake!"

"You didn't know. That's the point." Zane reached over and tucked loose strands of hair behind her ear. "You *didn't know*. You can't hold yourself responsible for that."

"But I'm always responsible for the bad things," she whispered, tears threatening to spill over with her admission.

"Who told you that?" Zane's gaze caressed her face.

Jennie didn't answer. She couldn't. She wasn't ready yet.

And that was okay.

Zane leaned forward and brushed his lips against her temple, then drew her into the security of his arms. "We've got all the time in the world, Jennie. And Milo needs you, so . . . I hope you're not planning on going anywhere."

Jennie had no words. She'd always found it easier to stay quiet and keep the peace. But in this moment, keeping the peace wasn't her responsibility. Someone else was keeping it for her, and they were beginning to chase away her monsters. And she was really very okay with that.

WAVERLY

TRAEGER HALL
NOVEMBER 1890

Preston had left Newton Creek, while Aveline had taken a position in Titus's home as a housemaid. Waverly was terribly grateful for that little burst of generosity.

Two days ago, they had laid Uncle Leopold and Aunt Cornelia to rest in their mausoleum. Thankfully, Waverly had listened to Titus when he'd told her the coffins she'd originally wanted wouldn't fit through the mausoleum's doorway. It would have been humiliating to have to increase the door's width and height just to hoist the deceased over one's shoulder and carry them inside. Also, there wasn't time for such modifications to the structure. As it was, Titus was an expert at what he did, so the burials had gone splendidly.

Uncle Leopold and Aunt Cornelia were encased in their stone sarcophagi for the rest of time.

Now Waverly took a final walk through Traeger Hall. She cradled a subdued and compliant Foo in her arms. Maybe even the cat knew that today was the end of Traeger Hall as they'd known it. Per Uncle Leopold's will, it was to be sealed off. The masons were already outside waiting, Mr. Grossman having made all the arrangements. And since she could take nothing with her but her own belongings, packing hadn't taken very long. She realized one might argue that Foo was not her belonging, but there was no way she was allowing him to stay behind.

She took a moment to slip into the bell tower to retrieve Louisa's locket. She would keep it for now. Perhaps one day she would return it to Louisa. Regardless, the poor young woman had no idea how awful her family was, and there was no need to invite that sort of pain into her life. If she herself could get settled, Waverly would invite Louisa to come to Newton Creek. Perhaps they could grow old together. Louisa could start a new life here.

Of course, if Traeger Hall was to be sealed, so too would its secrets be. Maybe someday Waverly would share what had taken place there. Meanwhile, Newton Creek was to move forward as though nothing had happened. They might retell the story of Leopold Traeger's death because, well, no one grieved him at all. All they knew was that the man who'd been taken from Traeger Hall that day the bell pealed a second time looked identical to Leopold Traeger. But Leopold Traeger was dead, wasn't he? And what was it the man had kept yelling about the art collection being his? No doubt Newton Creek would ruminate on that for years to come.

Waverly paused outside Uncle Leopold's bedroom. While she'd never been inside the room, now she pushed the door wide open. To her astonishment, she was met with a portrait of Louisa. How strange. How very strange indeed. Had Uncle Leopold allowed Theophilus to hang it there for when they swapped places? Perhaps this was another indication of why Aunt Cornelia had been so unhappy. She had lived in the shadow of a mysterious and beautiful woman, never knowing it was her husband's illegitimate niece.

And poor Louisa. She was the victim in all of this, yet she had no idea . . . would have no idea. This story of two brothers would not be passed down through the generations, not if Waverly had anything to do with it. It was a secret she would take with her to the grave. Leopold and Theophilus Traeger had ruined so many lives, played a wicked game of chess, and if by keeping silent, Waverly could spare Louisa the pain of the Traeger legacy? Then so be it.

On a whim she reached up and dislodged the portrait of Louisa from the wall and carried it down the staircase. She looked around and, seeing a hook, settled the portrait on the hook. It grazed the back of the portrait, and Waverly heard a ripping sound.

"Bother!"

"What happened?" Titus met her as he entered the room.

"I tore the backing." Waverly turned the portrait over, and to her surprise a miniature fell out.

Titus knelt and picked it up, then looked at Waverly. "This must be Louisa's mother, Fidelia Vallée."

"The miniature Theophilus panicked to find was behind Louisa's portrait the whole time?" Waverly couldn't help but smile. If Theophilus had insisted he have a portrait of his daughter hanging in their personal quarters, then Leopold had been vindictive in return and hidden the portrait of Theophilus's lover in a place Theophilus would not have thought to look. "Oh, Uncle Leopold," Waverly breathed, "you were quite the scoundrel."

She slipped the miniature back behind the painting, allowing Fidelia Vallée to keep watch over what would become her entombed art gallery, with Louisa keeping watch over the entrance.

Titus stood to the side, observing, and when Waverly stepped away from the painting, he mumbled, "Well, that's that."

"Maybe for you it is." Waverly sucked in a breath, trying to be brave. She was going to leave Traeger Hall now and go to Louisa—she supposed. If there were a teaching position, she would resign herself to that, assuming the school where Louisa taught would make a place for Foo. But it all felt so incomplete somehow. Her uncle's estate would be sealed until decades beyond her own death. Someday, someone would open Traeger Hall, and would they even know what had happened there? Would they piece together the puzzle of Leopold and Theophilus and Louisa and her mother? Or would it all crumble into dust and the story be forever lost in time?

Titus extended his arm to her. "Shall we go home?"

Waverly drew back. "What are you talking about?"

Titus's cool eyes glimmered, and she saw a tiny smile playing at the corners of his mouth that entranced her. The idea of a warm evening with Titus in his drapery-shrouded sitting room, his shirt hanging out, half unbuttoned . . .

She blinked. Rapidly. "What do you mean by *home*?" she asked.

"I made arrangements," Titus said. "If you're willing, Reverend Billings will marry us this afternoon, and then you will no longer be destitute."

"But I was going to . . ." Waverly couldn't swallow for a moment, and she was afraid she might swoon. Were her dreams coming true? What was she to do with the evening that awaited her with this untucked undertaker? She could hardly imagine it, and yet maybe—

Titus snapped his fingers.

Waverly raised her eyebrows. "Enough thumb-snapping, for pity's sake. Perhaps you forget that you said you are against marriage."

"Of convenience, yes." Titus was quick to respond with confidence. "Which this would not be."

Heat rose in her face.

"It also wouldn't be for money, for you have none," Titus went on. "And your association with Leopold Traeger will not win me any social status, I'm afraid. Not to mention your alliance with Traeger offspring of questionable origin."

"You dare not besmirch Louisa's name in my presence." Waverly defended her friend who knew nothing of the drama that had unfolded and never would.

"I do so appreciate your tendency toward loyalty. Such a wonderful companion you must be." Titus tapped her nose.

"So you would propose marriage to me for *companionship*? And because I am loyal?" A small part of her admitted that it hurt a tiny bit. While it was apparent Titus Fitzgerald was, well, a *man*, he had not mentioned affection or . . . love. But then what was love after all? She'd never really experienced love before, and perhaps it was all a rather inflated idea.

Oh, heavens.

Titus had moved quite close, and in that moment he kissed her.

He kissed her!

And he had such soft, fine lips. Passionate.

"Oh, heavens," she whimpered.

He pulled back and whispered against her mouth, "I have a strong affection for you, Miss Pembrooke. I have for a very, *very* long time."

"Why didn't you say anything?"

"Because I didn't suppose you would want to live in a funeral parlor."

"Why on earth would you make such an assumption? You've been wise in so many other ways," Waverly added. "Besides, I find the dead are far less trouble than the living."

"As do I, my dear. As do I."

AUTHOR'S NOTE

The inspiration for this story came from the life and death of George Harry Storrs. He's remarkably unremembered in the annals of true crime, and yet his murder is perhaps one of the most fascinating and dramatic from the nineteenth century.

For those who believe I was a tad too sensational by creating a man (Leopold) who was convinced he would be murdered and so installed a bell to be rung in case of such an emergency, well, that was exactly what George Harry Storrs did. Not unlike the scene in Traeger Hall when a bullet shatters the dining room window, so it happened one night in 1909 at Gorse Hall in Stalybridge, England. It was then that Mr. Storrs had a warning bell installed at Gorse Hall so that in an emergency, the bell could be rung and the town police alerted.

Not quite two months after the attempt on Mr. Storrs's life in his dining room, he once again convened there with his wife and their niece, Marion Lindley. Shortly afterward, an intruder forced his way into Gorse Hall, and the Storrs were alerted by their cook who had been confronted by the intruder. The Storrs retreated to the kitchen, with Mrs. Storrs momentarily startling the intruder with a shillelagh she'd ripped from its wall mount.

The intruder claimed he would not shoot, and Mrs. Storrs took the gun from the intruder as George Harry Storrs called for the bell to be rung. The police sprinted up the one-mile-long driveway, and once they arrived, they found Mr. Storrs lying on the floor and bleeding after being stabbed fifteen times by the intruder, who had stayed true to his word by not shooting anyone. Mr. Storrs died not long after. While there were several suspects, including two men who were both charged and acquitted of the murder, the death of George Harry Storrs remains unsolved to this day.

You can read more about this fascinating case in the book *The Stabbing of George Harry Storrs* by Jonathan Goodman, or by visiting https://gorse-hall.co.uk/.

ACKNOWLEDGMENTS

First and foremost, I would like to thank our ancestors for being so remarkably intrigued by the burial process that they created an entire volume of traditions I could choose from when writing this story. I was disappointed I couldn't use them all, but rest assured, when Uncle Leopold *did* finally exit Traeger Hall, he left headfirst through the front door so that his spirit wouldn't linger in the halls for eternity.

I would also like to extend my gratitude to every undertaker, funeral director, mortician, or whatever you prefer to be titled. You are the unsung heroes of the dead. You're the last ones to care for our bodies, to tend to our wounds, to bathe, dress, and make us presentable for the living. Or you are the ones who make sure we have entered the afterlife before assisting with our cremation. You also make sure our records are in order, our bodies entombed properly, and that nothing goes amiss as we reach our final resting places.

Continuing the gratitude, I would like to express my thanks to you, my readers, who generously buy these ghostly novels of mine, traipse through haunted hallways along with me, and leave me reviews online. You are all truly a blessing!

This book would not have taken place without the brainstorming assistance of Christen Krumm, some reading suggestions by Sarah Varland, and the podcast *Unsolved Murders: True Crime Stories*, which first introduced me to George Harry Storrs. Additionally, to my behind-the-scenes assistant I call my "mini-me" in many ways: you bless me, M!

Finally, many thanks to my publishing team for all that you do to make my books the absolute best they can be.

READING GROUP DISCUSSION GUIDE

1. After reading the author's note, were you surprised to learn that this story was inspired by a true, unsolved murder from the nineteenth century? What other unsolved cases from history intrigue you?
2. Aside from having a home security system, if you believed someone was intent on taking your life, what else could you put in place as a means of alerting others of an emergency?
3. In the novel, Jennie has a deep appreciation for classical art. How has the art world affected your own life and love of art? Who are some of your favorite artists and why?
4. Which period and style of art would you love to come across hidden in an old basement, for sale at a flea market, or hiding in a closet somewhere? What would you do with the art if you found something extraordinary or valuable?
5. There's a deep thread of family secrets and dysfunction

written into both time periods of the story. How do you think family dysfunction can be used both to strengthen a person and be turned into a motivating force in our lives?

6. The story includes a lot of twists and turns. Which elements surprised you the most, and what parts of the mystery did you solve before the end of the book?

7. If you were to inherit a mansion that had been closed up for more than a century, what sort of things would you hope to find after you opened its doors and looked around?

8. Have you ever read a true story or perhaps experienced it yourself where a deceased person's will included unusual clauses written in it? What were they, and why do you think they were put in the person's will?

Read on for a *sneak peek* at
the next book from Jaime Jo Wright

THE BOOKSHOP OF 99 DOORS

Available in the spring of 2026

Keep up to date with all of Jaime's releases at
JaimeWrightBooks.com
and on Facebook, Instagram, and X.

Minnie Tipton

Ambrose Fields, Pennsylvania
May 1910

If fear took human form, it would be a ghoulish creature. It would have talons for fingernails with serrated edges that ripped your soul if you tried to extricate yourself from those hooks. It would have eyes of black. Deep, soulless eyes that sucked you into them and swallowed you whole until trembling was all you knew, and gasping for air was futile but necessary nonetheless.

Minnie shut the book, clutching it between her hands. The bedcovers pooled around her waist as she sat up in her bed in the semidarkness. Gaslights illuminated her bedroom, but the effect was soft, the shadows deep.

The book she was reading had engulfed her with its imagery. She eyed the name of the author: Victor Barringsworth, Esq. An obscure English author who had penned these words around the same time that Edgar Allan Poe was creating his own prose of ravens and dead men trapped beneath floorboards. Few remembered Victor Barringsworth's writings. A person had to be a patron of books to discover his one 581-page tome.

Minnie slipped the book beneath her pillow and questioned her choices once again. The gruesome and the dark held a haunting mystery over mankind, this Minnie knew. But at half past midnight, she once again questioned her reasoning for reading it before she burrowed into her bed to sleep.

Though she was nearing thirty, a spinster who cared for her

ailing father, she had the stamina of someone half her age when it came to horror. And Victor Barringsworth, Esq. had done more than write horror. He had emoted it. He'd penned words that saturated Minnie's spirit and begged her to be afraid with him as he explored the long sleep of death.

If she allowed her romantic side to awaken, Minnie imagined she would have traveled to London in 1859 and engaged in conversation with the then-alive Victor Barringsworth. Instead, it was over fifty years later, and she was a husbandless female falling for a dead man and his writing.

She slipped from beneath the linens and padded barefoot across the velvety carpet that covered the scuffed wood floors of her room. She paused at her bureau and poured water from a pitcher to a washbasin, then splashed some on her face to awaken her senses.

There were no ghouls waiting outside her bedroom door. Her new home had been built in the late 1700s as part of a colonial plantation. A large addition had been designed and built by others in the 1840s, which included a second floor and attic. But while the century-old homestead might hold interesting secrets and lore, it didn't house any ghosts.

Minnie dried her face with a towel, lowering it to stare at her image in the mirror. Large brown eyes. Dark blond hair that hung well past her shoulders. White nightgown with a ribbon of blue at the scooped neckline.

No. Ambrose Fields didn't hold ghosts, at least not the spirits some of Minnie's acquaintances attempted to call upon as they socialized with spiritualists. Or the spirits they claimed moved the piece on the Talking Board they used as a parlor game. Despite her fondness for a thrilling read, Minnie avoided that game with an unease that told her there was more to the board and its alphabet than met the eye.

Minnie reached for her reflection, extending the fingers of her right hand toward the mirror. There wasn't anyone else at Ambrose Fields to confide in. Just Papa, who was not of sound mind, and Mrs. Pickston the housekeeper, who'd come with the place as if she were an inherited piece of furniture.

Minnie lowered her hand and moved to turn off the gaslights. She returned to her bed in somber silence.

Victor Barringsworth, Esq. was correct, Minnie determined as the remaining light dimmed at her touch and night's darkness conquered the room. Fear was an all-encompassing emotion. But it was an emotion, after all, and if Minnie had learned anything, it was that emotions could be wicked, unreliable. They doomed a person to shame, to assumptions larger than life, and to grief that overtook you. Emotions were not something to be followed or even believed. Emotions led one astray from the truth, from what was right and what was real. They betrayed you. They betrayed others. Just like Mama had betrayed Papa.

Minnie slipped beneath the covers and stared at the ceiling. "Don't be like your mother," she whispered.

In the darkness a scoffing laugh brushed over Minnie like a distant cold wind. Her mother's laugh. The one she heard every night in response to Minnie's whispered mantra.

And the vaporous words that followed were: *And yet you are. You're just like me.*

TRISS BELLAMY

AMBROSE FIELDS, PENNSYLVANIA
MAY, PRESENT DAY

"And through here . . ."

More doors opened, this time a set of French doors, with panes of sparkling glass framed by dark mahogany. The floors were also made of wood, and Triss Bellamy's footsteps echoed on the wood, making her wish she'd worn her leather mules instead of heels. But she'd wanted to make a good impression.

The woman in front of her was shorter, rounder, matronly. She spread her arms wide as if announcing the *pièce de résistance* of the entire estate. And Triss couldn't argue with that.

The bookshop at Ambrose Fields Homestead Estate was magnificent indeed.

Triss took a moment to drink it all in. To her right, large paned windows overlooked the south-facing lawn. Two of them boasted a window seat covered in lavender cushions and patchwork pillows of yellow, purple, and green hues. Two cats lay curled in the sun, claiming the window seat as their own. A black cat barely six months old and a smaller kitten, a silver tiger with white-rimmed yellow eyes.

"Emmy and ZoZo." Mrs. Nickle introduced the cats to Triss. "They come with the bookshop," she added with a laugh.

Aside from the felines who had already claimed Triss's heart, it was the bookshelves that drew her attention. They ran floor to ceiling, also of mahogany, with not one inch to spare between the hundreds of volumes to squeeze in another title.

Two smaller, double-sided shelves stood in the middle of the floor, with framed photographs of prior occupants of Ambrose Fields displayed on their tops. Strategically placed piles of vintage books were piled in a far corner to the left of a Victorian desk. On the desktop was a laptop, and on the wall behind the desk hung an impressive portrait of a pretty lady with large dark eyes, pale skin, her hair swept into an updo reminiscent of the turn of the century.

Triss didn't inquire as to who the woman was. She would find out soon enough. If she got the job, that is.

"And that's the main house here at Ambrose Fields," Mrs. Nickle said, concluding the tour of the sprawling estate home with its numerous rooms and hallways, so many that Triss had lost count. "As I mentioned before," Mrs. Nickle went on, "the east wing was built in 1790 when Rutherford Ambrose erected it. The rest of the place was added in 1856, less than ten years before the war broke out."

Triss nodded. Civil War history was much talked about in this part of Pennsylvania with Gettysburg less than an hour's drive away.

Mrs. Nickle leaned against the desk and crossed her arms over her ample chest. "It's been said that Rutherford Ambrose was a superstitious man who dabbled in . . . well, witchcraft. The estate was passed on to his nephew and was eventually sold to someone outside the Ambrose family in the early 1900s." Nickle craned her neck to look over her shoulder at the lady in the portrait. "That's Minnie Tipton, daughter of Bertram Tipon, who purchased the estate. It stayed in their family for several decades until it was willed to the village of Whipple Hollow and turned into a historic site and a museum."

That was it in a nutshell. Triss met Minnie Tipton's luminous eyes, which held something in their depths that would never be revealed now that she had passed away.

"I do love history." Triss attempted to be convincing, which wasn't hard when she was telling the truth. "And I adore books."

"Wonderful!" Mrs. Nickle, general manager of the estate and very friendly, seemed just a little bit desperate to find a manager for the museum's bookshop. "My previous bookshop manager left rather abruptly. With tourist season already in swing and with the Memorial Day holiday fast approaching, I must say you're a gift in heels." She shot a glance at Triss's navy heels. "Feel free to be a tad more casual when working here. We try to offer a relaxed and warm atmosphere for our guests."

With that, Mrs. Nickle pushed off the desk and held her hand out to Triss. "The job is yours. You've plenty of bookstore experience, and your aptitude for history will come in handy. The job won't make you wealthy, but we do offer a basic health benefits package. No dental, though." She shot Triss a worried look.

"That's okay," Triss said. She'd figure out her dental work when the time came for it.

"Good!" Relief was expressed in the form of a quickly expelled breath.

They concluded their handshake, and Mrs. Nickle eyed the two adolescent cats in the window seat. "You will need to care for them also. Their litter box is in the side room there." She pointed to a door that was mostly hidden to the left of the desk. It was built into the bookshelves with shelves in the door itself, and the only way a person would know it was there was that it was cracked open, probably to allow the kittens access to their bathroom facilities.

Mrs. Nickle clucked her tongue as she eyed the felines. "I do like cats, but I've no idea why I ever told the previous bookshop manager she could have them inside. If I'd known she would up and disappear a few months later . . ." She let her sentence hang as a shadow crossed her face. Waving it off, Mrs. Nickle met Triss's gaze. "Sometimes people vanish. Lazy, no-good people who want to make twenty dollars an hour to sit around and do nothing."

Triss had a feeling that the prior bookshop manager hadn't been all *that* lazy. Not with the bookshop so tidy and in order. But the word *vanish* captured her attention. It was a word Triss had despised for years and had come to Ambrose Fields to get away from.

Vanish.

Apparition.

Ghost.

Specter.

She came from a family of superstitious ghost hunters, and she wanted to put as much distance between her and them as she could. Triss neither liked nor believed in ghosts. She was more pragmatic than all that. She believed in history. In truth. Not in fiction and fanciful ideas. In fact, she'd always wondered why she'd never been that good at mathematics because the calculation of numbers aligned with Triss's desire for order, predictability, and logic.

But, she supposed, sometimes a person inherited things from their family they'd rather they hadn't. And so, in the true form of someone who'd grown up with Bohemian parents and a brother who saturated his life with apparatuses to capture evidence of the spirit world, Triss had made herself vanish.

She'd left her family.

She would reinvent herself here. At Ambrose Fields. In a bookshop inside a historic home that boasted ninety-nine doors. With two cats who now sized her up from their window seat, yellow eyes unblinking, and furry faces begging to be nuzzled.

Yes. *Vanish* was now a word that Triss had left behind.

The bookshop, with all its doors and history and cats, was far more preferable. A dream really. Triss's dream. She dared anyone, or anything, to haunt it.

Jaime Jo Wright is the author of fourteen novels, including the Christy Award– and Daphne du Maurier Award–winner *The House on Foster Hill*, and the Carol Award–winner *The Reckoning at Gossamer Pond*. She's also a two-time Christy Award finalist, as well as the ECPA bestselling author of *The Vanishing at Castle Moreau* and two *Publishers Weekly* bestselling novellas. Jaime lives in Wisconsin with her family and felines.

Learn more at JaimeWrightBooks.com.

Sign Up for Jaime's Newsletter

Keep up to date with Jaime's latest news on book releases and events by signing up for her email list at the website below.

JaimeWrightBooks.com

FOLLOW JAIME ON SOCIAL MEDIA

Jaime Jo Wright @JaimeJoWright @JaimeJoWright

Be the first to hear about new books from Bethany House!

Stay up to date with our authors and books by signing up for our newsletters at

BethanyHouse.com/SignUp

FOLLOW US ON SOCIAL MEDIA

@BethanyHouseFiction